Bernardine Kennedy was born in London but spent most of her childhood in Singapore and Nigeria before settling in Essex, where she still lives with her partner Ian. She also has a son, Stephen, and daughter, Kate. Her varied working life has included careers as an air hostess, a swimming instructor and a social worker. She has been a freelance writer for many years, specialising in popular travel features for magazines. Her other novels, EVERYTHING IS NOT ENOUGH, MY SISTER'S KEEPER and CHAIN OF DECEPTION, are also available from Headline.

Bernardine Kennedy's website address is www.bernardinekennedy.com

Also by Bernardine Kennedy

Everything is not Enough
My Sisters' Keeper
Chain of Deception

TAKEN

Bernardine Kennedy

headline

First published in 2004 by
HEADLINE BOOK PUBLISHING

First published in paperback in 2004 by
HEADLINE BOOK PUBLISHING

A HEADLINE paperback

1

Cataloguing in Publication Data is available
from the British Library

ISBN 0 7553 0091 2

Typeset in Plantin by Palimpsest Book Production Limited,
Polmont, Stirlingshire

Printed and bound in Great Britain by
Mackays of Chatham plc, Chatham Kent

Headline's policy is to use papers that are natural, renewable and
recyclable products and made from wood grown in sustainable forests.
The logging and manufacturing processes are expected to conform to
the environmental regulations of the country of origin.

HEADLINE BOOK PUBLISHING
A division of Hodder Headline
338 Euston Road
London NW1 3BH

www.headline.co.uk
www.hodderheadline.com

For Ian. LYFY.

Prologue

'Mummy, why don't I have a daddy to play with me on the beach?'

The little girl with a mop of Shirley Temple hair was crouched on the damp sand at the water's edge flapping her hands wildly to make waves. Kneeling alongside the serious-faced child was her mother, laughing as the water splattered over her.

'Because you've got me, sweetheart, and also you've got Grandad to play with you. Look – here he comes now on sandcastle duty, and I can see he means business.'

The five-year-old child looked up and waved happily at the man in the distance trudging towards them, but still continued her childlike interrogation of her mother.

'I know that,' she stated with childish exasperation, 'I can see him, but why haven't I got a daddy as well? Julie's got a daddy and he goes on holiday with her and they all eat dinner together every night.' Wide-eyed she looked up at her mother, waiting for an answer.

'Look, he's here, Jess,' her mother said, grateful for the distraction. 'Grandad's here.'

1

As her grandfather swept her up high in the air and pretended to throw her out into the chilly North Sea, Jess screamed with delight and instantly forgot all about her unanswered question.

Nobody could have disputed that Sara and Jessica Wells were mother and daughter. Bright red curly hair erupted from both heads, and the summer sun had caused a blossoming of pale brown freckles on every speck of bare skin it could reach.

Jess didn't bother to ask about her father again for several years; she hadn't forgotten, it was just that there never seemed to be a right time and, because she was happy, she only wondered about him occasionally. It wasn't a big issue because she was, and always had been, a well-balanced and mature child for her age with a unique bond with her mother, a bond that existed between a single mother and her only child.

It wasn't as if she missed having a father, but all her friends seemed to have two parents and she was interested to know why she didn't. All she knew was that her daddy had gone away when she was very small and had not come back. She didn't know any of the details. However, when she was eleven she once again broached the subject in a no-nonsense, direct approach that left her mother with no alternative.

'Mummy, tell me about my father. I really want to know. I mean, why doesn't he ever come and see me?'

The question was so perfectly phrased that Sara Wells knew the time had arrived.

'Do you really want me to tell you all about it?' she asked, knowing exactly what the answer would be.

'Mmm, everything. I'm old enough now, aren't I?' Jess replied as she waited impatiently.

'Yes, you are, darling.' Sara sat alongside her daughter

and gently stroked her hair. 'Well, here goes. As you know, your father's name was, *is*, Micky Wells, and I loved him madly. When we got married I knew he was a free spirit but he said he wanted to settle down, so we did. Then you were born and we both really loved and wanted you, but Micky couldn't cope with being tied down.'

'Why?'

'He found it hard not being able to go off and do whatever he wanted.'

'Why couldn't he?'

'Because we had no money, and I certainly didn't want to put you in a backpack and take off to India or wherever, so he went off on his own. He just never came back. In fact, I never heard from him again.'

'Where is he now?' Jess's expression was deadly serious and she stared into her mother's eyes as if daring her to even try and lie about it.

But Sara had no need to lie. She never had lied to her daughter, other than by omission.

'Australia maybe, that's the last I heard, but I don't know for sure. Micky had no family that I know of – in fact, thinking back over it, I actually knew very little about him. I just loved him and knew instantly that he was the love of my life.'

'Is that why you only had me?'

''Fraid so, darling. Despite the fact that he was a pretty useless husband and father, I've never met anyone else who could make me feel the same way.'

'When I get married I'm going to be really careful who I choose and then I'm going to have lots of children so they won't be lonely. I hate not having any sisters or brothers.'

Sara smiled sadly. 'I always wanted to have lots of

children too, but circumstances made it otherwise – but I've got no regrets. I've got you!' Sara planted a kiss on her daughter's head. 'I hope you get what you want, darling, but it's not as easy as it sounds. Best thing you can do is work hard at school and get your qualifications, then you'll always be able to keep yourself. Like I did.'

'I don't need to do that. I'm going to marry someone rich enough to look after me and all my children.'

'Really?'

'Yep. I'm going to marry someone who isn't a free spirit and we'll have five children, maybe six.'

'Okay, if that's what you want.' Sara smiled affectionately at her daughter.

'It is,' Jess stated categorically.

And Jessica Wells kept to it, waiting until she was thirty before she found the right man who would be safe and reliable. The man she was convinced would always stay with her and her children and keep them all secure.

She was sure, as soon as Sheldon Patterson came into her life and swept her off her feet, that he was the one she had been waiting for.

Chapter One

England, September 2001

Looking down at her watch, Jess focused hard on the hands, willing them to turn back instead of relentlessly sweeping on. She didn't need to work out the time that had elapsed, she knew exactly because it was only two minutes since she had last checked and it was also twenty-two hours and nine minutes past the agreed time.

The time that Sheldon, her husband, and CJ, her son, were due to have returned to their Cambridge home after a short holiday.

But they weren't back and Jess wondered if he was doing it deliberately to make the point that he was capable of being in sole charge of their son. Once again she peered through the window towards the end of the driveway praying that Sheldon's distinctive silver Mercedes would swing into view. Praying also they would both return safe and well, her fears of an accident unfounded.

Rubbing her eyes that were red and dry from lack of sleep she tried to drag her brain back over the day they had left five days before, the last time she saw her husband and son. The clearest thing in her mind was how happy CJ was to be going off on an adventure with his father, so happy that he was completely oblivious to the tension between his parents.

'I've already told you a dozen times, we'll be back at around one o'clock depending on the ferry times,' Sheldon had sighed dramatically when she had asked as they left, using the same falsely parental tone that was usually reserved for CJ. 'That leaves more than enough time for CJ to get ready for school. Now stop the fussing. I am able to look after my son on my own, you know – it is allowed.'

'Our son, Sheldon, he is *our* son,' Jess had replied angrily.

Standing in the porch she had waved them off, smiling happily, but as soon as the car, with CJ's excited little face pressed against the window, had disappeared from view she burst into tears.

It was the first time Jess and CJ had been apart for more than a day since his birth nearly five years before, and although she hadn't wanted it, Sheldon had said it was time for her to cut the invisible cord. He was insistent that their son should learn how to be more independent of his doting mother, insistent on taking him away without her.

His words echoed over and over in her head. 'Jessica, CJ is a boy. He shouldn't be hanging off his mom's skirt like a girl; he needs toughening up and as his father I'm the one to do it. Boys need their fathers, they need to learn how to become men.'

Scared of blocking the main phone-line, Jess went into her husband's study and picked up the other phone, quickly tapping in a number. Listening impatiently to the ringing at the other end, her over-active brain called up questions that had never crossed her mind before.

Suddenly they were jumping about in front of her.

Why had he been so positive that he didn't want her to go on the trip? Why were the arrangements so vague? Why hadn't she insisted that he give her an itinerary with contact numbers? Why had she even let CJ go in the first place?

Jess shook her head from side to side, as if to rid herself of the thoughts. Sheldon loved her, she loved him and they both adored their only child. There couldn't be anything worrying in their late return. They were just late.

It seemed forever before the phone was picked up the other end.

'Mum? They're still not back and I'm starting to panic. I have really bad vibes about this. I just know something has happened to them . . .'

Her mother's soothing voice wafted gently down the line, reassuring her, trying to calm her, and of course it all sounded so reasonable. Her mother was right. Sheldon was probably just making the point again that he was as much a parent to CJ as she was.

The same subject had been causing rows between the two of them recently, but it was something they were trying to resolve. Sheldon thought that Jess was babying CJ, Jess thought Sheldon was trying to make their son grow up too quickly. The bickering went back and forth and the compromise had eventually been that Sheldon would take CJ away for a few days without Jess for some quality father/son time together.

Jess listened carefully, desperately wanting to take on board all the things her mother was saying, wanting to believe that she was worrying unnecessarily. They were

7

the same things that she herself had thought the day before, before her mind had gone into overdrive.

Maybe he had lost track of time, maybe they had broken down in the back of beyond, maybe they had missed the ferry back, maybe his phone didn't work abroad . . . maybe, maybe.

Jess licked her lips nervously and tried to keep the tremor out of her voice. 'Can you come over, Mum? I badly need someone here. I know you probably think I'm being neurotic but I wonder if I ought to call the police?'

She paused a moment, then continued at breakneck speed, 'I don't know what else to do. Supposing there's been an accident? What if they're lying in a ditch somewhere and no one can see them? It happens. Remember that piece on the news a few weeks ago? That woman was there for three days, hidden in the undergrowth; she nearly died.'

As she was speaking and trying to keep the rising hysteria out of her voice, Jessica Patterson found her eyes drawn to the familiar framed photographs carefully placed on the desk and shelves all around the room that was her husband's inner sanctum. Although there were formal photos of the couple on their wedding day and at CJ's christening, the majority, she noticed, didn't include herself. There were holiday snaps of Sheldon with CJ, birthday snaps of Sheldon with CJ. It seemed that everywhere Jess looked there were colour images jumping out at her of her husband and son, together.

Just the two of them. Always just the two of them, father and son. It was as if she didn't exist.

After putting the receiver down she stood with her arms folded tightly around herself and her head on one side, studying the photos. Although they had always been there, and Jess herself had taken many of them, it was as if she was looking at them for the first time.

Her eyes flickered around at them all, aware that there was something she had not noticed before but now, with her senses heightened by trepidation, she tried to figure it out. Snatching down several frames, she took them into the light-filled kitchen, standing them side by side on the table to study them closely. She was still focused on them when the doorbell rang loudly, making her jump. Leaving them, she rushed to the door and flung it open.

It was her mother.

'Oh.' The disappointment in her voice was obvious. 'I thought it might have been them. I thought Sheldon might have left his key behind.'

'Oh, Jess, Jess – just look at the state of you.' The woman took Jess in her arms and hugged her close. 'Okay, now I'm sure there isn't a problem, not really, but just start at the beginning and tell me everything. That way we can work out if we really have cause to worry.'

Smiling tearfully, Jess walked ahead of her mother to the kitchen. 'There's nothing specific, but I just know something isn't right. It's a feeling, an instinct, you must know what I mean. A mother's instinct.' She looked at her own mother, her eyes wide, pleading silently for reassurance. 'For God's sake, they were only going to France,' she snapped in frustration, her eyes darting nervously around the room. 'Disneyland is hardly a danger zone on the other side of the world, is it?'

'No, it isn't, so stop panicking.' Sara Wells's tone to her daughter was sympathetically firm but Jess continued as if she hadn't heard.

'Like I told you earlier, he said they would be back

at around lunchtime yesterday. CJ is starting school tomorrow. It's his first day at big school and he's really looking forward to it. All his friends will be there, he's got to be there too – Sheldon knows that.' Her voice was getting higher as the words tumbled rapidly out, and her hands were waving about as if she was trying to communicate in sign language.

'Have you tried calling Sheldon again?' Her mother's voice was gentle.

'Of course I've tried bloody calling him! I've tried constantly, but his mobile is off or not connecting or something, which would happen if they were upside down in a ditch. God, they could be there for days. They could both be dead and no one would know.'

Sara Wells looked at her daughter for a moment before speaking. 'Okay,' she said, 'perhaps we ought to call the police, just to see what they have to say and check that there haven't been any accidents. Not that I think there's anything to worry about, but just to put your mind at rest.' Her smile and tone were reassuring. 'Sheldon and CJ will probably be back through the door before the police even get here.'

'Can you do it, please? You'll be far more coherent than me and they might take more notice.'

Sara put an arm around her daughter's shoulders. 'Of course I will. Now you go and have a quick wash and brush-up while I put the kettle on. Go and cool down, it'll make you feel better.'

Jess automatically reached her hand up to her hair and grimaced as she pushed it away from her face.

'What you mean is that I look a complete wreck and should go and smarten myself up in case the police think they're dealing with a madwoman?'

Sara shook her head and smiled. 'No, that's not what

I meant at all and you know it, although maybe you do look a bit wild and woolly. But then I shouldn't say that, considering that you got your hair and colouring from me, you poor girl!'

Jess nearly smiled back before taking off like a startled rabbit, terrified that she might miss the vital call. After splashing cold water on her face she tried in vain to drag a brush through the tangle of auburn curls that was splayed out around her neckline. Naturally shocking red, the colour had long been artificially toned down to russet, but the curls remained as uncontrollable as ever. Now, after not having seen a brush for nearly a day, it was completely wild.

With not enough time to tame it Jess clipped it up on her head with a couple of big combs and then half-heartedly brushed a layer of loose powder over her freckled nose and forehead.

Instinctively she looked at herself every which way in the unforgiving mirrors that Sheldon had tactlessly installed over and down both sides of the hand basin. Silently she bemoaned her wide hips and chunky thighs that seemed all the more obvious in the carelessly thrown on joggers and vest. 'A typical British pear-shaped body' she always described it whenever Sheldon commented on her widening bottom half. She wondered if she ought to change into something more flattering before Sheldon got back and made yet another remark about her increasing cellulite. But as soon as she thought it she felt ashamed. How could she possibly be looking in the mirror and thinking about her hated fat thighs when her husband and son were missing? Christ, she needed a drink.

Jess hurried back to the kitchen where her mother was busy making sandwiches and struggling with the top-of-the-range cappuccino machine that Sheldon had bought as an anniversary present.

From the back Sara Wells looked like a clone of her daughter, same hair although hers had faded with age and same pear-shaped body. Sara looked, dressed and acted considerably younger than her true age that was nudging slowly but surely towards sixty.

'Did you call them? What did they say?' Jess looked at the back of her mother's head.

'I'm afraid they want to leave it a little longer. They suggested you contact the hotel where they were staying. There have been no accidents reported locally, and if it had been anywhere else . . . well, they both had passports and Sheldon was in his own car.' Chewing her bottom lip Sara turned to face her daughter. 'I think they're right, you know. No news *is* good news.'

'But how can I phone when I don't know where they were bloody well staying?' Jess raised her voice, her tone defensive. 'Sheldon said they were going to book in somewhere when they got there, another part of the great adventure. He promised to phone, and when he didn't I was angry but just assumed it was Sheldon being his usual awkward self, just making a point about his ridiculous bonding session.'

The words tumbled out madly and when she stopped for breath Sara jumped in.

'That could still be the case. Maybe it's best to just wait and see. You know what Sheldon can be like, how intransigent he can be when the mood takes him.' Sara paused; it was obvious she was trying to find the kindest way to phrase her words. 'We both know that Sheldon can be a little self-important sometimes. He probably hasn't even realised the worry he's causing you.'

Sara turned and held out her arms to Jess. 'Come

here, sweetheart – it'll all be okay, I'm sure. Sheldon is a good dad, he won't have done anything to put CJ at risk. They're probably having the time of their lives and decided to stay on an extra day, completely oblivious to the fact that you're worrying yourself silly.'

Tearfully, Jess unclamped her hands from the tight fists she had made and walked straight into her mother's outstretched arms, the way she used to as a child.

Mother and daughter were very alike, and CJ was following in their footsteps. The dominant genes of red hair, green eyes and porcelain skin that freckled up at just a hint of sun had passed from mother to daughter to son.

However, looks were one thing, but Sara was all too aware that her daughter had inherited her personality as well. Both bounced happily along, ready to see the best in everyone, only to be surprised and get incredibly hurt when things went wrong.

Sometimes, she knew, they both set themselves up for falls.

Sara had done it with her own husband many years ago. She had fallen for a charming and handsome man who had seemed the answer to a girl's dream. But she could remember only too well her devastation when, without warning, he had announced he was leaving.

Still in her early twenties with a toddler to look after, Sara was left to scrape by while Micky Wells decided he had to 'find himself' and disappeared off on the hippy trail to India. He was never seen by either of them again. Micky. Baby Jessica's father. Tall and personable with his engaging smile, a happy nature and no sense of responsibility whatsoever.

Because she had no choice, Sara had metaphorically

13

shrugged her shoulders and got on with making a new life for herself and her daughter; and from then on it had been just the two of them.

Sara hated the expression 'just like sisters' that was often thrown at them because of their similarities, but she relished the fact that they were very close and always on good terms. Sara sometimes regretted not having met someone else but after Micky who, despite his all too apparent failings, had remained the love of her life, her guard had stayed well and truly up.

When Jess first introduced her to the similarly handsome and personable American guy whom she had met on holiday in Mexico, Sara's heart had sunk down into her boots. It was Micky Wells all over again, except that Sheldon certainly wasn't broke; in fact he seemed to be considerably wealthy.

Visually, apart from the fact that Micky was a hippy and Sheldon was conservative, Sheldon could have been a clone of her own husband when she had first met him. But despite her reservations, and also because she had promised herself never to question her daughter's judgement and choices, Sara had crossed her fingers and done her best to welcome him.

Sara was soon won over.

On the face of it, Sheldon Patterson had seemed to be the ideal partner for Jessica. Full of life, full of dreams and financially secure, he had promised Jess the moon and as many children as she wanted, while at the same time confidently assuring Sara that he would never in a million years do anything to hurt her daughter.

Sara, like Jess, had believed in him completely. Now she wondered if her initial judgement had been correct.

Sara physically jumped out of her reverie as Jess

sprang into life, banging the flat of her hand on the table.

'I know! I haven't contacted Carla! You know who I mean – her son Ben plays with CJ. She may know something, know where they were going to stay; her husband Toby is Sheldon's only real friend over here. If he's told anyone, it would be him.'

Jess pounced on the phone and then, hand outstretched, hesitated. 'No, I'll use the other line. If this one rings, you answer it and give me a shout.'

She disappeared into the study to make the call but was shortly back, looking even more bewildered than ever.

'This is really strange, Mum,' she frowned. 'Neither Carla nor Toby know anything. Apparently, they didn't even know Sheldon was taking CJ to France, which is fair enough, I suppose, but there's something not right.'

Sara leaned back against the doorframe. 'Go on.'

'Well, Carla sounded more distressed by this than I would have expected. She's on her way round now – says there's something she thinks I should know.'

Jess's sharp green eyes opened wide as she stared at Sara. 'Mum, I'm frightened.'

Chapter Two

Carla Barton's mind was in a whirl as she bustled about gathering up her handbag and jacket while at the same time reassuring her two young children that she wouldn't be long. At the same time Toby was chugging about in her wake trying to dissuade his wife from going to see Jess.

'This isn't a good idea, you know. It's really none of our business and we don't know anything for sure. You know the old saying about two and two making five. You could be making the situation worse for Jess.'

While running his fingers through his hair with one hand he grabbed her hand with the other, trying to slow her down.

'Listen to me, darling.' His voice was urgent. 'If you've got this all arse about face then Sheldon will never forgive us. Nor will Jess. It could be the end of the friendship for all of us.'

Carla hesitated for a moment then purposefully snatched up her keys from the dresser. Her voice was low so that the children wouldn't hear but at the same time it was determined.

'Toby, I'm not sure what to think, but I do know

I should have said something to poor Jess before this. God, I'm such a coward. If it was me, I'd want someone to tell me. Now just keep an eye on the children and their homework. Bloody *nannies*.' The vitriol in that one word made both children look up.

Toby lowered his voice to a whisper. 'Don't do this! It's all speculation and it'll backfire. No good ever comes out of interfering in other people's marriages, not to mention how it will affect my business dealings with Sheldon. His business is important to the company.'

Carla stared angrily at her husband as she interrupted him. 'Is that all you can think of? No, I have to go and see her. She's in a terrible state, imagining all sorts of horrors. All I'm going to do is tell Jess exactly what we know, or rather what we think, then it's up to her how she handles the information. Her child is missing, for God's sake! Imagine if it was one of ours.'

The hurt expression on Toby's face suddenly softened her anger.

'I'm sorry, sweetheart, I know none of this is your fault. If anything I'm angry with myself and, if I'm wrong, I'll take all the blame. You can tell Sheldon that if or when he reappears. It's all my fault, mea culpa and all that. I'll kiss his arse,' she paused and smiled, 'metaphorically speaking, of course.'

As she went over to kiss him on the cheek, Toby took hold of her hand. 'Take it easy on her.'

'Of course I will! Wish me luck, I think I'm going to need it. This certainly isn't going to be the easiest thing I've ever done.'

Carla drove the short distance to the Pattersons' house and, after hesitating briefly at the entrance to take a deep breath, she pulled into the curved driveway and carefully parked her car in front of the house alongside Sara's.

She didn't have to ring the doorbell. Jess was already there waiting on the doorstep moving rhythmically from foot to foot with her mother just a step behind her looking nervously over Jess's shoulder.

'You'd better come in.'

Jess didn't bother with the pleasantries she normally exchanged with the svelte and elegant woman in front of her, and as Carla moved forward to kiss her, Jess took a step backwards out of reach.

No matter what, Carla always looked cool and calm, Jess thought almost enviously. Not for her the bright red face and damp corkscrewed hair. Carla's hair hung glamorously straight and styled, just like her body!

'What's this all about, Carla?' Jess leaned her head on one side and looked quizzically at her friend. 'What is it you want to talk to me about? I need to know. I'm worried sick about Sheldon and CJ and if you know something, anything . . .'

'I know, and I'm afraid that's why I'm here.' Carla's tone was ominously neutral as she smiled sympathetically at mother and daughter.

Jess and Sara stepped to one side in unison to let her pass into the wide entrance hall of the modern house. Despite the circumstances of her visit, Carla couldn't help but notice the expensive new wallpaper and the cloying smell of fresh paint.

'Have you been decorating again, Jess? It looks lovely. You've got such a good eye for colour,' Carla murmured, making a half-hearted attempt at small talk as she slid out of her coat and handed it to Sara.

'Yes. I wanted to get it done before Sheldon and CJ got back. It was meant to be a surprise. I've had all the downstairs done – they didn't know . . .' Jess's voice tailed off as she tried hard to keep her emotions in check. She desperately wanted to know what Carla had to say but, knowing instinctively that it wasn't going to be good, she also wanted to delay it.

Painfully aware of her daughter's dilemma, Sara quickly moved in front of Jess and took charge.

'We haven't met before. I'm Sara – Jess's mother as you've probably guessed. Come through to the sitting room. I understand there's something you think you know about Sheldon and CJ's disappearance.'

Sara led the way with Carla close behind and although Jess knew she had to follow, her legs suddenly became leaden and she couldn't bring herself to move. Hesitating in the doorway, all her childhood superstitions were tumbling around in her brain.

Don't walk on the cracks, turn around three times and cross fingers, close eyes tight and wish but don't tell anyone . . .

'Jess? Are you coming through?'

Sara's voice brought her sharply back to reality.

'Yes, of course.' Feigning a confidence she didn't feel, and forcing her legs to function, Jess stepped towards her neighbour and friend. 'Well, Carla? What is it you want to tell me?'

The pleading in Jess's voice made Carla want to flee the house but she just turned away, then, looking for refuge, walked over to the furthest sofa and perched herself awkwardly on the arm.

'Look, Jess, perhaps I should have told you this before, but I still don't know if it's right or relevant. I just know you won't want to hear it.' She paused for several seconds and looked from Jess to Sara. 'Well, Sofia up and left without giving any notice just under a week ago.'

'Who's Sofia?' Sara, the frownlines between her eyebrows deepening, looked puzzled.

'You know Sofia, Mum. She's Carla's nanny – the Spanish girl who babysits sometimes for CJ.' Jess looked back to Carla. 'I'm sorry about your nanny, Carla, but right now your nanny problems aren't high on my list of concerns. I'm off my head with worry about CJ; they're so late getting back, I'm terrified there might have been an accident.'

'No, Jess, you don't understand. What I'm trying to say is that Sheldon must have left at the same time as Sofia.'

'So? What's that got to do with the price of fish?' Jess's voice was cold and detached. She could feel her frustration rising and she resented Carla for intruding in her personal life at a time of crisis for no apparent reason other than she was without a nanny. But, even as she was thinking it, a frisson of nervous apprehension ran through her.

'Look, Jess.' Carla hesitated and took a deep breath. 'I'm sorry, but I won't beat about the bush. It's just that I had suspicions – *have* suspicions – that Sheldon has been having an affair with Sofia.'

Looking from one to the other she sighed. 'There, I've said it. I'm sorry and I hope I'm wrong, but she's gone off at the same time as Sheldon and CJ, and I can't help but wonder if maybe they're together somewhere. They may have sneaked off for an illicit long weekend.'

Jess's hands flew up to her face. 'That is an awful thing to say and it's just not true! How could you even think it? Sheldon would never do anything like that!' Jess looked over at her mother. 'Tell her, Mum. How dare she waltz in here and feed me a load of old bollocks like that? I'd have known if he was having an affair, wouldn't I?'

As Carla silently looked down at her hands in embarrassment Jess felt an overwhelming urge to hit her, to lash out and stop her saying any more but Sara touched her on the arm.

'Hear Carla out, darling. Even if it's nothing, it's best to know what she thinks.' Turning to the other woman, Sara smiled grimly. 'Go on, tell us what you think and why. We're both so worried about them, they should have been back yesterday.'

Jess could hear what was being said but it all sounded distant and disjointed as if she were an eavesdropper on someone else's conversation. She couldn't understand how a virtual stranger could be saying things about her husband, things she never had any idea about, things that simply weren't true.

'I really am sorry.' Carla's voice took on a pleading quality. 'If CJ wasn't involved I probably wouldn't have said anything. Toby told me not to, but as I said to him, I know how I would feel if my child were missing.'

'I can understand that,' Jess heard her mother saying, 'but it's all speculation, isn't it? Couldn't it just be coincidence? I mean, your nanny must have given you a reason for leaving, given you notice.'

Frowning, Carla averted her dark eyes and furrowed her forehead before answering cautiously, 'Well, no actually, she just packed her stuff and took off nearly a week ago. Oh, she made noises about a terminally sick brother but I just knew it was nonsense. I knew she was lying but I had to let her go. After all, who wants a nanny who isn't committed? Anyway, it's not only that. There were other things, but you know how it is, benefit of hindsight and all that.'

Carla stood up sharply and went over to Jess who was silently leaning against the fireplace deliberately not making eye-contact with either Carla or Sara.

'Look, I may have got it all wrong, Jess, really I may,

but I've known for months that Sofia had a secret boyfriend. All the signs were there. I mean, I've had a stream of nannies and au pairs so I have a nose for these things now, but it's only recently that I've suspected it was Sheldon.'

Jess still wouldn't speak or look at Carla so the woman changed her direction to Sara.

'I don't want to go into details at the moment and make things even worse for Jess but I'm ninety-nine per cent certain Sofia is with Sheldon. But that doesn't mean that Sheldon has gone off with her, does it? He's got to come back, hasn't he? He's got CJ with him as well.'

Carla's rat-a-tat-tat voice tailed off as she saw the expression on Jess's face change dramatically. Until that moment she had appeared detached, looking vacantly around the room, but suddenly her shoulders drooped and she shrank visibly.

'Sofia! Of course,' she murmured so quietly she could almost have been talking to herself. 'Now I realise what was bothering me. Something wasn't right and then I got side-tracked, but now I know what it is that I couldn't quite put my finger on.'

Jess turned sharply and flew out of the door so quickly she tripped over the black Labrador that had taken up guard in his usual place just outside the door. 'Bloody stupid animal, get out of my way!' Pushing him away with her foot she disappeared back into the kitchen leaving Sara and Carla silent and bewildered. She was only gone a couple of minutes before she reappeared, holding aloft two of the photo frames she had taken from her husband's office. 'Look at these, just look at these and tell me! Look! Look!' The hysteria in her voice rose with each word until she was nearly screaming at them.

23

Jess sat down on the sofa and patted her hand impatiently, indicating for Sara and Carla to join her. 'Look, tell me what you see.' She had one in each hand and held them up for Sara and Carla to see.

The delicately embossed silver frame contained a beautifully posed and close-up wedding photograph of Jess and Sheldon. The two of them were gazing at each other, clasping hands in such a way that the rings glistened new and shiny in the bright sunshine, their total adoration of each other captured perfectly in their eyes.

The second wooden frame showed Sheldon and CJ, snapped informally at their son's fourth birthday party. CJ was on Sheldon's lap, his smile wide as he looked up at his father. Sheldon's expression was equally loving, a carbon copy expression of the one in the wedding photo.

Sara and Carla looked equally puzzled.

'I don't know what you mean, Jess. What's the relevance of the photos?' Sara screwed her face up as she concentrated.

Carla looked closer. 'Oh Lord, Jess,' she muttered, almost under her breath, 'I can see what you're getting at. Bugger, this is a mess. I was praying I was wrong, I really was, but now . . .'

Sara looked from one to the other. 'I can't see what you're getting at.'

'Look carefully.' Carla pointed at the second photo. 'Look at Sheldon's face, his expression.'

'Yes.' Sara's voice was puzzled. 'He looks happy and so he should – it was CJ's birthday. I know, I was there.'

'Yes, but who is he looking at? It's not CJ, is it? He's actually gazing directly at Sofia in the background!'

The three women studied the photo silently. There were several people in the background but it was only too obvious that Sheldon was gazing besottedly at the young woman on the perimeter of the frame and her expression as, apparently oblivious to the probing camera lens, she gazed back at him, was equally adoring.

Jess felt as if she had been hit in the stomach.

The encapsulated look of love and intimacy on Sheldon's face was the one that she had always thought was solely reserved for her.

'I'm going up to my bedroom,' Jess announced calmly. 'I'm okay, I just need some time to think. I have to get all this straight in my head.'

Chapter Three

In a few short, mindblowing moments, Jessica Patterson realised her life might just have changed for ever. When Sheldon came back she would have to confront him and if, as she feared, it was true, then she knew it would be almost impossible for the marriage to survive.

Infidelity was the one thing that Jess both feared and despised, and Sheldon not only knew that, but always professed to agree with her.

When they had first met, Sheldon was still suffering the fallout from the collapse of his first marriage to Kay. He told Jess all about it, how he had married Kay on the spur of the moment in Nevada, only to find that for her it was purely a marriage of convenience. The convenience being the crippling divorce settlement a few short years later, after which Kay went back to her previous boyfriend with enough cash to buy a house and set themselves up in business.

'Never again,' he used to say. 'Divorce is out – marriage and the family is for life.'

Was it fair then, she wondered, to prejudge him on the strength of Carla's speculation and one photograph, and at the same time undermine everything about her years with him?

Roaming the bedroom like a restless panther she nervously tried to piece it all together, but apart from what she had found out in the previous hour there was nothing she could find in her mind that she might have missed. No hints, no clues, there was nothing at all to suggest that Sheldon was playing away. But then, not being naturally suspicious and convinced their marriage was based on mutual trust, she certainly hadn't been looking.

Jess had known for some time that there were a few problems in their marriage, but it had never crossed her mind that their difficulties were any more than other couples face after the initial heady romance fades and real life takes over.

Once again she looked at herself critically in the mirror and wondered if she had let herself go. As clear as if she was in the room with her, Jess could see Sofia posing in front of her. The lively and confident Sofia, with a sexy Spanish accent colouring her perfect English, who managed to look incredibly sexy in battered jeans, muddy trainers and not a scrap of make-up.

Sofia, Carla's resident nanny.

Sofia, whom Jess had welcomed into her house to babysit regularly because CJ loved her.

Sofia, the young Spanish girl who was tall and slender to the point of being almost skinny with olive skin and thick dark hair. There was no getting away from it, Jess thought, the girl was attractive and confident as well as being very intelligent. Being a nanny, she had told Jess over a friendly cup of coffee, was a means of travelling, and she was saving as much as she could towards the day she would move to a new family in another country.

Jess in the meantime had been only too happy to pay well over the odds for the peace of mind that Sofia instilled in her. Momentarily mortified, she remembered the times she had given Sofia free access to the family home and maybe even free access to her husband.

She continued looking at herself critically. At about twenty pounds overweight, most of which was happily settled on her dimpled hips and thighs, Jess could see how in Sheldon's eyes, she could be seen to have let herself go. She could also see how her husband would prefer the lovely Sofia, a much younger and much more attractive model.

CJ! His name jumped ferociously back into her mind.

For a few short moments she had been distracted away from her prime concern. Where the hell were they? And when they came back, what would happen? How could she possibly survive as a single mother if the marriage was over? But then, how could her marriage survive if Sheldon had been unfaithful?

It had been at Sheldon's request that she had turned her back on her nursing career, albeit eagerly, and become a fulltime mother. It was because of this, and also because Sheldon spent a lot of time travelling, that Jess and CJ were inseparably close. Too close, according to Sheldon who had, from the beginning, resented the mother and son bond.

'Jess?' a voice called in the background. 'Can I come in? I just wanted to check you're okay. I know this has been a terrible shock.'

The sharp knock on the bedroom door, accompanied by her mother's voice, brought her back to reality.

'I'm fine, Mum, really. I'll be down in just a minute. Is Carla still here?'

'Yes. She's very upset at hurting you, not to mention deeply embarrassed at the turn of events.'

'Okay, I'll be down. I want to know everything, and I mean everything, so you go and warn her. I don't want her sparing my feelings.'

'Open the door, please.'

Jess took a deep breath. 'Mum, I'm okay, I'll be down in a minute. Just go and pour us all a stiff drink.'

Jess knew there was no putting it off any longer; she had to go down and hear what she didn't want to hear.

Not wanting to feel at even more of a disadvantage in front of the ever-elegant Carla, Jess quickly changed her clothes. Dumping the jogging bottoms straight in the rubbish bin in disgust, she pulled out a beige calf-length skirt that skimmed her hips, and paired it with a jade-green cashmere sweater that matched her eyes and set off the red in her hair. She knew she was being irrational but couldn't help herself.

Before going back down to face Carla, she picked up the phone in desperation and dialled Sheldon's mobile once again. The 'unable to connect' message continued to echo in her head as she made her way determinedly back to the increasingly nervous Carla who was sitting on the edge of her seat. Twisting a mug in her hands, she was distractedly watching Sara pottering around plumping the cushions and re-stacking a pile of books and magazines on the side table. She looked quite sick when Jess walked back into the room.

'Carla, I've been thinking about what you said earlier, and although I don't want to put you on the spot, I do want you to tell me absolutely everything. I need to be prepared for when Sheldon gets back.'

Chapter Four

Carla Barton's mind was in a whirl. She had the distinct feeling that she was in the process of unleashing something that could never be recaptured. While Jess was upstairs she had tried to voice her concerns about it all with Sara, but the woman had been adamant that they should not discuss anything without Jess being present.

Sara had poured herself a large brandy and put another to one side for Jess but Carla declined the alcohol, opting instead for a strong black coffee. The silence in the room was deafening as they both waited for Jess to reappear, but it gave Carla some thinking time to mentally gather everything she knew, or thought she knew, and to rationalise it all.

As she waited, her eyes were drawn to the photo frames that were laid flat on the coffee table and she studied them surreptitiously. The wedding photo was a classic, the pose familiar from photographers' shop windows everywhere, but it struck her that Jess and Sheldon were actually a fairly ordinary-looking couple behind the wedding glitz.

The bridegroom was taller than average with sun-bleached fair hair that stood to gel-assisted attention, and a Californian suntan. His smile was wide and genuine as he gazed down at the much shorter Jess, whose ivory wedding dress was perfectly cut to accentuate her narrow bust and shoulders, and detract from her noticeably wider hips.

By the time Carla had met the couple Sheldon's hair had darkened a little, the tan had faded and Jess was much more rounded, but until a few weeks before, Carla had thought they were a perfectly matched couple with everything going for them.

The impressive sprawling house they shared in the beautiful part of Cambridge en route for Grantchester, was tastefully furnished and decorated, and, a touch ostentatiously Carla had thought, they drove matching Mercedes in different colours. Sheldon worked from home but often commuted to Los Angeles, and occasionally Jess and CJ would go with him to visit Pearl, Jess's mother-in-law.

Although in theory Sheldon worked in the family real-estate business, he appeared to spend a lot of time wheeling and dealing in the financial market, which was where Toby came in. The company her husband worked for managed Sheldon's quite considerable portfolio of stocks and shares.

On the surface at least, it seemed a perfect lifestyle for a perfect couple with an almost perfect child.

To Carla, CJ came across as a well-balanced child who sometimes made her own two appear almost like hooligans by comparison. A touch too quiet and well behaved, she often commented to Toby, but she knew that might well be because she herself worked fulltime so when she was at home the pair vied rowdily for her attention.

CJ, of course, didn't need to compete; he was an only

child with his mother constantly on hand to provide all the attention he wanted.

In fact, Carla had, in the nicest way, envied Jess her carefree lifestyle.

Until now.

Jess sat down carefully on the edge of the chunky coffee table in front of her friend and deliberately made direct eye-contact. 'Okay, Carla, I'm ready. I want to know everything, every last little detail. Please don't try and spare me, I have CJ to think of here.' Unblinking, she fixed her eyes on Carla. 'If Sheldon *has* taken Sofia away with them then it means he's deceived me on several fronts.' Pausing, she shook her head. 'That I can live with if I have to, but I want CJ back. I *have* to have him back, I can't live without him, I can't! CJ is my whole life.'

As Carla raised her hands in a gesture of defeat and sucked in her cheeks, Sara, watching silently from across the room, felt sorry for her. She wasn't sure whether or not she would have had the courage to tell all if she was in that position.

'Of course, that's why I came over. I'll tell you everything I know, but if it all turns out to be a load of old nonsense, I hope you'll forgive me. I'd like us still to be friends regardless, and I also want you to know that I'll be there for you if the worst comes to the worst.'

'I know that and I appreciate it.' Jess waited.

As Carla prevaricated by sipping her drink and flattening her skirt, Jess watched her through lowered eyelashes. Although her friend's life was constantly hectic as she juggled career, home and husband she always looked groomed and relaxed and, despite the situation, her composure was still obvious.

'You know what Sofia is like.' Carla looked Jess in the

eye. 'She's a lovely girl, probably the best nanny I've ever had; the children loved her and, until recently, I always knew I could go to work and trust her completely. But lately . . .' She struggled to find the right words. 'Lately she's been distracted, her mind has been elsewhere. She suddenly acquired a top-of-the-range mobile phone, and a couple of times I found her whispering into it, almost slyly. She would cut off quickly when I appeared, which wasn't necessary as I've always been easygoing with her, as you know.'

Jess smiled. 'Yes, I always thought she had a good life, and job, with you.'

'So did I,' Carla responded grimly, 'but she obviously didn't think so. She started staying out late at night and asking for extra time off. When the children were at school, instead of coming back here to do a few chores, she would disappear for hours on end. It was obvious she was seeing someone and didn't want me to know.'

As Jess screwed her face up in concentration trying to make sense of Carla's words, Sara jumped into the conversation.

'But whatever makes you think it's Sheldon? It could be absolutely anyone, anyone at all. It could be a boy down the road.'

Carla moved her eyes sharply to Sara. 'I know that,' her tone was apologetic, 'and for a while I have to admit that I didn't have a clue, but with all the secrecy, I guessed it was someone who was married. What's more, she kept appearing with bits of jewellery and clothes that I knew she couldn't possibly afford herself.'

'That could still be anyone,' Sara intervened again.

'Well, yes and no. Jess or CJ always told me when Sheldon was working away and, with hindsight of course, that was when Sofia would either want extra time off or be at home, moping around like a wet weekend, and actually getting under my feet.'

Carla took a deep breath and then sighed. 'It was lots of little things, and all over a period of time, but the single deciding factor was when I went into her bedroom. I'd knocked to wake her up and then pushed the door open. On her dressing-table, with red glass hearts glued all round the large tacky frame, was a collage of photographs of Sheldon and CJ.' Again she hesitated before continuing. 'You weren't in any of the photos, Jess.'

The sharp intake of breath from Jess interrupted her and she reached out for her cup. Sipping nervously she said, 'Oh, I queried it but she said it was there because she was so fond of CJ. I knew that was ridiculous, but what could I say? She did babysit for you so it was almost feasible in a way, but I knew that it just wasn't true. Her whole defensive demeanour when I mentioned it, told me otherwise.'

'How can you be sure she's not just gone back to Spain to see her brother?' Again Sara spoke up, the desperate pleading in her voice all too obvious. 'I mean, that's just as feasible, isn't it? This could all be making mountains out of molehills, couldn't it? Two and two makes five?'

'Yes, it could – you're damned right it could – and I'm all too aware of it. That's why I don't want to be doing this!' Carla's tone was sharp to the point of anger. 'Look, I'm not here to hang Sheldon out to dry, and I'm certainly not here to upset Jess. I'm here because her husband and son are missing and Jess phoned me. I'm trying to help, really I am.'

'It's okay, Mum,' Jess intervened quietly. 'Carla is right – I did phone her and I do need to know where

CJ is. If Sheldon is with Sofia then there's not a lot I can do about it, but CJ? That's a whole different ballgame. Tell me, Carla, with the benefit of hindsight of course, how long do you think this thing has been going on?'

Carla's eyes narrowed at the veiled sarcasm in Jess's voice but her tone remained level. 'At a guess, I would say that if it is Sheldon whom Sofia was seeing, then about six months – possibly more. Possibly not far short of the year that she's been with us.'

'Do what?' Jess shrieked, standing so quickly she almost toppled over. 'Six months? A year?' The words were hurled aggressively across the room. 'No way, I would have known! Don't try and tell me that I'm so fucking stupid that I wouldn't have noticed something was up.'

'No one's saying you were stupid, just that Sheldon was very, very clever. And devious.'

'No, I won't have that. He wouldn't do that, he couldn't do that . . .'

Sara and Carla remained silent as Jess ranted at both of them. Her previous self-control disappeared as the information sank in. Sheldon, her husband, had been having an affair for months and she had been totally oblivious to it. It was just too much to accept.

After a few more uncomfortable minutes Carla stood up to leave. 'I really have to go now. I'm so sorry about it all – you will call me as soon as you hear anything? Any time, day or night. I've got the week off to get the children back to school and sort out a new nanny.' As the words came out, her hand flew up to her mouth. 'I'm so sorry, that was tactless in the extreme. I can imagine how you must be feeling.'

'Oh, I doubt you can, Carla. Even I don't know how I'm feeling.'

As Sara reached for her own coat as well, Jess panicked. 'You're not leaving, are you, Mum? You can't! I was hoping you'd stay a bit longer. I don't want to be on my own when he comes back.'

Sara reached out and stroked her daughter's cheek. 'I'm just nipping home to sort out someone to feed the cat and then I'll grab a few things and come back. I'm staying here with you for as long as it takes. Just give me an hour or so.'

Closing the door gently behind them, Jess went into the lounge and picked up the heavy silver frame that contained the wedding photo. Raising her hand high above her head she threw it full force at the marble fireplace and watched as the glass shattered and flew through the air to settle in the carpet.

All she wanted to do was curl up in a ball and go to sleep until it was all over.

After another sleepless night when neither she nor her mother even bothered to go upstairs, Jess presented herself at the local police station determined to get some action. All fired up, she calmed a little when introduced to a sympathetic young policewoman who led her through into one of the utilitarian interview rooms where she was handed a well-intentioned but unpalatable polystyrene cup of weak coffee.

'My name's Judy Simmons,' the WPC introduced herself. 'Now I understand from my colleague that your husband and son haven't come home from their holiday. I'm not sure exactly what we can do, Mrs Patterson, but just tell me everything and I'll do my best.'

Jess went through it all, including the suspicions that Carla had voiced, but although the young woman made the right noises in the right places, she offered little practical help. Jess had known they were going away, she said, and had countenanced them going away. There were no court orders, no custody proceedings in place. Nothing illegal for them to work with.

'But surely he can't just take my son and disappear? That can't be right. He can't do that!'

'I'm so sorry, Mrs Patterson, but Cameron is your husband's son as well as yours. You both have equal rights. I wish I could be more encouraging, but as it stands at the moment, our hands are tied.'

'But there must be something! Surely he can't just—'

The policewoman interrupted, her voice sympathetic but firm. 'I understand how you feel, I'm a mother myself, but your son is Mr Patterson's son as well.'

'Oh, come off it.' Jess stood up abruptly. 'Is that the best you can come up with?'

'I can give you the names of organisations that could maybe give you some information and offer you some support. Other than that, unless or until a crime has been committed . . .' The police officer shook her head and smiled before continuing. 'You told me yourself you have no fears for your son's safety with Mr Patterson. There's little we can do at the moment.'

Jess felt her frustration start to rise but she tried to stay calm. 'So what you're telling me basically is that there is nothing you can do until a couple of bodies turn up?'

'Be honest with yourself, Mrs Patterson. Do you really think there's been an accident? Realistically, the most likely scenario is that your husband has gone off on a holiday somewhere with his alleged girlfriend and taken your son along as well as an alibi. I'm sorry to sound harsh, but I think from what you've told me, that's the most viable explanation.'

WPC Judy Simmons leaned her elbows on the table

and crossed her hands in front of her. 'It happens all the time, I'm afraid. The accident theory is highly unlikely. We'd have heard something from somewhere by now, but I will double-check. I think you may have to accept that your husband has taken it into his head to go off somewhere on an illicit holiday.'

'Ten out of ten to the detectives. I sussed that one out yesterday,' Jess laughed dryly, 'but what can I do about it?'

'My advice is to phone everyone you know, here and, especially as he is a US citizen, in America. Check out everything you can think of and I'll give you a call tomorrow to see how you're getting on. Maybe you should also get some legal advice.' The policewoman stood up and smiled. 'I'll just go and find you some information to take home with you. Please call me if you hear anything or if they turn up.'

Jess felt her chest start to palpitate as the panic rose. She banged her fist hard on the desk in front of her. 'If that's the best you can do then you can shove your information and your caring smile. All I want is my son back, and if you're not prepared to help then I'm going to have to find him myself. I *have* to get my son back!'

She pushed her way past and slammed out of the office, tears of frustration pouring down her face. With no idea of where to turn next, Jess roared off in her car and drove halfway to London and back. Anything was better than going back home to a house without CJ.

Chapter Five

While Jess was out at the police station, Sara was on guard over the phone and at the same time busying herself working her way systematically through Sheldon's study. She was looking for anything that might provide a clue to his whereabouts, anything her daughter might have missed.

As more time had passed, her concerns had risen to the same level as Jess's. It was two days since Sheldon should have returned with CJ, and it was also the day that CJ should have started his new school. Sara was beginning to think sinister thoughts, but she knew she had to try and disguise them for her daughter's sake, and it helped to have something positive to do.

Despite scouring through Sheldon's office she found nothing at all out of the ordinary. His large office address book that lay neatly on the desk at least gave them a list of contacts, but they were all work related; there was nothing personal written in it at all.

During the long night before, Jess had combed through the rest of the house and found no clues or pointers at all.

It was all very strange.

Nothing was missing other than those items that Sheldon would normally have taken with him for a few days away, and nothing extra was missing from CJ's room.

The pair of them had allegedly gone away for a few days and then disappeared into thin air. The two burning questions both Jess and Sara repeated over and over again were, firstly, where were Sheldon and CJ? And secondly, did they go with or without Sofia?

But there was no one they were aware of who could answer either question.

Dispirited, Sara tugged the office door closed and went into the sitting room. She loved the room which, despite being square and barn-like, had been decorated and furnished to look cosy and warm. The long midnight-blue drapes framed the full-width French windows that looked out over the carefully tended garden that Jess loved so much.

Sadly Sara focused on the childishly fashionable two-wheeler bicycle with its wobbly stabilisers still attached. CJ's pride and joy, his last birthday present from Sara, his doting maternal grandmother.

Sara deliberately tried to shake off the gloom, aware that she had to be strong for her daughter. Just then she noticed the shards of glass picked out by the sun and glittering in the carpet. As she started to gather up the pieces her eyes settled on the battered frame that lay in the fireplace. Picking it up she tried to smooth the crumpled photograph. It didn't take a genius to figure out what had happened to it; she was sure she would have done the same thing.

Studying the scenario captured in front of her Sara literally ached with pain for her daughter, her only child who, in turn, because of unforeseen complications at CJ's birth, also had an only child.

It had been just Sara and Jess, mother and daughter, for so long. Jess had been nearly thirty by the time she took the plunge, convinced that Sheldon Patterson was the right man, the only man, for her. The birth of CJ had been a joyous time for them all and from the very first minute, Sheldon had been besotted with his adored son.

Sheldon Patterson. Sara's son-in-law.

Sara ran her fingers gently over his face. Was the man she thought she knew, and had eventually come to love and trust as her own, really capable of such unbelievable deceit and betrayal? Maybe, at forty, he was having a mid-life crisis? Maybe he would think twice and come back with his tail between his legs? Maybe, maybe . . .

Hearing Jess's car crunch loudly up the drive Sara hastily laid the battered and glassless frame and photo back on the marble fireplace face down and raced out to the rubbish bin with the broken glass.

'Any news, Mum?' Jess's voice preceded her as she walked quickly into the kitchen.

'Nothing, darling, apart from Carla – she's offered to contact the agency to try and get hold of Sofia's home address in Spain. She wanted to check with you first, she said. She doesn't want to step on any toes.'

'I'll phone her.' Jess's face was tight and pale with restrained anger. 'I got absolutely nowhere with the police so it looks like we'll have to play detective ourselves, although I haven't a clue where to start.'

'Didn't they have *any* suggestions? They must have said something.'

'Not really, or rather nothing helpful. The WPC did offer me the phone numbers of some bloody do-gooding support groups but I told her where to stick her phone numbers. I need practical help, not pieces of paper. I'm going to phone Carla – at least that's somewhere to start, and then I'm going to phone the mother-in-law from hell.'

Sara kept quiet, knowing it wasn't a good time to disagree with her daughter, but decided that she would herself contact the policewoman Sara was talking about and gather every scrap of advice she could.

Just in case, although she still hoped there was a simple explanation for it all.

But just in case.

'Tread carefully with Pearl, won't you, darling? You know how touchy she can be about her beloved son and heir.' Sara started to be sarcastic about Jess's mother-in-law then reined herself in. The last thing she wanted was for Jess to be defensive before she even got to the phone. 'Sheldon is her only son, and if she hasn't heard from him then you're passing on the news that her son and grandson are missing.'

'I do know that, Mum, I'm not daft! I've spent years making all the right, tactful noises to Pearl. I'm an expert at not upsetting the iron lady! She gives the expression *Mommy Dearest* a whole new meaning!'

Sara smiled, relieved that Jess still had a touch of the old spark in her despite the situation.

'Pearl's okay, I suppose, if you can accept her as she is. She has plenty of money and plenty of time to do whatever she wants, but she doesn't have the one thing she really craves – another husband to keep her in the manner to which she has become accustomed! That's why she spends her time flitting from cruise ship to cruise ship and getting in your hair between times.'

Jess opened her eyes wide and made her mouth into

a perfect O. 'Ohhh, Mum, that almost sounded bitchy. You're not jealous of her, are you?'

'Jealous? Good God, can you see me done up like a dog's dinner cruising the seas for six months of the year?'

The look that flashed across Sara's face amused Jess; her mother actually looked quite insulted.

'Well, yes, actually. I think it might suit you, you deserve a bit of pampering . . .'

'Not on your life. I prefer a cup of cocoa in front of the TV with the cat. The last thing I want is a husband to upset my well-earned equilibrium.'

Jess screwed her face up and shook her head vigorously. 'Yeah, right! I believe you even if no one else will. Anyway, I'm going to ring Pearl now. I can't really imagine Sheldon taking off and not letting his mother know where he is, can you?'

Sara's face went from light-hearted to deadly serious in a split second. 'I hope not, Jess. I really hope not.'

'Okay. I'll phone Carla and then Pearl, then the office in LA and anyone else I can think of. Back in a minute.'

As Jess dialled she once again let her eyes roam round Sheldon's office. His den. His personal space. His now empty, personal space.

First on the list of calls was Carla, who eagerly promised to set things in motion immediately.

'I'm so pleased you called, Jess. I've been racking my brains and I can't think of anything more apart from contacting the agency – and if they want to keep my custom they'd better come up with the goods pretty sharpish.' She laughed hesitantly; it was obvious that walking across hot coals would have been preferable to the conversation she was having. 'I know this is a really inane question, but how are you holding up? It's good that you've got your mother with you but I'm really worried about you. I feel almost responsible . . .' Her voice tailed off. 'Well, if you need anything at all then just tell me. Now I'll call the agency this minute and get back to you.'

Jess sighed and dialled her mother-in-law in California but she had no luck. Pearl Patterson was allegedly cruising somewhere off the coast of South America but was due back the following week. Her housekeeper did confirm that no one had seen or heard from Sheldon that she knew of, but Jess couldn't rely on that information; she was only too well aware of where the Patterson staff's loyalties lay.

Jess's mood dipped even lower when everyone else she contacted was just as negative. Because Sheldon worked from home when he was in England no one had even missed him, or so they said. The Los Angeles office of the Patterson Realty Company thought he was in England and his contacts in England thought he was in Los Angeles.

Sheldon Patterson had very cleverly managed to disappear without even being missed, which had allowed him plenty of time to get to wherever he was going.

'What am I going to do now, Mum? I can't just sit here and wait – I'll go crazy.'

Jess's normally pale face was almost translucent with worry, and pale blue rings were developing around her bloodshot eyes. There was no disguising the fact that she was teetering on the brink of hysteria.

Carla Barton was still trying to come to terms with what might have happened. She was fond of Jess and, like most women who came in contact with him, she also had a bit of a soft spot for Sheldon. Or *had* had! For the first time she found herself trying to analyse the man whom she thought she knew.

Although not exactly a ladies' man, Sheldon Patterson was definitely a charmer and he certainly had the gift of making anyone he was talking to feel as if they were the only person in the room. In fact, he was such flattering company in a social setting that Carla could easily understand how Jess had fallen in love with him and how Sofia might have developed a crush on him.

What she found difficult to believe was that Sheldon might have reciprocated, or even in the case of the worst scenario, instigated it. Despite living on the fringes of Newnham, in a small, exclusive suburb of Cambridge where Chinese whispers could do the rounds in minutes, there had never been any hint among their circle of friends of anything even remotely improper in connection with him.

The only other explanation that was too awful to think about was the one that Jess had put forward, the possibility that Sheldon and CJ had been involved in an accident in France, or even in England on the way back, and no one knew where they were.

As she wondered which would be the worse to contemplate if she was in Jess's position, the phone rang. As she had expected, it was Jess again and she had to give her the news that the agency refused to release any information on their nannies. Under duress they had said that they would write to Sofia's parents at the address they'd been given by her, and they had confirmed that Sofia had told them she was going back to Spain and didn't want another placement. But that was it. The manager had been so busy trying to distance the agency that the panic flowing down the phone-line had been palpable.

Jess sounded so dispirited by the end of the conversation that, on the spur of the moment, Carla phoned her husband to enlist his help. However, despite being the one person who knew everything about Sheldon's business dealings, Toby was reluctant to get involved.

'Look, Carla darling, I understand you're desperate to help, but it's just not good practice to snoop around after a client. I could lose my job, all for nothing if Sheldon suddenly swans back with a very good excuse for being away. Infidelity isn't a crime in the financial world, you know. It's almost commonplace.'

'Don't try and bullshit me, Toby Barton,' Carla interrupted. 'This isn't just a case of screwing around; every single one of your clients would be sympathetic under these circumstances. I'm not asking you to go out and plunder clients' funds, I'm just asking you to make a few discreet enquiries.' Her voice changed from confrontational to low and persuasive. 'Please? I want to know if there's anything that could point to Sheldon making advance plans to ship out.'

'But I can't. I daren't!' Toby's voice echoed desperately down the line.

'No buts, darling, do your best for Jess – she deserves it. Come on, put your head over the parapet and help me out here; no one else need ever know anything. Bye, darling, love you.' Smiling as Toby spluttered and stuttered his reply, she gently replaced the receiver into its base.

However, she decided against telling Jess that she had involved Toby, unless he came up with something positive. There had already been enough dead ends for her.

Chapter Six

It was after two heartbreaking weeks of non-stop activity and zero information that Jess finally received a phone call from the police that gave her what appeared to be her first lead. They told her that Sheldon's Mercedes had been vandalised in a private car park near Heathrow Airport, but to her horror she was informed that it had been there for nearly three weeks. Since the very day that he and CJ were supposed to have been driving down to Dover to catch the ferry to France.

Five minutes after Jess put the phone down, and before she had had time to fully absorb the information, she and Sara were on their way to London.

Oblivious to the speed cameras dotted en route Jess put her foot on the accelerator and gunned the high-performance car down the motorway at speeds of up to 130 m.p.h. Despite being aware of her mother's white knuckles and gritted teeth she didn't pull back; it was the last thing she was concerned with.

'I think you should slow down just a little, Jess. It won't do CJ much good when he does come home to find the pair of us in hospital.'

Jess could hear her mother's voice, she could even hear

the words, but she couldn't really understand them. She didn't want conversation and she didn't want to think too hard. She just wanted to get to Sheldon's car and maybe find an answer, a clue – anything at all that would point her in the right direction.

Sara had tried to persuade her to let the police deal with it, but Jess knew she had to see it for herself. The call from the police had momentarily raised her hopes but she had quickly realised that, far from being over, the sense of dread she had felt over the past weeks was deepening into something completely unimaginable.

For over two weeks neither Jess nor Sara had slept in the true sense of the word. Dozing and waking their way through the hours, day and night had blurred into a solid twenty-four-hour clock of catnaps and waking nightmares. When Jess did sleep it was usually alcohol induced and Sara was scared to leave her alone.

Word had soon got around, even the local newspapers and television stations had picked up on it briefly, and although Jess knew she should be grateful for all the support, she silently resented the kind-hearted phone calls and knocks at the door.

For a split second every time, they raised her expectations of an end to the nightmare.

Pearl Patterson had phoned when she got home to California, but by that time all thoughts of tact and diplomacy had flown out of Jess's head.

'What do you mean you haven't got a clue?' she had screamed at Pearl's apparent lack of interest. 'It's your son and grandson we're talking about here – they're missing, disappeared into thin air. Don't you care? You must know where they are, I know you do! Sheldon doesn't blow his own nose without your permission . . .'

As Jess's mood reached fever pitch Sara fought to take the phone away from her. 'Hello, Pearl, it's Sara here. Can you just hold on a moment?' She clamped her hand over the receiver. 'GO AWAY,' she muttered fiercely at her daughter. 'If you want Pearl to let you know if Sheldon and CJ turn up there, this isn't the way to go about it! Now GO and let me deal with her.'

Sara turned her back on her daughter. 'Pearl, I'm so sorry about that but Jess is very distraught, as you can well imagine. Don't take it personally, Jess is like it with me as well at the moment . . . Yes, I know she was rude but as I said, she's very upset . . . Yes, Pearl, I'll talk to her about it but in the meantime I really would like to pick your brains about where you think Sheldon and CJ might be.'

Her eyes blazing, Jess had grudgingly left the room but listened from outside the door to the one-sided conversation as Sara tried to smooth over her outburst. As the call ended she hurled herself back into the room.

'Stupid woman, she wasn't in the least bit interested in anything I had to say. She just twittered on and on.' Jess did a poor imitation of her mother-in-law. '"*Don't you worry your little head about Sheldon, he'll come home if he really wants to. He'll just have gone walkabout. You know how he is, honey – he just gets a bit stir crazy sometimes.*" She doesn't have a clue what I'm going through – she thinks it's all my fault.'

Sara smiled grimly.

'I know. I could bop her one quite easily if I saw her right now, but you have to be nice to her, you really do. If anyone knows what's going on then it's Pearl, and she's not going to co-operate with you if you go in there guns

51

blazing.' Sara spoke gently and persuasively, to try and take the edge off her words. 'Now you calm down, take a deep breath and then force yourself to ring her back and apologise.'

'I'm not ringing her back . . .' Her eyes wild, Jess paced back and forth in front of Sara. 'She knows what's happened, I *know* she does.'

'You have to call her back, Jess! If you really feel the need, you can tell her what you like after we've found CJ, but in the meantime be nice – it's the only way. Now I'm going to cook us something to eat. We haven't had a proper meal in days.'

'Oh come on, Mum, I don't want to eat. Nor do I want to phone Pearl, or keep on being nice to all the do-gooders who think they know how I feel. *I just want CJ back.*'

When the phone call had come from the police about Sheldon's car, Jess's emotions had see-sawed rapidly between anger and complete bewilderment. But although the tears were hovering near the surface, the anger won out.

'What the hell is his car doing at Heathrow? They were going by ferry, that was all part of the trip for CJ, sailing across the Channel. He'd never been on a boat before. He was really excited about it, so why would they fly instead?'

Sara didn't answer, she knew that whatever she said would be wrong. It was all too obvious that Jess was having problems holding it all together.

The race to Heathrow had continued until they hit the traffic and Jess had to slow down. But after much cursing, hooting and drumming of hands on the steering wheel, they eventually arrived at the car park that was really only a fenced-off piece of land just outside the perimeter of the airport.

Pulling up outside the ramshackle shed that passed as an office, Jess impatiently held her hand on the horn. The man who eventually sauntered out was short and wide and as bald as a coot. Scruffy and unshaven he lumbered over to the car, a look of irritation on his face as he casually eyed Jess's car.

'Oi! Any more of that and I'll have you thrown off my site. Now what do you want?'

Sara explained calmly while Jess steamed silently in her seat.

'Yep.' Flicking through a sheaf of dog-eared pages on a clipboard the man confirmed they were in the right place. 'Spot on. Got any ID with you? Can't let you near the car without ID. We've got to be careful here, you know.'

'Did the vandals who broke into my husband's car have to show their ID?' Jess asked in a pseudo-polite tone.

'Yes, we've got ID. Here you are,' Sara quickly interjected, handing over their driving licences with a wide smile. 'This is Mrs Patterson, it's her husband's car. He's actually listed by the police as missing, along with her young son. I'm her mother. What information can you give us? We would be really grateful if you could help us.' Sara tried not to show her distaste as she continued smiling.

The man looked the two women up and down almost suggestively as they got out of the car, before glancing back down at the clipboard.

'Booked in advance, paid in advance but he's now overdue. There'll be a penalty charge for each day over, and then the rest of it is between you and your insurance. We don't take responsibility for this sort of thing, don't normally get many Mercs in here.' The patter was monotone and bored.

'Yes, yes,' Jess snapped. 'I'll pay whatever you want. Now what else do you know?'

'Not a lot. Says here he was going to Spain, that's all the information we've got. Could have been going to Timbuctoo, for all I know. Our shuttle bus dropped him at Departures and that was the last we heard. Vandals got in last night and wrecked a couple of cars. Smashed the windows, took the stereo, and keyed it down both sides.'

'Spain!' Jess literally spat the word. 'He wasn't going to *Spain*!'

Sara's warning look stopped her mid-sentence.

'Can we see the car, please? Then we'll make arrangements to get it transported back home,' Sara asked, forcing herself to disguise her impatience with a smile.

'Yep, it's over on the far side – probably why they picked it, little bastards. I'll swing for 'em if I catch 'em. String 'em all up, I would. Come on – jump in and I'll drive you.'

The van swerved through the sea of parked cars then pulled up behind Sheldon's familiar Mercedes.

Jess was out of the van before the engine was off and frantically pulling at the door handles. They were locked despite the broken windows and she was about to reach in through the broken glass when Sara stopped her.

'Keys – I've got the spare key. Here you are.'

Apart from the broken glass that littered the seats and floor, the car was as pristine as Sheldon always kept it, neat and tidy with not so much as a sweet wrapper in sight.

'I don't understand this. Sheldon was always so particular about his car. He never left it at the airport, not even in the main area. He wouldn't have left it here, where there's no security at all.' Jess was turning out the glove compartment.

'I beg your pardon, sweetheart! We have got security, but you get what you pay for, and whatever you might say, he did leave it here, didn't he? Obviously didn't want it to be found too soon, so don't go all arsy on me just because your old man's done a runner.'

Gritting her teeth, Jess chose to ignore him and carried on desperately rifling through every nook and cranny of the car.

'Where in Spain?' asked Sara. 'Do you have his flight number?'

'Come on, look around you. How can we keep track of all this lot? All that's here is the date out, date due back and *alleged* destination.' The man's emphasis wasn't lost on either of them. 'When the passengers get back they give us a call and we go and pick them up from wherever they tell us they are. We don't give a toss where they go.'

He looked her over again with a leer. 'Just 'cos he said Spain to us don't mean nothing. As I said, he could have been on his way to anywhere in the bleeding world. Not going to tell us, now is he?'

'When was the car actually dropped off?' Sara asked.

Again he checked his clipboard. 'About nine, morning of the thirtieth. Now look, I've got to get back to the office, I can see the bleeding queue from here. Here's my number – let me know when the motor's going to be collected. You gonna settle up now?'

'Thank you so much for your help and your kind understanding of my situation.' Jess looked him up and down distastefully. 'NOT!'

The man laughed. 'Jump in again, I'll take you back to your motor. Don't worry, luv, he'll be back. We get loads of 'em sneaking off where they shouldn't. I can spot 'em a mile off!'

Jess couldn't believe that she had driven all the way from Cambridge and found absolutely nothing. There was no clue to suggest where Sheldon and CJ might be. Apart from Spain, with his Spanish girlfriend, and even Jess's befuddled brain took on board that if they really were going to Spain he probably wouldn't have told the car-park man that.

Returning to the gate in silence, they paused only to hand over a cheque then got back into Jess's car but she didn't pull away immediately.

'We need to check all the flights to Spain that morning. Let's go to the terminal.'

'Jess, sweetheart, that will take for ever. Why not let us go home and talk to the police. At least they've got something to go on now – or maybe you could employ a private detective? You certainly need to talk to your lawyer.'

Jess leaned forward onto the steering wheel, resting her head on her hands. 'He's done it, hasn't he? He's taken CJ away from me. He's abducted him. Why? Why would he do something like that? What have I ever done to him to deserve this?' Her face bright red with angry frustration and wet with tears, she battered her fists on the steering wheel.

'I really don't know.' Sara looked sideways at her daughter. 'But I'm sure as hell going to find out! This whole thing must have been pre-planned; he knew no one would trace the car for weeks. We probably still wouldn't know if it hadn't been trashed.' Sara's expression was grim, her voice angrily restrained. 'Now no arguing, I want you to change places with me. I'm driving home and then we'll really get this show on the road. Your husband's a selfish bastard and we're going to find them whatever it takes. Trust me, we'll find them.'

'But what about CJ? He must be so scared and he must be missing me. He won't know what's going on. He should be at his new school with all his friends. What on earth could Sheldon have told him?'

Sara took hold of her daughter's wrist and pulled her firmly round to look her in the eye. 'CJ will be okay. For all that I think of him at the moment, Sheldon is a good dad. I don't know why he's done what he's done but he'll take good care of CJ.'

'But I'm . . . his . . . mother.' Jess's sobs were so fierce she could barely get her words out.

'I know, I know.' Sara reached up and took hold of her daughter's face with both hands, kissing her on the forehead the way she had done when Jess was a child. 'But you have to trust me. Sheldon is his dad and won't hurt him. I know that with certainty.' Her voice was intense. 'I also know with certainty that we'll find them, but in the meantime I just know that CJ is safe. Sheldon would never hurt him, and deep down you know that, don't you?'

Jess sat silently on the drive back, huddled like a little girl against the car door with her arms crossed and her hands up her sleeves. She wanted to try and figure it out but her brain just wouldn't work.

The only thing she could think about was the abandoned car with naked wires dangling inside, dumped, abandoned and wrecked.

Just as she herself felt.

* * *

As soon as they got back home Jess, who had spent the whole journey in the foetal position, went to work like a woman possessed, checking and double-checking everything in Sheldon's office before maniacally filling two boxes with anything connected to him. Then she dragged them out and deposited them in the garage before cleaning the room from top to bottom.

Dusting, polishing and vacuuming, Jess worked to remove all trace of her husband – and his own personal space was as good a place as any to make a start. She wanted him out of her life but she desperately wanted her son back, and she knew that in order to do that, she would have to find Sheldon and possibly Sofia.

As she rubbed and sprayed, her mind kept springing back to Sofia. Jess couldn't even remember the girl's surname and that bugged her. She knew she had to ring Carla as soon as she got home from work.

If Sofia was somewhere with CJ then Jess wanted to know everything about her. Yes, she may have been an excellent nanny and babysitter, and yes CJ might well have loved her in that role, but as a substitute mother?

Jess could feel her emotions hurling to the surface; anger, grief, sorrow and despair were all fighting against each other as she determined not to cry. She knew that if she really let go then she would never be able to stop – and that wouldn't help her find her son.

'Mum?' she called through to Sara, who was busying herself cooking a meal for them both that she knew wouldn't get eaten. 'Come and have a look! I've finished.'

Jess stood back to let her mother into the room. Apart from the actual furniture there was now nothing in the room that connected it with Sheldon. The mahogany desk was still home to his computer, but it was now tucked behind the door with the matching bookshelves framing the comparatively small window that looked out over the front drive. All of Sheldon's chosen photographs were gone and in their place were Jess's own selection of favourites.

'It's lovely, darling, but why are you doing this now? We need to sit down together and sort out a strategy to search for them.'

'Yes, I know,' Jess's voice was almost triumphant, 'but this room signified something that I wanted gone. Now I can think. I need legal advice, I need information and most of all I need CJ home.' Her voice started to tremble but she determinedly held it in check. 'So, where shall we start?'

Later that night, after rolling around restlessly, Jess crept out of her bed and headed back down to the room. Turning on the light she looked around, and for the first time she realised the implications of the computer.

She clicked it on and waited as the monitor sprang to life.

Jess had never learned much about computers. She owned her own laptop, a present from Sheldon, but apart from writing a few letters she had little idea of anything more advanced. Sheldon had tried to teach her and as she looked at the screen she cursed herself for not having taken much notice.

Moving the mouse around she tried to remember.

A flicker of daylight was trying to break through the crack in the curtains when Jess finally gave up. She had found nothing. Everything she clicked into was 100 per cent innocent. Work, work and more work. Sheldon had either wiped it clean or been clever enough not to put anything incriminating on it in the first place.

Sighing loudly, she thought about the Sheldon that she thought she knew and loved; work and family were all that was important to him, and the remnants of his office typified that. A family man.

Or so it had seemed.

The man who could sneak around behind her back for months on end, having an affair with a girl nearly young enough to be his daughter was someone she didn't know. The man who could then disappear off the face of the earth with Sofia while at the same time taking CJ away from his mother was a complete alien.

More dispirited than ever, Jess went back upstairs, but instead of going into her own room she turned along the galleried landing and quietly went into CJ's room.

A large airy room decorated in several different shades of blue, CJ had loved it. The fitted wardrobes were navy blue and decorated with luminous stars and planets to complement his bed. Big and silver, it was a replica of a spaceship. Jess had seen it on display in a shop window and rushed straight in to pay the exorbitant six hundred pounds for it that she knew was silly, but she also knew that CJ would love it.

Bedtime was always a set routine and CJ wouldn't allow anyone or anything to break the routine. Wearing his favourite spaceman pyjamas he would clamber over the end of the bed and, after several kisses and cuddles, he would snuggle up with his head in the tail fin of the spaceship and his feet tucked into the nose cone.

Usually Jess, but occasionally Sheldon, would then sit beside the bed on CJ's favourite chair and read him a story. An unwanted thought popped into Jess's head as she pictured Sofia sitting on the same chair beside the same bed if she was babysitting, for a few hours until Jess and Sheldon got home. At which point Sheldon would kindly offer Sofia a lift back to Carla's and then inevitably return, saying, 'Sorry I was so long. Had to have a word with Toby – business and all that.'

Jess blocked the thought; she didn't even want to think about Sheldon, let alone Sofia. She just wanted to think about CJ. To picture him in his bed, to smell him. Picking up his raggedy stuffed dog, she held it to her face. She wanted his blanket, his torn and worn security blanket, but she knew he must have taken it with him, smuggled it into his bag.

Sheldon hated the blanket and CJ always knew it wasn't a good idea to hold it tight and suck a screwed-up corner when his dad was around. Jess wondered if Sheldon would let him have it; the thought that Sheldon might just have thrown it away was too much to contemplate. CJ would need it more than ever now he was away from his mother.

Jess climbed over into her son's bed and snuggled down with the toy dog cuddled close under her chin. She wished she hadn't changed the bedding after CJ left, hadn't washed the clothes that he had been wearing before he went away. But more than anything she wished that he was tucked up in the bed and that the events of the past few weeks had never taken place.

The last time Jess had felt so bereft had been after Zoë, but then she had had Sheldon to share her loss with. Thinking hard about her, Jess suddenly realised what it was about Sofia that seemed familiar and why she herself had always felt comfortable with her.

She was just like Zoë.

Zoë, Sofia . . . Zoë, Sofia. As she dozed off, the two

names buzzed round and round in her head like two bumble bees.

Sara woke up with a start and looked around. For a split second she couldn't figure out where she was.

Then she remembered.

Grabbing her wrap, she went downstairs expecting to find her daughter hyperactively cleaning the house as she had been doing constantly. But she wasn't there.

'Jess?' she called as, with rising panic, she checked every room. 'Jess, where are you?'

Running back upstairs she checked Jess's bedroom and then cautiously went into CJ's room to find Jess sound asleep in the spaceship. Sara stood over her daughter for a few seconds before turning and quietly leaving her sleeping.

At that particular moment she knew that if Sheldon should walk in the door then and there, she would be hard pushed not to kill him stone dead. Squatting on the top stair with her head in her hands, Sara knew she had to do something. She didn't know what, but she knew that Jess wouldn't keep herself together for very long unless something positive happened.

The ring of the doorbell sent Sara down at breakneck speed to open the door before Jess was disturbed.

'Carla, hi. Ssshhh – Jess is asleep.'

Silently Carla followed Sara through to the kitchen. 'Any news yet?' she asked softly.

'No, nothing at all. It is just so bizarre. Sheldon must know that Jess will be going frantic, I really can't understand it. Marriages break up all the time and it gets dealt with, so why did he have to sneak off like that? And to take CJ away from his mother . . . well, that's just so unbelievably cruel to both of them.'

Carla leaned forward. 'There's still nothing from the agency. They're being a bit precious about their confidential information. Honestly, you'd think that a business that allegedly cares about the welfare of children would be a little more concerned. However . . .' She paused and Sara's antennae twitched. Carla knew something. Looking down at her hands Sara stayed silent, waiting for her to continue.

'Sara, if I tell you something, can you promise it won't go any further than you and Jess? Only as you know, Toby's business relies on confidentiality.'

'Go on.' Sara looked up and set her gaze directly into Carla's eyes.

'No, you have to promise that no one will know that it's come from Toby.' Carla's face was intense as she looked questioningly at Sara. 'Well?'

'I'll do my best but I can't promise anything. My prime concern is finding CJ.'

'I know that,' Carla responded sharply, 'but this is important.'

'Okay, I promise. Let's hope I don't regret it.'

Carla breathed in deeply before exhaling slowly. Sara could see she was wondering what to do.

'Okay, Sara. I asked Toby to do some surreptitious digging around and it turns out that Sheldon has been selling or moving his assets for quite a while, in fact virtually all his investments in the UK. It looks as if this has been a long time in the planning. Jess really needs to think about checking her financial situation. I don't know if she's got any money of her own . . .'

Sara paled as the implications of the news sunk in. 'What do you mean, selling his assets?'

'Stocks and shares mostly, as far as we can tell. Even Toby knew nothing about it, so he feels a bit betrayed.

Toby thinks he was probably getting everything out of the country. Do you know anything about the house? Is it in joint names? Jess has to check everything, and check quickly. Apparently he recently re-mortgaged the house as well. Up to the hilt!'

Sara shook her head. 'How can I possibly lay this on her? As we speak she is curled up in a heap in CJ's bed gripping his soft toy. This will be too much.'

Carla reached out and took both Sara's hands in hers. 'You have to be practical. You have to get Jess to check—'

'Get me to check what?'

Both the women physically jumped before quickly looking round. Neither of them had heard Jess come into the room. Still clutching CJ's toy dog she looked from one to the other.

'Well, come on, tell me exactly what it is that I should be checking. What do you know about my husband that I don't?'

Her eyes still bloodshot and her head muggy from restless dreams and nightmares about Zoë, Jess looked from one to the other expectantly.

Chapter Seven

Mexico, 1996

Sitting on the deck of a magnificent white catamaran waiting for the orange sun to slide slowly under the horizon, Jessica Wells nudged her friend Zoë and, without moving her head or mouth, whispered quietly, 'Don't look now, but that incredibly sexy guy over there leaning on the rail keeps looking at us.'

Zoë's head instantly swivelled in the direction Jess was talking about.

While the majority of the revellers were casually lolling on the divided deck, some with their feet hanging through the rails, he was standing scanning the horizon. His tan was golden and his fit-looking body was clad only in cut-off denims and a pair of high fashion sunglasses pushed uselessly on the top of his head.

'Mmm, not bad I suppose, but not my type – too much of a poseur! I like my men dark and moody. That one looks a bit soft and flaky to me, and he knows we're looking at him. Wonder if he's a Brit?'

'Zoë! I said *don't* look. God, you're just so tactless.' Jess then couldn't resist a second sly glance herself but he turned and caught her eye. The man held her gaze for a split second before looking towards Zoë and then lowering his glasses onto his nose.

Jess thought he looked as if he was on his own but he also had an air of detachment that didn't seem to encourage communication.

'Oh well, there you go, Zoë, so much for my feminine intuition. He just blanked me – didn't even smile, smug bastard.'

'Never mind him, look at the sun. It's going, it's going . . .' Zoë's voice was an excited highpitched squeak.

A murmur went up across the catamaran that was full of holidaymakers taking the regular sunset cruise in the Gulf of Mexico, a nightly event off the coast of the resort that attracted all ages and nationalities.

As the big flaming ball slipped slowly below the horizon, a loud cheer went up across the water from all the other boats that were there in time for sunset before the partying began.

An hour or so later, many of the revellers were past happy and into drunken jollity. The cry of 'One, two, three, TEQUILA!' echoed back to the shore at regular intervals as cheap tequila slammers were tossed back down dozens of throats to the throbbing rhythm of the Eagles and UB40.

Jess and Zoë were having the time of their lives. The two friends had intended to head for the Mediterranean for a holiday but the last-minute booking had just about put the cost of two weeks in Mexico within reach.

The first week had gone in a flash and so had most of their spending money, but neither of them cared. It was the trip of a lifetime and they both wanted to stay for ever.

They had met at Italian evening classes a few years before and had quickly paired up when they discovered that most students in the class were a lot older. They had soon found they had a lot in common, and both shared the fantasy ambition to learn another language, leave their day jobs and travel the world in search of adventure.

Jess the midwife and Zoë the art teacher both dreamed of making their mark in life before settling down to the more mundane business of marriage and children.

The calm and sensible Jess still lived at home with her mother in the same house she had been brought up in while Zoë, who was completely off the wall, shared a flat with another teacher, Mike, with whom she had an on/off relationship. Currently it was off – which was why she was in Mexico with Jess instead of in Greece with Mike.

The Italian language had proved harder to learn than they expected, and the travel dreams were hindered by a lack of cash, but a firm friendship had been quickly established.

'One, two, three, TEQUILA!' The cry went up again, but by this time both had to miss their turn.

'No more, no more or I'll fall overboard,' Jess laughed and leaned on Zoë, who in turn hung on to the rail as if her life depended on it. Both were wearing minuscule bikini tops but while the tall and leggy Zoë sported a deep bronze tan and an almost indecently cut-away pair of white shorts, red-headed Jess, who was a good six inches shorter, had a cover-all sarong wrapped around her wider pink hips and thighs. No amount of reassurance from her lithe friend would persuade Jess that she didn't look like a sun-burned beached whale.

'We're heading back to shore, thank God, Zoë. I

don't know if it's me or the water that's swaying but the horizon is moving up and down much faster.'

They both dissolved into hysterical tipsy laughter as the alcohol, combined with the sun from earlier, affected all their senses.

The catamaran pulled back into the small dock and everyone happily surged off, eager to get back to their cars or find a taxi to ship them back to their hotels. Jess and Zoë were last off and still hanging on to each other, giggling as they made their way from the dockside when a car pulled up beside them.

'You two look as if you need a ride home.'

The man from the boat smiled up at them from the open roof of a convertible VW Beetle, the favoured hire car in the resort.

'I'd be glad to drop you off at your hotel if you like. Save waiting for hours in the cab line.' He had barely finished the sentence before they were pulling at the door handle. The taxi fare was an expense they could do without.

They exchanged surreptitious glances and the unspoken thought between the two girls was that it was only a lift, there were two of them and one of him, and he looked normal enough.

The warm air breezing on their faces sobered them a little as they chugged along in the direction of the main hotel strip where they were based, albeit at the cheap and cheerful end.

'I should introduce myself. I'm Sheldon Patterson, and I'm from California. You two here on vacation?'

Zoë took up the conversation as she was sitting in the front beside him. 'Yep. I'm Zoë and that's Jess behind you. We came for two weeks, and have just under another one to go. It's so great here, we love it, and we're going to come back next year if we manage to save up enough. She's a nurse,' Zoë nodded her head in Jess's direction, 'and I'm a teacher, so we both earn crap money. And you?'

'Just got here but I try and visit whenever I can. It's easy from the States for a long weekend. I'm based in Los Angeles but I travel a lot for business. Where are you two from?'

Jess listened to the conversation but didn't add anything. She was too busy savouring his sexy American drawl and studying the perfectly shaped brown neck and shoulders that were naked in front of her. She stared fascinated at the way his perspiration-damped hair curled very slightly along the nape of his neck and around the backs of his ears. She also noted that the sun had highlighted the top layer while the underneath was dark blond. Very sexy, she thought drunkenly. Very, very sexy.

Zoë directed him to the front of their hotel.

'Oh wow, this sure is a dump. Are you two safe staying here?'

The girls looked at each other and grinned idiotically.

'We thought it was quite nice, actually. It's got beds, it's cheap, there's a bar next door and a cheapo restaurant up the road that does a deadly chilli. What more do we want?'

Zoë looked at Jess and crossed her eyes as Sheldon continued, looking bemused, 'But you're in the centre of town! Don't you want to be on the beach with a view of the ocean? I mean, that's what everyone wants, surely?'

Jess snorted but still couldn't speak, she left it to her friend.

'I want doesn't always mean I get. Well, not where we come from anyway.' Zoë shrugged her shoulders. 'No, seriously, we're okay here, we only use it to sleep – and that, I'm afraid, is what we really have to do right now. That tequila on the catamaran was a killer, the dollar a bottle stuff – cheapest they could find, no doubt.'

Although Zoë was speaking Sheldon was looking at Jess who was still silent. 'I'm sorry, have I offended you? I didn't mean to be critical. That was so bad mannered of me – I wasn't thinking.' His voice was apologetic but his face was bemused.

Jess didn't answer. She wanted to, her brain was telling her what to say but her mouth refused to co-operate. Also, the cheap alcohol and the car that seemed to have square wheels had combined to make her feel quite sick.

As Jess swayed in the rear seat with a silly grin on her face Zoë started giggling again. 'Take no notice of her, she has a bit of a problem holding her drink. Thanks for the lift though, we owe you.'

Quick as a flash, as Zoë jumped out and pulled her seat forward to let Jess climb through, Sheldon was out and round to help her.

'We can manage,' Jess blurted out as he took her hand, her senses suddenly coming back. Good-looking and charming as he was, and much as she wanted to drag him physically from the car herself, he was still a stranger and Jess didn't want Zoë impulsively inviting him back to their room. Their tip of a room in a dump of an hotel that, until that moment, they had both thought quite okay.

'Well then, Zoë, Jess.' He held out his hand and smiled. 'Great meeting you. I'm sure I'll see you around. I'm here for a while longer – staying at the Palms.' He watched them into their hotel and then, with a friendly wave he was gone.

'Jessica Wells, you disappoint me! I knew you could be as daft as a brush but not that daft,' Zoë muttered as she linked arms with her friend to lead her along. 'You reckon he's gorgeous and hunky and the man of your dreams, and you've let him walk away, tut tut!'

'Yeah, well, I could see it was you he fancied, even though he was being tactful and talking to both of us. Anyway, I feel *soooooo* sick . . .'

They both collapsed onto their beds as soon as they got to their room and stayed there, still clothed and almost comatose, for the rest of the night.

The next morning Jess groaned pitifully as she raised her head from the pillow. 'Bloody hell, never again, never, never again!' Letting herself fall gently back, she pulled the sheet over her head, determined to sleep until the throbbing in her temple eased, but Zoë wasn't having it. Pulling at the single cotton sheet that Jess had wrapped around herself she laughed loudly.

'Come on, you lazy cow, have you no stamina? We're going shopping today. It's absolutely pissing down so no beach unless you want to swim down the road to get there.'

She tugged the curtains apart and looked out. 'I reckon we should get the bus to the Mall for an alcohol-soaking breakfast and then burn the plastic, now the cash has gone!'

'NO!'

'Oh yes, Tequila Queen, I've decided for both of us. You'll feel better once you're up and running. It's a waste of good holiday time to pander to a hang-over.'

Grudgingly, Jess eventually admitted defeat as she

always did when she was with the ever-exuberant Zoë. But they never got as far as the mall.

As they left the hotel a car horn tooted vigorously at them. It was Sheldon, leaning against his car with one hand on the horn, looking tanned and gorgeous in a crisp white shirt, expensively cut knee-length khaki shorts and deck shoes. Jess immediately felt a thumping in her chest. 'What do you reckon?' she muttered under her breath. 'Shall we go over?'

'Too bloody right we go over. Looks like a decent free lunch beckoning, and anyway, I can see you really want to shag the arse off him!' Zoë replied, equally quietly.

'Zoë! How could you?'

Their neutral expressions gave no inkling of this conversation. Trying not to look too eager, the two girls sauntered over to where he was parked under the canopy out of the rain.

'Hi there again. I saw the rain and wondered if you fancied a day out of town? I was just going to come in and get them to call your room.' His smile was open and enthusiastic. 'Come on, take pity on a poor lonesome guy who's here all alone, abandoned in Cancun by his so-called friend who had to cancel at the last minute.'

The deciding factor for Zoë was the hope of a decent lunch, but for Jess it was Sheldon's smile and sexy shoulders. Nudging each other in silent agreement they grinned in unison.

'Okay then, where are we going?'

The first day out set the scene for the rest of the holiday, and the three of them became a strange item. Where one was, so were the other two.

Despite Sheldon's perseverance, Jess and Zoë continued to proudly reject his offer to pay for them to move into his hotel so instead, Sheldon would drive

downtown every day from his five-star hotel to pick
the girls up from their barely one-star lodgings. They
enjoyed his hospitality and his company and the feeling
seemed to be mutual, but they bluntly refused to let him
subsidise them.

If Sheldon treated them in a restaurant they reciprocated by treating him to burning-hot fajitas and cold
beers in the ridiculously cheap beach café. He took
them to see the cabarets, they took him to local bars
with live music that echoed for miles. It worked well
and all three enjoyed themselves, but for Jess it was a
different enjoyment.

Jess had fallen in love; completely and hopelessly
in love.

She found out that he was thirty-six, divorced, had
no children and was a partner in the family real-estate
company in Los Angeles. It wasn't long before she was
fantasising about becoming the second Mrs Patterson.

At nearly thirty herself, Jess had had a couple of close
relationships but she never found what she called 'the
big one' and had certainly never been tempted to set up
home with anyone.

Although she had never known her father and adored
her mother, there had always been a gap in her life.
Jess had determined at a very young age that when
she got married it would only be when she was 100
per cent sure.

Now Jess *was* sure. Sheldon seemed to have the perfect
combination of character assets. Fun-loving but not
over-familiar, polite but not uptight, and although he
obviously wasn't short of a few dollars, he wasn't brash
about it.

The singing of his praises was a constant source of
amusement to Zoë, who took great pleasure in trying to

set Jess and Sheldon up together by pleading headaches and sunburn. It never worked because the three of them stayed as three throughout, and although Jess laughed and took Zoë's gentle teasing in good part she was deadly serious in her ambitions. She wanted Sheldon Patterson and, despite the niggling little ache that told her it was Zoë he wanted, she was determined to go for it.

Taking full advantage of Sheldon's hire car, Jess and Zoë went out and about seeing far more of the country than just the usual beach and shops. They visited ancient ruins, swam with dolphins and snorkelled in the Gulf of Mexico. They were light-hearted, carefree days, and the two young women were each having the time of their life in different ways. Jess was happy to be with Sheldon and Zoë was savouring the whole holiday experience.

But none of them knew that in a split second it was all going to change.

The flash summer storms that had burst on and off throughout the holiday did little to damp their enthusiasm as the trio set off for a day out on the nearby island of Cozumel. As quick as the skies opened and dumped inches of water in minutes, the rain would suddenly stop and the sun would shine brightly, drying the landscape in an instant.

It was one such day when, as usual, Sheldon had picked them up. The rain stopped as they came out of the hotel and Sheldon quickly rolled the top back on his hire car.

As part of the ongoing teasing about Jess's infatuation, Zoë had quickly jumped into the car first, dragging in with her all the snorkelling gear and beach towels. To her delight, Jess was left with no alternative but to sit in the front. Alongside Sheldon.

As the little car rumbled along, the morning sun beat

down, giving them advance warning of the hot day to come. Scared of being too late they raced down to the coast to catch the ferry and Zoë threw up her hands, waving them about in the warm, humid air. Jess raised her arms as well and all three of them laughed happily and sang the Mexican chorus of songs they had heard in the bars. None of them knew what the words meant but it didn't matter.

They were all happy.

As Sheldon put his foot down on the clear straight road, the ever-exuberant Zoë went one step further and, amid the excitement, stood up to catch the full force of the cooling breeze.

Suddenly, with no warning, the car hit a puddle of water that had settled in an almost invisible dip in the road. Despite Sheldon's maniacal efforts to regain control of the vehicle, it aquaplaned smoothly across the glistening rainwater and, almost gently, slewed round across the road. Both girls screamed in fear as the car spun around like a bumper car before slowing to a stop just short of a ramshackle little house by the side of the road.

The seconds of the skid had occurred in slow motion and Jess had thought the car was about to flip over. But it remained upright. Jess took a deep breath as she noticed Sheldon's sickly white face and then looked round at Zoë. Her relief that the car was still the right way up was overwhelming. But the space where Zoë had been sitting was empty. Her friend was no longer in the car.

'Sheldon! Where's Zoë? She's not in the car, where is she?' Jess shouted at the top of her voice as she threw herself out onto the road, running round uncontrollably and signalling hysterically at the curious locals who were gathering.

'Zoë's gone, I can't see her. ZOË! ZOË!' And then she started screaming and screaming, unable to stop.

The ferocity of the swerve had flung Zoë straight out of the car with such force that she was lying several yards away on the opposite side of the road. She was found by an hysterical Jess on the verge opposite, her head battered and bloody and her face unrecognisable from the direct impact with the fat trunk of a tall, firm tree. She lay on her back like a rag doll that had been carelessly cast away.

Sheldon ran over and violently pulled Jess away, almost throwing her across the road in his attempt to get to Zoë. Heaving her body towards him, he tried frantically to revive her but Jess, a trained nurse, could see instantly there was nothing that could be done for her friend.

The vibrant twenty-five year old was pronounced dead at the scene: she had died on impact.

The next few days passed in a blur of officialdom. Jess moved into Sheldon's hotel along with Zoë's grieving parents who had flown out to take her body home for burial. It was a long drawn-out process before the accident was formally declared an accident, after which they were allowed to leave Mexico and fly home, arriving just in time for Zoë's funeral.

Jess and Sheldon had clung to each other in the aftermath both physically and emotionally and, from then on, were never apart. Grief and guilt encompassed them both, Sheldon because he was driving and Jess because she saw it as her fault that Zoë was in the back and able to stand up.

They both needed each other because only they understood what the other was going through. The shared grief had, without doubt, joined them together and, in the months after, kept them together. Their closeness was so great that it was only a matter of time before they formalised their relationship. The grief that had thrown them together proceeded to glue them together permanently and there was an inevitability about their marriage.

It wasn't long after they had set up home in California that Jess gave birth to Cameron John. Jess had heaved a sigh of relief when she discovered her unborn baby was a boy; she knew that their combined guilt would have forced them to name a girl after Zoë.

When Sheldon's family wanted to expand their business interests into Europe, it had seemed logical for Sheldon and Jess to move back to England, which was an ideal base for them. Jess was also delighted to be back home near her mother again.

But the shadow was always there. Sheldon Patterson and Jessica Wells were joined together not only by marriage but also by tragedy.

Mexico would forever be a bittersweet memory for both of them. Jess had known with certainty that Zoë was not the least bit interested in Sheldon but deep down, hidden away inside her, was the knowledge that he had maybe fallen in love with Zoë. Knowing she was second choice wasn't a problem to Jess – she had loved him, wanted him and married him – but she did just occasionally wonder how things would have turned out if they hadn't had the accident.

Chapter Eight

Cambridge, England

'What do you mean, he's been selling assets? What the fuck makes you think that?' Jess, her eyes wide and cold, stared at Carla as the implications of what she was saying sunk in. Her instant reaction was one of disbelieving anger that she instinctively directed at Carla. 'Who said you could nose around in our personal affairs?'

Carla looked at Jess open-mouthed as Jess continued aggressively, 'You've got no right to interfere.'

'Stop it, Jess,' Sara intervened. 'All we're trying to do is find CJ so it's ridiculous to criticise Carla for wanting to help. Surely any news is helpful?'

Jess was defiant. 'Only if it's true. Toby had no right, not without asking me first. You should have consulted me.'

Carla stood up. 'Hey, hey, don't shoot the messenger. I realise you're distraught and I understand completely, but we were only trying to do what we could. I thought we were helping.'

Jess suddenly crumbled in front of them; she didn't

cry but in just a few seconds she seemed to shrink visibly into herself.

'I'm sorry, I didn't mean it. It's just that I don't know if I can take much more. I'm so tired and this is all going from bad to worse; it's a waking nightmare and it's all my fault. This is my punishment for Zoë. I was thinking about her while I was upstairs.'

'Zoë?' Carla asked curiously. 'Who's Zoë?'

'Oh, I'll explain that later.' Sara moved her gaze to Jess. 'You're confused, darling. Zoë was a long time ago and it's got nothing to do with this.'

But Jess continued as if neither of them had spoken. 'Zoë died because of me and Sheldon, so now I've lost CJ. It's retribution, that's what it is. If I hadn't fancied Sheldon then Zoë wouldn't have been in the back and if I'd been in the back I wouldn't have stood up and no one would have been hurt. Now Sheldon has found Sofia who looks just like Zoë and he's gone off with her.'

Sara, her face a mask of concern, rushed over and grabbed her daughter's upper arms tightly while at the same time shaking her hard.

'Don't talk such nonsense! Sofia is *nothing* like Zoë. You're confused and angry, but you're certainly not to blame for any of this. This is Sheldon's fault, nobody else's. It's Sheldon one hundred per cent.'

Leading Jess over to the chair she forced her down into it and then knelt in front of her. 'Listen to me: he cold-bloodedly planned this, it's obvious. He planned it and executed it without a thought for you and your pain. He's obviously not even given a thought to how CJ must feel away from his mother.'

Despite Jess trying to wriggle away, Sara didn't release her grip. 'It's not your fault, it's not my fault and it's certainly not Carla and Toby's fault, so let's sit quietly, gather all the information we have and then go from there. Zoë has nothing to do with this, nothing at all.'

Just as Jess was on the verge of falling apart there was a knock at the door. Amid all the shouting, none of them had heard the car transporter pulling onto the drive with Sheldon's car strapped on the ramps. The unfortunate driver had no idea of the circumstances surrounding his delivery and he certainly had no idea that he was going to be confronted on arrival by a screaming banshee.

Jess broke away from her mother, then, when she saw what was happening, threw herself out of the door and ran barefoot down the drive, oblivious to the sharp gravel under her feet.

'What the fuck is that doing here? This is supposed to be going to the garage for repair. You were supposed to take it straight to the garage, NOT HERE, you stupid dumb bastard! Now take it away!'

Jess's face was beetroot red with tears running unchecked down her cheeks as she launched into a tirade of abuse at the man who just stood silently with his mouth agape.

'Get rid of the damned thing! Watch my lips: *I don't want it here, get rid of it, get rid of it!*'

As her voice became hysterical Sara had no choice but to intervene. 'Carla, can you take Jess indoors, please. I'll deal with this.'

Carla reached for her arm to lead her back but Jess brushed her away like an irritating fly. 'Are you saying I'm not capable of dealing with this? Are you? *Are you*?' she screamed at Sara and Carla. '*You* go back indoors. This is *my* house, *my* problem. Now get off me, the pair of you!'

During this exchange the driver had gone from being taken aback to bored in a couple of minutes.

'Look, luv, I don't know what your problem is but my instructions are to deliver the car to this address. Now if you don't want it, I'll take it back – but trust me, you'll never see it again. I'll dump it straight at the breakers, no problem.'

Holding his hands out towards the three women who were ringed around him he sucked air in through his teeth and shook his head back and forth theatrically.

'So, come on then, ladies, what's your choice? Take it or leave it. I haven't got the time to piss about while you lot stand around arguing the toss.' He looked from one to the other expectantly.

'Just unload it and put it over there. I'll deal with it later,' Sara stated firmly.

'You sure? Once it's off it doesn't go on again.'

'I'm sure, now unload it.'

Jess watched the exchange between her mother and the driver and then, without a word, spun round. With Carla hot on her heels, she marched back into the house leaving Sara to calm the situation and make their apologies.

Once indoors, Jess headed straight for the window where, motionless, she watched as Sheldon's car, the car that was once his pride and joy, was quickly unloaded and left carelessly on the drive. Her mind wandered as she tried to imagine exactly what could have happened to her husband and son since she had last seen the car outside their home.

Folding her arms and leaning her head slightly to one side she racked her brain to try and find something she might have missed, but there was nothing out of the ordinary that she could think of, nothing that should have made her suspicious.

Sheldon had packed the car the night before with the

cases that Jess herself had prepared for him and CJ. She had allowed CJ to pick his own clothes and, apart from a few essentials that he had forgotten, Jess had stuck to his choices.

Sheldon had been working late the night before, or so he had told her, so she had actually packed his as well. Enough of everything to cover the five days that they would be away, more than enough, in fact, but certainly not enough for the time they had already been away.

With his excitement levels bouncing off the ceiling at the thought of the adventure Sheldon had been promising him for weeks, CJ had been late going to sleep that night but had miraculously dropped off just before Sheldon got in.

Still looking at the car, Jess continued to trawl her memory, trying to recall every little detail.

Sheldon had been perfectly normal, maybe a little impatient when he got in but that wasn't unusual. Jess had prepared dinner and they had eaten together; they had also bickered and sniped a little because Jess was dreading CJ being away from her, but it was no more or less than usual. He accused her of being over-protective, she accused him of being overbearing – it was the same old things that always set both of them off but nothing more or less.

In fact, Sheldon had even made love to her that night.

Jess clenched her fists and gritted her teeth as she remembered it. How could he? she asked herself silently, aware of Carla's presence in the room. How could he have done that, knowing exactly what he was planning to do the next day? Yes, the sex itself had been a little perfunctory and over quickly, but then their love-life had never been full of mad passion, not even in the

early days. Sex had never really been important to
Sheldon.

Jess had always consciously put it down to the long
hours that her husband worked, but the tiny pocket of
memory that was reserved for Zoë sometimes prompted
her to think otherwise.

The next morning they had all been up and about
early, and after breakfast father and son had skipped
out to the car. Just a father and son going away for a few
days together. No way could she have anticipated that
it was father and son leaving for destination unknown
with no return time-scale.

There had been nothing to raise any suspicions, she
told herself. The normal glancing kiss on the cheek
from Sheldon, the huge bear hug from CJ and they
had gone.

The light touch on her shoulder made her flinch, but
it was only Carla.

'Jess, I have no idea what to say or what to do, but
whatever you want or need we're here for you.'

Jess smiled tearfully. 'I know, and I think you were
right – firstly I need a good independent lawyer and
then I need to employ someone to search for them . . .
somewhere.' Her desperation was palpable. 'I have to
find CJ but I also have to find Sheldon to learn why he
has done this to me. I've never done anything to him
apart from love him and love his son. Our son.'

Carla stayed silent as Jess continued.

'Did you know I fell in love with him at first sight?
We were on a boat trip in Mexico and he was standing
looking out to sea when I saw him.' Still gazing out of the
window at the car her voice softened as she remembered.
'I knew straight away that he was the one I had been
waiting for. I knew nothing about him at all, but still

I knew that I wanted him. Unfortunately, I also knew that he really fancied my friend, but he wasn't her type. I was the consolation prize in more ways than one, but I didn't mind, not really. I loved him and I really thought he had grown to love me.'

'Sheldon did love you, I know he did. He never said a single detrimental thing about you – in fact, he was always talking you up. You seemed such a perfect match.'

'Oh yes, I don't doubt he loved me,' Jess smiled, 'but he was never *in* love with me. I was a good wife and mother and he loved me in the same way he loved his own mother. I was never a great passion for him but he was for me, he was the love of my life.'

She kept glancing out at the car as she spoke; her tone was no longer angry, just bewildered.

'I've been going over it all again and again, and I still can't understand. Why couldn't he have told me there was someone else? Why did he have to do it like this? Yes, it would have hurt – but this? I just can't get my head around it.'

Sara came into the room just at that moment. 'I'll tell you why he did it like this. I've been thinking about it, and it's because if he had left you and set up just around the corner with Sofia, then CJ would have stayed with you and he would have had to support you.'

Sara's face was a mask of cold fury. 'He did it like this because he wanted to keep everything that he perceived as his. His son, his money and his control. And he's done it, he's got the lot. The lousy bastard.'

'Maybe,' Jess pondered, 'but I would guess that Pearl is behind it.'

'She might have told him how to implement his dirty little plan, but the idea had to have come from him in the first place. I doubt Pearl suggested that he took up with Sofia – that was all Sheldon's own work.'

Jess looked down at the floor as her chin started to tremble again.

'I'll talk to Toby about legal advice. He'll know who the best person is for this sort of thing, I'm sure.' Carla looked and sounded hesitant. 'If you want me to, that is. I really don't want you to think I'm being pushy or intrusive.'

Jess tried to smile but it was more of a grimace. 'Yes, please. I'm sorry for being a bitch, I really do appreciate your help, you're the only friend I've got right now. Everyone else is so embarrassed by it all they don't know what to say so they're keeping away.' Walking over, she grabbed Carla in a tight embrace and kissed her on the cheek. 'Thank you again – I mean it.'

'I'll call you tonight,' Carla smiled, struggling hard to keep her composure. 'I'll phone Toby straight away and get him onto it, but can I make a suggestion? Gather up everything you can find relating to your, and Sheldon's, finances, absolutely everything. Whoever you see will need as much info as possible. Also things like CJ's birth certificate, anything formal relating to him, to you, to your marriage.'

As Carla was speaking, Jess returned her gaze to the window and continued staring at the car, not really hearing it all. 'I guess I don't have a lot of choice. I'm going to have to go to Los Angeles,' she announced, still looking through the draped curtains at the car. 'As soon as I can arrange it. I can't believe Sheldon wouldn't contact Pearl, and if I see her face to face I'll know if she's lying – I've seen her do it often enough. If I can find out exactly where Sheldon is, then I can go straight there.'

Sara tried to keep her expression neutral as she took in exactly what her daughter was saying. 'But what about legal advice? You need to do that as soon as possible, and supposing the agency gets back with the details of Sofia's family? Maybe that's where they are. You could be going off at a tangent. I really think you're better off staying here until we have a clearer idea.'

Jess turned quickly towards Sara. For the first time her demeanour was calm but her normally lively green eyes were completely devoid of any expression.

'Maybe, maybe not, so what I shall do is give you the authority to deal with all that crap while I go and see Pearl. I have to do something positive, and if it means flying to LA then that's what I'm going to do. I'm going to check out all his contacts there. If I'm on their doorstep and in their face then I might just find something out. I might even find *them*.'

'I don't think it's the right thing to do. You'll only inflame the situation if you confront Pearl with all guns blazing. Surely it makes more sense to use the legal system as best you can?' The words were spilling out faster and faster as Sara became agitated.

'It's what I want to do,' Jess stated. 'If Sheldon thinks I'm going to lie back and let him walk all over me, he's wrong. I'm going to find them by fair means or foul, and I'm going to get CJ back where he belongs – with me – and if needs must I'll destroy Sheldon Patterson in the process.'

Carla had remained silent throughout the exchange between mother and daughter, but the sheer hatred in Jess's voice made her look up and lock eyes with Sara. Neither of them said anything but their thoughts were easily understood; they were written all over their pained faces. She meant business, but in the process it could just be Jess herself who ended up mortally wounded.

It was when Carla phoned Jess later with the names of three specialist lawyers that the enormity of the situation hit her. Thinking about CJ had completely absorbed Jess, but it was how she wanted it to be; she didn't want to think about anything else. However, she soon realised that she would have to. Unfortunately, she didn't have a clue where to start.

Sheldon Patterson was wealthy, Jess had known that when she married him, but she had no idea at all about exactly what they, as a couple, were worth. She knew the house was in both their names, but apart from that Sheldon had kept everything to himself. Jess had never had anything to do with any of the bills and they didn't even have a joint bank account.

As soon as they had become engaged, Sheldon had given her a generous allowance as well as a credit card, and she used that for everything – but she never saw any statements or bills outside of the sealed envelopes that she regularly laid on his desk. Until recent events Jess had thought how lucky she was to be so cosseted and protected, but now she knew that she had been stupid in her complacency and would probably have to pay a high price.

Jess actually had nothing of her own.

The fact that Sheldon was wealthy had played no part in Jess's feelings for him because, although she had guessed he was comfortable she had had no idea about his true financial standing until they had gone off to California to meet his family.

The excitement of the whole experience of getting engaged and travelling to Los Angeles with Sheldon,

had meant that Jess hadn't even realised the implications of the chauffeur car that had met them at the airport, but the sight of the Patterson house had made her sit up instantly.

Tucked up in the hills behind Los Angeles, it was actually quite modest by LA standards but to Jess, who had yet to have the Hollywood guided tour, it was the most beautiful house she had ever seen.

A sprawling pink and white stucco bungalow, it twisted and turned around the gardens like three separate buildings. The building itself was encircled by wide tiled terraces that edged a staggered hillside garden overflowing with trailing and climbing plants, and the property was surrounded by a high wavy wall. Unusually, inset at the front of the house, was an irregular-shaped floodlit swimming pool surrounded by enormous terracotta pots planted with palms and a gently tumbling waterfall that appeared to flow out of the bushes.

The whole thing had a very Mediterranean feel and Jess fell in love with it at first sight, although her feelings changed slightly after she met the woman who lived there. Pearl Patterson, her future mother-in-law and supreme matriarch of the Patterson family.

Jess had been excited at the prospect of her trip to California but although Sheldon had told her that he was taking her to meet his mother he had failed to mention that she was actually going to be interviewed by the head of the family. Much in the same way as if she was applying for a job in the company.

Sheldon's father had passed away a few months prior to his trip to Mexico and although Sheldon, along with two of his cousins, had taken over the day-to-day running of the family business, Pearl retained ultimate control without actually doing any of the work.

Not just the control of the company but also control of her son.

Her beloved only son Sheldon.

As soon as Jess had walked into the room alongside Sheldon she was immediately so overawed that, as she had later related humorously to Sara, she felt as if she was being received for an audience with royalty. The delicate hand that was proffered almost reluctantly, accompanied by an immediate up-and-down glance that took in her future daughter-in-law from top to toe, spoke volumes and Jess felt exactly the same as she had on her first day at work.

Jessica Wells knew she had been assessed and judged in a few short minutes, but she didn't know immediately whether or not she had passed muster.

Pearl was tall, lean to the point of emaciation and perfectly groomed from top to toe. Framing her carefully made-up face was a helmet of white blonde bobbed hair that gleamed brightly above a shocking pink velour jogging suit. Although she looked casual it was a contrived designer casual.

'Excuse me, Jessica, but I've just come in from the tennis club. Exercise keeps me in trim.' She waved her hands over her body dismissively before continuing in exactly the same tone. 'Now tell me, what business is your father in?'

The question had come out of the blue and Jess fumbled for words as Pearl used a perfectly manicured talon to delicately brush her eyebrow.

'I thought Sheldon would have told you. My parents separated when I was a baby, and my mother brought me up on her own.'

The raised eyebrow was the only expression change. 'And what does your mother do, Jessica?'

It passed through Jess's mind to lie, to make up something exotic enough to wipe the disinterested expression off Pearl's face but she couldn't bear to betray her mother.

'My mother is a nurse, like myself.' Smiling to take the edge off her words Jess continued, 'She doesn't earn a lot but she managed to raise me and support me. In fact, I'm very proud of my mother; she has worked hard all her life to give me the best opportunities.' Jess spoke gently but firmly; she wanted to make her point but at the same time she didn't want to antagonise Sheldon's mother on their first meeting.

A flicker of a smile crossed Pearl Patterson's face. 'Hmm.' The single sound made more impact on Jess than any of her words. 'Coffee, Jessica? Or would you prefer English tea?'

For the first time since the introductions Sheldon spoke. 'Mom, I have some good news for you. Jess and I are going to be married. I wanted to tell you in person.'

Still her expression remained enigmatic. 'I guessed as much. Jessica is the first girl you've brought home since Kay. Now away you go and find something useful to do, Sheldon.' Pearl shifted her gaze back to Jess. 'I think we should get to know each other. Follow me and I'll show you the garden.'

It had been the start of a very superficial relationship between Jess and Pearl. Sheldon had been very persuasive, so despite his mother's very vocal reservations about Jess's lack of financial stability, the wedding went ahead.

Sheldon had got his way over the marriage but Pearl won out on everything else.

The wedding had taken place in the grounds of the

family home which was also to become Jess's home for the next few months until they were offered a rental property nearby.

Their son Cameron John Sheldon Patterson was born while they were there, and although they were happy, Jess had been ecstatic when it was suggested that Sheldon should spend some time investigating the property market in the UK.

They had soon moved back to Cambridge, Jess's home town, bought a gorgeous brand new house on a very select development and settled happily, Jess had thought, into married life in the pretty University town.

Everything had seemed perfect at the time and had, in her eyes at least, stayed that way until the day her husband ran off with CJ. But now she was going to find them. Find Sheldon and beat him to a pulp and then bring CJ back home where he belonged.

Chapter Nine

'As soon as I'm dressed I'm going to sort out my flights to LA. Do you mind standing guard over the phone again while I'm out?'

Jess had accepted that the odds on Sheldon getting in contact after so many weeks were lengthening, but she harboured the hope that CJ himself might try to phone her, so she couldn't bear to leave the phone unmanned for even a second.

While Jess was ensconced in the walk-in wardrobe attached to the bedroom, looking for something to wear, Sara absentmindedly busied herself folding the assortment of clothes that Jess had spread over her bed.

'I wish you'd think again,' she fretted. 'I'm worried that you'll upset Pearl at a time when we really need her on our side.'

'Mum, I promise. I'm going to see Pearl but I'll be nice to her and then I'll throw myself at her mercy. She's a mother, look how she dotes on Sheldon. She'll understand how I feel if I can just get to see her. Sheldon could have told her all sorts by now.'

For the first time in weeks Jess had put a touch of make-up on her face and changed out of her jogging pants. Pulling on a pair of classic cut cords that usually disguised her hips, she was surprised to find that they were quite loose. She stripped them off and looked for something else.

'I must have lost weight,' she said. 'I can see my arse in the mirror again. I might even get back into my jeans soon.'

Sara smiled. 'You've lost quite a bit, love, I've noticed, but it's because you're not eating. You need to keep your strength up, we've got a long fight ahead of us.'

Jess put her head round the door and smiled albeit sadly. 'You're not eating either; your arse is shrinking as well!'

'Maybe, but I'm too old to worry about that any more.'

'Nonsense! You don't look anywhere near your age and you know it.'

Sara smiled. 'Not as ageless as the lovely Pearl, though. I wish I could afford to have everything lifted and shifted, sucked and tucked, then I could rediscover my cheekbones and hipbones. I haven't seen them since I was about ten.'

Jess came back into the bedroom. 'Right, this'll do. I just needed to look a little more human. I know that if I let myself go too much then it'll be the first step on the slippery slope and I won't be able to fight Sheldon when I find him.'

'Have you thought about how you'll react if Pearl tells you she knows nothing? You won't find it so easy to be nice then, will you?'

'No, but I promise I'll still try.'

Because she felt she was doing something positive, Jess was almost upbeat as she drove into the city. Only another few days and maybe she might find something out. Just maybe she would get to LA and persuade Sheldon to let CJ go home with her.

It had seemed such a simple thing to do, book a flight and then, as soon as possible, go off to confront Pearl in person, but when she presented her credit card to pay for her ticket the card was rejected. As soon as she checked with the company she discovered that Sheldon had cancelled it. Not only that, when she went to the bank Jess discovered that he hadn't paid her allowance into her account and she was overdrawn.

Without any warning Jess suddenly found herself with no money and no access to any. Sheldon had well and truly pulled the plug on her life.

Sitting unwillingly in front of the lawyer, whom she knew she could not afford, all Jess really wanted to do was curl up and go to sleep and preferably never wake up again. She didn't want to be there sharing her embarrassment and confiding her worst nightmare to a complete stranger, and she certainly didn't want to have to confront the reality of the situation.

But she had little choice. Sheldon had taken everything from her.

'I'm really sorry, Mrs Patterson, but on the surface it seems as if your husband has literally cleaned you out. He's sold up from under you. I don't want to sound too harsh, but realistically, at this moment in time, you are in a very difficult position.' The lawyer's voice was sympathetic, his expression concerned, but there was no way of taking the sting out of his words.

After she had got back from an embarrassing meeting with the bank manager, Jess had ripped the house apart looking for any personal papers that might help her, but there was nothing at all. It was almost as if Sheldon hadn't ever been in her life.

She couldn't believe how stupid she had been when she searched Sheldon's office. Her relief at finding nothing incriminating about her husband and Sofia had clouded her judgement and she had missed the biggest clue of all – that there was *nothing* there. Now she could see it, but at the time all she was looking for were signs of his possible involvement with Sofia and clues to his whereabouts.

There was no paperwork relating to everyday bills and accounts, no receipts, no account details. Absolutely nothing to give Jess any information. She hadn't even noticed that his precious laptop was missing. If she had, she would have realised earlier that something was up. Sheldon would have had no reason to take it with him on a short holiday.

'I don't know what to do,' she whispered now. 'I've got no money – how can I look for CJ when I have no money? My mother is funding me at the moment but she has little spare cash. I'm at my wits' end, really I am.' Her voice quivering, Jess bit her lip hard. She knew it wouldn't help if she burst into tears and started shouting and screaming.

'It's a difficult situation, certainly. Your husband appears to have already transferred everything out of the country and we can't start proceedings against him for maintenance if we don't know where he is. Also, he is a US citizen, as is your son.'

Jess laughed. It was a dry brittle laugh that sounded eerie in the small, bookcase-clad office.

'I know that – I keep being reminded about it, unfortunately. I know that they're both US citizens, I know we're both his parents and I know I was fully aware that

Sheldon was taking CJ out of the country and that I fully agreed with it. But I certainly didn't know he wasn't going to bring him home again. It just never entered my head – in fact, I still can't believe it.'

The man sitting opposite her leaned his elbows on the heavy mahogany desk and, pushing his fingertips together, rested his lips on them pensively. As Jess waited for him to respond, she watched him surreptitiously and tried to make a thumbnail assessment. She guessed he was around fifty, and although he was suited and booted to perfection, his physique was wide and gently rounded, his hair a sombre gunmetal grey and his persona soothing and gentle.

Jess thought he looked caring in a legal sort of way and figured that if she could get him really interested, to care about the case, then maybe she could get somewhere.

Anywhere other than where she was at that moment would be a bonus.

When she had made the appointment, she had given little thought to the person she would see; her sole focus had been to find someone who could help her out of the mess she found herself in.

Of the three lawyers that Toby had recommended, Jess's choice had been quickly narrowed down to Barry Halston, of Halston & Jones – for no other reason than he was the only one who could see her immediately.

'Okay, Jessica – you don't mind if I call you Jessica?'

'No, of course not.' She frowned at the unexpected question.

'Good. The first thing you have to do is make an appointment to see your bank manager and explain the situation fully. I'm sure there's something they can do for you, at least in the short term. Then contact the mortgage company and find out how much is outstanding and what help they can offer you by way of reduced payments. The mortgage is the most important bill to pay. You need to keep a roof over your head. Did you know your husband had re-mortgaged your home?' he asked gently.

Jess screwed up her face. 'I may have signed something, I don't know. Sheldon dealt with the finances. Stupid, aren't I?' Jess lowered her eyes in embarrassment.

'Not at all,' he smiled. 'You had no reason to be suspicious. Now, I want you to contact this agency.' He handed her a familiar leaflet. It was the same one the police officer had tried to give her right at the beginning of the nightmare.

'The people there are experienced in this sort of thing and can help you through the minefield that is parental abduction. There are strict laws in place governed by the Hague Convention, but the more you can do yourself, the better. I really don't want to take your money unnecessarily, believe it or not.'

Smiling, he made eye-contact with her. 'This is just the first step of a long journey, I'm afraid, but you've made it. Denial is a big time and energy waster, you know. We have to be realistic but at the same time optimistic.'

As Jess looked down at her hands that were gripped in tight fists on her lap it struck her that not so long ago she wouldn't have been able to do that because her well-manicured nails would have dug into the flesh. Now her nails were back to how they had been when she was a child. Bitten and chewed away to nearly nothing. Unclenching her hands she studied them carefully as she responded tonelessly.

'Yes, Mr Halston, I'm sure you're right but denial is all I have to keep me sane. I have to believe that this is all a ghastly mistake, that Sheldon has had some sort of brainstorm and that as soon as he gathers his senses everything will be as it was.'

In much the same way as a psychiatrist would pause to slow down the emotions then so did the lawyer.

'Barry, call me Barry. I need you to feel comfortable with me.' Again the reassuring eye-contact as the man leaned back in his worn leather captain's chair. 'I'm going to have to dig deep into you and your husband's life if I'm to find anything to go on, and you have to not feel embarrassed about anything I may ask or find.'

Jess stood up nervously. 'There's nothing *to* find.'

'Well, Jessica, I really hope you're wrong about that because we need to find a few pointers to be able to proceed. If you truly want my help then you have to stand back and let me dig and delve into everything about you and your husband.'

'Dig and delve?' Jess frowned. 'I can't think of any-thing that I haven't already told you. I'm not keeping anything back.'

'I'm sorry, Jessica, that wasn't what I meant.' Again the kindly smile spread over his face up towards his eyes. 'I just need to prompt you to tell me things that you may not think are relevant. The problem we have is that it's going to be difficult to trace his financial movements because you know nothing about them. There is so little to go on.'

His quizzical expression silently asked the question that Jess had asked herself over and over again. Had Sheldon, her husband and the love of her life, actually been clever enough to have a contingency plan in oper-ation the whole time they were married?

'I know what you're getting at and I feel so incredibly stupid. I don't know why he's done this, I didn't have any idea that anything was wrong in our marriage, and I haven't got a clue how I could have been so abysmally stupidly naive.'

Now she had actually put it all into words to a stranger, Jess was suddenly overcome with embarrassment.

'No, not stupid, not stupid at all – and you've done nothing to be ashamed of.' Barry Halston looked directly at her. 'You trusted your husband implicitly and that's certainly not wrong. Trust should be the linchpin of a marriage.'

He stood up and Jess realised it was time for her to leave. 'My secretary will schedule another appointment but in the meantime, if anything comes to mind then call me.'

He held out his hand and Jess grasped it tightly. All her hopes were pinned on the man in front of her and she didn't even know him.

When she pulled up outside the house, Jess turned off the engine and stayed where she was, just looking at the house, her home, as if she had never seen it before. It was similar to the others on the exclusive development, but each house had a slightly different feature, obviously an attempt by the builders to personalise the expensive properties.

The wide in-and-out block-paved drive passed closely to the front of the house and the adjoining double garage where Sheldon's car stood forlornly with its window blocked out by a single poignant sheet of polythene that was being sucked in and out by the gentle wind.

Jess couldn't face trying to drive it into the garage.

From the outside, the pseudo-Georgian flat-fronted

house was actually quite bland, but when the array of exterior lights were on at night they reflected down from the eaves and up from the flowerbeds, illuminating it with different shadows of light and dark.

Despite the size, Jess always thought it looked cosy and nestlike in the evening glow but now, as she looked at it from a completely different perspective, she hated it. Like everything else in her life at that moment, she knew it wasn't what it seemed. The family home that she thought she had known and loved was suddenly an alien building that meant nothing to her any more, other than a highly mortgaged financial millstone around her neck.

It was all a lie. Her marriage was a lie. Her life was a lie.

Sara had been watching her daughter sitting as still as stone in the driver's seat, her eyes flickering over the profile of the building. She had to fight hard with herself, not to go out to her daughter, and she breathed a sigh of relief when Jess eventually pushed her key into the lock.

'Are you okay, darling? You've been out there for ages. I wondered if you were all right?'

'I was looking at the house and trying to work out how much it's worth. It's too big for just me and CJ and I hate it now. I'm going to pack up and sell, get something back from the bastard. I could come and live with you, couldn't I? Both me and CJ?' Jess phrased it as a casual question but there was an underlying pleading in her voice. Marching over to the drinks cabinet, she poured a huge slug of vodka into a glass and then gulped it greedily.

Sara was troubled as she looked at her daughter's distant expression. 'What made you come up with that all of a sudden? Haven't you seen the lawyer? I didn't think you could sell it.'

'I'm going to have a damn good try. Sheldon gave up his claim to anything the day he walked out of here.'

'Yes, I know.' Sara tried to keep her tone calm. 'But legally I'm sure you can't do anything with the house without his permission.'

Jess swung round, her eyes wild and disorientated as she faced her mother. 'I thought I could rely on you but you're just as bad as Sheldon, telling me what I can and can't do. This isn't fair, it's just not fair!'

Sara tried to keep her voice calm and sensible although she found it increasingly difficult to reason with Jess, especially when she was drinking.

'I know it's not fair, none of this is fair, but there are legal processes – didn't the lawyer tell you that you can't sell the house if it's in both your names? Sheldon would have to agree. Come on, Jess, you have to get a grip on all this. Tell me exactly what he had to say and then we'll try and work out the best way forward. It's still early days.'

'Oh for Christ's sake!' Jess screeched, her face screwed up in frustration. 'I'm getting so pissed off with you and po-faced Carla. My life is falling apart and all you're interested in is telling me about legalities. Sheldon's gone and I need money. Who's to tell me what I can or can't do with my own home?'

Sara watched her daughter's anger rising as she picked up a large and expensive figurine, one of a pair that had been a gift from Sheldon, from the window-ledge and passed it from hand to hand slowly.

'Certainly not Sheldon,' she continued, 'and certainly not some dumb-ass lawyer who doesn't know me from Adam. This is my home and I'll do whatever I damned well want with it and with everything in it.'

The figurine suddenly flew across the room over the

top of her mother's head before smashing against the ceiling coving and shattering back down to the floor.

It took all Sara's willpower not to respond but she knew that Jess was under the most unbearable pressure. However, at the same time she wanted to shake her to try and get through to her. Well aware that the other matching figurine could come flying her way at any moment, Sara decided her best course of action would be to give her daughter some space.

Keeping her emotions tightly in check, Sara turned silently and went up to the spare bedroom where she was temporarily camped. To her relief, Jess made no attempt to follow her.

As each hour of each day passed, Jess was becoming more and more irrational, and Sara feared for her daughter's sanity. In her own mind she likened her to a sealed pressure cooker that was bubbling away, building up to boiling point and likely to blow at any second.

Jess was eating virtually nothing, hardly sleeping and having no contact with anyone apart from herself and Carla. It physically hurt Sara to see her daughter roaming the house in distress, chainsmoking her way through packet after packet of cigarettes and drinking almost neat vodka at every hour of the day and night.

With no idea what to do for the best and also knowing she couldn't do right for doing wrong, she made an instant decision to telephone Pearl Patterson, Sheldon's mother, in Los Angeles.

Hoping that Jess didn't take it into her head to pick up the phone downstairs, she sat on the floor as far away from the door as possible, dialled the number and waited. Pearl's housekeeper answered the phone and, as always, tried to hedge but this time Sara was having none of it.

'No, I'm sorry, this time I will not call back. Tell Mrs Patterson that it is Sara Wells on the phone and I'm going to keep calling until she picks it up.'

After a long silent interval the phone was picked up. 'Sara! I'm so pleased you called. Tell me, how is Jess? This must be so hard for her—'

'You're right it's hard, Pearl – in fact, that's an understatement. It's actually bloody unbearable. Have you heard from that son of yours yet?'

'Sara, if I knew anything that I thought Jessica should know then I would have told her, but as I said, you know what Sheldon can be like – so single-minded.'

Sara was seething; she could feel her blood pressure soaring as she gripped the receiver in her palm. 'Pearl, I'm sorry but that just isn't good enough. Now I'm sure you've either heard from Sheldon or you've heard something about him and I want to know – I *need* to know. Jess is off her head with worry about CJ.'

'I understand that,' Pearl murmured gently, 'but Jess has to be a little more understanding of Sheldon's position as a father. He loves his son—'

'Understanding? *Understanding?*' Sara interrupted furiously. 'Your son has cut off all her finances and she is virtually destitute. Now, either you give me some positive feedback or I'm going to make sure everyone knows about it. I know you don't want the good name of Patterson being bandied about. I'm sure you'd lose a lot of business goodwill.'

The momentary silence at the other end of the phone let Sara know that Pearl was thinking about exactly what she had just said.

'Don't try and blackmail me, Sara.' Her tone was controlled and carefully modulated, but the underlying anger in Pearl's voice was electrifying. 'This is all very inconvenient for me, you know. I really do not want any involvement in Sheldon and Jessica's marital difficulties.'

'Pearl, please help me here. This is my daughter we're talking about!' Sara snapped, her exasperation slowly but surely overflowing.

'Okay, Sara, mother to mother I tell you what I'll do: as a gesture of goodwill, I'll transfer some funds into Jess's account to tide her over, but in the long term . . .' Pearl paused and her silence told Sara far more than her words, 'well, I'm afraid that in the long term Jess will have to think about being independent of this family.'

'But she's your daughter-in-law, the mother of your grandson!'

'I'm aware of that, Sara, but if Sheldon doesn't want to be with her and if CJ is with him then I'm afraid there's nothing more I can do. Your daughter isn't my responsibility. She and Sheldon will have to sort something out between themselves, eventually. Now I have to go, I'm already late for my appointment.'

Before Sara could think of anything to say that wasn't overtly threatening Pearl had hung up, but Sara knew the first bullet had been fired on both sides. She just hoped it wouldn't ricochet back to Jess.

Sitting on the edge of the bed Sara tried to think it all over logically, and in the order of events; she tried to piece it all together and look for something. Anything at all that could maybe help in the search for CJ and give her daughter her life back, as well as her son.

Sara still had the phone in her hand when it rang loudly, causing her to start up in shock. She let it ring a few times, thinking that Jess would snatch it up but the ringing continued unanswered. Sara pressed the button.

'Hi, is that Jess Patterson I'm speaking with?'

The accent was familiar but the voice was one she hadn't heard before.

'No, this is her mother, Sara Wells. Who's speaking?'

'You don't know me, but I'm sure you've heard all about me. My name is Kay Cacherton, previously Patterson. I'm Sheldon Patterson's ex-wife.'

'Oh,' was all Sara could think of to say, silently grateful that it was she who had answered and not Jess.

'I'm calling because I've just heard a little of what has happened and want to help if I can.'

Sara couldn't understand what was going on. 'If you don't mind me asking, what exactly do you think you can do?' She paused and then continued as a thought flashed into her head. 'And how exactly do you know what's happened?'

'Pearl's been talking about it all over town but I probably haven't got the true story. She can be economical with the truth when it comes to her precious Sheldon, but I understand he has taken custody of his son.'

When Sara didn't respond, couldn't respond, the woman continued, 'I heard he's spirited him away and gone underground to keep CJ away from his mother, who Pearl so lovingly describes as over-protective and mentally unstable. Be sure I'm not saying that at all – I don't believe a word of it. I know the Pattersons work in mysterious ways. She's justifying his actions so that Sheldon looks like the victim in all this when he re-surfaces in LA.'

As the implications of what the woman was saying were permeating into her brain, Sara heard Jess heading up the stairs.

'Look, I can't talk now, I don't want my daughter

upset any more than she already is. Give me your number and I'll call you back as soon as I can.'

The woman rattled off a number and then spoke quickly. 'My husband and I will be in London shortly for a conference. Call me and we'll arrange to meet up. I'm sure I can help you with some background information.'

As Sara put the phone down the door opened.

'Who was that? I didn't want to answer the phone in case it was Saint Carla being bloody benevolent again.'

Again Sara was concerned by her daughter's irrationality. She could see that Jess had been drinking again.

'That's not fair, Jess, she's been good to you and so has Toby. Right now you need all your friends, especially ones like Toby who was prepared to stick his neck out for you. Anyway, it was only double glazing.'

Sara hated lying to her daughter, but looking at her hollow eyes and dreadful pallor, she knew she had no choice. She had to protect her as much as possible. *Keep CJ from his over-protective, mentally unstable mother?* The words went round and round in her head in a repetitive loop as she tried desperately to keep her face neutral in front of Jess.

'Mum, I'm sorry, I just can't help it. I don't know what to do but I do know that if I let myself get too upset then I won't be able to handle any of this so I take it out on you.'

The red-eyed sadness etched on her face upset Sara far more than any words spoken in the heat of the moment ever could.

'Am I forgiven?' Jess said shakily. 'I have to try and keep it together for CJ. How can he understand what's happened? Sheldon can't go on pretending to him that it's just an extended holiday. Can he? *Can* he?'

'It's okay. We'll deal with this and we'll get CJ back, I promise.'

'I'm not so sure any more. They've disappeared into thin air, and how can you fight something if you can't confront it?'

Sara didn't answer. She just didn't know what to say to reassure her daughter.

Chapter Ten

Santa Monica, LA

Sheldon Patterson's ex-wife Kay stood immobile, arms crossed, looking out over the ocean from the wide wooden slatted deck at the front of her house. When, after hearing the story from a friend, she had initially brought the subject up, her present husband Ryan had suggested that, for her own sake, she should not get involved with any of the dreaded Pattersons again.

A part of her, the sensible part, told her he was right, that they should be left as her past, but there was another part that reasoned it was once again time to put her head over the parapet with regard to her ex-husband.

The family had tried, almost successfully, to destroy her and she could sense that they were now trying to do the same with Sheldon's current wife. Kay didn't know Jess but her instincts told her that the Pattersons were again playing games with other people's lives.

Although he was a part of her life she would have preferred to forget, the constant high-profile presence of Pearl Patterson, her ex-mother-in-law, badmouthing

Kay and Ryan, albeit oh so politely, meant it was sometimes difficult.

Kay and Ryan had dated briefly before she met Sheldon; in fact it had been through Ryan that she met him. The Patterson company had many offices and Ryan was one of their many employees – one of the best, Kay found out later, much later after she was well and truly entwined with Sheldon. Kay and Ryan had met in a bar and clicked instantly but then, just as the relationship was blossoming Ryan had introduced her to his boss.

Ryan because he had worked for the Pattersons, and Kay because she had been married to one, both had experience of the real-estate business so the next logical step after they got back together had been for them to start up their own company. The plan hadn't gone down too well with Pearl and Sheldon even though they deliberately steered clear of direct competition, but Kay and Ryan had persevered and opened an office in nearby Malibu.

At the height of the none too subtle harassment she had wanted to move away, to go back to her home city of New York, but as Ryan had said, why should they run away and hide when neither of them had done anything wrong? Contrary to what the Pattersons had said, she hadn't been the one at fault in the marriage breakdown, she hadn't even wanted it at the time but, after an emotional battering, Kay had quietly given in and taken the paltry Patterson pay-off.

It had been sufficient to buy the beach house in Santa Monica and a fancy convertible, with enough left to invest in starting the business. It had also bought her peace of mind. With Ryan back in her life, her first disastrous marriage, or rather the disastrous ending of it, had in time become a distant memory.

Until now.

With the rumours and gossip flying back and forth about Sheldon and his disappearance, it all came flooding back and she could once again smell a rat. Kay had firsthand experience of the workings of a family which always wanted its own way. Regardless.

Ryan came out onto the deck. 'Shall we go for a run? It's a beautiful evening and it might just clear the mind and stop all those irrational thoughts in their tracks.' Walking up behind her he wrapped his long and muscular arms around her waist before kissing her gently on the nape of her neck. 'Come on, Kay. I know the Patterson business is bugging you, but it's history.'

'Not history for long, Ryan, not if that goddamned guy has done something to his son. I have to try and do something, I just have to. I have an instinct for this and it tells me that Sheldon and Pearl are making mischief again.'

'If you truly feel like that then so be it, but give it some more thought first, huh? Think about what you might be getting back into, but you know I'll support you whatever.'

Kay turned round to face him. 'I love you so much, Ryan. You're just so . . . so incredibly nice! And sexy too, of course.'

'I know!' He smiled down at her.

Kay and Ryan were an attractive couple who complemented each other perfectly. She, blonde and tiny with an evenly tanned, well-honed bikini body that belied her age by about twenty years. He, on the other hand, was tall, black and smoothly muscular with not a hair on his shiny shaven pate. Both were fighting fit from their daily runs along the beach trail and workouts in the gym. They were also very busy and popular, with working days that were long and hard and a social life full and active.

As Kay looked at Ryan she found it hard to imagine how she could ever have thought Sheldon Patterson was the answer to her dreams.

'I've got everything now, Ryan. Well, almost everything, and I'm so grateful, especially to you.' Reaching out, Kay took Ryan's face in her hands and kissed him gently on the lips. 'It's because I feel so lucky that I have to try and help the current Mrs Patterson. Poor woman!' Smiling sheepishly she ran her fingers up and down his thigh. 'Actually, I've got a confession to make. I've already phoned.'

Pausing, she looked up at him. 'You're not mad at me, are you? I spoke with her mother and I told her we're going to be in London. The ball is in her court now, so if she calls back then I'll arrange to meet her. If I don't hear any more then I'll leave it.'

A flicker of concern flashed across Ryan's dark eyes but his voice remained gentle and uncritical. 'Okay, honey, sounds a good compromise. Now let's run while it's cool.'

They ran together down to the beach and set off down the trail that ran along the sands.

'Race you to the pier!'

Kay stepped up her pace to match his long-legged lope and smiled. She still couldn't believe how lucky she was to have turned her life around to become the person she now was.

Mrs Ryan Cacherton, with a perfect husband and two perfect step-daughters who lived with their mother, Ryan's ex, about 100 miles up the coast but spent a lot of time at the beach house with them. They had no children of their own but, as Kay often told herself, 100 per cent of everything going right was really too much to ask for.

Sara thought long and hard about the call from Kay. She tried to recall everything she had heard about Sheldon's ex-wife and the divorce but, without asking Jess, it was difficult to remember something she hadn't taken a lot of notice of. All she could trawl from her memory was that Kay had married Sheldon, left him, fleeced him and then run back to her previous boyfriend who, rumour had it, she had been seeing all through the marriage and whose baby she aborted.

Sara couldn't imagine how the woman could possibly have any information that would help find Sheldon and CJ, but she also couldn't figure out why Pearl would be gossiping about Jess. How could she possibly have said that Sheldon had to protect CJ from Jess? And as for describing her daughter as mentally unstable . . . Sara steamed silently at the mere thought of it.

'Mum? You're miles away, you haven't answered my question.'

Sara shook herself back to the present where her daughter was standing beside her. 'Sorry, love. You're right, I was just thinking. What did you ask?'

'I said I'm going to see Carla. Do you mind me leaving you to phone-sit?'

'Ah, I really have to pop home and sort things out there. My own bills will be piling up and Whisky will think I've abandoned him totally to my neighbour Hilary if I don't make at least a fleeting visit. Could Carla come here instead? Or could you have your calls diverted to your mobile? I know you don't want to leave the phone.'

Jess's face dropped even lower than before. 'You're

not thinking about going home for good, are you? I'm sorry about how I was earlier. I really couldn't have got this far without you, you know. I'd be in a padded cell by now.'

'I know. I've just got some things to do that can't wait any longer. Give me a few hours and I'll be sorted. I won't be any longer, I promise. If anything happens, call me straight away.'

Despite being well aware that Jess didn't want her to go, Sara smiled and kissed her on the top of her head while at the same time waving her mobile. 'See? I've got my phone. I'll be contactable all the time.'

As she pulled up outside her small terraced house on the other side of the city off the Newmarket Road, Sara breathed a sigh of relief. Guilty as she felt about it, she knew she had to get away from the situation for a while, and a trip home had been the only excuse she could think of. As she put her key in the lock she heard the echo of the cat flap, and by the time she was in the hall Whisky was there to greet her, rubbing enthusiastically around her legs and mewing as loudly as he could.

'Hello, puss, have you missed me?' Sara reached down and stroked him. 'Come on then, I'm going to put the kettle on and then you and I can sit down and relax for a while. I've missed you as well, you know.'

Ever since Jess had got married it had been just Sara and Whisky and, although she missed her daughter dreadfully in the beginning, she had gradually got used to the solitude and eventually had come to enjoy her peaceful life. Now, in circumstances she could never have imagined, she was back in the thick of Jess's life but the impotence that she was feeling at being unable to help was unbearable.

Opening one of the cans of catfood with which she had

stocked the cupboard, she tipped the contents into the cat's dish and watched as Whisky devoured the lot, purring loudly. Oh to be a cat, Sara thought. Just eat and sleep and chase the occasional mouse. But much as she wanted the break, her mind couldn't stay away from Jess.

Kay! She fumbled in her bag for the piece of paper. A quick bit of mental arithmetic told her it wasn't an unreasonable time to call her so she dialled the office number and, when she was put through, re-introduced herself.

'I wondered what it was you thought could help us? My daughter is frantic with worry. Not knowing where her son CJ is or what's going on is driving her insane.'

'I can understand that. I'd be crazy too if Sheldon Patterson had disappeared with a child of mine.'

Curiously Sara absorbed her words. 'What exactly do you mean? Despite everything Sheldon has always been a good father to CJ.'

'No doubt,' the sarcasm in Kay's tone was hard to miss, 'but I bet everything had to be done *his* way and I bet your daughter had to do exactly as she was told although, to be fair, she probably didn't realise it at first.'

'Maybe,' Sara replied tentatively, 'but I thought they were happy – more relevant, *Jess* thought they were happy. There were no rows, no arguments. A disagreement maybe, but nothing to warrant this.'

'I learned that Sheldon isn't good at confrontation but he is good at running back to Mom. Sheldon likes to be in control but he's also a coward. Running off with his son would be a typical Sheldon answer to things not going his way. Just run away and pretend nothing has happened. Just run away and start again.'

The panic was quickly rising up into Sara's throat; she found it hard to speak clearly. 'How do I know that you're not just being malicious? From what I understand, you ripped Sheldon off for a small fortune after you yourself had run off.' Sara was stopped mid-sentence as Kay's laughter echoed down the line.

'Not true, not at all true, but I can understand that being the story you were told. I've heard it myself in fact, plus a few others. Look, I'm trying to help. If you want to meet up with me in London then I'd be more than happy to talk about it all, but if not then I understand.'

Sara knew the pause was for a response but she couldn't get the words out.

'Pearl Patterson has dedicated her life to protecting her son,' Kay continued, 'and will say anything to do so. I shall be staying at the Martinet Hotel in Kensington. I'll call you when we arrive. I'd love to meet your daughter and offer her some support.

'Tell me what you know, or rather what you've heard, and then I'll tell you the real story.'

After Sara had replaced the phone she sat back down and the cat jumped straight onto her lap and started purring. Sara felt guilty about Whisky; he had been her constant companion for so many years and now she felt as if she was deserting him. As she stroked his silky coat and whispered sweet nothings to him in the absolute knowledge that he understood, she thought about the strange conversation she had just had.

Should she tell Jess? Should she tell Pearl?

Suddenly Sara felt apprehensive. The conversation worried her mainly because, much as she didn't want to believe it, she had the rising fear that Kay had been telling the truth about Sheldon and his mother.

If not, why would she have bothered to phone in the first place?

Chapter Eleven

Cancún, Mexico

Sheldon Patterson leaned back in his chair and impatiently watched his son playing with the assortment of new toys that had arrived in the post that morning.

The boy had been so pleased to receive the birthday presents from Pearl, his grandmother, that Sheldon had decided to let him have them for the time being – just for a short while, he decided, then he would take them away. Having already stated that they weren't the most suitable playthings for his five-year-old son, it irritated him that his own mother was being so thoughtless, so dismissive of his opinions.

He didn't want his son to waste his time with remote-control cars and male dolls. CJ was going to learn to be a man. He would be independent and highly educated in the ways of the business world, he would also play first-class golf and study the stock market on the top-of-the-range laptop computer that Sheldon had bought him. The five year old's study timetable was already drawn up, a timetable that covered all the things that were important for CJ's future in the family business, things that would mould him into a son to be proud of. Character-building pursuits.

The boy needed neither toys nor mollycoddling. That was where Jess had failed as a mother.

My son. Pleasurably he rolled the words around in his head. That was all he had ever wanted for as long as he could remember.

My *son.* Lots of sons, in fact, but at the grand old age of forty-two he only had the one. The relief at being able to call him that was wonderful. No longer would Jess be able to smother the boy and ruin his future.

It had been a heartbreaking disappointment to him when it hadn't happened with Kay and, as far as he was aware, with any other of his girlfriends over the years, but then Jess had come along.

For a few short days after they first met, Sheldon had felt himself being pulled towards the fun-loving and effervescent but highly unsuitable Zoë; however he had soon decided that his future lay with the more homely and malleable Jess. His instincts had told him that Zoë would have been as hard to handle as Kay had eventually turned out to be, but Jess was different; she had openly adored him and without a second thought, acquiesced to him on all counts.

But whereas he had thought originally that soft and gentle Jess would be a good wife and mother, after CJ was born she had started to be more assertive. It had been subtle, but Jess had gradually started to make decisions without first consulting him. Sheldon Patterson didn't want an assertive wife and he certainly didn't want his son to have an assertive mother who might try to usurp his authority and scupper his plans and dreams.

He felt a slight tingling of guilt at keeping CJ away

from Jess on his fifth birthday, but blindly convinced himself he was doing the right thing for all of them.

Jess had been a perfect mother when CJ was a baby, even a toddler, but then she hadn't let him grow up; she had even over-ruled Sheldon and insisted on enrolling him at a run-of-the-mill little nursery school that let the children waste time with crayons and Playdough.

That had been bad enough, but when she had tried to insist that he went up to the local junior school instead of Sheldon's careful choice of exclusive private school, it had been a step too far. The deciding factor. Or that was the way that Sheldon justified the situation to himself.

That, and of course Sofia.

Sofia, who completely idolised both him and CJ, and agreed absolutely with his views on the upbringing and discipline of children. Sofia, the brilliant lover and carer who would happily tend to his every whim without having any legitimate say whatsoever in CJ and his future.

Sheldon smiled at the thought of the gorgeous young Spanish girl pottering around their rented house, turning it into a home for them all even if it was only going to be temporary.

'Sofia? Sofia, are you there?' he called out in no particular direction. He knew she wouldn't be far away from him.

'Coming, Sheldon,' her heavily accented voice tinkled seductively in the room as she appeared, a wide smile on her beautiful young face. Walking straight over to him, she leaned forward and sensuously wrapped her arms around his neck from behind the chair. The movement encouraged her almost waist-length chocolate-brown hair to fall over their faces, obscuring them both from CJ's view.

Very gently she let the tip of her tongue snake around his earlobe, while at the same time sliding round in front of him. Absentmindedly Sheldon reached out and touched the erotic diamond ring he had bought her that pierced her taut belly button. He turned it gently before letting his hand roam up under the short T-shirt that showed off her well-honed midriff before running his fingers over her bra-free breasts which were suddenly a hair's breadth from his face.

'I was thinking, perhaps we ought to move to the East Coast for the sake of CJ's education – maybe Boston? Or even New York? I'm not sure. I'll ask Mother what she thinks. I have to phone her later, thank her for the presents even if they are too goddamned stupid for him.'

'Whatever you think is right, darling. I just want to be with you wherever you go.' Sofia leaned further forward and sensuously kissed him around the edge of his lips. 'You will always do what is correct for us all, I know. Now I am going to prepare the dinner. What do you want?' Smiling happily she looked over at CJ who was out of earshot and raised her voice. 'And you, CJ? What for you today?'

The little boy looked up. Neither of them had noticed the tears that were plopping one at a time on to the floor where he sat cross-legged and dejected. 'I want Mummy. It's my birthday and I want to see Mummy!'

Sheldon and Sofia exchanged glances.

'You know what I've told you, son. Your mom is busy right now, she has other things to do, that's why you're here with me. You do like being here with me, don't you?'

The emotional blackmail oozed from the carefully spoken words but CJ just looked at him sadly and silently, his little face, with down-turned lips, openly defiant.

'Come on, son, you've got me and now you've got Sofia, so let your mom have some fun without us around. She doesn't need us and we don't need her. She didn't even send you a card, did she?'

Without a word CJ stood up and, after a swift kick at the brand new Action Man, abandoned the toys. Head hung low he stomped out of the room, but there was no mistaking the words that he muttered when he was through the doorway. 'I hate you, I want my mummy. I hate you, I hate you . . .'

One big disappointment to Sheldon was that CJ looked just like a small version of his mother, albeit a little watered down. He had the same fair skin that freckled at the hint of sun but his hair wasn't quite as bright, more of a sandy red and straighter. It had never occurred to Sheldon that he could have a child with red hair but he was hoping that a little sun and sea air would brighten up the boy's pallid complexion and maybe even lighten his hair a little. Now, with red eyes and his mouth turned down, he annoyed his father even more.

'Get into your room now and stay there until you learn some manners.' Sheldon's raised voice made the child scamper away to his room. 'That boy needs to harden up a bit. I was brought up without my mom around and it never did me any harm. Jeez, I had a nanny from the minute I was born and Pop would take me hunting in the mountains nearly as soon as I could walk.'

Frustrated, Sheldon pushed Sofia away.

'I could shoot a tin can off a log by the time I was three and I want my son to be like that. I want to take him hunting and fishing and be proud of him, not embarrassed by him being soft and effeminate.

Mother hates all this New Man crap; she likes men to be men.'

Sofia smiled sympathetically. 'CJ will be okay. Soon he will forget his mother and then he can be just like you. Soon. Maybe then we can be married? I could be his mother instead. I could love him like a son.'

A shadow passed over Sheldon's face. 'I've told you, Sofia, it's not an option. Anyway, I'm still married and I'm not going to divorce Jess. If I do, she'll try to take my son away. I know what she's like. Her life revolves around the boy and the house. She'll come and take him back to England, I know she will.'

Biting his lip nervously at the thought he didn't notice the very slight tightening of lips and narrowing of eyes that flashed across Sofia's face but, as if realising the harshness of his words he reached out and pulled her close again. 'One day things will be different. CJ will settle down and eventually Jess will want to marry someone else and then we can make some permanent plans.'

Gazing at her, he stroked her hair tenderly and she put her arms around him. 'Aren't you just happy that we are together?' he asked. 'That's what we wanted, isn't it? You, me and CJ, just the three of us?'

'Of course I am. I love you, Sheldon, and what you want, I want.'

Satisfied with her response, Sheldon again untangled her arms from around him and stood up.

'I'm going to have a chat with the boy, explain a few things to him about his new life with us, and then we can jump straight back into that gorgeous new bed that's been beckoning me since we got out of it. Okay with you?' Sheldon smiled and pressed himself against her.

'I shall be waiting for you, do not take too long.' Sofia laughed and gently pinched his cheek. She knew that

Sheldon was about to punish his son to bring him into line. She doubted that he would lay a finger on him, but his verbal berating and the deprivation of privileges, including, no doubt, every single item that Pearl had sent, would wound the already unhappy child.

Sheldon was brilliant at psychological punishment.

Then, of course, CJ would be confined to his room for as long as he and Sofia were in their room making love.

Sofia had a way with children; she loved them and they nearly always loved her so she didn't agree with Sheldon's views and ideas on parenting. But she would say or do nothing about it because she knew how Sheldon wanted to play it and Sofia had every intention of playing whatever game was necessary to ensure her own secure future.

The first time she had entered the Patterson family home in Cambridge to babysit and had locked eyes with him, she had known exactly where that future lay. She had instantly sensed he was there for the taking. Consciously she had played him like a fish on the end of a line, pulling him in, letting him swim away a little, until she was ready to reel him in for the final time.

By then, of course, he was convinced that it had been all his idea in the first place. However, although he didn't know it and would never believe it, for once Sheldon was the one being used.

It had been obvious to the sharp young Sofia from first glance that Jess was contented with her life and completely oblivious to Sheldon's faults and foibles. Therefore, inveigling herself into the family had been amazingly simple, with the added bonus of Carla, her employer, unwittingly providing her with all the information she needed to know to capture Sheldon Patterson.

Friends with the child first, then the mother and finally the father.

Sofia wasn't a bad girl but she wanted the best things in life, the lifestyle that she had witnessed as a nanny, and with Sheldon she knew she could have it, just so long as she played the game and let him think that everything was his own idea.

The occasional twinge of guilt flashed through her for Jess as CJ's mother, a mother who Sofia had seen at first hand in her home environment. Sofia hadn't intended CJ to be part of the package but now he was, she would use the boy to make herself indispensable to the father.

Sheldon Patterson, heir to the Patterson family fortune, was an attractive prospect as a future husband and Sofia knew that he would marry her. Eventually. When it was all his own idea.

It was the worst day so far for Jess. Two months on and there was still no news. Sheldon, CJ and Sofia had all disappeared into thin air. Hiding in CJ's bedroom, completely grief-stricken, Jess couldn't even cry any more. Drained of all feelings and reactions all she could do, all she wanted to do, was sit silently with her eyes closed and try to imagine her son.

She wanted to know where he was, what he was doing and what he was thinking, and she desperately wanted to project her love to him somehow. Screwing her eyes tightly shut she silently spoke to him, hoping that there might be some natural telepathy between a mother and child that would help her communicate with CJ, to let him know that she hadn't abandoned him.

It was her only son's fifth birthday, a day that should have been celebratory, and she had no idea where in the world he was. Repeated enquiries had turned up nothing but false hopes and alarms; all the publicity and the press appeals had been in vain and it seemed that everywhere she turned she hit a dead end.

Barry, her lawyer, was working hard over and above his remit considering her lack of funds and was ever the optimist as he opened all the official and legal channels – but there was still nothing to raise Jess from her despair.

Even the desperately requested response from Sofia's family had been negative. According to the Agency, her father had reacted angrily and was adamant that they had not heard from her. He also stated that if it was true that she had run off with a married man, then they didn't want to hear from her anyway. A staunchly Catholic family from a rural Spanish town in the north of the country, they wanted their shame at their daughter to remain secret and refused to talk to anyone.

Barry Halston was sure they were telling the truth.

He was equally sure that Pearl Patterson was not.

Pearl continued to portray herself as sympathetic and caring, but every time Jess or Sara called, she simply reiterated that she knew nothing at all and, despite Sara's polite disbelief and Jess's white-hot anger, nothing could shift the woman from her stance.

Both emotionally and financially Jess was in ruins. The large mortgage was becoming impossible to maintain and the bills that dropped daily onto the mat were mounting up.

Jess and Sara had optimistically shopped for CJ's birthday as if he might just come home, but now the day had arrived with no news of him. The pile of brightly wrapped presents and unopened envelopes in the centre of the room mocked her. Kneeling on the floor in front of them, gently stroking the ribbons and bows, Jess thought back to the day he was born.

The happiest day of her whole life.

Sheldon had been delighted at her pregnancy, ecstatic in fact, and he had savoured every milestone alongside her. All her clinic appointments, scans and classes had been arranged around Sheldon's diary, and he had planned meticulously around the birth date. Jess had, however, drawn the line at his suggestion that a pre-arranged caesarean would be more convenient.

Sheldon had read all the books, watched all the videos and questioned all the professionals. He thought he knew everything there was to know; in fact, he had bordered on obsessive throughout.

In the end it had been a difficult birth and surgery had been the only option anyway, but Cameron John Patterson had arrived safely to a world full of flowers and blue helium balloons. Only once had Jess wondered to herself whether Sheldon's enthusiasm would have been so great if the baby had been a girl, but in the end it hadn't mattered; after the complications of CJ's birth Jess had been devastated to find out that she was unable to conceive again.

Her long-held plans of a large family were suddenly thwarted.

As she continued to think back through it all she subconsciously noticed her mother quietly slip into the room and crouch down on the floor beside Jess. Mother and daughter sat together in silence for a few minutes before Sara stood up.

'I've just made a pot of coffee – will you come down?

There are things we need to talk about, to set in motion if we're going to get through this.'

Jess looked at her mother as if she was seeing her for the first time, almost as if she was wondering who she was. She said nothing.

'Come on, come down with me.' Sara took her daughter's arm and, the same as when Jess was a child, she pulled gently at her, making her stand, and then led her down the stairs.

'Jess, we have to think about the immediate future. You have no money and I have no money so we have to plan ahead now.'

Jess's head moved slowly around as if she had just woken up and realised where she was. Huge bloodshot eyes gazed out from under an uncontrollable mass of shocking red curls. Jess hadn't been to the hairdresser since before CJ went missing and her natural colour was creeping back but it was dull and dishevelled.

In fact, Jess as a whole looked unkempt. Despite her dramatic weight loss she was still wearing the same clothes that now hung off her and it was all too obvious that she once again was severely hung over.

'I'm not planning anything. I can't plan anything until CJ comes home.' The fire had gone from her voice, along with the anger; now her tone was flat and almost robotic in response.

'Well, you have to. You have to decide what to do. I've spoken to Barry and we have two options. You can come and stay with me and rent this house out, or I can sell mine and live here. Our money has run out and I have to go back to work properly. I've had so much time off that I'll lose my job completely soon. They won't be this understanding for ever.'

Jess looked at her mother, a slight smile on her mouth

but not in her eyes. 'Do you think CJ has forgotten me yet? Does he think Sofia is his mother now? He's still a baby, really. I suppose he will have forgotten. He's probably quite happy with his new life wherever it is. He'll have everything he wants with Sheldon, won't he?'

'Of course he's not forgotten,' Sara murmured comfortingly, 'the same as you haven't forgotten him, but it won't do CJ any good if he comes back to find he hasn't got a home any more. I think that if you come and live with me we can rent this house out and it will bring in enough to pay the bills. Will you at least think about it?'

'I'm too tired to think – you decide. I'm going to have a shower.' Jess turned and walked away, but instead of going up to the bathroom she hurried through to the utility room and snatched open the cupboard under the sink. As her hand reached in her mother's voice echoed through the open door.

'Jess, alcohol won't do any good in the long run, you know.'

'But it helps in the short term, thank you very much!' Jess shouted back as she pulled out a bottle and poured a slug of vodka into the same glass she had used the night before. She hadn't realised that Sara knew where she kept the bottles.

'I'm thirty-six years old,' she continued, 'and I can drink if I want and however much I want without asking my mother's permission.'

Jess added a splash of tonic water to the triple vodka and then downed it in one. Without thinking, she chucked the glass into the sink, forgetting that the utility butler sink was china. The glass smashed on impact and Sara flew into the small closet-like room.

'What on earth are you doing? For God's sake, Jess!' she snapped.

Jess smiled humourlessly. 'It's only a glass, cut-glass maybe, but still only a glass, not very high on my list of priorities at the moment, I'm afraid. Now I am going to have a shower.'

'Jess, you have to get a grip. This isn't doing anyone any good. You're a nervous wreck and at this rate you're going to turn me into one as well.'

Ignoring her mother completely Jess walked out and went upstairs.

Standing under the piercing jets, Jess could feel the alcohol working its way into her system and clearing her mind a little and, as the guilt sneaked back in, she thought about what her mother had said.

Although grateful for her help she could see no way that she could let Sara sell her house, her only security. But at the same time Jess couldn't imagine having to pack up her home, CJ's home, and move back to the house of her childhood.

Jess had moved on from there a long time ago, both physically and financially, and she knew that as soon as she moved out of the family home she was accepting the situation. Accepting that the previous six years of her life were a complete waste of time, and also accepting that CJ wouldn't be coming back.

Jess knew she could never do that; she simply couldn't let herself consider a situation where CJ didn't live with her.

Shaking off the excess water she stepped purposefully from the shower and, wrapping herself in a couple of towels, ran downstairs to find Sara picking glass out of the sink as round globules of tears dropped unheeded from her eyes.

'Mum, I am so sorry, I really am. I'm going to get myself together, I promise.'

Jess wrapped her arms around her mother, realising that it was the first time she had done that since CJ went missing. It had always been the other way round. 'And you're not going to sell your house – that's stupid,' she continued, the excitement in her voice hard to disguise. 'I've decided I am going to go to LA, after all. I'm going to see Pearl – she owes me, owes us. And I'm going to make sure she knows it.'

Almost feverishly, she waved her arms around as she spoke, her face animated again. 'I'm pissed off with being polite about this, it's not got us anywhere so far. I'm going to camp on her doorstep for as long as it takes.'

The shock on Sara's face took Jess aback.

'You can't do that! You can't go and see Pearl! She won't help you and it could make things worse.'

'How can anything be worse than it already is? I've not seen her since Sheldon slunk off like the snake he is.'

'You can't afford it.'

'I'll find the money. I'll sell something – I'll sell the car. I'm going, no argument.'

Sara's shoulders visibly slumped as she tried not to look her daughter in the eye. 'Jess, there's something I have to tell you. I should have told you earlier but I didn't want to upset you any more than you already are.'

Suddenly alert, Jess realised her mother knew something. 'You'd better not tell me you know where they are. If you know that . . .'

'No, of course not,' Sara interjected sharply, 'but I'm afraid there is something you should know. Please don't be angry with me, I was just waiting for the right moment.' Sara hesitated before continuing. 'Kay phoned here a couple of weeks ago – Kay, Sheldon's ex-wife. And then I met up with her in London.'

Jess frowned and bit her lip as she thought for a moment about what her mother was saying. The cogs of her mind were whirring and it was reflected in her face.

'Kay? What the fuck has this got to do with her?'

'I went to London to meet her. I didn't tell you in case there was nothing to tell. I didn't want to raise your hopes.'

'And?' Jess glared angrily at Sara as she tried to mentally collate exactly what her mother was trying to tell her.

'And I think we may all have underestimated both Sheldon and Pearl.'

Chapter Twelve

The guilt Sara had felt at sneaking off to meet Kay was overpowering, but she was so concerned about her daughter that she knew she had to go; she also knew that she couldn't tell her beforehand. Jess wouldn't be able to take another dead end.

The fast train to London pulled into King's Cross leaving Sara with barely enough time to grab a cab to reach Kay's hotel on time.

Puffing up to the intimidating reception desk, a polished length of mahogany that swept along the back wall of the vast lobby, she asked nervously for Mr and Mrs Cacherton. Following a short, polite conversation and a phone call to the room from the receptionist, she was pointed in the direction of the lift that would take her up to the correct floor.

As she knocked hesitantly Sara was expecting to be let into an ordinary hotel room, but as the door was pulled open she could see straight away that it led into a large and airy sitting room that was part of the suite that Kay and her husband were staying in. Before a word was spoken Sara could feel her guard getting even higher. Suspiciously she wondered why, if Kay could afford a suite in a top London hotel and money wasn't an issue to her, she would be bothered about Jess's problems.

'Hi there.' The woman who stood back welcomingly as she opened the door, smiled widely and held her hand out. A man stood close behind with a hand pressed protectively on her shoulder. 'I'm Kay and this is my husband Ryan. We're so pleased to meet you although I wish it hadn't been necessary.'

Sara looked at Ryan and blinked. If Kay had been deliberately searching the polar opposite of Sheldon then she had found him in the handsome and athletic Ryan.

'Hi there.' The man's smile was big and genuine also.

'Hello.' Sara gathered her wits together quickly, hoping that neither of them had noticed her surprise. 'I'm pleased to meet you too, I think!'

Kay's eyes flickered past Sara. 'Is Jess not with you?' she asked curiously.

'No, I'm sorry, I thought it was best not to say anything to her just yet. She's really not very well; this whole sick business is destroying her.'

Kay and Ryan, standing side by side, smiled sympathetically in unison.

'We can understand that. Come in, come in, now can I get you a coffee? Tea? Or would you feel more at ease down in the coffee shop? I don't want this to be an ordeal for you, we're happy to go wherever you feel most comfortable.'

There was no mistaking Kay's New York twang that echoed loud and clear.

'No, here's fine and yes, I'd love a coffee, thank you.'

As Kay called down to room service and ordered coffee and sandwiches Ryan led Sara over to a large comfy sofa that was set squarely opposite two tapestry easy chairs with a polished oak coffee table in the middle.

'Just tell me if you would prefer me not to be here, but I thought Kay could use some support. This is hard for her also.' His drawl was soft and calming as, very gently, Ryan leaned forward and touched her arm.

'It's no problem to me,' Sara smiled, 'but I'm still curious about how you feel you can help me. As far as I was aware, Kay hasn't seen Sheldon in years. I also understood that the divorce was particularly nasty.'

Kay moved over to Ryan and Sara hesitated, torn between not wanting to offend the couple in front of her and wondering what exactly they thought they knew.

'I don't want to appear rude but if this is your way of getting back at Sheldon and his family at the expense of my daughter and her misery, not to mention a little boy who is God knows where without his mother . . .' Sara paused for breath, giving her words time to penetrate but Kay jumped straight in to respond.

'Sara, I know you are rightly very angry and probably suspicious of my motives but I promise you, I have no axe to grind over this.'

Kay's tone of voice told Sara that the woman in front of her really wanted to be believed.

'I just know how I would feel if I had a child and its father had taken it away, any father, but especially Sheldon and his control freak of a mother. I don't believe either of them is likely to be put up for a good parenting award.'

In an instant it hit Sara exactly why she was there and a huge feeling of guilt swept over her for sneaking about behind Jess's back. But it was too late, she was there and her deception was complete. Now she had the feeling that she was going to hear things that she didn't want to hear, and certainly things that she might not want to, but might have to, share with her daughter.

'All right, Kay, I'm all ears. Tell me what you think I need to know.'

As Ryan sat down Kay placed the tray on the table and then perched on the arm of his chair. She put a hand on his shoulder in what Sara could see was a gesture of both natural affection and reassurance.

'When I met Sheldon Patterson I thought he was the best thing in my life. Back then I didn't look the way I look now. I was a little overweight, with mousy hair and not a clue about make-up, clothes – things like that. I was just the optimistic fat kid from downtown New York who thought she could make it in Tinseltown. Wrong! Sooo wrong!' Kay grimaced at the memory. 'Like thousands before me, I ended up waiting tables and cleaning hotel rooms just to survive. I didn't want to go back home and admit my failure. That's how I met Sheldon; he was in the restaurant and I was waiting on him. He was Ryan's boss and they came in to eat. It was love at first sight – well, it was for me, anyway. I now know differently about him.'

'Big mistake taking him to meet Kay. I thought I was showing her off and he decided she was up for grabs!' Ryan laughed dryly. 'I was slowly and carefully wooing Kay, doing all the right things when Sheldon came at her full on and I lost out!'

'Come on,' Kay slapped his leg, 'you never told me how you felt. I thought you and I were just having fun. Anyway, that's history, we got there in the end!'

Kay's laugh was a loud raucous guffaw that didn't match her delicate beach-girl looks. Irrationally Sara

t. She contacted me because she heard rumours
around – bad rumours, I'm afraid.'

ah, right,' Jess snapped. 'Like I'm sure she gives
about me. I bet she was laughing her socks off.'

ignored her and carried on. 'Kay is one hundred
nt certain that Pearl knows where Sheldon is. She
s that there is no way he would not contact her.
's a lot of stuff that's been said about Kay that
ntly not true, as well as a certain amount of
linging about you, I'm afraid.'

king quizzically at her daughter, Sara tried to
her words gently. 'Darling, I have to ask you,
erything really okay with you and Sheldon? Was
ly the caring, sharing husband and father that you
think he was?'

ening her mouth to automatically defend her hus-
Jess hesitated. 'Why do you ask? Is it because of
hing the bitch Kay said?'

n attempt to avoid any unnecessary confrontation
eliberately didn't make eye-contact. Sitting on a
ool she propped herself up with one elbow on
akfast bar and her chin in the palm of her hand.
gh she intended to be selective she also knew she
be honest. CJ was the most important person in
, not Jess, not Kay and certainly not Sheldon.

it is because of something that Kay said. Lots
said, in fact. Please tell me the truth, Jess. Trust
is important. Tell me everything and then I'll
about what Kay said.'

oured herself another drink. 'With hindsight
hat's the only time I seem to see things clearly
h hindsight Sheldon wasn't all he seemed, but
now that he's not here that I can see it.'

tears welled up Jess started talking, and once

thought that if Kay tried to make it in Hollywood now she probably would.

Ryan didn't laugh at all, he just smiled gently up at her.

Sara felt herself being drawn to the couple against her will.

'I didn't realise then,' Kay continued with a rueful smile, 'that I was merely selected. Sheldon wanted a hausfrau, good breeding stock to be the mother of his sons. Of course, as soon as he realised that I was infertile I was on the way out. Paid off and sent packing.'

Sara continued to be puzzled.

'What do you mean, you were infertile? I heard that you had an abortion behind Sheldon's back, that it was Ryan's baby.'

'Yep, that's another rumour that made its way back to me – completely untrue again. When we didn't conceive Sheldon became quite frantic and we went for tests, so many tests, but I soon sensed I was going to be sidelined. Sheldon wanted sons more than anything in the world so I was dumped to make way for a more successful brood mare.'

Sara bristled, unsure whether that was a dig at her daughter or purely Kay saying it as she saw it. Kay noticed and quickly tried to backtrack.

'I'm so sorry, I shouldn't have said that, it was thoughtless. I didn't mean Jess.'

'It's okay.' Sara's tone was abrupt. 'Just carry on. So far you've given me nothing to go on, nothing that will help me find CJ – and that is all I really care about.'

Kay and Ryan exchanged glances. 'May I ask you a couple of questions before we start? Firstly, are you going to tell Jess about our meeting?'

'Oh, probably an edited version and I'll have to pick

my moment. She has more than enough going on in her head right now: one wrong push and without doubt my daughter will topple over the edge. Next question?'

Kay looked intently at Sara, so intent that Sara felt uncomfortable. 'Why did your daughter only have the one child?'

Sara certainly hadn't expected that and was visibly taken aback. She wandered over to the window and looked out across the London skyline. An early dusk was settling outside blurring the view. She watched the lights flickering on.

'She had problems when CJ was born and as a result had to have surgery. She can't have any more.' Out of the corner of her eye she saw the look that Kay and Ryan exchanged.

'Then I'm afraid the chances are he's gone looking for a younger, more fertile option. Poor Sheldon.' Kay's laugh was humourless. 'First me with my problems that gave him no kids at all and then Jess with only one when his sole obsession was a gang of kids, his progeny, living proof of the masculinity that Pearl has been carefully eroding all his life.'

Sara frowned as she tried to take in exactly what Kay was saying. 'He's already found the younger model,' she said, 'he's gone off with a twenty-two-year-old Spanish nanny. He's taken CJ and everything else. Not only has Jess lost her son, she is also destitute. Sheldon pulled the plug on her finances.'

'That figures.' Ryan rolled his eyes to the ceiling.

'Now trust me, Sara, Sheldon doesn't change his shoes without seeking approval from Pearl first. That woman knows where they are, I'd stake my life on it. Don't waste time seeking out Sheldon, just keep an eye on the mother and the son will eventually surface.' Kay

leaned forward. 'Now let me tell how I think I can help.'

By the time Sara left to rush was completely confused. Kay's de her separation from Sheldon mirro only differences being Kay hadn't she had been covered by US legisl Jess, Sheldon disappeared tempoi understanding mediator and the went into overdrive.

Apparently Kay could have rea under Californian law but, in her whole episode, she had settled out that barely dented the Patterson for

Sara wondered at what point Pe settlement approach to Jess and sh out the least damaging way to tell Ryan, but by the time she arrived t Cambridge, Jess was already drun right time to tell her.

'Well, come on then – tell me al little chat you've had with Sheldoı even if I don't understand how you that. You're my mother, you're s fucking side!'

Jess was struggling hard not to mother. She couldn't understand and she also couldn't believe people had betrayed her.

'There's no need to swear a the circumstances.' Sara smiled words but the point was made. meet Kay and her husband to

releva
going

'Ye
a toss

Sar
per ce
recko
There
is pa
mud-

Lo
couch
was e
he rea
let me

Op
band,
some

In
Sara
high s
the br
Althou
had to
all of i

'Yes.
that Ka
me, thi
tell you

Jess
again?
now. W
it's only

As the

she had started there was no stopping her. The flood-gates were opened for the first time and the words gushed through.

Sara listened without comment; she knew it was not a good time to interrupt, especially as Jess was unwittingly confirming much of what Kay Patterson had said.

'Now listen to me, Jess, I think you can have a good ally in Kay. In Ryan her husband as well, actually – he's a lovely man. If you really are intent on going to LA, then call them. They want to help.'

'Why should they? Why would they give a flying fuck about me?'

The doorbell stopped them both. It was Carla and Toby.

'We may have a solution to one of your problems,' Carla announced. 'Some friends of ours are looking for a house to rent for about six months, maybe longer, if you're interested. They're even prepared to look after the dog for you.'

Jess looked at her mother in panic. The reality of her situation was snapping hard at her heels.

Chapter Thirteen

Waiting in the airport departure lounge it took all of Jess's willpower to keep away from the bars that twinkled their lights seductively and beckoned her in with the subtle aroma of alcohol. Aware of her promise to both Sara and herself that she wouldn't have a drink before or during the flight, she gritted her teeth and looked round for the smoking area. Although at that moment in time Jess would have killed for a huge slug of vodka, a huge slug of anything in fact, she was determined to stay strong. It was hard but she knew her mother was right.

Wandering nervously through each and every one of the shops as a distraction, she wondered how she was going to handle the inevitable confrontation with her mother-in-law. Part of her was looking forward to getting it over and done with and finding out what was going on; the other part was dreading it. Far too much depended on it and she knew that a fruitless visit could easily signal the end of her self-control. The film *Down and Out in Beverly Hills* flashed into her mind and momentarily made her smile.

When Sara had finally to accept that Jess was going to go to LA either with or without her support, she had persuaded her to accept the offer of help from Kay and Ryan. It had been a difficult decision for her to make but, under duress, she had agreed. LA was expensive and Jess had already had to sell her car to fund the trip, so the generous offer of rent-free accommodation with Kay was too good an offer to refuse.

Jess found it ironic that the ex-Mrs Patterson, now a successful businesswoman in her own right, appeared to be the one person she could rely on in Sheldon's home town. Jess had no illusions about the fact that any friends she had had when she lived there would undoubtedly side with Sheldon and Pearl. Sadly she accepted that she didn't have any friends of her own in LA. All of them were via the Pattersons, even the neighbours at the house that Pearl herself had chosen for them to rent.

With difficulty Sara had managed to persuade her suspicious daughter that Kay was genuine in her desire to assist them. She wanted to help Jess get CJ back, mainly because she doubted Sheldon's ability to be a good parent, but there was also the memory of her own treatment by the Patterson family.

Jess determined to use the time before and during the flight to try and collate in her head all the information that she had; it wasn't much but it was all she had to go on. Firstly she wanted to make sure she hadn't missed anything, and secondly she wanted to distract herself from the tempting thought of having just one drink to calm her nerves.

The temptation grew stronger with each passing minute, but her mother's carefully worded warning, that a drink problem would be yet another weapon to add to the Patterson arsenal when the inevitable custody issue came into the open, echoed in her brain.

The initial shock and anger that had raced through her at finding out that Sara had been to see Kay had abated, but hadn't gone away completely; still she saw it as a betrayal by her mother, the one person whom she thought she could trust. It had hurt her deeply that, albeit with the best of intentions, Sara had gone behind her back and had not been completely honest with her. After Sheldon's betrayal she found it difficult to wholly forgive Sara, however hard she tried.

For two long days she had stubbornly resisted all of Sara's explanations, but finally her curiosity had got the better of her and she had agreed to ring Kay and make up her own mind, to find out for herself all the things that she really didn't want to confront.

The content of the subsequent conversation with the woman whom she had always been led to believe was the cause of so much unhappiness to Sheldon, angered Jess even more than she could have thought possible. Thread by thread, Jess's relationship with her husband had unravelled like the wool from an old familiar sweater that was then knitted back into something else. The texture of the wool and the colour shades were familiar but the re-knitted product was virtually unrecognisable.

Although Sheldon had never been abusive or aggressive towards her, Jess could now look back, unblinkered by her previous devotion to him, and see that the potential was there. He had just never had to resort to any of it because Jess had always been blindly subservient. That was, until CJ passed his third birthday and, following a long telephone conversation with his mother, Sheldon had casually announced his plans for their son's future. Plans that were so bizarre to Jess's way of thinking that, for the first time since the day they had met, she had vehemently disagreed with her husband.

He had been angry out of all proportion at his wife's dissent.

'He's just a baby, you can't plan his future like that,' Jess remembered saying.

'Not any longer. He's a boy and he needs to be treated as a boy. I'm going to give you a list of the rules that I want you to stick with. He has to be trained.' To Jess's amazement Sheldon had repeatedly banged his fist on the table as he spoke.

'He's not a dog! You can't have a list of training rules for a three year old! Good parenting is instinct.'

'You're right, he's not a dog, but he's not a girl either, and you seem to have forgotten that.' Sheldon had thumped his fist again. 'This is the age when the ground rules need to be set. I have plans for my son. He needs a firm structure to his life, he has to be disciplined and focused on his future right from the start.'

'Not at three years old he doesn't. At this age he should be having fun; learning should be fun, not a chore.'

Jess had found it hard to believe they were having this conversation; something had fired Sheldon up, but she had no idea what it was. And so it had gone on into the night, the night of their son's third birthday, and by the end of it Jess thought she had talked Sheldon round just a little. They had reached a compromise of sorts where CJ would have fun but would also spend a portion of the day in structured activities that Sheldon himself would organise.

Looking back, Jess could see that Sheldon had merely acquiesced to her face. Behind the front he had put on, he had probably already been plotting and planning from then on to take her son away, to have him to himself. She even wondered if the fact that Sofia had come along might just have been a lucky bonus, simply nothing more than good timing.

Again she pondered her husband's close relationship with his mother, Pearl. Someone, and she could not recall who however hard she tried, had once commented that Pearl and Sheldon were more like a couple than mother and son and the more she thought about it now, the more it seemed true.

Sheldon would, without fail, go out of his way to please his mother and the two of them rang each other sometimes several times a day, wherever either of them were, even when Pearl was away cruising.

Sheldon admired his strong and ambitious mother and Pearl openly adored him, no doubt she always had, but the situation had worsened after the death of her husband. Sheldon had instantly, and willingly, taken up the mantle of head of the family although he had failed to see that he was the head in name only.

Pearl Patterson was supreme matriarch and her son was her beloved puppet.

Even his two younger cousins, who did most of the leg work, were in awe of her despite getting little recognition, either verbally or financially, for their hard work. They were the invisible men, Pattersons in name only whereas Pearl and Sheldon were truly 'The Pattersons'.

Now, with it all crystal clear in her mind, Jess was mortified that she could have let herself become so cocooned in her life that she had never thought the family dynamics and behaviour unusual or, even worse, threatening.

Because of thinking so much about the mother and the son, Jess analysed her own relationship with her mother. Although very close it was certainly different to Sheldon and Pearl's, but without any doubt, it was normal. Sara was always there for Jess, but she had never interfered and sometimes they went for weeks without any contact. Both knew they didn't need it. Each would always be there for the other if it was necessary, but neither had ever thought they would be drawn back together in such tragic circumstances.

Throughout the long flight, even during the meals that she had rejected in advance, Jess kept her eye mask on and feigned sleep; the last thing she wanted was a meaningless conversation with any of her co-passengers.

For twelve hours she was captive in her seat with her feet tucked up on her vanity case and her head cushioned against the window but, uncomfortable as she was, it gave her the time to continue to assess her situation without interruption.

Finally the aircraft's tannoy system jumped to life and announced the arrival of the flight at Los Angeles. Jess could feel her panic rising to an almost unbearable level. The idea of hot-footing it to LA and confronting Pearl had seemed a good one at the time, but as the wheels hit the tarmac of the runway she seriously thought about catching the next flight back.

Just turn around, she told herself, get a flight back home. But Kay would be waiting for her.

After the usual time-consuming formalities were over Jess had no choice but to go and face Kay Cacherton. Walking out into the arrivals hall she scanned the crowd for a few seconds before her eyes settled on the hand-held sign that proclaimed her name. Before acknowledging that she had noticed, Jess studied it for a few seconds along with the bearer who bore little resemblance to the nondescript woman she had seen only in photographs but who certainly matched the description that Sara had given her.

Casually dressed in lime green slacks and a pristine white blouse, she had her hair tied back in a pony tail with a pair of sunglasses pushing back her fringe. Kay Cacherton looked nowhere near the age that Jess knew she actually was.

Nervously inhaling a deep breath and wishing it was nicotine instead, Jess approached the woman. 'I'm Jess Patterson,' she said, cautiously holding out her hand. She smiled thinly, feeling distinctly uncomfortable. This was the woman about whom Jess had heard so much but now, it seemed, most of it was untrue.

Another part of the unravelled sweater that she no longer recognised.

Kay dropped the sign and before Jess could react she found herself in a tight embrace.

'It's good to meet you, Jess, but I wish it had been under other circumstances. Ryan, my husband, is waiting in the car. I'm sure you just want to change your clothes and chill. It's a long flight from London – I did it just a couple of weeks ago and I was completely whacked.'

The words were fast and the New York accent stood out. Jess half-heartedly returned the embrace then quickly broke away, busying herself with her luggage. Chatting non-stop, Kay snatched the suitcase away from her and started pulling it along in the direction of the car park.

'As your flight was delayed Ryan had to park the car. Were there any problems? I like delays, gives you time to gather your thoughts and do some last-minute shopping. Oh look, there he is.'

Kay's chatter was incessant but Jess was relieved; it meant she didn't have to respond other than with the odd yes or no. The short ride out to Santa Monica was made up of small talk about the weather, the traffic and other associated chit-chat, interspersed with loaded silences. Jess found it hard to get her head around her situation sitting in a car with Sheldon's ex-wife, the woman she had been led to believe was his personal spectre, and heading out to stay in her house.

And what a house it was. Ryan swung the car down underneath the two-storey clapboard building that was raised on a vast deck that encircled the front ranch-style and was painted classic pale grey and white. Although only half the size of the Patterson property it was just across the road from the long wide beach that ran for miles along that part of the California coast.

Jess had loved Santa Monica from her very first visit with Sheldon and had quite fancied the idea of living there. But that had been a lifetime ago, before everything had been so dramatically turned on its head. Now she didn't have a penny to her name and was being supported with charity, first from her mother and now from a virtual stranger.

The dusky evening was cool and fresh, and after unpacking her case, Jess sadly savoured the atmosphere of the oceanfront from her bedroom window. Sadly, because the last time she had been in LA it had been with Sheldon and CJ and, as usual, they had all stayed at Pearl's. If someone had told her that her next visit would be like this she would never have believed them.

Before going into the living area for supper with Kay and Ryan she touched up her make-up, changed into jeans and sweatshirt and forced a smile on her face.

'I've ordered pizza for tonight,' Kay smiled. 'We were thinking about taking you out to a restaurant but decided this would maybe be better. I'm sure you just want to sit and talk?'

'Thanks.' Jess nervously fingered the cord of her sweatshirt. 'I really need to know everything you know. Mum told me about your meeting but I'm sure she didn't tell me everything. She can be protective, sometimes too much so even if it is with the best of intentions.'

'That's no problem,' Ryan joined in, his wide friendly smile spreading across his face. 'We'll talk over dinner, unless of course you just want to be alone with Kay? That's no problem either. I can disappear off into my den and catch up on some overdue paperwork. I must have six trees of paperwork waiting patiently for me.'

With the ball firmly in Jess's court she studied the man to whom Kay was married and wondered at the circumstances. If she had met the couple six months ago she knew she would have wondered what Kay saw in Ryan that would make her choose him over Sheldon, her ideal man. But now all her preconceptions had become muddled and she no longer trusted her own judgement.

'I don't mind either way. I don't want to embarrass you by talking in front of you about Kay's ex-husband.'

Kay's laugh echoed through the open-plan building.

'Honey, there's nothing Ryan doesn't know. He was the one who picked up the pieces and put me back together again. Without him I probably would have dissolved totally – I was so low I was almost scraping along the floor, but just look at us now.'

Jess frowned. It was all too much for her to take in. 'I thought it was Sheldon who was devastated? I was told that it was you who sailed off into the sunset with your ex-boyfriend and Sheldon's money.' As she realised what she had said, Jess's hand flew up to her mouth. 'I'm sorry, that came out all wrong. I'm just repeating what

I was told, but I really should think before speaking, I know.'

Again Kay laughed. 'Don't worry, I'm sure there's nothing you can tell me that I haven't heard before. It's what *you* haven't heard before that may just help you. It's for sure you will have been told the Patterson version so I can tell you the true version.' For the first time her smile faltered. 'Unfortunately I can't tell you where your son is, but I'm damned sure Pearl Patterson can, and I can maybe help you deal with her. I know the bitch and how she works only too well.'

Both the situation and the conversation were so bizarre that Jess didn't know whether to laugh or cry. Biting her lip she looked down at her handbag. 'I'm going outside for a smoke if that's okay with you. It goes against all things Californian, I know, but I'm addicted. I'm smoking too much, drinking too much and worrying too much, but there's nothing else I can do.'

Ryan smiled and stood up. 'I'll come out with you, Jess. I confess to enjoying the occasional cigar and beer myself.'

Opening the wide sliding glass doors that led out onto the deck, he stood aside to let Jess through first. With a gentle hand in the small of her back he led her over to the table and chairs that, although well used, were tastefully expensive, as was everything else she had seen in the house.

It occurred to Jess that she hadn't asked what they did for a living. Being a member of the Patterson family Jess had a good idea about the cost of real estate in and around LA and guessed that the beach house was probably worth a good couple of million dollars.

'What business are you in, if you don't mind me asking?'

Ryan smiled widely. 'I thought you might have guessed that, Jess. We're realtors, but we only work in and around Santa Monica and Malibu, and mostly vacation rentals.'

Jess opened her mouth but no sound came out.

'I know what you're going to say.' Ryan laughed gently. 'Patterson Properties. Well, I've been in this business since I left college and we don't step on their toes. There's room for everyone around here and we've deliberately stayed small. We're not entrepreneurs, we earn a good living and still have lots of fun.'

'Didn't Pearl try to shut you down?' Jess frowned.

'Of course, in the beginning, out of principle, but we're small fry to them, and the Pattersons eventually decided to just ignore us. We may only get the leftovers but we make a good living doing what we do.'

His wide and genuine smile again caught Jess off guard. She realised she would have to blank out everything she had heard about Kay and Ryan and start again with a clean canvas.

'But enough about us,' Ryan continued. 'Tell me about CJ,' he asked, his tone compassionate. 'I'm sure he's a great kid if he has a mother like you to bring him up.'

Jess looked across to the beach before answering. 'But he hasn't got me to bring him up though, has he? He's got Sheldon and Sofia. And of course he's also got Pearl when they come out of hiding. I don't have a chance against the Patterson name and money, do I?'

Jess let her eyes focus on the beach and bay that swept wide in front of them; even in the dark there were roller bladers and cyclists whooshing athletically along the beach path. She wondered at the peace of the vista in front of her – and yet her own life was in complete turmoil.

'I'm already broke,' she continued sadly. 'I even had to sell my car to get here. Pearl deposited some money in my account in the beginning but since then she's been harder to contact. Even my lawyer is at a loss to know where to go next. The long arm of the law is actually very short when it comes to parental abduction, especially as no one has a clue where Sheldon is hiding out.'

Her eyes came back to Ryan who was listening intently to her.

'I've only got two weeks to try and find them before I have to fly back. I can't imagine going back without my son, I really can't.'

Kay walked up behind them. 'Jess, honey, I don't want you to feel offended but don't worry about money when you're with us. It's not a problem, really it isn't. Ryan and I are doing just fine and we're more than happy to help you out. Anything you need, just ask.'

'Why?' Jess asked and looked around, but she was unable to judge their expressions in the dim light. 'Why would you want to help me out? I'm a stranger to you, and I could really be the psycho bitch from hell for all you know. Sheldon could be right to take CJ and protect him.'

'Oh, I doubt that,' Kay responded dryly, 'and we're offering you help because we want to. Sheldon would have wiped me out completely if it hadn't been for Ryan. Up against the mighty force of the Pattersons it's easier to lie down and accept defeat, as many of their business rivals have discovered to their cost. I'm sure that's not what you're going to do, is it? Let the Pattersons have your son all to themselves?'

Jess gritted her teeth, just the thought of it made her angry. Eyes blazing she stared at Kay.

'Now you look real mad and that's good.' As Kay smiled, her perfect teeth gleamed in the half light. 'That's how you have to stay. Mad as hell and ready to take them on.'

Chapter Fourteen

Pearl Patterson was deep in thought. She wasn't overly concerned because her belief in her own power and control was absolute, but she did wonder about the most beneficial way to tackle the problem.

The best way, she thought, was to ensure that Sheldon and CJ stayed undiscovered for the time being, until the dust had settled and all the proceedings were fully in motion. Sheldon had told her he wanted full custody of CJ, and Pearl agreed with that. CJ was a Patterson and as such should be within the family, not closeted away on the other side of the Atlantic.

It had been a surprise when a friend who had been collecting her daughter from LA airport had mentioned in passing that she had seen Jess, Pearl's daughter-in-law, in the arrivals hall being met by a woman who looked not unlike Kay, her ex-daughter-in-law.

Pearl wasn't completely convinced whether the part about Kay was correct. She couldn't imagine why those two should be together, but until she knew for sure she decided to work on the assumption that it was true until proven otherwise. She hadn't got where she was by being complacent.

Jess without Kay certainly wasn't a problem; however, Jess with Kay might be a little more complicated.

Kay had, at the time of the divorce, proved to be tougher than expected when the gloves had come flying off, and in a detached way Pearl admired that. Sheldon could really do without Kay behind Jess, pulling the strings. Still, she smiled to herself, the problem certainly wasn't insurmountable.

After weighing up the pros and cons she decided against phoning her son straight away. Better to see exactly what Jess was going to do first, she thought.

When her son had told her he was going to leave his wife and was taking CJ with him Pearl had advised caution and planning, and it had been her idea to cut off the financial lifeline and pre-empt a long-drawn-out legal battle. In Pearl's eyes, no cash equalled no legal representation and therefore no battle could occur. Sheldon would be home and dry with full custody of CJ and in time Jess would probably be allowed to see CJ but her influence would be satisfactorily diluted by then.

However, now she knew Jess wasn't going to give in gracefully, she did decide to have an informal chat with the family attorney first, just to be fully prepared for when Jess turned up.

As she did two days later, without any advance warning.

Pulling up outside the gates in a rental car, Jess, oblivious that Pearl was already well aware of her arrival in town, was prepared for hostilities, but the gates were opened instantly and Pearl, immaculately turned out as always, was waiting by the pool to welcome her.

'Jessica! How lovely to see you! Why didn't you call and let me know you were in town?'

Wrong-footed from the start Jess had no option but

to accept the air kisses that flew past both cheeks and the perfunctory hug that was so fast there was barely any body contact.

'Come on inside, you can join me for morning coffee. The smog's just too low for us to sit on the verandah – such a shame, don't you think? I know how much you love it out there.'

Pearl held her arm out in the direction of the house. Jess automatically started to walk, then stopped.

'Pearl, I haven't come to be sociable, I've come to find out where Sheldon and CJ are. I'm sure that you know. Sheldon tells you everything—'

Pearl's tinkling laugh jarred instantly on Jess's nerves. It wasn't natural and it wasn't genuine. It was Pearl playing games.

'Oh Jessica dear, I've already told you. Sheldon is a grown man and a law unto himself. He doesn't have to tell me what he's doing but I know he'll come back home if and when he's ready.'

'Where do you mean by home? Cambridge where our home is, or here?'

'Well, as you're asking then I would say he'd come here – if he's left you for good, that is.'

Jess itched to smack Pearl right across the face, to remove the supercilious smile and silence the nerve-jangling laugh. But she knew she couldn't, not until she had CJ back safely where he belonged. Instead she forced a smile and changed tack.

'I know how difficult this must be for you, Pearl. After all, Sheldon is your son, but CJ is *my* son and I desperately need to know, first and foremost, if he is okay and—'

Pearl's return smile was as insincere as Jess's as she interrupted her mid-sentence. 'Don't be ridiculous,

Jessica! You know CJ will be safe and happy with his daddy now, don't you?'

Pearl didn't so much sit, as place herself carefully on a throne-sized upright chair that held pride of place in the expensively furnished split-level sitting room. The more she spoke the more condescending she became.

'They're just having some quality time together and getting to know each other without you there to keep them apart. Like fathers and their sons should. You know, Sheldon loves his son more than anything else in the world.'

'Hardly,' Jess snapped. 'If he loved him so much he wouldn't have taken him away from his mother and his home – that was cruel to both CJ and me. I may have missed his birthday but trust me, Pearl, I've no intention of missing Christmas with him.'

Pearl's eyes chilled but her mouth remained fixed in the same pseudo smile. 'Do you not think it was cruel of *you* to try and come between father and son? To try and force your own silly ideas of parenthood on CJ? To undermine Sheldon's role as a father? CJ is a Patterson and will one day be heir to the family. We have to have high expectations.'

Even Jess was surprised by the laugh that escaped unbidden from her own mouth. It was Pearl at her obnoxious best.

'That's bullshit, Pearl, and you know it. I'm sorry, but you're talking complete rubbish. I am a good mother and CJ loves me, he should be with both his parents. I know that you're not going to tell me where Sheldon is but please, please reassure me that everything is well with CJ.'

'Well, of course "all is well" as you put it. I would have been told if it wasn't.'

Jess started pacing the highly polished wood floor that spread throughout the whole property. She could feel herself becoming hot and clammy as she struggled to keep control. She was on the edge of losing it but was trying hard to cling on.

'I know Sheldon won't come back to me now that he has Sofia to tend to his every whim, and I wouldn't want him now anyway, but I do want CJ. Please, Pearl, please help me.'

The quizzical expression that flickered across Pearl's face told Jess that Pearl wasn't au fait with all the details about Sofia. Temporarily exhilarated that she had found a chink in the woman's supreme confidence Jess tried to stand still as she pushed the point home.

'I know I can't compete with a leggy twenty-two year old who is in love with his money, and I don't want to. But for God's sake, Pearl, she's young enough to be his daughter.'

'Sofia is only the nanny. She's with Sheldon just to help him look after—' Pearl stopped suddenly, aware that, unusually, she had made a mistake.

Jess jumped straight in, eager to capitalise on her advantage. 'How do you know about Sofia if you haven't heard from Sheldon? And purely by the by, they've been at it like rabbits for months behind my back. Pearl, they've been having an affair for nearly a year.'

Pearl's expression didn't change; her well-practised smile remained firmly in place on her mouth but her eyes wide and hard, told a different story to Jess.

'You might as well tell me what you know. I intend to find them and then take CJ home with me, home where he belongs.'

'CJ belongs with his father, Jessica, and that's where he will stay. You're in no position to provide for CJ

– you and your mother are broke. The Pattersons will provide for CJ, he will want for nothing.'

'Nothing except a mother! And Sofia? Have you met her yet? Certainly not up to your standards, Pearl. A mere whisper away from trailer trash is Sofia with her pierced belly button and naked midriff, and certainly more impressed with your son's financial standing than his riveting personality and blinding good looks.'

Although Jess fired the words like bullets, she knew she was losing the battle. 'You're going to look a bit daft when everyone finds out exactly what he has done. And I shall go public, trust me. I have to put the record straight.'

'That sounds like Kay putting words into your mouth.'

Jess was determined not to let Pearl see her surprise. So Pearl had known that she was in LA and that she was with Kay, she smiled to herself. The jungle drums were as efficient as always.

'I don't need anyone to put words into my mouth. I can think and act for myself, unlike your son – and, surprise surprise Pearl, you've got yourself a fight that you're not going to win. Neither you nor that sonofabitch Sheldon.'

'But Jessica darling, you can't possibly afford to compete with Sheldon. We employ only the best.'

'Money isn't a problem. Believe me, I can raise as much as I need,' Jess lied easily. 'I'll see you in court unless you tell me what I need to know. I'll call tomorrow and if you don't tell me then, I shall have to start things moving legally. I don't want to put CJ through that but if necessary, I will.'

She looked at her mother-in-law, hoping to connect with her, to make her realise just how much pain she was in. 'Please, Pearl? I'm begging you, for CJ's sake. Will you help me?'

Pearl looked back at her with power written all over her face. Slowly she shook her head. Jess locked eyes with Pearl. Although it wasn't what she had intended, she knew that the battle-lines were drawn. There was no going back. Fumbling in her bag she pulled out a card with her rental mobile phone number on it.

'If you change your mind, this is the number I'm on. Don't bother to get up, Pearl, I can see myself out.' Jess threw the words over her shoulder as she marched out looking far more confident than she felt.

As she drove away Jess could see Pearl standing straight and still watching from the rail of the verandah. Her expression gave nothing away but her stance was adversarial. For an instant Jess regretted having shown her hand but the feeling soon passed. CJ was her son and there was nothing she wouldn't do to get him back.

As Jess gunned the rental car at speed out through the remote-control gates that had swung wide ahead of her, Pearl went straight back indoors to call her son and tell him the latest news. Jess was far more determined than she had anticipated, far more aggressive and showing a lot more fire than Pearl would ever have thought possible.

Jess the mouse had started to roar.

In a way she admired her daughter-in-law's newfound spirit, the same as she had admired Kay when she had finally tried to stand up for herself, but she wasn't about to let that get in her way.

Pearl never accepted any less than total victory as her due.

It was a standing family joke that Pearl never admitted her true age to anyone; she never had, especially now that she was sixty-seven, an age that had such negative connotations. Too old to be sensual and sexually attractive to men, but too young to start bragging about achieving a great age.

Carolina Patterson, her dynamic late mother-in-law, Pearl's role model in life, had touched eighty before anyone found out exactly how old she was, and Pearl fully intended to do the same. Eighty would be her first celebratory party, she had decided. However, despite all that, she knew very well that she looked good, courtesy of her subtle cosmetic surgeon, a healthy but minimalist diet and a rather handsome young fitness trainer who cajoled and flattered her in the extreme.

Tall and upright with carefully maintained hair framing her perfectly made-up face, Pearl dressed conservatively but expensively, and exuded an air of authority that could part crowds in her path in much the same way as Moses parted the Red Sea.

Waiting impatiently for the phone to be picked up the other end she tapped her foot in annoyance. She adored her only son but just sometimes she wished he would assert himself a little more instead of constantly expecting her to sort out his problems. Her annoyance was exacerbated by the answering-machine picking up her call.

'Sheldon? It's your mother here. Call me as soon as possible. Your wife has turned up in town and is getting up close and friendly with your ex-wife. You may be happy as a hog in mud down Mexico way but trouble with a capital T is brewing for you in Los Angeles, my darling. Speak soon.'

Pearl knew a short sharp message on his answering-machine would get the quickest response from her renegade son.

Walking slowly out to the poolside she thought back over her life – a good life, no doubt, but with more ups and downs than a big dipper.

Like her age, Pearl never confided in anyone about her past before Patterson her husband. Her well-buried English past as a high-class call girl in London during the late 1950s, that she had used as a rung on the ladder to a better life.

She had met Rod Patterson, who liked to be called just Patterson, at a private party and attached herself to him like glue in an instant. The snaring of the wealthy American, with a wife who, Pearl had thought, looked more like a well-bred horse than a woman, started as a challenge. But as it turned out, it had been almost too easy for Pearl to sideline the 'Arab Mare' as she liked to call her and become the next Mrs Patterson.

It had also been easy to bury her own past and immerse herself in the role of Mrs Patterson ex-London Society Girl! Fortunately for Pearl, Los Angeles was a long way from London.

So much work over so many years to build her reputation and financial standing in LA had made Pearl paranoid about any break-up of the family fortune. It had hurt to hand over a chunk to Kay and it would hurt even more to hand over another chunk to Jess.

She decided that Sheldon her son definitely needed some maternal assistance. She would find him a suitable wife with an independent cache of security who would provide him with the family he desired without being a drain on the Pattersons.

Pearl picked up the small silver handbell that was on the table by the pool and tinkled it. 'Bring me some iced tea,' she ordered the maid without so much as a nod. 'And make sure I am not disturbed.'

Chapter Fifteen

Despite working together, Kay and Ryan always travelled in separate cars during the working day and it was often the luck of the draw which one of them managed it home through the traffic first. Kay had the advantage of a sporty two-seater BMW whereas Ryan preferred the more sedate, and much larger Lexus, so often she was able to nip out into the traffic-flow way ahead of him.

Kay arrived home that evening from their office ahead of Ryan again and, gasping for a drink to wash away the traffic fumes from her throat, she headed straight for the kitchen, pausing en route to the fridge to click on the answering-machine. She had already pulled open the door and grabbed a carton of juice when the first message kicked in.

'Get the hell out of my life, you interfering bitch. This is none of your goddamned business. If you don't send my wife straight back to England then the Pattersons will bring you to your knees – we'll screw you both and your business. Mess with me, Kay, and you'll regret it. You *and* your new best friend. I'm warning you.'

As her ex-husband's disembodied voice echoed angrily around the room Kay stood stock still in front of the open fridge, oblivious to the carton that started to slip from her hand. It hit the floor with a squelch and as Kay started to run back into the living area she slipped in the juice and sprawled full length on the shiny floor.

'Did I hear what I think I just heard?'

Kay looked up from the floor to see Ryan standing over her holding out his hand to help her up. His eyes said far more than words.

'Kay?' Ryan raised one eyebrow, the way he always did when he was puzzled. 'I only caught the end of it, but that was Sheldon Patterson, wasn't it?'

He pulled her up and immediately reached for the floor cloth to wipe up the yellow mess that was quickly spreading across the floor.

'Okay,' he smiled ruefully when she didn't answer, 'I take that as a yes then. How did he know Jess was staying here? I thought she wasn't going to tell anyone where she was staying.'

Kay's expression was grim as she faced him. 'She called me earlier after she had seen Pearl. Jess just turned up there but Pearl already knew she was in LA and that we were in contact. Jess didn't confirm it to her and she certainly didn't say she was staying with us.'

'Oh come on, Kay,' Ryan raised his hands in disbelief, 'she must have done. How else would Pearl know? Jeez, we could do without the Pattersons resurfacing right now. Everything is so good with us . . .'

'I'm so sorry, Ryan. I didn't mean for any of this to happen.'

In tandem Kay and Ryan both spun round at the sound of Jess's voice. It had never occurred to either of them that she was already home and in the guest room. Now she stood at the top of the open-plan staircase rooted to the spot, her eyes bright with tears.

'I never said a word to Pearl. I don't know how, but she already knew I was here and that I had seen you. Someone must have told her – Pearl has eyes and ears everywhere. I'm sorry, I'll go and pack and find a motel. It's not fair to lay this on you.'

Kay kicked off her juice-sodden pumps and ran up the stairs to the balustrade where Jess was leaning. Taking her forearms in both hands Kay shook her gently.

'You will not. Sheldon doesn't scare me any more and neither does that walking talking dummy from up in the hills. Don't forget, *I* got me involved. *I* called *you*, remember?'

Jess could see Ryan's expression from out of the corner of her eye and she attempted a smile despite the quivering chin that was on the verge of getting out of control. 'I know you're not happy about this, Ryan, and I don't want to come between you two.'

Ryan shrugged his shoulders and grimaced slightly. 'Hey, what the heck! If Kay is happy about it, then so am I. Patterson power doesn't rule in this house. We knew we were poking at the sleeping dragon when we met up with your mom.'

'Do you know something?' Jess looked around help-lessly. 'Apart from missing CJ more than I could ever explain, the worst thing about all this is the fact that I was married to the man for six years and it's only now I realise I didn't know him at all. I knew nothing about him, his business, his life away from home . . .'

Jess opened her eyes wide to stop the tears from falling. She didn't want to look pathetic. 'You must think I'm a complete dumbo. I mean, I know that was Sheldon leaving the message, I know it was him, but I've never heard him speak like that or even use that tone. It was so . . .' she hesitated '. . . so aggressive, so angry.'

'Oh Jessie, Jessie, I did the same, remember? I'm no dumbo, you're no dumbo but Sheldon Patterson is a complete jerk and Pearl is nothing but a bored old woman with not enough to do now she's killed off her old man. Remember that! Pearl will see this as just another competition to be won. This is just another contract race to her.'

Jess ran her forefingers under the rims of her eyes, trying to halt the running mascara that threatened to stream down her cheeks. Her nerves were ragged to the point of hysteria.

'I'm going for a walk,' she said in a choked voice. 'It'll give you two some time to discuss how you feel about all of this. Sheldon, and no doubt Pearl, will already be plotting their next move.'

Then Jess jogged quickly down the stairs and walked out of the front door before they could stop her.

With her head down and shoulders hunched up, she strode quickly towards the beach. The high of the morning when she had thought she would be able to reason with Pearl had plummeted back down to an all-time low.

Turning it over in her mind again and again, she still couldn't make sense of any of it.

Before going to see Pearl that morning Jess had dressed for effect, knowing that whatever the time of day, her mother-in-law would be groomed to perfection from top to toe.

Although a trip to the hairdresser was out of the question, Jess had made the best of a bad job by pulling her out-of-control curls tightly back into a knot and fixing it firmly with a large clip and masses of spray. Meticulously putting her make-up on for the first time in months she had been horrified to see up close the baggy black circles around her eyes and her pale translucent skin that reflected the light over the bathroom mirror.

Jess realised that she looked ill, she also felt ill, but knew there was no way she could actually *be* ill, not if she was going to put up a fight for CJ. No, as far as Pearl was concerned, she had wanted to make certain she was not at an instant disadvantage by looking like a bag lady.

When she had been packing her case back in England, Jess had found several items of clothing tucked away in the back of the closet that she had bought too small, 'for when I lose weight'. Now the weight had dropped off without her even noticing, and the clothes fitted perfectly. She had teamed a pair of classic suede trousers with her favourite, and most flattering, soft beige sweater and a pair of black boots with killer heels that had cost a fortune and hurt like hell.

'Very classy.' Ryan had looked her up and down appreciatively as she set off. 'You go get her!'

'Yeah, you look great. Call me when you're done. Good luck!' Kay hugged her close.

Feeling confident, Jess had set off early, eager to catch Pearl on the hop. But unfortunately Pearl had been ready and waiting to shoot her down in flames.

Now Jess felt utterly deflated and, spying a payphone on the road running alongside the beach, she decided to ring Barry Halston, her lawyer in England, on his home phone number. His slurry voice told her that she had woken him up, but she didn't care.

'I really think the best thing you can do is get back to England and carry on fighting within the system. There's nothing more you can do there unless you can afford the exorbitant charges of a specialist attorney. Let me deal with it from here.'

'You know damned well I can't even afford next week's dinner, but I can't come back, not yet.' Letting her frustration overtake her Jess had spat the words down the receiver. 'I *have* to find him! I'm sure he's here somewhere. I'm going to try and trace the call Sheldon made to Kay's phone. Maybe that will give me a clue.'

Barry's voice, still thick with sleep, washed soothingly down the line as he tried to persuade her that the best way forward was legally. '*Not* a good idea. Sneaking around LA like an amateur detective is going to be counter-productive to your case. I've already been in touch with the LA authorities—'

'NO! That's not good enough. I have to be near CJ.'

'But you don't know if you're near him, Jess. Sheldon and CJ could be anywhere in the world. You may be wasting time and money on a wild goose-chase—'

But before he could finish Jess had slammed the phone down.

Perching herself on the edge of a bench Jess hugged her arms around her body. She physically ached for body contact with her son, but the ache for CJ was slowly being joined by a feeling she had never before experienced.

Hatred. Pure and simple hatred for her husband. There was no doubt in her mind that if she had to actually kill him to get her son back then she would.

Chewing over the events of the day, Jess didn't notice the filthy old down-and-out who shuffled up wearing several layers of old clothes and dragging all his belongings with him wrapped in a grubby and tattered sheet of polythene. Cautiously he sat on the other end of the bench.

'Have you any spare change, ma'am?' the man muttered sideways at her, his voice hoarse but the tone polite.

Jess's instant reaction was to recoil in horror, but she

forced herself to stay calm. 'Sorry, I don't have my purse with me.'

'That's okay, thanks anyway.'

Not wanting to get up and run off, Jess stayed where she was wondering exactly what would be a reasonable time-lapse to leave.

'You look pretty sad, ma'am – you okay?' he asked without looking at her.

For the first time Jess looked at the man and realised that he wasn't old at all. Probably similar in age to herself, maybe even younger she decided, after trying to see past the hair and grime to the face that obviously had a story to tell. But Jess wasn't interested in anyone else's story at that moment.

'I'm fine,' she replied, looking out to sea, not wanting to make eye-contact and encourage conversation.

'Boyfriend trouble?'

'No.'

'Been fired?'

'No.'

'Kids playing up?'

'NO!' Jess jumped up. 'I don't want to talk about it, and I certainly don't want to talk to *you* about it. Now leave me alone.'

The man didn't move a muscle but his eyes flickered nervously back and forth. 'Got somewhere to sleep tonight?'

'Yes, of course I have.' Jess hesitated.

'Then things can't be so bad for you.' He stood up and pulled his makeshift polythene suitcase towards his feet. 'I got no job, no family, no home and half a lousy cigarette to last me till fuck knows when. Count your blessings, ma'am.' He started to shuffle away.

It was the polythene that did it. It reminded Jess of

Sheldon's wrecked and abandoned car with the piece of polythene fluttering in the space where the window had been.

'No, come back!' Jess called after him. 'I'm sorry. I don't have any money but I do have half a pack of cigarettes.' She dug into her pocket. 'Here, take them.'

She held them out to him and for the first time he looked at her directly. Piercing blue eyes stared straight at her from under a matted fringe that had probably been blond in the far distant past. He was much taller than her but his frame, under all the clothes, looked scraggy and thin. A bony hand with dirt ingrained so deep that it looked naturally dark grey reached out for the packet.

Resisting the urge to snatch her hand away Jess smiled. 'You asked me, now I'll ask you: how come you're here living on the streets?'

'The big d's – divorce, debt, drink and drugs. Where are you from?' Not one part of his body moved but the blue eyes probed.

'England.'

'What are you doing here? Vacation?'

'No.' Jess stepped back. 'I have to go, nice meeting you.'

The man laughed. 'Yeah, right.'

'Yeah, right! If you're here tomorrow I'll buy you a coffee and a burger at the pier but I won't give you cash.'

'Yeah, right!' He laughed again, a dry, depressing sound that was hollow and humourless.

'What's your name?'

'Brad. What's yours?'

'Jess. See you around, Brad.'

Jess turned and, resisting the urge to run, made her way back to Kay and Ryan's by a deliberately circuitous route. The man had affected her deeply. She wondered how on earth someone who seemed so ordinary could end up as a tramp in Santa Monica.

'Jess, you've been so long, we were worried.' Kay was waiting on the deck. 'I saw you with that guy. I was just going to send Ryan out to rescue you.'

Jess smiled. 'He wasn't a problem. Actually he was good for me. For a brief time I was more interested in someone else's problems.'

Looking out from the deck she could just make him out in the distance trudging off in the direction of the pier dragging his pathetically few belongings with him. For what they were worth.

'Imagine living like that, carrying your stuff around with you all day and sleeping rough at night. It doesn't bear thinking about.'

'Hey, you get used to it here. There's a good pro-gramme to help the homeless and dispossessed, that's why they gravitate here – that and the good weather. Better to sleep under the pier in California than freeze to death in a New York subway in winter.'

'He said his name is Brad.'

'Oh right, I couldn't see from here. Yeah, we know of him. Brad is always up and down the beach. Story is that he's a Gulf War vet. Came back from the war to find his wife had upped and gone off with someone else and cleared him out. He cracked up and was hospitalised, post traumatic stress so they say. Now he lives on the streets with all the addiction horrors that go with it.'

For a second there was sympathy on Kay's face but she quickly brushed it away. 'Anyway, enough about down-and-outs and wars and whatever. We're going out to eat tonight so go get yourself dressed up. It's time you had a break.'

Chapter Sixteen

In his office, tucked away in a small mews in the centre of Cambridge, Barry Halston, Jess's lawyer, was at his desk with a thick file open in front of him and a pen in hand staring into space. The tiny sash window behind him overlooked the pavement that always bustled with tourists and students alike. He spun his chair round and gazed out through the opaque blinds. The quaintness of the mews attracted sight-seers despite being a cul-de-sac and Barry usually relished working in the heart of Cambridge as it was the complete opposite of the sleepy village that he went home to at night. But at that moment his mind wasn't on work or home, it was on Jessica Patterson; in fact, his mind had been on her ever since their first meeting. As a lawyer, Barry was all too aware of the invisible but immovable line between him and his vulnerable clients and, up until he met Jess, he had never even thought about crossing it.

But there was something about his client that kept her in the forefront of his mind whatever else he was doing. Now he wanted to jump on a flight to LA and help her, he wanted to support her but most of all, for reasons he couldn't even explain to himself, he wanted to be with her.

Leaning back in his chair, he put his feet up on the desk and closed his eyes as he tried to analyse his feelings.

Pity had been the first emotion he had felt when she had rushed in like an out-of-control whirlwind and begged for his help, but the initial sympathy had soon been overtaken by something else. Something that he had recognised instantly but tried to deny. Jessica Patterson was a client and he was her legal adviser. There could be nothing else.

Barry Halston was just fifty years old, a milestone that he had long dreaded but could do nothing about, and well aware that he was lounging in a very comfortable rut. His very amicable divorce had taken place many years before, and although he had had several relationships since he was currently footloose and fancy free, he was not enjoying it like he used to.

Emma and Piers, his children, were grown up and off leading their own lives, leaving Barry rattling around alone in a house that was far too big and unnecessarily expensive, and now Christmas was again looming on the horizon with a New Year not too far behind it.

He was dreading both.

The previous couple of years he had celebrated with his ex-wife and her new family up in the Highlands of Scotland. But, much as he appreciated it, even enjoyed it in an embarrassed kind of way, he was determined not to again be the spare part saddo for whom they all felt sorry.

His ex-wife Fiona was constantly trying to match-make among her circle of unattached friends and acquaintances; even his daughter had managed to rake up a few although they were nearly always mothers of friends, but no one had sparked with him.

No one had given him that breathless ache under his ribs that he associated with being in love.

Until Jessica Patterson.

Fit and healthy, with a full head of hair and just the hint of a middle-age paunch, Barry knew he had worn quite well and his partnership in the practice gave him a good standard of living and no financial worries. The fact that his ex-wife had had an affair with, and then married, an extremely wealthy barrister with far more ambition and the accompanying rewards than Barry, had actually turned out to be a bit of a bonus. Barry, who had long accepted that his marriage was in its death throes, had got to keep the house and everything in it.

But suddenly it all seemed lacking in purpose.

All because of Jessica Patterson.

Without warning, his inbuilt caution suddenly flew out of the window and he flipped his legs back to the floor while at the same time purposefully pressing the intercom on his desk.

'Helen? What have I got in my diary that can't be rearranged? I want to take a week out of the office starting now. Come in and we'll go through it.'

He guessed that Helen, his secretary of fifteen years, would be overcome by curiosity at his request but, professional as always, she appeared instantly in front of him with his diary in her hand and a blank expression on her face.

Together they went through the lists, rearranging and reallocating. Barry had no qualms about piling some of the work onto his partner Anthony, who had spent the previous summer on a yacht in the Aegean.

'Okay, that's all clear, now I want you to book me a

flight to Los Angeles for tomorrow and find me a hotel room in or around Santa Monica. I have an emergency with Mrs Patterson that needs dealing with.'

Helen said nothing but she looked curiously at her boss over the top of her reading glasses. The raised eyebrows and pursed lips told him more about her disapproval than words ever could.

'I want to liaise with a US attorney about the case. I worked with him some years ago on a transatlantic fraud case. He may be able to help her as a favour.'

The lips pursed a fraction tighter.

'It's work, Helen. I have to do my best for my clients . . .' His words trailed off and he busied himself pretending to study the diary page.

'I'll arrange it now, Barry, but have you thought this through? Is it really necessary? We are both aware of Mrs Patterson's immediate financial status. Who do I charge the flights and accommodation to?'

Barry was starting to feel defensive but his legal brain automatically warned him against reacting. Feigning interest in his diary page again he replied almost absent-mindedly, 'Oh, just charge them to me personally. I have other business I can take care of out there so I can kill two birds with one stone. I'm thinking about buying a holiday home . . .'

Helen smiled tightly. 'Yes, Barry. I'll arrange it right away.'

As she reached the door she turned back to him. 'It's only a couple of months since Mrs Patterson's husband abducted her son and ran off abroad, isn't it? It must be hard for her – in fact, it's going to take for ever for the poor woman to get over it even if she *does* get her son back.' Her expression was blank, the words spoken professionally. 'I would imagine any sort of normal life will be out of the question for quite some time.'

Slipping quietly out of the door she pulled it to behind her sharply, leaving Barry in no doubt about her unspoken comprehension of the situation, and also her obvious disapproval.

Barry smiled to himself. Helen was so good at hitting the mark with the minimum of emotion; that was why she was excellent at her job and indispensable to him.

He picked up the phone and dialled. 'Hello, Mrs Wells? Barry Halston here – Jessica's lawyer. I'm ringing to let you know that I have business in Los Angeles next week. I'm flying out tomorrow and I'm going to try and look up Jessica. Is there anything further I should know before I see her?'

After he finished the call Barry felt exhilarated at his own impetuosity but at the same time quite dejected about his inability to solve the problems that were piling up rapidly for Jess. Everything that could be dealt with by the British courts was in place but with Sheldon on the run, and no one having a clue where they might be, his hands were tied.

He knew her mother was working flat out to pack up Jess's belongings and clear the house out ready for the new tenants, Carla's friends, to move in. He could only imagine how traumatic it would be for Jess, on her return, to have to leave her marital home, CJ's home, and move in with her mother.

So much had happened in such a short space of time.

Suddenly Barry couldn't wait to see her. Maybe he could help while he was out there, maybe liaise with the mother-in-law, maybe find the despicable Mr Patterson and CJ. Maybe . . . maybe . . . Contrary to Helen's scepticism, he really did have a contact in LA, albeit an old friend he hadn't seen since law school. He wondered if he could throw himself on his mercy . . .

Aware that he would have to shoulder the costs personally, he hoped Jess would never find out. He could imagine her being horrified at the thought that she might be in his debt.

It passed fleetingly through his mind to confide in his partner but then he thought better of it. The fewer people who knew, the less likely he was to end up with egg on his face publicly.

Waiting for Carla to arrive for a last visit, Sara Wells wandered despondently from room to room in her daughter's house. It was hard to think of it as a home now all the personal knick-knacks of life and living were no longer there. The basic furniture was still in place but that was all. Pictures and photos were all boxed away, along with ornaments and books.

All the things that Jess wanted to keep.

Everything that belonged to Sheldon was packed up in one box although Sara had no idea what to do with it, and all CJ's toys were in another. All Jess was taking to her mother's were her clothes and personal bits and pieces; everything else was going into storage in Carla's garage for the time being.

It broke Sara's heart to see her daughter's life packed up in one room ready to go into storage but she was relieved that she had got it all done while Jess was not around to see it. On her return from LA she would be heading for the other side of the city; mother and daughter would be living together until Jess could get CJ back and recover financially.

Sara's own hard times from the early days paled into

insignificance by comparison to what Jess was going through. Never to have had it was one thing, to have it all and then see it snatched away in a moment was even more unfair, and, even during the really bad times, Sara had always had her daughter.

However, the phone call from Barry had raised her level of optimism. She guessed he had to have a good reason for going to see Jess.

The unexpected image of herself jumped out as she walked past the ornate gold-framed mirror on the wall. Her rapid weight loss had caused everything else to drop a bit. Where previously there had been relatively smooth rounded cheeks, now there were wrinkles that streaked randomly down to her jowls and the outside of her lips turned down. With a start Sara realised that, despite her slimmer hips and defined waistline, she looked haggard and worn.

'Hellooo? Yoohoo?' A voice echoed through the hollow-sounding building and Sara went through to greet Carla who was standing there with her cleaner in tow.

'Sara, this is Betty. She's going to give the place the once-over for you.' Sara opened her mouth to protest but Carla held her hand up. 'No, I insist. You're going to run yourself into the ground and that will do no one any good. There's no need for you to do all this.'

Sara tried again but Carla was adamant.

'This is my leaving gift. I'm really going to miss having Jess nearby, so are the children. I'm going to miss you as well, Sara. It'll be quite lonely when you both move on. But you'll all be back, I just know it. I can feel it in my bones!'

She turned to the woman who was standing slightly behind her. 'Take as long as it takes and do whatever needs doing. I leave it all to you, Betty.'

Sara managed to find a pause in which to break in. 'This is all so difficult. I feel completely impotent. She's my daughter, I should be able to make everything right for her, but I can't. I can't even help her stay in her own home.'

'It's not for you to feel guilty, it's that asshole Sheldon who's caused all this. You're just trying to pick up the pieces.' Smiling sympathetically, Carla put a comforting arm around her shoulder. 'Come on, Sara, let's go and have a natter in the kitchen while Betty is beavering away upstairs. She's wonderful. I don't know how I'd manage without her, and not only that – she's happily married with several children so she's not going to run off with any of my friends' husbands.'

Sara managed a laugh. She was so tired both physically and emotionally, it would be good to sit and have a chat while someone else did all the work.

Linking her arm into Sara's, Carla tugged her along. 'Come on, caffeine and nicotine beckon. I've had a bastard of a day and you look completely trashed!'

'You're right, I am. This has taken over my whole life. I think about it all day and have nightmares all night. It's so hard to just sit and watch Jess disintegrate in front of me.'

Carla leaned her head on one side. 'Tell me about you and Jess. I don't really know anything about her life before Sheldon. She never spoke of it, although thinking about it she never spoke about anything much except Sheldon and CJ. They were her whole life.'

Sara frowned. 'I know what you mean. It's hard because Jess's father was a handsome, charming, personable waste of space as well. God, I was so in love with him. He just waltzed into my life and we had such fun and then Jess came along.'

Taken

'Sounds perfect,' Carla smiled. 'So what went wrong?'

'Life changes when you have children and he didn't want it to change. Jess was a toddler when he just went out one day and never came back. All he said was that he wasn't cut out for responsibility and off he went. That was the last time we saw him.'

'Did you try and trace him?'

'Of course. He was last heard of working his way to Australia aboard a cargo-ship. So we just got on with our lives. We've always been good friends – no teenage tantrums, no nothing.' Sara's eyes focused on the middle distance as she reminisced. 'Jess finished her nursing training and then progressed to midwife; she was doing really well. Then of course she met Sheldon.'

'Excuse me.' Betty appeared in the doorway. 'I've just found this down the back of the unit in the master bedroom.' She handed a fat paper wallet to Sara, who flipped it open.

'It's just some old photographs.' Sara shuffled through them quickly before singling one out. 'Now there's a coincidence. These must be from the holiday in Mexico – it was when Jess met Sheldon. Look,' Sara held one up to Carla, 'that's Jess with Zoë. Oh dear, it's so sad – just look at her, so full of life.'

Carla frowned. 'Zoë? I've heard that name before.'

'Jess went to Mexico with her friend Zoë, who was a teacher. There was a terrible accident while they were out there. The car they were in skidded and Zoë was thrown out, killed instantly. Neither Jess nor Sheldon had so much as a scratch on them.'

'God, that must have been so awful for Jess!' Carla gasped.

'It was, but it was actually Sheldon who supported her and then they got married not long after. Jess was completely fixated on the idea that Sheldon had preferred Zoë and only settled for second choice after the accident. It always made her insecure as far as he was concerned.'

'Maybe she was right,' Carla replied quietly, reaching her hand out to touch Sara gently on the arm.

The photographs were dusty and a little dog-eared; there were so many that Sara just scanned them quickly.

'Maybe she was – who knows?' She carried on flicking through. 'Sheldon must have taken these, there's only a couple of him in among them. I suppose I'd better keep them. No point in giving them to Jess and opening up old wounds at the moment, is there?'

Purposefully she gathered them together and pushed them back into the envelope. 'Jess would never go back to Mexico again after that, although Sheldon wanted to. I think they even had a disagreement over it, but I don't know all the details. Oh well, best not to tell Jess, eh?'

'No, I suppose not.'

Sara slipped the photographs into her handbag and continued telling Carla all about Jess when she was a child. Talking about the past reassured her somehow. She and her daughter had managed before with the odds against them, she was sure they would manage again.

Chapter Seventeen

Santa Monica

'Oh Barry, that's great! I look forward to seeing you.'
Jess put the phone down and turned to grin at Kay. 'That
was my lawyer from back home – Barry Halston. He's
got some business in LA this week and he wants to meet
for an update. Maybe we're going to get somewhere
after all.'

With her optimism rising, although only minimally,
her smile got wider. 'If I turn up at Pearl's with a lawyer
in tow she might well take me more seriously. She made
so many digs about me not being able to afford legal
representation.'

'That's great, Jess. He must be good if he's coming
all this way! Where's he going to be staying?'

The question from Ryan was innocent enough but
Jess instantly decided she knew what he meant.

'You're okay,' she laughed, 'he's staying in a hotel
downtown. Don't panic, you're not going to have any
more strangers checking into your guest room!'

'I wasn't thinking that at all, as you well know.'

'Yes, you were,' she punched Ryan playfully on the

arm, 'and I understand. I would feel the same. No, I'm only a passing query to Barry; he's got far more important clients than me and they can actually afford him. It's just a stroke of luck for me that he's going to be here at the same time.'

'Well, he must rate the chance of success or he wouldn't be even thinking about your case, let alone looking you up in LA. It's looking good, girl, looking good!'

'Ryan's right,' Kay interrupted. 'Sounds positive to me as well. Now, are you going to join us for a run or do you want to use my bike? How about rollerblades? We have it all at your service, ma'am – the advantages of living at the beach!'

So far, Jess had managed to avoid being coerced into any exercise. 'I'm not in the mood for anything energetic,' she told them now. 'I'll just watch the TV if you don't mind, catch up on the news and hope that Pearl rings.'

Laughing, Ryan shadow-boxed around her. 'Your choice if you want to be a couch potato. We're just going to run there and back and some! We'll see you in about an hour.'

Watching from the deck Jess smiled to herself as they jogged away together looking the perfect Californian couple. Kay was wearing pale-blue shorts and a matching crop top, while Ryan was in a grey sweatsuit. Jess thought they could have been running straight into a fitness video.

Leaning on the wooden rail that edged the deck, she waited until they were out of view before lighting a cigarette. Having spent most of the day roaming around inside the house like a caged animal, she wanted to go out, to escape, but it seemed so inappropriate to wander along the beach in the sun or look in the shops when her son was missing.

At dinner the night before she had felt uncomfortable just being in what should be an enjoyable situation. Everything she did that was remotely pleasurable seemed like a betrayal of her son. Even something as simple as putting a touch of make-up on her face before going out or enjoying the excellent food that was placed in front of her by a gorgeous young Hispanic waiter with a smile as wide as the bay outside her bedroom window.

The waiter had smiled at her and she had smiled back reactively before the wave of guilt washed over her. How could she even notice a good-looking young man when her son could be crying into his pillow, missing his mother? she had asked herself before gazing down at her dinner-plate.

It wasn't right.

So she had stayed home all the next day waiting and hoping in vain that Pearl would soften her stance and ring, but knowing deep down that her bluff had been well and truly called. She should have known better than to confront her mother-in-law before finding out where Sheldon and CJ were.

Jess really wanted, needed, a drink. Anything that would deaden the senses and block out the pain for just a short while. But just as she was about to raid Kay and Ryan's drink cabinet that seemed to be calling her from the corner of the living room she spotted a tattered figure in the distance on the bench by the beach.

Brad! Jess remembered that she had promised him a burger. Shit, she thought. She didn't want to go, she didn't want to see anyone, least of all someone like him. At that moment in time Jess needed some TLC herself;

she wasn't in the mood to dish it out. It had been a stupid thing to say in the first place; in fact, she shouldn't even have got into conversation with him.

She went indoors and flicked the TV on, but the only image in front of her was Brad with his filthy face and bony hands and a battered sheet of polythene wrapped around his pathetic bundle of possessions.

Her guilt got the better of her, so clicking off the TV she grabbed her bag and slipped on her trainers. After scribbling a short note to Kay she walked over to the beach bench where he was still sitting.

'Hi there, Brad. How are you doing?' Deliberately she kept her voice upbeat. 'I've got some cash on me today, do you want that burger now?'

Lifting his head from his hands the man looked at her. His glazed eyes were vacant and his brow etched in a deep furrow, as if he had never seen her before. The sickly aroma of stale alcohol that was engrained in his clothes and on his breath wafted across to her before she even got close.

'Remember me? We met here yesterday, and I promised you a burger.'

Without answering he looked down again but not before she had registered the dark bruises and scratches on his face and hands that weren't there the day before.

'You look a mess – what happened to you?' she asked carefully.

'They took my smokes. I only got to have one and then they fucking took them all, the whole packet.' His voice wasn't aggressive or angry, merely accepting.

'Who took them? Did you get beaten up for half a pack of cigarettes?'

'That's life here, ma'am. I'd have done the same if I had none.'

The silence between them was deafening as he carried on looking at his hands and she watched the passing people.

'Please don't call me ma'am,' Jess smiled as she spoke. 'It makes me feel old – call me Jess. Do you want that burger now?' she asked casually, trying not to spook him. A part of her was wary of moving away from the now familiar bench with the man, but at the same time she could feel herself being inexplicably drawn to him. There was something there that she felt.

A connection of some sort.

'Nope.' He shivered.

'A soda then?'

'Nope.'

'Oh for heaven's sake!' Jess retorted in frustration, but still he sat in the same position with his elbows on his knees, staring at his hands that were clasped together in front of him.

'I could really use a drink.'

Jess opened her mouth to snap an emphatic no, but before the words came out she remembered that only a few minutes previously she had been thinking exactly the same. The thought made her smile: being nicely turned out and taking the bottle from the cabinet or from under the kitchen sink wasn't really any different from Brad scavenging round the streets looking for dregs in discarded cans.

'Me, too. I was thinking that myself just a little while ago. I had to get out of the house before I gave in and drank the cabinet dry,' she said.

At last there was a reaction. The man turned his head slightly and looked at her. 'Why do you need to drink?'

'It's a long story, too long to tell now, but I know

alcohol isn't the answer. It only blocks out today and then come tomorrow everything is still the same and you've got a hangover as well. Why do you drink yourself?' Jess asked.

'It's all I can get now I'm off the drugs – one out one in.'

Jess didn't respond; she was sure that the last thing he needed was advice. He seemed all too aware of his circumstances.

'Come on, let's walk to the pier and get that burger.'

They made an unlikely pairing. Jess the middle-class clean and fresh wife in suede and cashmere walking alongside Brad the dishevelled tramp in rags with his territory of polythene separating them.

Neither spoke and when they reached the burger bar Jess went in alone to make the order and took it back to him in a paper bag. 'Here, soak up the booze a little and warm you up.'

They sat side by side on the seat but with a good distance between them, each uncomfortable with the other. Jess only had a Coke but she had bought Brad burger and chips and a large coffee.

'Thanks.' He hesitated and then looked sideways at her, making eye-contact for the first time that day. 'Do you know someone's following you?'

Her head spun round, expecting to see Kay and Ryan hovering protectively but they were nowhere to be seen. 'No. What makes you think that?'

'That guy over there with the baseball cap. He sure as hell isn't following me so it must be you. You pissed him off or something? Is that the husband?'

Jess looked over to where Brad was indicating. The man was leaning on the railings looking out over the ocean.

'No, never seen him before. You've got it wrong, there's no reason for anyone to follow me.'

'He's on your ass all right, but if you say so . . .'

'I do say so. Now I must get back – see you next time, Brad.' She handed him another pack of cigarettes. 'Hide them this time, yeah?'

'Yeah. Thanks . . . Jess.'

As she was nearly out of earshot she heard him mutter something. Turning round she looked at him questioningly. 'Sorry?'

'I said, you be careful.'

Jess walked away and headed back to the house by a slightly roundabout route. Much as she was convinced that Brad was harmless, she still didn't want him knowing where she was staying, considering that his patch was on Kay and Ryan's doorstep. She stopped halfway to look back, to see where he was, and was surprised to notice the man in the baseball cap not too far behind.

Kay and Ryan's house was actually on the road that ran parallel with the beach so there was really no need to turn off again but she took another unnecessary detour just to see. He was still behind her. Far enough away for her not to feel threatened but too close, for too long, for it to be a coincidence.

Turning into the driveway she slowed and he walked on past without a glance, but once inside she rushed up to her room and peered through the shutters just in time to see him getting into a white convertible further up on the other side of the road.

Still as a stalking cat and looking straight ahead, he sat for a while, apparently doing nothing, but she was sure she could see his eyes flickering over to the house before he finally drove off.

Brad could well be right, she thought. Maybe she was being followed.

Her eyes scanned along the beach and she breathed a sigh of relief as she saw Kay and Ryan jogging towards her. She decided not to tell them what she thought, what Brad thought, just in case there was nothing in it, in case it was a touch of paranoia.

Jess motivated herself to make good use of her time in LA and phoned every single person she had ever known in an attempt to find some information, any information but it was all to no avail. The shutters were down as everyone either sided with Pearl Patterson or pleaded complete ignorance of it all. Jess felt so alone, and for the first time she had an insight into how Kay must have felt when the Pattersons had tried to 'persuade' her to move away. There was nothing as cruel as exclusion.

Just as her spirits were way back down in her boots again, Jess had a call from Barry who had not long arrived in LA. It was a very casual call inviting her to lunch the next day at a restaurant in the centre of Santa Monica. He told her it was a modest eatery that his contact in LA had recommended as quiet enough for them to be able to talk about the case.

Although he offered to pick her up en route Jess volunteered to walk there and meet him inside, aware that on foot she could keep more of an eye out to see if she was actually being followed.

And she was. Same man, different baseball cap. But she couldn't see the car.

Varying her speed from saunter to power walk and back again she tried hard not to look round although she did drop her bag about a third of the way there and get a non-existent stone out of her shoe when she was almost at the restaurant.

He was still there each time, hesitating and looking around as she glanced furtively in his direction.

'Hello, Jessica, how are you holding up?' Barry was already there and jumped up politely as the waiter pulled out her chair. 'It's nice to see you somewhere other than my office.' Expressive eyes looked at her appreciatively. 'You look well – the California weather must suit you. Is there any progress to report on the dreaded Mrs Patterson senior?'

Jess took her seat before answering. 'No, not really. I tried to back her into a corner but she just wriggled out past me when I wasn't looking. She's mentally very agile, that one, and I haven't a clue where to go next.'

Barry smiled and Jess looked at him as a person in his own right for the first time. She hadn't seen him away from his office before and she had never seen him without a suit and tie. Taller than she remembered and less chunky without a bulky jacket on, she thought he looked as if he had been stretched.

He was wearing artificially faded but perfectly laundered blue jeans and a pristine white polo shirt with a small designer logo that seemed to reflect up onto his face and make his navy-blue eyes shine. His well-groomed grey hair was quite coarse, making it look even thicker than it actually was.

For a very British lawyer he actually blended rather well, she thought. Visually he could easily have passed for a relaxing local straight off the golf course. 'Casually formal' was the contradictory description she decided suited him best.

When she didn't respond he continued, 'I take it there's still no news of CJ then?'

'No.' Jess's face dropped. 'Not a thing from anyone. I can't believe that no one is coming forward with any information. Kay and Ryan are the only people I seem to have on side right now. But,' she looked him in the eye and smiled hesitantly, 'I know this is over and above your remit, or rather over and above my financial capacity, but I wondered if, as you're here anyway, you would come·with me to see Pearl.' Although her voice was neutral, her face pleaded. 'Just one visit, then I promise I won't take up any more of your time here. I'll let you get on with your trip in peace.'

Jess hated being girly and needy but she really wanted him to go with her and turn the screws. After threatening Pearl with an attorney she knew she had to try and prove that it wasn't just an empty threat. Seeing Barry looking confident and attractive she wondered if she might just be able to fool her mother-in-law into thinking he had been shipped over especially.

'Well,' he frowned at her, his best acting skills coming into play, 'if you really think it will help then of course I will. What do you intend to say to her?'

'Give me back my son now or I'm going to blow your brains all over your precious garden with this rather fetching designer Kalashnikov I am aiming at you from under my right arm.'

Barry leaned back in his chair and laughed out loud. 'Oh dear, I'm sorry, I know none of this is even remotely amusing but I think that would be a bit of an overkill if you'll excuse the pun. Why don't we just try and talk to her – blind her with good old British legal jargon?'

'Oh, okay then if you insist!' Jess laughed back but just as suddenly she stopped. 'Barry, there's something else you should know. I think someone is following me.'

As he listened attentively she told him about everything that had happened since she had arrived.

'So you're telling me that you've been meeting up with a tramp for evening tea on the beach?'

''Fraid so! But if I hadn't then I wouldn't have known. Brad spotted him.'

Barry shook his head. 'You amaze me, do you know that? Everything that has happened and you're still holding it all together and also finding time to do good works.'

Jess didn't smile. 'That's not how I see it, Barry. It's not good works as you put it, at all. Yes, I feel sorry for him, and I don't know why when there are so many others around, but without intending to, of course, he made me look at myself. I needed that.'

She looked at Barry, her expression serious.

'He's well known around here, apparently. He was just an ordinary bloke in the Army who went away and came back to find his old life gone. I've never met anyone before who's actually fought in a war. But apart from that, that could be me out there, you know. If I hadn't got Mum I could easily have distintegrated in a haze of despair and alcohol. It would have been so easy.'

'Oh, I don't think so,' Barry smiled.

'Well, I do. I was already taking the first steps down that road. Anyway, enough of that. When will you be free to visit the lovely Pearl with me?'

'Whenever. Just tell me and I'll arrange my schedule around it.' Barry didn't look at her; he fumbled around in his pocket for his wallet as she continued.

'Have you got time this evening to call round and meet Kay and Ryan? I'd like you to meet them – they've turned out to be the most unlikely supporters. I've found out more about Sheldon in my short time here than I did in all the years I was blindly married to him.'

'I'd love to. It'll be nice to socialise with real Californians in their own home.'

'Actually Kay is from New York!' Jess smiled.

'Oh well, that's just as good.'

When they left the restaurant Barry offered to walk her back to the house via the beach path.

'Don't look round but he's there again, the man who's been following me.' Again he stayed a distance away but there was no doubt he was tracking them.

'Okay, this is what we'll do.' Barry's voice was hesitant as he thought on his feet. 'As soon as I leave you at the door, you go in and stay in. I'll see if he follows me. I have to walk back again to get my car. I'll try and figure out if he's just a chancer looking for someone to rip off, or whether he's really following you.'

'Be careful, Barry. I mean, if he is a mugger . . .'

'Then I'll keep my hand on my wallet and stay in sight of other people.'

After walking Jess to the door, he kissed her politely on both cheeks and then purposefully retraced his steps to collect his rental car. As he got close to the car park and the hairs on the back of his neck stood to attention, Barry Halston was suddenly aware that he was getting into something that really was well outside of his remit. He cursed himself for trying to be Macho Man in front of Jess.

The man had been behind him all the way, but there was no point where Barry could get a good look at him. The most he could see was someone of average height dressed from top to toe in neutral beige and grey and with a deep peaked baseball cap pulled down low over his features. Strolling casually along behind Barry with his hands in his pockets and his head down, he looked just like any other lone walker.

As Barry approached the covered car park he stepped up his pace and then ran the last few steps to the car, zapping the locks from a few feet away. By then he was really frightened – all he could think was guns! He knew the man was getting closer and he could feel fear coursing through his veins making his heart thump furiously.

Frantically pulling open the door, he pushed his leg in ready to swing his body in after but the man got there first. The last thing Barry remembered was the door being ripped out of his hand and a hefty crack on the back of his head.

By the time Jess was contacted, Barry was in the Emergency Room being treated for a superficial head injury, a cracked cheekbone and possible concussion. He had called her because his wallet had been stolen and he had no proof of who he was or why he was there.

'My God, Barry, what happened?' Horror was written all over her face as she took in the purple and red bruise that was spreading down the side of his face and the stitches in the back of his head. The pristine white polo shirt was grubby and splattered with blood.

'Your man jumped me and stole my wallet. You know what? I really think he might just have been a straightforward mugger waiting for the right opportunity. Stupidly I gave him that opportunity in the shadows of the car park.'

Barry grimaced in an attempt to smile. 'I got carried away with your tramp's conspiracy theory and led him right there.'

'Bullshit!' Jess was incandescent with anger. 'Muggers don't follow someone for at least two days just on the off-chance. They're mostly instant opportunists. You said earlier that you thought he wanted to know who you were so I think he took your wallet to find out. Have you cancelled your cards?'

'Yes, as soon as I realised what had happened. There was a bit of a delay, so he's probably whooped it up with my plastic already. But I need you to go to my hotel room and collect my passport and insurance documents.'

As they were talking, two police officers came in the room.

'Mr Halston? You'll be pleased to know we found your wallet, sir. It was in the trash can outside the parking lot.'

'Is there anything in it?' Barry asked.

'Yes, sir. We'd like you to check the contents.'

Barry took the wallet and flicked through it. 'Everything's there – credit cards, cash, even my travellers' cheques, but my driving licence is missing. That's strange. Why would someone batter me and steal my wallet and not take the cash?'

Jess let out an involuntary snort but didn't say anything.

'I don't know, sir. It's certainly unusual. Did you see anyone suspicious?'

'Yeah, I did.' He stopped as he caught Jess's eye. Almost imperceptibly she was shaking her head. 'Well, yes and no. I saw a shadow coming up behind me and then felt the crack on the back of my head. He must have been following me.'

The policeman turned to Jess. 'You are?'

'I'm Jess Patterson. I'm staying in Santa Monica. We

went for lunch and then Mr Halston walked me back. I wasn't there when it happened.'

After a few more questions, the police left. Barry looked at Jess through his double vision. 'Why didn't you want the police to know you were being followed?'

'Because, I want to stay low profile for the time being. You were no more randomly mugged than I was. They wanted to know who you were and your wallet was the best bet.'

Jess moved aside as the nurse entered the side room.

'Now they know who you are. If Pearl isn't surprised when you and I turn up there together, then we'll know for sure that she or Sheldon was behind it. It'll give us more ammunition for bargaining.'

'Hmmm.'

As Barry closed his eyes and leaned his head back wearily, the full impact of what had happened hit Jess for the first time and she was suddenly scared that her lawyer would think twice about helping her.

'Barry, I'm just so selfish! It's my fault you're in here and you were only trying to help me. Oh bugger, this is such a mess and it's stupid of me expecting you to tolerate it. I can understand if you don't want to represent me.'

'No. No, I wouldn't do that. I'm finding this case a challenge, although I could really have done without the headache! Jess,' Barry reached out and patted her hand, 'we'll get CJ back, I promise. We'll get him back.'

'So you're not going to fire me then?'

'Not just yet, although I think you owe me a dinner date.' He smiled.

Chapter Eighteen

Pearl was quickly losing patience with her son. She loved him dearly, adored him in fact, but sometimes she despaired over his habit of running for cover and leaving her to deal with the problems he caused, especially with women. First Kay, then Jess and now, apparently, Sofia.

'Sheldon, I want to know about Sofia. You told me she was the nanny.' Her voice was authoritative as it travelled down the line to him.

'She is a nanny – that's how I found her. She was the nanny for a friend's children in Cambridge and she babysat for CJ. They get on really well, you know; she's great with him.'

Pearl sighed, her exasperation quickly growing. 'That's not what I asked. I want to know in what capacity she is with you. Sheldon, is she your latest obsession?'

'No, of course not.'

'SHELDON! Don't lie to me. I always know when you're lying.' Her voice reverberated into the phone.

'And what if she is, Mother? What difference does it make?' Sheldon's tone was defensive, the way it always was when he was in the wrong in his mother's eyes.

'You fool, it makes all the difference! It makes me look ridiculous, for a start. I've told everyone that you had to leave England with CJ to get away from your psychotic wife. Now I find you're living with a twenty-two-year-old Spanish nanny with no money and a pierced navel. How does that look?'

'I'm in love with her, she loves me – what difference does it make how old she is? And who told you about her navel anyway?'

'Oh Sheldon. You were in love with Jess, you were in love with Kay, you've been in love more times than Casanova, more times than your father even, but at least he had the sense to limit his wandering to just affairs. Why couldn't you just settle for an affair the way other men do? Why does it always have to be love?'

'That's not fair.' Sheldon's voice whined loudly in the receiver. 'You agreed with me about Jess, you agreed that I should have CJ. You know what she's like.'

'I know what you *told* me she was like. I hadn't realised you had someone else in line. Now listen to me, Sheldon, you have to leave Mexico straight away, get away from that girl. You can both stay here with me and we'll fight for CJ correctly. We'll win, you know. Jess cannot afford to take us on.'

'If that's what you think, but Sofia is coming with me.'

'It is what I think, but you can't bring your girlfriend with you. She has to go.'

'No way, Mom. Where I go, Sofia goes. She loves me.'

'Oh, do grow up,' Pearl snarled dismissively. 'If you bring that girl here then I will cut your financial umbilical cord. In fact, unless the girl goes I'll cut it off wherever you are. I mean it, Sheldon. Jess has got her lawyer in town with her now, and she means business.'

'How the fuck can she afford to do that? She hasn't got a penny, I made sure of it. She can't get her hands on a goddamned cent of mine and she's got none of her own. She can't fight me, she can't.' His almost childlike anger flew down the line at his mother.

'Well, it looks like you screwed up again, doesn't it? She's here and her lawyer is here. I've spoken to our attorney and he agrees that in view of Jess's actions the best way forward is for you to be upfront about everything. Now you go off and think about what I've said. The girl has to go and you have to face up to it all. No more hiding.'

Before Sheldon could respond Pearl clicked the button on the phone. Sometimes she wished she could still slap his legs and send him to his room for a couple of days.

Pearl Patterson's tolerance threshold as a mother had always been low.

Sheldon sat back in his chair deep in thought, unaware that CJ had heard every word from the hallway outside, tucked up tight in his child-sized hidey hole, a hard-to-access alcove that was used for storage.

Obliviously Sheldon thought hard about Jess and what his mother had said, but he knew she was wrong. He had never been in love with Jess, same as he had never been in love with Kay and he certainly wasn't in love with Sofia.

He always professed it because it was the right thing to say at the time but he knew he had never truly been in love with anyone. He had certainly loved them at the time but had never been *in love*, never felt that all-consuming passion that he had heard about, fantasised about even, that he knew must exist out there somewhere for him.

The nearest he had come to passion was what he felt for his son, his own flesh and blood rather than someone he had just met somewhere, sometime. Having a son had given meaning to his life and he was determined that in CJ, he would provide his mother with a reason to be proud of him.

He often wished he could experience true love, just so that he would know exactly what all the fuss was about. Both his wives had been in love with him, he knew that without a doubt, but he hadn't been able to respond in kind.

Kay had been chosen as a potentially good wife, attractive and fun but down-to-earth at the same time, but she couldn't give him the one thing he truly desired. Children.

Then he had chosen Jess but even she hadn't lived up to his expectations. At least she had given him his long-awaited son but she hadn't actually wanted to share him, she had wanted CJ for herself. And of course she couldn't have him any more.

A mother's love. How he hated that expression. No one ever spoke of a father's love in quite the same way and yet he loved his son passionately. His son and heir, a Patterson through and through. Not a Wells-Patterson, but a Patterson.

And now that he actually had CJ to himself, Jess was trying to take him away again. Also, to top it all, his mother wanted him to get rid of Sofia.

Methodically as always, he weighed up the pros and cons.

Sofia was good company, she adored him and had few

inhibitions. It amazed him when she confidently walked around the house naked and revelled in making love whenever the mood took her. Anywhere. Sofia was the kind of young woman most men fantasised about, but still he knew he wasn't in love with her.

If it came to a straight choice between Sofia and CJ there was no contest. CJ was the route to his mother's attention, Sofia wasn't.

'Sofia!' he called through the open door, knowing she was sunbathing topless in the garden. 'Sofia!'

Again he smiled when she came bounding barefoot into the room like a graceful gazelle, all long-legged and sleek, her perfectly shaped brown breasts bouncing slightly with the movement. Stray dark hairs escaped from under a minuscule thong that left very little to the imagination and her hair hung over one shoulder, twisted round in a band.

So like Zoë, Sheldon thought, or rather so like how he imagined Zoë would have been, had he got to know her. A part of him regretted that he had cold-bloodedly chosen the homely Jess at the time. If he had gone with his heart and chosen Zoë then maybe she wouldn't have died and maybe he would have experienced true love. There was still a pang of pain when he thought about her.

Apart from wanting to get CJ as far away from Jess as he could, Zoë was one of the reasons he had brought Sofia and his son to Mexico. He loved the country and it brought back both good and bad memories for him, but Sofia wasn't Zoë and much as he loved her and was flattered by her adoration, CJ would have to come first.

'You called me, Sheldon?'

'Sofia, I have to take CJ to Los Angeles. Mother rang

and there are some hitches – I have to apply for custody formally in the States. Jess has already filed papers in England and it looks as if there may be problems. She's in the States with her bloody lawyer.'

Sofia flung her arms around his neck. 'Don't worry, my darling, it will be better to arrange it properly, it will be okay. You are a good father and CJ will stay with you . . . and me. I've been hoping we will go there, just as you promised.' She nuzzled into his neck. 'I have always wanted to go to America and I will love to live in California!' Pulling him close excitedly she tried to kiss his face but he gently pushed her away.

'Yes I know, but there's a problem. I can't take you with me. You have to stay here or go back to England or Spain until it's all resolved. It's too complicated and I can't afford to risk being seen as the bad guy in court.'

He didn't look at her as he said it, he didn't have to; he could well imagine the expression on her face. Looking away he continued trying to justify his actions.

'Sofia, I'm sorry but you know the most important thing to me is to have my son with me. I can't risk losing him. You know how it is, the father is always second best and if they find out I'm with you . . .' He paused and tried not to catch her eye. 'My mother says—'

'Your mother?' Sofia shrieked, catching Sheldon completely off-guard. 'Your *mother*? I thought you were a man, yet still you take notice of your mother? You cannot do this, you cannot leave me here alone. I know no one here, it is not my home!'

'Sofia, it may not be for long. I can still visit, or you can go home to Spain for a while—'

But she interrupted him, her anger making her lapse into her native Spanish. Sheldon didn't have a clue what she was saying but he could tell it wasn't complimentary.

He did however understand her only too well when she reverted to English again.

'You cannot do this, Sheldon, you cannot leave me. Shall I tell you why? Shall I tell you why?'

'Honey, you can tell me whatever you want, but that's the situation, like it or not. I'm going to LA, you're not!' Sheldon was becoming irritated; he had expected her to be upset but acquiescent.

'You cannot stop me. I shall follow you – I will always be there with you whatever you say.'

Suddenly Sheldon felt trapped again. He wondered why women were always so demanding of him. Why couldn't they just do as they were told?

'You're not coming with me and that's final. I'm telling you.'

'And I'm telling you that I am. I am pregnant with your child, Sheldon, your child. So yes, I am going to LA with you.'

Chapter Nineteen

Unfortunately, Jess and Barry didn't get the chance to turn up unexpectedly at Pearl Patterson's house. As was her wont, Pearl cleverly wrong-footed Jess again.

It was just 8.30 on a bright Saturday morning when the electronic buzzer at the gate of the Cacherton house reverberated irritatingly through the house. Kay and Ryan were already down at the local gym while Jess was in the kitchen struggling with the complicated juicer that seemed to do everything except make ordinary orange juice.

Still in the old grey jogging suit she used as pyjamas and with her hair dishevelled and mad, Jess went through to see who it was.

To her horror, standing by the locked gate on the pavement, dressed and coiffeured as if she were about to go out to dinner, was Pearl smiling brightly. Like an alligator eyeing up the prey before clamping its jaws around its victim's legs, Jess thought, as she saw her mother-in-law's teeth shining from behind scarlet lips.

With her chest thumping and nausea rising in her throat Jess flung open the door and went out onto the deck.

'Good morning, Jessica. Can you spare me some time for a chat?' Pearl's eyes wandered over Jess from the top of her unbrushed hair to her bare feet. 'I know it's a little early for you but it is important.' The slash of red stretched tighter across her face, pulling the already over-stretched skin back taut across her lips.

'What do you want, Pearl? This isn't my house, as you well know. I can't invite just anyone in.'

'But I'm not just anyone, am I, Jessica? I'm your mother-in-law. I'm also Kay's ex-mother-in-law just in case you, or she, have forgotten.'

Grudgingly Jess buzzed opened the electronic gates.

'You're welcome to come and sit on Kay's deck or alternatively, if it's that important, I'll come up to see you at your house later on today.' Jess paused for effect. 'With my lawyer.'

The other woman didn't react. 'The deck is fine,' she said coolly. 'I've told my driver to come back in an hour – that should be long enough for what we have to discuss.'

Jess started to panic. She hadn't bargained on seeing Pearl again without Barry alongside to support her. Now she was instantly at a psychological disadvantage, but to go back in the house, change her clothes and brush her hair would let Pearl know how uncomfortable she felt. She decided to stay as she was.

Tripping up the wide wooden steps and balancing herself daintily on the edge of one of the upright chairs, Pearl crossed one leg carefully over the other and pulled gently at her brilliant white linen slacks to avoid any unnecessary creasing. Jess was left with no option but to sit opposite her feeling like the female equivalent of Brad.

Pearl glanced at her watch. 'Just got up, Jessica?' The question was loaded.

'No, I haven't actually, I've been up for hours. I look a mess because I was tossing and turning all night, the same as the night before and the night before that. I haven't had a night's sleep since your son kidnapped CJ.' *Be calm, she told herself. Don't let her get to you, that's what she wants. She wants you to lose it. More grist to the mill.*

'Now, Jessica,' Pearl wagged a manicured finger at her, '"kidnapped" really is a dangerous word for you to be throwing around, very slanderous, but I'll make allowances for you at the moment. I think "rescued" is more the correct word, don't you agree?'

Don't react. Stay calm until Kay and Ryan get back. Get Barry over to mediate.

'No, Pearl, you can dress it up how you like but "kidnapped" *is* the right word. However, I don't want to argue with you. Just say what you have to say. Have you come to tell me where they are?'

'Noooo.' The word was drawn out dramatically for effect.

'Then that's the end of the conversation. All I'm interested in is the whereabouts of my son.'

'You don't need to know where they are, Jessica. Providing we can come to an agreement regarding custody of CJ then Sheldon will let you see him. I've spoken with him since I last saw you and of course he wants to see this resolved satisfactorily.'

Don't lose it Jess, don't lose it. Hang on for Kay and Ryan to come to the rescue.

'Satisfactorily for whom? And exactly what sort of agreement are we talking about here, Pearl?'

Pearl opened her briefcase with a flourish, pulled out several sheets of A4 paper and a dainty pair of reading glasses. Then with all the aplomb of an actress with a script in her hand, she proceeded to read from them.

'In brief, and I shall of course let you keep a copy of this, Sheldon will have full custody of CJ, full parental rights and full control over everything to do with his life in the future. They will live with me in the short term until Sheldon finds a suitable property in the same district.'

Pausing for effect, Peal set her face with a wonderfully magnanimous expression before continuing in the same tone.

'You will, of course, be able to visit CJ during school vacations but only with myself present. We have to consider what is best for CJ and, as you know, we can provide for him far better than you ever can. Sheldon will pay you alimony and I will pay for your airline tickets but you will not, I repeat not, live in the States. You will stay in England. That really will be the best place for you to get on with your life, near to your mother.'

Breathe deep, breathe deep and smile. Be the alligator yourself for once. Creep up and chew her head off before she knows what's happened.

'Anything else?' The sarcasm appeared to go right over the top of Pearl's head.

'There are a few minor conditions but we can go through them later, and a whole heap of legal minutiae that you don't need to bother with. You know how wordy these attorneys can be. Now do you agree in principle?'

Jess didn't reply. She looked out across the beach and to her relief saw Kay and Ryan heading home.

'Sorry to disappoint you, but I don't agree to anything. I want to see Sheldon face to face and I want to see CJ. Then I want him to live with me. Non-negotiable. The only thing I will concede is that yes, CJ does need his father, so if needs be I'll live here with CJ and Sheldon can have unrestricted access. That's my only concession.'

Pearl started to laugh but Jess kept it together.

'This is really none of your business, Pearl, is it? Surely it's for me and Sheldon to sort out our differences?' She smiled. 'Anyway, haven't you got a cruise to go on or something?'

They're getting closer, only another couple of minutes, Pearl hasn't seen them.

'Don't try and be clever with me, Jessica, because you won't win. Now these are the conditions and they are non-negotiable. The alternative is, of course, a lengthy legal battle which the Pattersons will win and then,' Pearl looked almost motherly as she leaned forward and patted Jess's knee, 'you'll never see CJ at all because you won't have any money left!'

Jess frowned as she looked closely at the woman sitting opposite her. A deep frown as fake as Pearl's smile.

'I'm puzzled, Pearl. Tell me, why are you doing this instead of the lily-livered Sheldon? What exactly is in this for you? Just what is it that makes you such a vindictive old shrew?' As she put the majority of her emphasis on the word *shrew*, it coincided with Kay's foot on the bottom step.

'What the fuck is she doing here?' were Kay's opening words as she took in the scene in front of her. She made it up the rest of the steps in one long jump.

'Kay, darling! Still as bad-mannered as ever! Just having a chat with my daughter-in-law about things that don't concern you. I really wish you would mind your own business. You're making this all so difficult for Jess.'

For a split second Jess felt a certain admiration for Pearl. The woman didn't move a muscle in her body or face as she locked eyes with Kay, her son's ex-wife. The stand-off lasted only a few seconds but it seemed like for ever as Jess wondered what would happen next. It was Ryan who made the first move.

'Mrs Patterson, I'm not usually impolite but I'd like you to leave my home. You're not invited and you're certainly not welcome.' Ryan spoke loud and clear but his tone was polite. 'You have no business here.'

Slowly Pearl rolled her eyes from Kay to Ryan. Before speaking she looked him up and down from head to toe before shaking her head dismissively.

'Surely you're aware that my son actually paid for this house? Your wife screwed him for every cent she could, she may well do the same to you.' She paused again. 'Not that you appear to have much for her to screw.'

Jess stood up and moved out of Pearl's line of vision. 'I'd like a few more minutes with Pearl if that's all right with you. We could go over to the beach if you'd prefer it.' *Call Barry*, she mouthed at Kay, who blinked twice in acknowledgement.

'It's okay, Ryan, the woman's nuts, I learned that a long time ago. Just ignore her. I'll make some coffee and we'll let Jess and Pearl continue their conversation in private.' Kay grabbed his sleeve. 'Come on inside, honey. You can help me.'

It wasn't hard to keep Pearl talking. Jess just asked a few questions and let the woman ramble on, hoping that Barry would be able to get there in time. Kay had brought the coffee out and winked so Jess knew she had contacted him.

It was about half an hour later, by which time Jess was getting jumpy, that Barry pulled up outside in a cab.

'Well, how fortunate!' Jess smiled with relief. 'I'd like you to meet my legal representative from England, Pearl. I'm sure he'll just love a chance to peruse your little document.' She smiled at him. 'Barry, say hello to Mrs Patterson, my husband's mother.'

Barry held out his hand. 'Pleased to meet you, Mrs Patterson. I'm Barry Halston.' He hesitated for a second and then theatrically banged the palm of his hand on his forehead. 'Oh, how stupid of me! You know who I am already, don't you? You sent a pet goon to beat my head in the other day. Would you like to see my stitches?' Barry's tone couldn't have been more polite.

Pearl's smile was fading rapidly. 'I'm sure I don't know what you're talking about, Mr . . . Sorry, I've forgotten your name already. You must give me your card.'

Barry laughed. 'Very good, Mrs Patterson, you should be in the movies. Still, no matter, I survived. Let's take a close look at this document.'

With his face straight and devoid of all expression, Barry went through the whole thing word by word as Pearl and Jess sat opposite each other silently sipping their drinks.

Jess glanced absently out across the beach and could see Brad in the distance, head down as he trudged along looking in the bins for any scraps of food worth eating or cigarette butts worth a couple of puffs. She guessed he wouldn't find much. Californians were careful about their rubbish, especially on the pristine beach.

Her distracted thoughts were abruptly cut short by Barry's growling laugh that started as a gentle snigger and then slowly built up into a full belly laugh.

'You are joking, I assume, Mrs Patterson? Come on, tell me this a wind-up. Never in a million years would I advise my client to sign this load of old baloney, and even if by any chance she did have a lapse of intelligence and put pen to paper it would never stand up in court.'

Barry dumped the papers on the table with a flourish. 'If that's the best you can come up with then I suggest you seek legal advice elsewhere. You've just wasted a lot of good money on that nonsense.'

Pearl looked slowly around then stood up and straightened her clothes carefully paying particular attention to the back of her trousers.

Kay and Ryan were standing in the doorway, arms entwined around each other.

'Still not good at housekeeping, are you, Kay? These chairs are really quite dusty.'

Ignore her, Kay, don't give her the satisfaction. She wants a row.

'Well, I have to go now,' she continued when no one responded. 'It's been a pleasure to meet you, Mr Halston. I look forward to introducing you to the family attorney whenever it's convenient for you.'

Pearl looked round distastefully before picking up her bag from the table with two fingers as she saw her car pull up outside.

'Mr Halston, let me just point out that this document is Jessica's only hope of seeing her son. If she doesn't sign then I can assure you we will see you in court and by the time we've finished we'll prove that she isn't capable of looking after a stray dog, let alone a five-year-old child. The woman is a mess, an out-of-control mess.'

Jess gripped the arms of her chair tightly. *Keep calm, she wants you to retaliate.* 'See you in court, Pearl,' she smiled grimly.

'I'm sure I will. Oh, and a word of advice. Don't listen to Kay, she's bad news for anyone. Trash, nothing but trash.' The accent on the word *trash* echoed along the deck.

'Fuck off, Pearl,' Kay snarled.

'See what I mean? Trash with a bad mouth as well.' Pearl laughed lightly and almost skipped back down the steps.

'If you think Kay is trash then just wait until you meet the lovely Sofia!' Jess simply couldn't resist the final word as Pearl climbed into her car.

'So, that's the charming Pearl Patterson. Verbally adroit, I have to say. I feel you'd have to get up early to put one over on her – she's definitely a force to be reckoned with.' This time Barry wasn't smiling.

'I'd forgotten how much I hate the bitch. Jeez, don't you want to just lay her out cold?' Kay snarled angrily.

But Jess could see that she was just a blink away from tears. Poison arrows had always been Pearl's favourite form of attack and her aim was impeccable.

Barry still had the document in his hand. 'She forgot to take this with her.'

'Bull, she meant to leave it. If she'd meant to take it, she would have. She doesn't make mistakes.' Kay's face was red with anger but Ryan was silent. He was saying nothing.

'Ryan, are you okay?' Jess asked, aware of his lack of response to any of it.

'Sure, just thinking it all over.'

'Thinking that it would have been better not to have got involved?' Barry asked.

'Something like that, I guess. I'm sorry, I wish I didn't think like that but I can see what this is going to do to us. Pearl Patterson will start chipping away at us . . .' Ryan's normally sunny face was dejected.

Sadly Jess knew he was right. 'Well, I'll be out of your

lives next week. I'm sorry. If I'm not here she'll leave you alone. She's got nothing to gain from it any more. It's me she wants to destroy.'

'If you want to stay longer, you're welcome.' Kay jumped in quickly. 'Really. Ryan doesn't mean it, he just knows what Pearl and Sheldon did to me before. But I'm stronger now and I'd just love to see Pearl get screwed deep into the ground. As for Sheldon, I kind of feel sorry for him. With his doting mama always clearing up behind him he doesn't have to be responsible.'

'I'd better get back.' Barry suddenly came to life. 'I'm meeting someone for lunch who may just be able to give me some advice. We need to move quickly. I've only got a couple of days left and I want to get somewhere with this before I go back.'

Before anyone could say a word Barry was gone, leaving the three of them looking more than a little bewildered at his hasty departure. Dejectedly they trooped inside. Pearl could cast a cloud over anyone.

'You know something, Jess? I think that man has the hots for you,' Kay suddenly announced over breakfast. 'He's like a lovesick hound drooling around behind you. It's so sweet to watch!'

Jess froze with her fork midway to her mouth. 'That's a ridiculous thing to say. I'm just his client.'

'Yeah, right,' Kay laughed. 'How many lawyers do you know who fly across the Atlantic to check how things are going? Especially a client with no cash to her name who can't pay her bill. Come on, Jess!'

'That's not true! He had business in LA, he was coming here anyway. It was just good timing that I happened to be here.'

'Yeah, yeah, yeah.'

'Kay! Cut it out. I'm going frantic here trying to find

my son. I haven't got time for all this crap.' Jess was angry that Kay could even make jokes about things like that. 'I *need* Barry Halston. He is my only hope, considering the complete lack of interest from the authorities both here and in England. No one seems to give a toss about CJ caught up in the middle of all this. They pass the buck from one to the other, agency to agency.'

'Hey, hey, enough now!' Ryan intervened, his tone was calming but firm. 'Kay didn't mean anything – it was an observation, just an observation to lighten the mood. Chill, Jess – it's not worth getting upset about.'

Jess looked furiously from one to the other, then slamming down her fork she pushed her chair back and ran into her room.

'Wow, that was some outburst.' Kay looked bewildered as she focused on the upturned chair. 'I was only making conversation, trying to give her a shot of confidence. She needs a lift.'

'Yeah, but maybe you went about it all wrong. Sorry, but you asked for all you got back there. Jess isn't in the right frame of mind for that kind of thing.' Ryan paused and smiled. 'Even if it is true.'

Kay clapped her hands. 'You noticed as well? Jeez, he couldn't take his eyes off her when he was here the other night. He seems like a straightforward guy and quite a hunk too in a British sort of way, just right for Jess.'

'Not now, Kay!' Ryan leaned forward and playfully clamped his hand across her mouth.

Jess wasn't in tears, she was too angry to cry. Pulling open drawers and cupboards she dragged her clothes out and started pushing them at random into her suitcase. She couldn't understand how Kay could even think something like that. Did she really think that it would be that easy? 'So long Sheldon, so long CJ, hello next available man?' Was that how Kay thought of her?

But as she stamped around the bedroom she slowly started to calm down a little. Not enough to see the funny side of it but enough to stop chucking her belongings about. Maybe, she thought wryly, she had been down for so long she had forgotten what it was like to have a laugh, to interact with someone humorously. Her life had revolved around Sheldon and his needs and wants for so long that she had lost the art of friendly banter.

With a start she realised that Zoë would probably have said the same thing as Kay, a flip comment to try and make her laugh in the face of it all.

Suddenly Brad flashed into her mind again. The man from the beach was morphing into her conscience; every time things looked as bad as they could get, his image would spring into her mind as if to prove that they weren't so bad after all. There were others who had been dealt an even worse hand than she had, others who didn't have the advantage of family and friends for support during the bad times. At least she had the power, the means and the help to fight for CJ.

Brad wasn't even able to fight for a few lousy cigarettes.

Throwing on a pair of jeans and a T-shirt she ran out through the house, calling to the bewildered couple as she went, 'Something I have to do, won't be long. Sorry, sorry, sorry for being such a crab.' Before they could reply she blew a kiss at them and was off out the door, running across the road to the beach.

But when she got to the beach bench there was no sign of him. She knew he wandered about during the day; there were so many places to go she wasn't sure where to look, and also she didn't want to approach him if he was not alone.

Reaching the pier and still finding no sign of him, she gave up and leaned back against the railings, momentarily enjoying the sun's rays on her face and trying to analyse her feelings. For a reason she didn't understand, she had searched him out almost every day since the first meeting. She had hardly touched the surface of Brad, didn't even know his surname, and yet she had confided in him and felt strangely at ease with him.

Was she just thinking of herself, she wondered, using Brad because he was noticeably worse off than she was, because he made her feel better about herself? She hoped not; she hoped that her concern was for him, not for herself, but she couldn't be sure.

Scanning around as far as she could see, Jess suddenly spotted the man with the baseball cap. Only he wasn't wearing a cap and he was togged out in jogging clothes but Jess knew it was him.

So! He was still following her.

Jess put two fingers in her mouth and whistled, a shrill piercing whistle that echoed around. Even the man looked over.

Jess smiled widely and waved at him before turning to head home.

Chapter Twenty

Sheldon Patterson felt as if he had been dealt a heavyweight body blow. All the years that he had spent desperately wanting to be a father and now, when it was the last thing on his mind, Sofia had actually got pregnant. He couldn't believe it could happen – unless, of course, Sofia had planned it.

'How did that happen?' he snarled. 'How could it happen? You know this isn't the right time, not now, not with Jess trying to flush us out and discredit me, to take CJ away from me.'

Sofia managed to look sheepish as she snaked her arms up around his neck. 'I don't know, Sheldon, my darling. I take the pill every day. I don't understand also, but it will be okay. Maybe you will have another son like CJ?'

'No!' The word was sharp and vehement, causing Sofia to step back. 'I just told you, this isn't the right time. It wouldn't look good in court, it could ruin everything. You have to get rid of it.' Almost scornfully he looked her up and down. 'And go and get some clothes on before CJ sees you.'

Sofia didn't scream and shout and she didn't disintegrate in front of him; all she did was let him see her disappointment and sadness before, shoulders drooping, she walked silently back to the garden, leaving Sheldon feeling incredibly guilty.

CJ was still in his hiding place listening and absorbing as much as a five year old could. He desperately, desperately wanted to be back with his mother, to feel her all-enveloping arms around him and to inhale her comforting smell.

Wrapped around his chubby fingers was his precious blanket that he kept hidden, tucked behind an abandoned packing box. When it all got too much for the little boy he would slide in behind the boxes and gently rub the blanket with his eyes closed. Sometimes his thumb found its way into his mouth and he would soothe himself with the memory of his mother's lap. He knew that his father must never see the blanket and certainly never see him with his thumb in his mouth.

Despite his young age CJ was well aware that if Sofia had a baby then he would be pushed out. He didn't want a brother, he didn't want his father or Sofia, all he wanted was his mother. The tears fell silently as he tried to stay hidden and quiet.

Sofia knew that CJ hid in the alcove and also that he kept his beloved blanket there, but she had no intention of telling his father who didn't understand these things. Mostly she also modified her conversations with Sheldon if she knew CJ was in hiding, but in her fury at Sheldon's betrayal she had forgotten. Now she was unsure how much the already sad little boy might have heard.

Life with Sheldon Patterson was turning out to be nothing like she had anticipated. Working for the Bartons in England she had seen the lifestyle that both they and the Patterson family led, and that was what she had wanted for herself. Exactly what she saw: the house, the clothes, the cars, the hardworking provider. It had been the whole package that had seduced her into thinking that was how life could be for her.

But it wasn't turning out like that at all.

Instead of the promised house in Beverly Hills she was living in isolation on the outskirts of Cancún in Mexico. The rented bungalow was merely adequate and the furnishings basic, but worst of all was the isolation Sheldon had imposed on them all. He promised it was temporary, just until the problems over CJ were resolved, but now it looked as if he was going to walk away and leave her with nothing. Sharp as a knife, Sofia knew that if she let Sheldon get away then he would never come back and she would have to start all over again.

From as far back as she could remember Sofia had wanted to break out from her claustrophobic existence back home in rural Spain. A natural-born rebel with a wild streak, she had known she could never settle for the traditional female role that was expected of her.

She wanted more, much more, and at eighteen, against her parents' wishes, she had set off to England for her first au pair position. It wasn't long before she had realised that nannies had a much better time of it than the lowly au pairs who were only one step up from general dogsbodies, so she amended her CV accordingly.

By the time she had gone to work at the Cambridge agency she had even acquired the fraudulent qualifications to go with the role. Having been brought up in a large family with numerous young children she knew exactly what to do with them, how to look after them. Not only that, she was honest, ambitious and hardworking, so by the time she went to work for

Carla and Toby everyone easily believed she was a bona fide nanny.

It had never been her intention to break up a marriage – she had certainly not set out to do it but once the seed was sown her initial reservations about starting a relationship with Sheldon Patterson had been quickly dismissed by Sheldon himself.

The marriage was long dead, he kept telling her during their secret meetings on Sofia's day off when Sheldon purported to be working away. Sheldon had justified his every move and Sofia had let herself believe him, because she wanted to.

Jess was an obsessive mother, he told her, who was smothering CJ and wanted to exclude Sheldon from his life. He had no choice but to get CJ away, especially now that he had found Sofia, the love of his life.

The deciding factor in her agreeing to leave with Sheldon had been the promise of a very comfortable life in Beverly Hills where she would want for nothing. It wasn't until they were already on the way to the airport that Sheldon had told her they were going to lay low in Mexico for a while.

Yes, the bungalow was okay, more than she was used to, but it wasn't what Sheldon had promised. Sofia had perfected her English by watching as much TV as she could and reading English and American magazines. She knew what Sheldon could afford to provide her with and that was exactly what she wanted. Nothing less.

Sofia flexed her arms and legs before stretching out on the sunbed and thinking about her next move. Sheldon Patterson had promised her everything and she was damned sure she was going to get it.

One way or another.

She had played the game by his rules so far, but with the latest bombshell still echoing in her mind she knew she would have to have a re-think. Stay in Mexico on her own? Get rid of her baby? 'Not a chance,' she muttered to herself as she stretched out catlike under the hot Mexican sun. 'Not a chance.'

Meanwhile, inside the bungalow, the rumbling rhythm of the ceiling fan lulled Sheldon into closing his eyes as he tried to come to terms with the latest complication in his life. If his mother thought Sofia could harm his case for custody of CJ then a pregnant Sofia could blow it completely out of the water. As soon as Sheldon surfaced, or someone found him, court papers would be flying around like confetti, especially if he was back in the States. A pregnant twenty-two-year-old ex-babysitter would go down very badly indeed with the courts.

Decisions, decisions, he thought. Decisions that Sheldon knew he had to make very quickly.

But Sheldon wasn't really very good at making decisions for himself.

'I have to leave tomorrow. I'm flying back to England.'

Although Jess was speaking to Brad she wasn't looking at him. Side by side but with enough space for two people between them, they both looked straight ahead. She wasn't even sure why she was confiding in him. She wondered if it was the psychiatrist thing? Brad didn't offer advice, he didn't tell her whether he thought she was right or wrong, he merely sat quietly and let her unburden her thoughts and feelings.

'I don't want to go – in fact, I'm dreading it. I feel as if I am abandoning my son by flying in the opposite direction but I can't afford to stay, and I have to go to court in England, try and plead my case.' Sadly she gazed out across the spotlessly clean, raked and flattened sand that stretched in front of them. 'I just can't imagine Christmas without CJ. Until my husband abducted him I had never been away from him for a single night, not one single night.'

Brad was silent. He was a good listener, Jess thought – if, of course, he *was* listening; his thoughts and feeling were impossible to read.

The first time the conversation had veered away from generalities to the more personal, Jess had said more than she intended. Her idea at the time had been to try and get Brad to open up to her. Naively she had thought that he might give her the opportunity to help him. But the man was adept at turning conversations round and, each time she met with him, it was only after she had gone home that she realised he had said nothing and she had said everything.

'Why go, then? You can do what you want.' Still Brad didn't look at her.

'I have to go, I'm broke and now my mother is broke. I have to go back. I'm going to have to live with her – it'll be like being a teenager again. Back home to Mum, who'd have thought it?'

'A mom to go home to? You should be that lucky.'

Jess froze at the unexpected chink in Brad's self-erected defences. 'Where are you from?' she kept the tone light, as if she was asking the time.

'California.'

'No, I mean originally . . .'

'Yeah, I know. California, then the military, then Nevada now California. Home.' He snorted his disgust. 'Born and bred in LA, land of the fucking beautiful, land of all or nothing depending on who you are.'

The sarcasm that poured from his mouth was matched by the look of distaste on his face. The first time Jess had seen a reaction from him.

'So? What happened to change it for you? To bring you here?'

As his face blanked out again Jess realised that it was a step too far for him. 'Brad, I'm going home tomorrow. I like you and I'd like to help you, but even if I can't do that I'd like to stay in touch.'

For the first time she touched him, very gently on the back of his hand, much in the way that she would have reassured a nervous kitten.

'Please, Brad? You've been such a help to me recently, you've listened. Tell me what you need me to do to help you. I feel as if you're a friend.'

'Nothing. It's too late for me, I've blown it.' The words weren't self-pitying or sympathy-evoking. It was a statement of fact.

'It's not, Brad. It's never too late to turn things around.'

His eyes flickered over her face. 'For me it is. Sorry, ma'am!' Cautiously he raised himself from the seat and pulled his polythene tight around his belongings. Touching his forehead with his free hand in a humorous salute he smiled. 'Good meeting you, ma'am. Good luck.'

'I'll be back soon. I'll be back for my son and I'll see you then.'

The smile was another first but it was more of a bitter widening of his mouth. 'Right.'

'I'll keep in touch.'

'Right.'

'What's your surname?'

'Walden.'

'Okay, Brad Walden, I'll be seeing you – you can count on it.'

He shuffled away without looking back and Jess, feeling strangely bereft, headed home to pack and leave.

Leave California. Leave her son, wherever he might be.

Barry had arranged to travel home on the same flight and he had offered her a lift back to Cambridge. She was expecting him at any time.

The mood on the final evening was sombre to say the least.

'Is there nothing else you can do here?' she had begged Barry, her frustration reaching boiling point. 'I can't believe that the law isn't on my side.'

'The law isn't on anybody's side, apart from CJ's and if, as we suspect, Sheldon and CJ aren't even in the US right now, then we're at an impasse. All the custody orders in the world are worthless if we don't know where they are.'

'Is there anything else we can do?' Kay asked eagerly. 'We'll do whatever you suggest. How about a Private Investigator, Barry? He or she could keep track of Pearl, bug her phone, follow her, torture her, dump her body in the ocean.'

A flicker of horror shot across his face before he realised she was trying to lighten the mood a little.

'Right! The only thing you can really do is keep your eyes and ears open. If you get so much as a whiff of Sheldon and CJ in LA then let us know immediately and I can brief my friend here. If we find them in the country we can proceed legally.'

Ryan looked thoughtful. 'If Pearl knows you've gone back and tells Sheldon, then maybe he'll surface. He won't be able to stay away for too long.'

'I'm definitely coming back for Christmas,' Jess suddenly announced. 'I can't believe Sheldon will stay away for Christmas. I'm sure he won't.'

'He didn't come back for Thanksgiving, or not that we know of,' Ryan interrupted tentatively.

'I know, but Christmas is different. CJ will be excited about it – surely he won't deprive him of a family Christmas? No, I've thought about it. I'm going to come back one way or another, but this time I won't intrude on you both. I'll stay in a motel.'

'No, Jess, it's okay, you really can stay here,' Kay intervened excitedly. 'Ryan and I are taking his kids to New York for the holiday, so you can stay here and house-sit for us. Bring your mom, bring whoever you like. We're taking extra vacation and will be away for around two weeks. You'll be doing us a favour.'

'Oh my God, that would be great – if you're sure . . .'

'Of course we're sure, aren't we, Ryan?'

Ryan raised his eyes up and sighed before letting his face split into a wide grin. 'No problem, Jess, you're welcome to use our home as your home!'

'I know I'm pushing it a bit but can I ask another favour?'

'Sure, ask away, but don't expect me to be nice to Pearl.'

'No, nothing like that,' Jess laughed, 'but can you watch out for Brad? And if I send an email, will you print it out and give it to him? I feel a touch responsible for him. It's daft, I know, but he's so vulnerable.'

Kay and Ryan looked surprised.

'He's vulnerable?' Kay looked bewildered. '*You're* vulnerable, you mean. You're experiencing a far bigger trauma than I can imagine and you're worried about Brad? Beware, Jess!'

Shrugging her shoulders up high around her neck Kay sighed. 'Brad has been around for a while and until he wants help no one can give it to him. But I'll try, for you.'

'Thanks,' Jess smiled. 'That's all I'm asking, just one eye!'

'Of course we'll keep an eye out for him,' Kay flicked away a stray tear, 'and we'll do what we can, but I can't promise to present you with a cleaned-up version of him when you come back.'

As they all laughed, Kay continued more seriously, 'And trust me, if anyone can do for Pearl and Sheldon Patterson then it's you. Sheldon is a sonofabitch of the first degree for letting you go. Literally a son of a bitch, I mean.' She blew an exaggerated kiss across the table.

Trying to ease the atmosphere Ryan got up and hugged Jess from behind in his long arms.

'You'll get there in the end, honey, truly you will. As soon as he shows his face, just give it him with both barrels . . . and Pearl.'

Chapter Twenty-One

'Well? Have you decided what you're going to do?'
Pearl's voice rang loud and clear down the phone
receiver, making Sheldon feel distinctly uncomfortable
and childlike.

Sofia was causing him problems, not by being difficult
but by being exceptionally gentle and understanding.
Once her initial anger at the turn of events had worn
off she had been so calm and reassuring that Sheldon
was starting to relent.

Maybe his mother was wrong, he thought as she
berated him down the phone line. Maybe he could find
a way to keep CJ and Sofia and the new baby.

'Not sure, Mom. I'm still trying to work out what to
do.'

'Sheldon! This is becoming ridiculous! Do you want
your son, or don't you? Make up your mind.'

'Of course I want CJ with me, that's all I've ever
wanted, but Sofia is something different . . .'

'No. Sofia isn't a part of this. You told me, and I told
everyone else, that she is only the nanny. So fire her.'

'I can't.'

'Okay, if you can't then I shall have to do it for you.

I'm flying down tomorrow. Why do I always have to organise your life for you?'

With that Pearl hung up, leaving Sheldon muttering, 'You don't have to,' while listening to a distant buzz.

'Is something wrong, Sheldon?' Sofia went over and sat closely beside him. Sliding her arm along the back of the sofa she ran her fingers down the back of his neck.

'You are so tense, shall I give you a massage? You should not worry about your mother. It's not good for you to rely on her so much, you have me now.'

Like a gymnast she slipped gracefully over the back of the sofa and started rubbing his neck muscles firmly. Her hands kneaded the muscles from behind his ears down over his shoulders, all the while whispering how much she loved him. Then, almost imperceptibly her hands roamed forward, very slowly, over his shoulders and, stretching her arms at full length, she moved her fingers down his chest towards his stomach.

'Come to the bedroom, Sheldon, and I shall massage your whole body.'

As Sofia's loaded words entered his brain, his mother's image exited and he allowed himself to be led across the room by her. The deliberately ragged shorts that she was wearing were in danger of disappearing between her buttocks and, as usual, she was topless.

Sheldon could feel himself becoming aroused at the thought of what was to come. Although Sofia wasn't the love of his life, she certainly knew what to do to distract him.

'Daddy, can I see Mummy at Christmas? I hate it here, I want to go back to Mummy. I want to see Nana, *pleeeease*.'

Like a bucket of cold water over his head CJ's voice whined from the doorway.

'Go back to your room, CJ, we're talking!'

'No!' The word was fierce and firm and his expression insolent.

Both embarrassed and angry Sheldon shouted reactively at his son. 'Just get in there and don't come out until I tell you. I'm getting really ticked off with you creeping around like a fucking house-breaker.'

The little boy's face visibly crumbled. The burning Mexican sun had reacted badly on his fair skin; his freckles had spread over his entire face and were slowly working their way down his skinny back to the extent that some of them were beginning to blend together. Much to Sheldon's dismay, no amount of the high-factor sunscreen that Sofia caked on him regularly could stop the relentless spread.

At the end of the tirade from his father, CJ's pale, almost colourless eyes opened wide with horror. He stared for a few seconds before turning and scampering away, screaming and crying, 'I hate you! I hate you! I hate you!'

Sofia's expression showed no emotion but Sheldon knew she was dismayed; he was dismayed himself, and the situation was getting him down. Maybe he hadn't done the right thing after all.

With CJ sobbing in his room, Sheldon and Sofia went to their room and tried to make love but the moment had passed for both of them. Sofia's enthusiasm had waned and for that Sheldon was almost relieved.

For the first time he wondered about letting CJ go back to Jess. Maybe if Sofia's baby was going to be a boy, he thought tentatively, maybe he could start over with her. She was still young and fit enough to give him another family. He decided to wait for a scan before making any decisions, but he was only too aware that if Pearl arrived on the doorstep then things could get very nasty.

No, he thought, even if he wanted to, he couldn't let CJ go back to Jess. His mother would be incandescent at the waste of time and energy. His mother was once again at the forefront of his mind and although he could usually blank the memories out, this time he couldn't.

Thinking back to his own childhood always made him feel uncomfortable. It was easier to keep the rose-tinted glasses on than look at it realistically, but the guilt he felt at treating his own son so badly stripped them off.

Sheldon had loved his father and he adored his mother but there was no doubt in his mind that he was a trophy child. Everything he did well was greeted with heaps of praise and bucketloads of presents, while failure earned a disappointed silence. However, for the day-to-day, run-of-the-mill things they were never around, either of them. His father was a workaholic who put his all into the business while Pearl tinkered around on the periphery and arranged a non-stop round of entertaining and socialising.

Nannies who cared for him came and went, house-keepers who fussed over him came and went, even the chauffeurs, who took him here, there and everywhere, changed regularly. There was little stability and certainly no continuity.

His parents were around on the outskirts of his life but they never involved themselves in the minutiae of their child's everyday life. As well as hating the constant changes, he had hated being an only child, which was why he had always fantasised about having a bevy of children himself one day and being there for them, involved in every aspect of their lives.

In his mind Sheldon imagined being Master of the

family, Father with a capital F dispensing discipline and love and receiving unequivocal respect in return. But it frustrated him that CJ didn't understand how it should work and for that it suited him to blame Jess totally.

Now that he had CJ all to himself he wasn't so sure it was what he wanted; it certainly wasn't how he had imagined it would be. CJ just didn't love him the way he wanted to be loved and now Pearl was about to appear and take charge of his life once again.

To reinforce his failure.

He wished he had never told her about his plans but it was so hard not to talk to Pearl, who had an inbuilt radar system for detecting secrets and deceptions; constantly seeking approval from his mother was Sheldon's biggest failing. With a start he realised that he still had to tell Sofia that his mother was en route to organise their lives, and that night was a restless one for all three of them, albeit for different reasons.

As the hired chauffeur-driven car pulled up outside the bungalow the following day Sheldon felt the familiar waves of apprehension washing over him again. Without fail just the sight of her could reduce him to a little boy again.

'Sheldon!' she cried as she padded across the patio that encircled the bungalow. She proffered her cheeks to him one at a time taking care not to touch flesh. Looking around she shrank into her powder-blue linen shirt coat. 'This is very . . . er . . . how can I put it, basic? Yes, basic. Surely you could afford better than this?'

'It's good for the moment. We like it and it's only temporary.' Sheldon's tone was defensive.

'We?' The word was quizzically delivered for effect.

'Yes, Mom, *we*, Sofia and I. I told you, we are a couple.'

'Oh, do grow up! You're forty-two years old and acting like an adolescent. Twenty-two-year-old nannies are for playing around with, why couldn't you just leave it at that? Why do you have to fall in love with every goddamned girl who so much as blinks at you?'

Pearl was busy telling him that he was forty-two but she was using the tactic she had used when he was a child. Going on and on, repeating the same thing over and over until she won out eventually.

'Leave it, Mom.'

'No, Sheldon, make up your mind. If you want your son, then the girl has to go.' She looked around as if something had just occurred to her. 'Where is she anyway?'

'She's got a name. Sofia's taken CJ to the shops to get some lunch for you. They'll both be back shortly. Please be nice to her, Mom, she's helped me a lot.'

'No, Sheldon. She's doing what suits her. She's using you, taking advantage of you. She's patently after the Patterson kudos.'

The face-to-face stand-off between mother and son came to an abrupt end when CJ hurled himself into the house.

'Grandma! Grandma!' The little boy clung to her legs like a monkey.

'Well, well, CJ, you've grown a little since I last saw you, and all those freckles . . .'

Gently but firmly she removed the child from her legs almost distastefully while at the same time eyeing up Sofia who came in behind him.

'So! You must be the nanny. Thank you so much for helping my son out with my grandson.'

Pearl looked Sofia up and down critically, the dismissive look that she had honed to perfection over the years.

The statement, combined with the look, was meant to demean and disable the girl. But for once Pearl had made a serious error of judgement.

'Oh no, Mrs Patterson, I'm sorry but you have got it wrong, I'm not the nanny.' Sofia raised her eyebrows and an expression of pure innocence swept over her face.

'No? Sheldon told me you were, but much as we appreciate your help, Sheldon and CJ are coming back to the States with me so we don't need your services any more. Of course you'll receive some severance pay to compensate for the inconvenience.'

Sofia smiled innocently. 'No, no, Mrs Patterson, you're wrong. I am Sofia, Sheldon's fiancée and I am soon going to be the mother of his child, your grand-child. That is good news, yes?' Sofia opened her eyes even wider and smiled politely.

It nearly made Sheldon laugh to see his mother stuck for words.

'Sheldon! A word in private. Now!'

Still Sofia smiled sweetly. 'Come, CJ, we shall go and look for lizards outside.' Taking his hand she led the child out.

'What are you playing at? Have you lost your mind? Pregnant – with your child?'

Her usually immovable face was screwed up in rage as she fired the questions at him one after the other, giving him little chance to reply to any of them.

'You took CJ away from Jess because you wanted him to yourself. Now what are you going to do? One mother out, another mother in? Rather counter-productive, don't you think?'

'I didn't know, it wasn't planned.' He hated himself for blushing but he couldn't help it. Pearl always succeeded in making him feel like a silly boy.

'Not planned? NOT PLANNED?' Her voice wasn't that loud but the words struck him like punches. 'Not by you maybe, but definitely by that manipulative little bitch. I can spot them a mile off.'

'It's not like that – she loves me.'

Pearl was about five foot six, Sheldon around six foot but with no effort Pearl raised the flat of her hand and slapped him full force across his cheek.

'How dare you hit me, Mom?' Sheldon tried to stand his ground. 'How dare you lay a finger on me!'

Pearl merely laughed. 'I'm your mother. Now we have to sort this out. Get rid of her, deny the child is yours, and that will buy us some time to deal with the problem of CJ. We can pay her off at a later date.'

Sheldon rubbed his cheek angrily. 'No, Mother, that's *not* what I'm going to do. This is my child, my chance of another family, with Sofia.'

'Rubbish, Sheldon. That's what you said about Jess after you divorced Kay. Girls like Sofia are two a penny. Just wait a while and then grab yourself another one as she passes by. Now get her back in here and I'll deal with her.'

'I'm not doing this, Mom.'

'Yes, you are. Jessica is about to leave LA – this is the right time to come back and apply for formal custody. It'll look good that you're doing it correctly. Don't blow it all now for the sake of a silly little gold-digger.' Pearl paused and looked at her son carefully. 'Unless of course you're regretting running away with CJ already?'

'Of course not,' Sheldon muttered, but he couldn't look her in the eye as he said it.

Chapter Twenty-Two

Cambridge, England

'Well, here we are. You're home at last.' Barry glanced sideways at Jess who was immobile beside him, her gaze fixed firmly ahead. She had barely uttered a word after leaving the airport.

'This isn't home,' she sighed. 'This is my mother's home. My home has strangers living in it now, laughing, cooking, sleeping in my bed, even playing with my bloody dog. This is just somewhere to stay.'

By the time they reached Sara's, Jess was functioning on nervous energy alone. Each mile of the flight home had distressed her more. The photographs of CJ that she had taken with her were shuffled over and over again on her lap but, although she was aware she was being repetitive, she couldn't help it.

Barry had tried unsuccessfully to persuade her to eat and sleep during the overnight flight but she couldn't, she didn't want to. It had taken all her energy not to lose it as she walked down the tunnel to board the plane. Only the photographs kept her comparatively calm.

It was nearly three months since she had last seen her

son and she was terrified she would forget exactly what he looked like.

At least in LA she had felt as if she was doing something positive, but all of a sudden there was nothing. As far as she could see, it had all been a waste of time. She had achieved nothing other than to really rile Pearl.

As the car drew up outside the house, the door flew open and Sara ran out. 'Jess, darling, it's so good to see you. I've missed you.'

'I'm glad to see you too, Mum.' Her response was robotic. 'But I'm so tired, I just want to go to bed.' Ignoring the open arms, Jess pushed past her mother, leaving Barry to follow with her suitcase.

'Okay, I'll make you a hot drink first.'

But Jess was away up the small path.

'Did you have a good flight?'

'Not particularly.'

'And how did it go? Any more news since I last spoke to you?'

Jess turned to her mother, her shoulders sagging. 'Not really. Look, I'm sorry, but I wish I wasn't here. It doesn't seem right. I need time to think about what I'm going to do next. I feel as if I've abandoned CJ.'

'Nothing of the sort. Now, let's go in and you can tell me all about it.' Sara turned to Barry who was looking lost and unsure what to do. 'Come in, Barry. I know you've been a godsend to my Jess and I imagine you're probably knackered as well but come in, please. Join us for a cuppa before you carry on home.'

'Thank you, I'd like that.'

'Whereabouts do you live?'

'Oh, I'm in a small village called Oakfield – do you know it? Not too far away from the bypass, easy access to town and work, but dead as a dodo most of the time. Picturesque though!'

The terraced house was small but cosy. The front door opened onto a tiny lobby with a door to a straight narrow staircase going off it. There was barely room for three of them in the lobby together so one at a time they filtered through into the sitting room.

The house was a classic two up two down, but over the years an extension at the back had added a bathroom and a small modern kitchen where once the old scullery had stood. Because of the extension the back yard was minuscule and paved, but brightened by an array of ceramic pots and two small garden chairs crammed into a corner.

The house had been home to Jess and her mother from the day she was born until the day she and Sheldon married; she had never thought about it, but suddenly it seemed extra small and claustrophobic.

The fact that Barry was tall and wide compounded it for Jess. He looked big and uncomfortable in the surroundings, different somehow from the attractive and confident man that she lunched with in the Californian sunshine. The upright, self-assured Barry that she had seen behind his desk and on the deck in Santa Monica now seemed distinctly out of place. Jess herself felt out of place. She thought that the house was part of her past, not her future.

'Sit down, Barry, you're making the place look untidy.' Jess tried to make a joke of it to cover her all-consuming embarrassment. She hated herself for it, but as she looked around, as if for the first time, she was aware of the drabness, the shortage of living space and the lack of colour, but most of all she disliked the clutter that her mother had collected and hoarded.

It brought home her circumstances, her loss of everything.

'I know what you're thinking, Jess. I know it's horrible for you to come back here after living in your own beautiful home, but it won't be for ever.' Sara's smile was understanding but sad.

Jess laughed. 'I don't know about that: you might just be stuck with me for ever. There's no way I can dig myself out of this. All I can do is jog on the spot until Sheldon decides to sell the house – and then what will I have? The mortgage is absolutely fucking enormous, the collateral wouldn't even buy me a new car after Sheldon's taken his share.'

Barry intervened. 'We'll deal with all that. It'll take time but Sheldon has to support you. He has to pay you a settlement.'

Jess looked at him closely. He was a nice man, a kind man who was doing his best, more than his best probably, but he didn't understand. Everything was gone. Her son, her house, her life. All of it, gone. All in one hit.

'You have to pursue Sheldon through the courts in LA. I've told you that over and over, it's the only way.' Barry was trying hard to make the legal point but Jess wasn't in the mood to listen to reason.

'How can I start arguing about money? It's almost obscene. It's my son that's important. If I make an issue about money it takes me down to *his* level, to Pearl's level. I don't want to do it.'

'I know how you feel, I really do, but everything is linked together. When you get CJ back there will be his future security to consider. The Pattersons are millionaires many times over, they have to pay.' Barry was using his hands to make the point, stabbing his fingers at the air.

Sara came back into the room and joined in, siding with Jess. 'We can manage without any money. We've done it before, we can do it again, but CJ is another matter.'

'That's not the point.' Barry was tired and he was getting frustrated as he tried to put his point across. 'The man owes you. That is what the legal system is all about. There are procedures, and it's my job to go through those procedures. The correct way, the only way.'

'Oh come on, where has the right way got me?' Jess sighed, her own tiredness getting the better of her. 'The law is crap and so are the so-called procedures. It can't even get my son back for me, so how is it going to get Sheldon to cough up a cent? Face it. I'm destitute.'

As she said the word, a mental picture of Brad jumped into her mind along with a tremendous feeling of guilt and shame. Brad Walden epitomised the word 'destitute'. She didn't. Brad had nothing and, by comparison, Jess had everything she needed – apart, of course, from her son CJ.

'I'm sorry, Barry, and you too, Mum. I really appreciate everything you're both doing, but I can't see where I'm going to go from here. I just don't know what to do next but I know I shouldn't take it out on you.'

By the time Barry left the mood couldn't have sunk any lower and, without a further word, completely disheartened, Jess trudged up to the bedroom of her childhood. She had thought she wouldn't be able to switch off but, completely exhausted, she slept through until the following day.

For a split second when she awoke mid-morning, Jess forgot where she was but she soon dropped back down to earth with a thud when she realised she was curled up in her old single bed in her old bedroom.

Once downstairs she was greeted by Sara, dressed in her uniform and getting ready to go to work for the afternoon shift.

'Morning, sweetheart, feeling better now? I checked you earlier but you were dead to the world, snoring for England.'

Jokingly Jess flexed her muscles. 'Snoring for England, eh? Well, I've been thinking and today I'm going to motivate myself. I'm going to see if I can get some agency work, then I can be flexible and fit in all the legal stuff and nonsense.'

Looking sideways at Sara she continued, feigning nonchalance, 'I'm going back to LA for Christmas. Kay and Ryan won't be there and they've offered me their house, you as well if you want.'

Knowing Sara wouldn't agree with her she waited for the reaction. It came immediately.

'Jess! Is that sensible at the moment, given your circumstances? Surely that money is better spent on legal fees here? Let Barry deal with it, let him get your finances stabilised first. You didn't get anywhere while you were there, why should it be any different next time?'

Jess shrugged. 'Perhaps it won't be, but I know, I just know, that Sheldon and CJ aren't too far away from Pearl. I want to be there, on her tail. Anyway, you deserve a bit of a break, you haven't been to LA since the wedding.' Jess's voice trailed off and the tears threatened again. It only took a chance remark to set her off every time.

Her wedding day. The happiest day of her life.

Pearl had really pushed the boat out for the Pattersons' only son and no expense had been spared. But the joy she had felt at the beautiful wedding had been nothing compared

*to her happiness at marrying Sheldon and her anticipation
of a life with the new husband that she absolutely adored.
The whole day had been a dream.*

Her mother's voice dragged her back to the present.
'I'm sorry, love, I don't want to put a dampener on your
enthusiasm but I'm just trying to be realistic. I have to
get off to the hospital now. We'll talk later, see if there's
a way.'

Sara kissed her daughter on the top of her head. 'I
understand, you know. I really do understand. I just
have to play devil's advocate now and again!'

Jess thought about breakfast but quickly dismissed it;
her brain had gone from semi-comatose to hyperactive
in a few minutes and she wanted to get moving, to carry
on searching albeit at a distance. She knew that as soon
as she let the momentum fail it would be hard to start
it up again.

But before she could even shower and get dressed,
there was a knock on the door that stopped her in her
tracks. Fortunately, it was only Carla.

'Jess, welcome back! How did it go? I've been thinking
about you all the time.'

Dressed in faded jeans and a battered leather flying-
jacket Carla bounced into the house, making Jess wonder neurotically if she had dressed down because she
was visiting the downmarket side of town. However,
the sight of Carla's hair pushed back with a narrow
velvet Alice band made Jess smile to herself. Carla was
the only forty year old she knew who could get away
with it.

'Not very successful, I'm afraid, but I'm glad I went.
I really saw Pearl in her true light, but Kay and Ryan
were wonderful. Apart from that? Zilch.' Jess grimaced.
'It was like battering my head on a brick wall – all

pain and no gain, unfortunately. I'll tell you about it later. Right now my brain is numb from going round in circles.'

'Okay. Whenever you're ready to talk, I'm ready to listen.' Carla patted Jess on the leg. 'But tell me about Barry Halston. I hear he was out there as well – how did that go?'

'A nightmare, Carla. I felt so bad. He got thumped on the head, probably by one of Pearl's henchmen, and ended up in the ER being stitched up. I persuaded him to keep quiet about it. How sad is that?'

Carla frowned. 'Why keep quiet? Surely that would have given you some clout over Pearl.'

'Not really. Who could have proved anything? Even the police were satisfied that it was a random mugging attempt.'

'Mmm, well, I'm sure you know best, but what I meant was, how did you get on with him personally? He plays squash with Toby who is quite bewildered by the whole thing; apparently it's completely out of character for him to take off like that.'

Initially Jess didn't hear the undertones. 'I think he sees the case as a bit of a challenge but he didn't go out there for me, he had to meet someone else there, a contact of some sort.'

'Oh, I see.' Carla's words were loaded. 'How very strange that he just happened to have to see someone thousands of miles away, the very same time you're there.' Carla winked knowingly and Jess finally caught on.

'Not you as well, Carla! Kay made the same comment. Neither of you are any good at maths: two and two don't make five, however hard you try.'

'What do you mean? It's not my fault if you've made

a conquest. How lucky is that? You've got yourself a pet lawyer!'

As Carla smiled Jess found herself bristling defensively. 'It's not like that. Come on, Carla, a mere three months or so ago I was blissfully happy and deeply in love with my husband. Conquests, as you put it, are the last thing on my mind right now.'

Carla sat forward on the edge of her seat and looked Jess in the eye. 'Listen to me. Toby has known Barry for years and he is speechless. Barry is professional, cool, detached and any other adjective you can think of to describe a hardworking lawyer.' Sucking her cheeks she looked up at the ceiling and laughed. 'The Barry Halston we know simply would not jump on a flight to LA to help out a client, especially one with no money, so sit back and enjoy a little adulation. You deserve it with everything you're going through right now.'

'Now you're making me feel guilty! Okay, I give in, tell me about him.'

Carla moved her chair a little closer to Jess as if she was in a crowded room and wanted to avoid being overheard.

'Well, he was married but is now divorced and single. His marriage was in trouble for a while so it was no surprise when she left him for someone else. It was all terribly civilised. The two children who are nearly adult now, go backwards and forwards between the two homes and they're all good friends.'

Wistfully Jess looked at her friend. 'That must be so nice. I wish Sheldon could have seen it like that. I could have accepted that, accepted that he had fallen for someone else. I could even have accepted sharing CJ but no, he had to go one step further. I still can't work out why he did it this way.'

'Darling, people with loads of cash operate differently from the rest of us. Your mother-in-law could probably see the family business being weakened if he had to pay you off. The very wealthy seem to resent any kind of redistribution.'

'But she must have known I wouldn't try to milk them. She must know me better than that.'

Jess stood up and went into her familiar pacing routine but it was harder in a small room bursting with furniture. Sitting back down, she silently wished her mother wasn't such an inveterate hoarder.

'Maybe, but the urge to keep the finances whole is probably ingrained. And, from what you've told me, Sheldon also likes to be in control. He couldn't do that if CJ was based with you. He also probably wanted to go back to the States anyway but knew that you would never let him take CJ for any length of time.'

Watching and listening to Carla it suddenly occurred to Jess that her friend, as an independent observer with no axe to grind, was probably right.

'I doubt if you could ever change that mindset,' Carla continued. 'Mind you, he's still a little shit for doing it. A coward. I can understand how awful this is. I don't know what I'd do in your situation . . . yes, I do! I'd cut his nuts off and let him slowly bleed to death!'

Carla laughed as she banged her fist on the arm of the chair. 'But then you might still do that when you find him, eh? Joking apart, I think it would be good for you to have a little light relief. I'm not suggesting you marry Barry, for heaven's sake. Just get yourself back into a little light socialising.'

'But I don't want to. I can't imagine going out anywhere with anyone, let alone a man. Firstly I'm still married and it would be disloyal to CJ.'

'No, it wouldn't. The one good thing in all this is that you know, deep down, that Sheldon and Pearl love CJ. No doubt the poor kid is missing you like crazy but he's with his dad and, dare I mention it, we do know Sofia and she is basically good with children.'

Jess glared a warning at Carla. The last thing she wanted to be reminded of was Sofia acting as surrogate mother to her son.

'Don't even go there. I really cannot deal with hearing that . . .'

'I would have thought that it would be reassuring to you. At least there is a voice of reason in CJ's life. She has to be better than CJ or Pearl.'

Jess thought about it. Maybe Carla was right. Sheldon had never had to cope with CJ on a twenty-four-hours-a-day basis. In fact, he had barely had to deal with him for twenty-four hours a month.

'I suppose you're right, although it offends me beyond belief to think of those two together. Honestly, I can't imagine what's got into him. He was always so . . . so almost staid in many ways.'

'Staid?' Carla repeated. 'I certainly never thought of Sheldon as staid. He was always charm personified . . .'

The phone ringing interrupted her.

'There you go. I bet you lunch at The Pasta House that's Barry now.'

Jess smiled as she picked up the phone. 'It's Sheldon here. Who the fuck is living in my house? I called and they redirected me here. I want you to stop being so godamned malicious and sign the agreement. Sign it and I'll go back to LA and you can see CJ. Don't sign and you'll never see him again. Understand?'

'Please, Sheldon, listen to me. I don't want any of this, let me speak to CJ—'

But Jess didn't even have a chance to finish her sentence before the phone crashed down. Just before the silence she heard her son laughing in the background.

'Bastard, bastard!' she screamed into the silent receiver. 'You fucking bastard, how can you do this to me?'

But there was no response.

Chapter Twenty-Three

Smiling smugly, Sheldon replaced the phone. He was looking forward to getting away from Mexico. Spending a few days there on holiday was one thing, but living there had turned out to be no fun at all. In fact, because he wasn't working he was actually bored witless.

The old-fashioned Mexican bungalow he had rented on the spur of the moment was in a residential area several miles away from the bustling resort. He had thought it would be a romantic adventure, but it wasn't, and now he yearned to be on the beach sunning himself outside his favourite five-star hotel complex in between relaxing in his favourite suite.

He wasn't enjoying slumming it in a three-bedroomed rental that had looked far better on the internet photograph than in the flesh. His mother had, quite predictably, refused to stay at the property and was currently holed up at the exclusive hotel where he wished he was and, no doubt, being waited on hand, foot and finger.

He wanted to be there with her instead of ensconced on a rattan sofa having to listen to Sofia acting like a child herself, playing hide and seek with CJ. In a way though, he was pleased. Although it hadn't been intentional, he knew that Jess would have heard CJ in the background and he hoped it might motivate her to sign. As soon as she did that, he could get back to some normality, get back to working and living in LA and having a life.

He smiled at the thought; he had really missed that. But then the sobering thought of Sofia jumped into his head. He had to decide what he was going to do before Pearl reappeared.

'Sofia?' he called without bothering to get up. 'Aren't you going to get the shopping? We need something for breakfast.'

'But it is so early.'

'That doesn't matter, they'll be open by the time you get there. Buy some fresh bagels or croissants, whatever they've got, nothing fucking Mexican.'

Even if it was the crack of dawn he wanted her to go out; he needed time to think without hearing her voice chuntering away in the background. He hoped to get his head together before his mother showed up again demanding action.

'I'm going now then.' Sofia put her head round the door and smiled. 'Shall I take CJ? He's playing in his room with the puppy.'

'No, it's okay, leave him here!' he shouted, still not moving. If it wasn't for the pregnancy he would have left Sofia without a backward glance. The sex was good but that was about it, and he knew he could easily live without that. Much as he enjoyed it when it happened, it wasn't a priority in his life.

His mother was right, he thought. At twenty-two Sofia really was too young and it had been a stupid idea to let himself get carried away on the romance of it all. But then again, he ruminated, at that age she had quite a few childbearing years ahead of her. He needed someone young if he was going to achieve his dream of having a large family.

And also, if he did get out of it, how could he let her have his child without him around? His child. His second child.

Sheldon was still alone in the bungalow, deep in thought, when he heard a car pull up. Without even glancing out of the window he knew it was his mother. He waited for the knock before getting up.

Pearl almost tiptoed in, as if it was embarrassing for her to even put her shoes down on the floor. Pearl was the Queen of Disdain, always able to make her disapproval known without saying a word; all it took was a subtle glance or a slight movement, and she could put her point across quite succinctly.

'I really have to get you out of here, Sheldon,' she announced, standing on the multi-coloured rug that Sofia had bought in the local market. 'It upsets me to see you living in squalor, not to mention my grandson. Have you come to your senses yet?'

'This is hardly squalor and I can't just leave her. She's pregnant with my child.'

'We can easily deal with that. Where is she now?'

'At the shops.'

'And CJ?'

'In his room.'

'How long will Sofia be?' Pearl was firing the words at her son.

'An hour or so, I suppose, by the time she gets there and back and chats to everyone en route.'

'Good. Gather up CJ and only what you need and we'll leave now, before she gets back. You can deal with the rest of it from home. Pay her rent for a few months and leave her enough for an abortion then that'll be the end of it.'

'But the baby—'

'Sheldon,' the exasperation in her voice and on her face was intense. 'There are enough young ladies in LA who would stick hot needles in their eyes to get a date with you. You don't need a Spanish pauper. Now get packing.'

'What about Jess? She'll find us.'

'I have it on good authority that Jess is currently completely broke and looking for a job. How will she be able to get back to LA unless she signs the agreement? Now hurry, we have a flight to catch.'

'But what if we can't get on it?'

Pearl smiled victoriously. 'I've already booked three seats. I knew you'd see sense, darling. Deep down you know I'm right, don't you?' She picked her way over to the window and looked out, her expression wonderfully smug. 'If you'd listened to me in the past then neither Kay nor Jess would have been part of your life. If it's more children you want then you have to choose the mother more carefully next time.'

Her voice continued berating him as he gathered everything up. 'Don't leave any paperwork here, make sure you have everything that connects you to the girl. In fact, take everything that connects you to anything!'

As always, Sheldon put up a minor fight then gave in and let his mother make his decisions for him.

Within fifteen minutes Pearl, Sheldon and a bewildered CJ were en route to the airport leaving Sofia to return to an empty bungalow, a short note, three thousand dollars in cash and the address of a local abortion clinic that would ask no questions.

Pearl Patterson had done her homework.

* * *

Completely demented, Jess was storming around, shouting and waving her hands about, with Carla hot on her heels trying to calm her.

'Listen to me, Jess. I know you don't see it this way right now, but this is positive. Sheldon has phoned, albeit briefly, and you heard CJ laughing. Now that's good, you know they are safe and sound.'

'No, I don't. I don't know anything. I don't know WHERE they are, do I?' Jess screamed. 'What am I going to do?'

Raising her rarely used authoritarian voice Carla stopped Jess in her tracks. 'Stop this now! You have to be rational about this. Sheldon would never have phoned if he wasn't having second thoughts. You said CJ was laughing so he's not in any danger. Now first things first, check the phone and see what 1471 gives up then call Barry.' She paused to check that Jess was actually listening.

'Okay? Are you listening to me? You're too close to it, so let me do the thinking, right?'

Although her eyes still moved wildly, Jess stopped still. 'Is that what you really think? Shouldn't I try and catch a flight back?'

'No! Leave it to Barry. You have to let Sheldon and Pearl relax, let them think you're backing off, thinking of signing. That way you're more likely to catch them off-guard in the long run. Now, 1471 – I'll do it.'

She dialled and then cursed. 'Bugger, international as I expected but worth a try. Okay, now I'll call Barry. You go and put the kettle on.'

As Jess stood in the small kitchen with her back to the cooker, she breathed deep and hard. She hoped it was a breakthrough but she couldn't share Carla's optimism.

CJ was still somewhere unknown and she knew nothing about three months of his life. It tore her apart each time she thought about it.

And she thought about it constantly.

Opening the drawer to get a teaspoon, Jess struggled to close it but there was something in the way. Pushing her hand over the cutlery she found an envelope that had jammed up the back. Jess wasn't naturally nosy and it was only because she was distracted that, almost without realising what she was doing, she opened it.

It took a few moments for her to register what it was. Slowly she flicked through the dozens of images of herself and Zoë on their holiday to Mexico and it all came flooding back to her. The fun, the sun, Sheldon and the accident – it all flashed in front of her; suddenly it all came back and she was there again.

The photo of the catamaran where she and Sheldon had met, she and Zoë drinking the tequila slammers that had befuddled their brains. It occurred to her that she had never noticed Sheldon taking those very first photos. There was the beach where she had manipulated her place in the sand next to Sheldon, but most vivid of all was the clear and sharp image of Jess and Zoë, leaning up against the car.

The car that, a mere half an hour or so later, Zoë had been thrown from and killed.

The first time she had flicked through them haphazardly, the second time she had studied them a little closer, but now, the third time, she peered at each photograph in turn, taking in every detail and looking at each one from every angle.

Then it hit her like a speeding bullet straight between the eyes.

'Carla! Carla! I bet I know where they are. I bloody know it, I just know it!'

'I'm on the phone to Barry,' Carla shouted through. 'Do you want to speak to him?'

Jess pounced and snatched the phone. 'Barry, I reckon they could be in Mexico, in or around Cancún. The more I think about it, the more it seems a possibility. I just found some old photos and it came to me. Sheldon loves it there and, before the accident, he used to run off there all the time . . . No, I haven't got time to explain, I have to think . . . Yes, okay. I'll meet you here at one.'

Carla looked bewildered. 'What brought that on?'

'These old photos – look.'

'Yes, I've seen them. They were down the back of your bedroom unit. My cleaner found them and gave them to Sara.'

'Why didn't anyone tell me?' Jess snapped, her eyes wide with stunned surprise.

'Sara probably didn't want to upset you.' Jess could see Carla trying to backtrack. 'And anyway you were in LA at the time. But what makes you think that Sheldon is there now? It was a long time ago, wasn't it, when you met?'

'God yes, that's why I never thought of it, I suppose, but it all fits. It was always Sheldon's bolt-hole and Sofia speaks Spanish so they could easily fit in out there. I'd bet my life that's where they are.'

'Hang on a minute.' Carla tried to calm her down. 'Even if they are there, how are you going to find them? It's a big place, is Mexico, and I'm sure they wouldn't be in a hotel all this time. They'd be too conspicuous.'

'Probably not, but if they get wind that we're on their trail then they may move on, maybe back to Pearl. At least then we can serve some papers or something. Oh I don't know, I'll talk to Barry when he gets here.'

'Ah ha! Barry again! The lovely Barry who, once again, is dropping everything to come to your aid. Your knight in shining armour. Take a word of advice from me, Jess. Barry is a nice man – you could do a lot worse, and he's a bloody good lawyer. Utilise both, my dear!'

'That's a bit hard-nosed, isn't it?' Jess's tone was distinctly disapproving.

'Not at all, just realistic. Now sit down quietly and calmly and tell me exactly what you think you know.' Folding her hands in her lap Carla looked expectantly at Jess, waiting for her to start.

'Instead of going through it twice, why don't we wait until Barry gets here? You're calmer than me, you can intervene when I start rambling,' Jess asked her friend with a plea in her voice.

'Okay, you've twisted my arm. But give me the wink if you think I'm in the way and I'll disappear like a puff of smoke!'

Jess smiled for the first time that day and whacked Carla on the arm with the envelope of photos. 'Stop it! You're being flippant.'

'You need flippant sometimes. I tell you what, I'll make the drink and you can go and make yourself look gorgeous.'

Sofia bounced up to the corner of the street just in time to see the easily recognisable limo that Pearl had hired, narrowly miss an accident as it pulled over the cross-roads without stopping. She could see the peak-capped chauffeur in the driving seat and tried to peer in through the tinted rear windows as it whisked past, but the sun was shining too strongly for her to focus.

Sheldon hadn't told her that Pearl would be visiting again so soon and it infuriated her to think that she had been sent to the shops purely to get her out of the way. Increasing her step she broke into a run, with a heavy bag of shopping in each hand, ready to do battle with Sheldon who, she was well aware, had become even more dictatorial in the way he dealt with both her and CJ.

Running up to the door she was surprised to find both the door and the security gate locked tight. Cautiously she let herself in, shouting as she went through, 'Sheldon? Sheldon, I'm back! What did your mother want? You did not tell me she was coming today again.'

But at exactly the moment she registered the lack of response her eyes settled on the note propped up against the fruit bowl. The only sound in the building was the distant whimpering of CJ's puppy that was locked in the gated courtyard at the back.

Then she saw the money, neatly piled beside the note, and her instincts went into overdrive. Pearl had persuaded Sheldon to leave her. Skimming the note she could barely believe what she was reading. Sheldon had gone. His bitch of a mother had persuaded him away just when Sofia had thought she was safe and secure for the foreseeable future.

Sliding down the wall she settled desolately on the cool tiled floor. It didn't need a genius to figure out they were en route to the airport but she knew that realistically, a confrontation at the airport would not be a good idea, especially with Pearl present. Her next move would have to be carefully planned, the same way she had meticulously planned her unexpected pregnancy!

She would go to LA as soon as possible, confront Sheldon there and persuade him to have her back. She knew she could do it but there was one problem she was well aware of and hadn't planned ahead for. She didn't know for sure where Sheldon would be. He had run out on Jess and taken CJ along without telling her where he was going. He certainly wouldn't make it easy for Sofia to track him down, she knew that only too well. Pearl would be easy to find but Sheldon might prove more of a problem.

Sofia started pulling out drawers and looking through piles of papers but Sheldon had been scrupulously careful and left no clues to his whereabouts. All she knew was that Pearl lived in LA although she did not have a note of the phone number.

Sofia was incensed at his deception but she was also determined to deal with it sensibly and methodically. Sheldon Patterson would not do the same to her as he had done to his wife, she determined. Unlike the naive Jess, Sofia had an inbuilt security system that had been activated from the word go. During the time that she had been with Sheldon she had gathered just about enough information to hopefully secure her future. Providing of course she could actually find him. But if not, then Pearl Patterson herself would have to do.

Sofia chewed her lips thoughtfully as she mentally collated what she knew and the best way to use the information. If she couldn't have Sheldon in her life then she would have a fair chunk of his money instead.

Crossing herself, she murmured a silent prayer for her commonsense and foresight in getting pregnant. Something had made her do it and it certainly wasn't the fact that she wanted children at her age. No, her pregnancy was her security blanket for the future.

Leaving her in that cowardly fashion was going to cost Sheldon Patterson dear but, unlike Jess, she had no intention of wasting her energy on fruitless journeys around the world.

Her approach to, and/or revenge on Sheldon would, when she was ready, be sharp and to the point.

Chapter Twenty-Four

'Barry, hello. Long time no see.' Carla hugged him affectionately and then stood back to let him in. 'Jess is upstairs getting dressed. She's a bit behind today with everything that's going on.'

'Tell me what's going on.' Barry faced her, looking serious.

'No way, that's Jess's territory. I'm just the support back-up.' Her expression was wide-eyed and innocent. 'So how are things with you, Barry? How was LA? And the jetlag? And the stitches? I'm surprised you even made it into the office today under the circumstances!'

'Questions, questions!' Barry laughed. 'One at a time, Things are busy, busy, LA was just LA, jet lag is alive and kicking, and the stitches are out. Anything else?'

'Well yes, actually. I hear you were a great help to poor Jess even if you did get battered for your trouble. You are such a hero rushing off to her side like that.'

'Hey, hey, stop right there.' Barry held his hand up in the air and smiled. 'I was actually in LA on business. It was pure coincidence that Jess was there at the same time, as you well know. Don't let your imagination go into overdrive.'

'As if! Nothing out of the way even crossed my mind, why should it?' If Carla had opened her eyes any further they would have popped out of their sockets.

'I don't know. And if it did, then what would it mean?' Barry asked.

Before Carla could answer Jess came into the room. 'You look nice, all slender and sleek.' Carla smiled knowingly as she looked her friend up and down.

Jess had decided that she would match Carla's dressed-down look so she had put on a pair of needle-cord jeans and a fitted cable-knit sweater. Now her hair was longer it was actually a little straighter and she let it hang loose in waves over her shoulders.

'Thank you so much, Carla,' Jess replied, her tone syrupy sweet, while glaring at the same time. Then instantly she smiled and swung her glance to Barry.

'Barry! I'm sorry, I didn't give it a thought when I phoned that it was your first day back in the office. You must have so much to catch up on at work and I'm dragging you back almost immediately.'

'Don't worry about it. This is my lunch-hour anyway.'

Carla looked across at her friend meaningfully but Jess wouldn't meet her eye.

'Thanks, I appreciate it. As I told you, Sheldon actually phoned me today. It was short and sharp and then he hung up on me but I could hear CJ laughing in the background. He sounded so happy . . .'

'Well, that's one good thing,' Barry said positively, but Jess cut him short.

'I know, I know! That's what Carla said but I can't think like that. I need to know what he was laughing at, what he was wearing. Hearing his voice was like being punched in the stomach. The pain was physical.'

Carla and Barry stayed silent, waiting for her to continue.

'It would have been early morning there and I tried to imagine what he was doing. It's just so damn wicked of Sheldon to do that to me. Why? *Why* has he done it? What have I ever done to him?'

Again the silence was tangible before she continued.

'I don't understand any of it. I'd never have thought of Sheldon as a psychologist but he must know me well. He knew that was the one way to get me to sign Pearl's bloody piece of paper.'

As Jess's voice wavered, Carla took over and told Barry all about the photographs that had jogged Jess's memory back to Mexico.

'That's not such good news, I'm afraid. I really do hope they're not in Mexico. It will be even harder to get the co-operation of the authorities there, than in the US. They don't react at the same pace as we're used to.'

Looking perplexed, Barry scratched his head absent-mindedly. 'You'll have to leave me to think about this. What we need is someone on Pearl's tail, but cost is a factor. It would be exorbitantly expensive . . .'

The laugh that sprang from Jess's throat was dry. 'I know, you don't have to remind me that I'm skint. The rental from the house is enough to keep me from having to prostitute myself on the streets but I'm still "financially embarrassed". Don't you just love that expression? And I owe Mum as well.'

'As I said, leave it with me.' Barry stood up. 'I can't promise anything but I'll do some digging, try and check out the best way forward if they are in Mexico. Now I have to get back and catch up. I'll call you later.'

Jess saw him to the door. 'Thanks, Barry. You've no idea how grateful I am to you.'

'No problem. I'll do my best for both you and your son, I promise.' Reaching out his hand he very lightly squeezed her shoulder before kissing her on the cheek. A brief but lingering kiss accompanied by a hint of expensive after-shave that could be interpreted either way.

The tingling that swept through her body and made her blush took Jess by surprise. She couldn't remember the last time she had felt like that.

'Speak soon, Barry. Thanks again.' Firmly she shut the door and then leaned on it. No way did she want to go back in and face Carla until the embarrassing blush had receded.

Jess's emotions roller-coastered in seconds. Surprise at her electric reaction to Barry's touch was quickly superseded by disgust that she could even be thinking such thoughts while CJ was missing.

Damn Sheldon, she thought. Damn him to hell for doing this to her.

After Barry had gone Jess made tactful excuses to Carla. Suddenly she wanted time alone, time to collate her thoughts and feelings without someone beside her.

Instead she clambered her way through the over-crowded room to the corner where Sara had thoughtfully set up her laptop. Turning it on she wondered about what she was going to say to Kay.

Arrived safely, thanks for having me. She smiled to herself as she thought it, knowing that Kay and Ryan would see the joke.

Her excitement had waned since she had realised that, despite her earlier optimism, she knew nothing more than she had done the day before.

CJ could be in Mexico but he might not be.

CJ could be in LA but he might not be.

That was it. Although she knew now that CJ was

probably safe, she was no nearer to finding him and bringing him home.

After she had told Kay the latest and begged her to keep her ear to the ground, she typed a separate email to Brad. Knowing that Kay or Ryan would read it, she limited the mail to just a few chatty lines and a brief update, just enough to let him know she hadn't disappeared and forgotten about him. Why it was important to her she couldn't quite understand, but it was.

Switching off the machine, she leaned back in the chair and thought about him. Not too long ago she would have run a mile away from someone like that. From her stand on the moral high ground she had lumped alcoholics and drug addicts together under the heading of hopeless. Just losers with no self-control and no desire to seek the help that was on offer.

But she knew that was because she had taken on board Sheldon's intolerance of weakness. Now, after having got to know Brad as a person rather than a shuffling, bumbling old drunk, she realised that amid it all was a very grey area, an area where Brad and all the others like him just about survived.

The urge for a drink washed over her. She needed a good long swig of alcohol to calm her down, to help her think straight, and it was only the image of Brad that stopped her.

When Kay opened the mail from Jess that also included the mail for Brad she was torn. The right thing to do, she knew, was to take it over to him that evening but she wasn't convinced that Brad was as good for Jess as she thought he was. Down and outs hanging around the streets was a problem in Santa Monica and Kay didn't want to exacerbate the situation by getting too familiar with one, especially on her own doorstep.

Tucking the printout in her bag, she tried to convince herself that it would be in Jess's interests not to pass it on, but her inherent honesty won the day. She had promised to keep an eye on Brad and she would, after a fashion.

Several evenings later, she waited on the deck until she saw Brad shuffling aimlessly along then jogged over to him. 'Hi! You're Brad, aren't you?'

Suspiciously he raised his eyes from the pavement. 'Yep.'

'I'm Kay, a friend of Jess, the Englishwoman you met with on the beach. She's asked me to give you this. It came today – she emailed it to me for you.'

Her discomfort was only too apparent as she stepped back and handed him the letter at arm's length, holding it out with her fingertips. A slight smile crossed his face as he took it equally carefully.

'Thanks! You're okay, I don't bite and I'm not infectious.' Dropping his belongings to the ground he quickly scanned the piece of paper.

Standing silently as he read the printed note, Kay surreptitiously looked him up and down and tried, as Jess had suggested, to look past the outer layers to the man hidden underneath.

'Nothing resolved then?' he mumbled.

'No,' Kay replied shortly, still unsure if it was a good idea for him to know chapter and verse about Jess's personal life. Digging in her pocket she pulled out a ten-dollar bill. 'Jess asked me to give you this. It's for a meal, says she trusts you not to blow it on the booze or whatever.'

His hand reached out but he quickly pulled it back.

'Nope, I can't. I can't promise that. Thanks anyway, but I have to go.'

'No, you don't, Brad. You don't have to go anywhere. Stay right there and I'll get you something to eat. Just stay there, don't you dare move.'

Kay took off at a run to the small back-street convenience store and bought him a pack of cigarettes and an armful of snacks and cans. Running back she couldn't see him at the same spot but then she spied him sitting immobile on the bench he used to share with Jess.

'Here, from Jess. You made quite an impression on her. Tell me about yourself.'

'Nothing much to tell,' he muttered as he ripped open a pack of cookies.

'Don't bullshit me, man. You can't kid a kidder. Come on . . . spill,' Kay smiled but Brad remained silent. 'Okay, if that's how you want it then no problem. See you around.' She stood up again and started jogging on the spot, ready to run back up from the beach.

'Just tell her I'm doing okay.'

Kay didn't look at him but, despite the monotone, she sensed his desperation.

'I'm starting a programme down at the centre next week.'

She sat down again. 'Hey, that's great! And some good news for Jess. She'll be pleased to hear that as things aren't so good for her right now.'

'Yeah right, but one day at a time. I'm starting, don't mean I'll finish.'

Still there was no eye-contact but although Kay was perturbed she tried not to show it. 'I'll mail her just as soon as I get home and let her know.'

'Fine by me.'

Kay opened her mouth and the words were out before

she could stop herself. 'I'll do you a deal. You get yourself clean on the programme then come and see me. I'll try and fix you up . . . for Jess. I'm sure we can do something.'

His eyes met hers for the first time. 'Thanks, ma'am. I'll sure try.'

Brad watched from the corner of his eye as Kay made her way back home. He knew where she lived, where Jess had stayed, of course he did, but he didn't want them to know that he knew. Quite rightly they would be fearful of their home and their belongings, but he knew they were safe. He might be a down and out and a beggar, but that was all: despite the permanent haze that enveloped his life Brad Walden had never stolen a single solitary thing.

But he could understand how the residents of the area felt. He would have felt the same not too many years previously, in his past life, the life that was his before he was sent to the Gulf as part of the Desert Storm attack on Iraq. The life when he had a career in the military, a nice house and a perfect family.

His time in the Gulf was something he tried desperately not to think about. Alcohol and drugs in varying degrees of strength had helped to erase most of it, but each time his head cleared, so it came back. He could remember it all, from arrival to departure, but certain things fought to the forefront of his tormented mind every time.

The blinding, unrelenting gritty sand that sneaked into every crevice of his body no matter how tight his clothes, the stench of burning oil and the accompanying black smoke that invaded his lungs, the screech of Scud missiles whistling past, sometimes without warning. But most of all it was the sight and sound of the dead and dying, the mutilated and the tortured. Men, women, children – even animals – he could picture them as clearly as if they were on a movie screen in front of him. In glorious, special effect Technicolor. Not for Brad Walden the relief of black and white.

Drunk or drugged he could forget most of it most of the time, but it was during his rare forays onto the wagon, that the memories were most vivid, as was the physical discomfort he had suffered as a result of his short time in the Gulf.

Was the sickness all in his mind, as they said before they dumped him back into society with an honourable discharge? Or were the crippling aches and pains and constant debilitation 'Desert Storm Syndrome' as so many declared?

Brad didn't know. But he did know that when he had left for the Gulf he had been a fit and healthy young Marine with a lovely wife and two young daughters. Just a few months later he had returned a mental wreck to find that his wife was shacked up with his best friend on the other side of the country and that his daughters were no longer his. Never had been, so his wife said, and as the subsequent DNA tests confirmed.

Now, more than twelve years on, he had nothing. Nothing to show for his life apart from ailing health, a few old rags and the crumpled family photograph he had taken away with him to war.

But now someone unlikely cared, a complete stranger had shown compassion. He knew he had to return that compassion somehow.

'Stop!' he shouted after Kay. 'Stop a second! I want to ask you something.'

Kay paused, unsure, then doubled back to him.

'Does your husband have any old clothes I could use?

Old jeans, sweats, anything . . . I don't want to ask, but I can maybe help Jess.'

'With all due respect, how can you do anything practical to help Jess?'

'I was a Marine.'

'What's that got to do with anything?'

'Once a Marine, always a Marine.' He could see Kay's brain ticking over trying to figure out just what he was getting at. 'I'll explain.'

They both sat back down and Brad pulled out one of the cigarettes Kay had bought him from the packet. Dragging a solitary red-headed match along the concrete he waited until the flame caught before breathing deeply. Suddenly he doubled up and his racking cough echoed along the beach.

'You should quit.'

'You think smoking cigarettes caused this?' Despite the watery eyes he managed a smile and Kay saw exactly what Jess had seen.

A tormented soul.

'Okay, point taken.' She smiled back. 'Tell me what you think you can do.'

Kay didn't notice the time passing until Ryan appeared beside her.

'You okay? I wondered where you were.' He looked quizzically from Kay to Brad and then back again.

'Fine, Ryan. Say hello to Brad. He's going to help us help Jess, but first you have to find him some clothes and boy does he need a shower!'

For the first time in years Brad could see a very slight flicker of light at the end of his tunnel of tortured darkness.

Chapter Twenty-Five

Barely had the car pulled up at the airport than Pearl was impatiently out and away, leaving Sheldon and CJ to follow in her scented wake as she marched purposefully up to the check-in desk.

'That's the wrong desk. This is for the Miami flight.' Sheldon pointed out the destination board.

'I know it's Miami. That's where we're going, just in case that ridiculous girl tries to follow us. We don't want her tracing you to LA, do we?' Pearl handed over the documents with a flourish before continuing. 'You haven't told her where I live, have you? I don't want her turning up on my doorstep the same way Jess did. It's getting so tiring, having to deal with your women for you that I've decided *I'm* going to choose the next one. That way we can be sure she's right for us.'

Sheldon felt about six inches tall as the check-in clerk smirked slyly. Pearl's carefully enunciated voice carried great distances and Sheldon guessed, without looking round, that several other people were probably listening in on his humiliation.

'Keep your voice down, Mom. I don't need this, not here.' He looked around to see where CJ had got to and was relieved to see him straggling far behind, unaware of the conversation. 'I am over forty years old. Don't speak to me like that in public!' he snapped angrily at his mother.

Pearl smiled benevolently. 'Well, maybe if you acted your age then I wouldn't need to. A pregnant nanny, for God's sake. It's like a bad movie. *So* predictable.'

The desk clerk's smile widened as he handed the travel documents back to Pearl.

'That way, please,' he pointed, 'through to the waiting lounge. Enjoy your flight, madam.' His eyes flickered over Sheldon. 'Sir!'

'This is so fucking unnecessary.' Sheldon was marching along beside his mother. 'Of course Sofia knows you live in LA – *everyone* knows you live in LA, so it won't take a genius to find you – us – so why Miami?'

As well as being profoundly embarrassed Sheldon could feel his heart palpitating as he became increasingly stressed. He had briefly forgotten just how overbearing his mother could be, and the thought of actually living with her didn't, right then, seem such a good idea. He wondered why, once again, he had given in to her manipulations so easily.

'I thought we could have a couple of days together – just you, me and CJ. We can use the time to discuss CJ's future. I've found an excellent school just outside of Miami, ideal for a Patterson son.'

Sheldon sucked in his breath in a noisy protest. 'I don't need to discuss his future with you and I don't need you to choose a school. I've got it all planned.'

Pearl's sarcastic laugh tinkled irritatingly. 'Not that well planned, Sheldon darling. The child's been out of school for months. He's way behind already, one can see it just by looking and listening.'

Sheldon raised his eyes to the ceiling in frustration. 'Sofia's been teaching him. She's got experience and it was better for him to have one on one education. He's doing just great now.'

'Baloney!' Pearl uttered the word venomously. 'She's no more than a child herself, how could she possibly teach him anything?' Placing herself elegantly on a seat she continued without looking at either of them, 'The purpose of all this trouble you've put me to, was allegedly to get CJ away from your wife, to make certain he would not be what Jessica wanted him to be. And then, because it suits you, you happily hand him over to a twenty-two-year-old Spanish girl! Again, baloney!'

'Are we going on the plane to see Mummy?' CJ's voice caught them both unawares. 'Are we going home now?'

'Not yet.' Pearl drew her lips back and patted the child on the head in much the same way she would her pet dog. 'We're going on a trip. You're going to see your new school.'

'I don't want a new school, I want my old one and I want to see my mummy and my nice grandma.'

The child's voice contained the element of whine that grated on Sheldon as nails down a blackboard. He also knew that Pearl was likely to pick him up on his words.

'Come on, CJ.' He tried to take his hand. 'We'll go and look around, maybe check out the planes.'

CJ, still wearing shorts, T-shirt and beach bumpers, slumped back in his seat with his arms wrapped tightly around his chest. Kicking his skinny little legs back and forth his face was a picture of unhappiness.

'I want to go home, I want my mummy, I really want my mummy.' The frown on his face was deep as he swung his legs faster.

Pearl glared and stopped him mid-sentence. 'Stop that right now, CJ. When the time is right you can see your mother. But in the meantime sit up straight and smile. You're not a baby any more and I certainly don't expect you to behave like a Mexican street urchin.'

The child's face crumpled completely at the unexpectedly harsh words from his grandmother.

'I want Sofia, I want my puppy, I want my blanket,' he cried.

'Oh, do be quiet, you annoying little child.' Pearl slapped her magazine across his legs sharply and turned to Sheldon. 'You see what you're doing? You're raising a monster. He needs a good school and some discipline to bring him back into line right now.'

Sheldon looked helplessly from one to the other. His instinct was to support his son but he also thought his mother was right. In his twisted perception of childhood he thought that by wrapping him in cottonwool Jess had stopped CJ from growing up – even Sofia had been too soft with him. And now he was behaving badly and embarrassing his grandmother.

'Maybe you're right, but he is *not* going to school in Miami. What do you have in mind? Packing me off out of sight in Miami also? Well, no way. I'm going home to LA and CJ is coming with me. I'll put him in school there, maybe get a tutor as well to bring him up to speed.'

Pearl sighed, the long deep sigh that Sheldon remembered only too well from his own childhood. It was her '*you've disappointed me again*' sigh.

'We're booked to Miami now, Sheldon, so we may as well stop off there and have a look. I know what you could do, you could set up an office in Miami and live in the company vacation apartment. You'd soon get used to it, I'm sure, and it would be a great help to the company.'

When Pearl smiled benignly into the middle distance before purposefully opening her magazine, Sheldon knew it was the end of the conversation.

By the time the Pattersons' flight took off Sofia knew exactly where they were going. After three months in Mexico she had secretly made several friends outside of the home. Sheldon may have thought they were isolated but it wasn't in Sofia's nature to be solitary. Being a natural Spanish speaker had helped her integrate into the local community very quickly, so it had only taken one phone call to a taxi-driver friend who regularly did the airport run to find out exactly where and when they were going.

Miami, he had said, much to her surprise.

Sofia chewed that over for a few moments but guessed that it was probably a smokescreen. They were obviously heading home to LA via a different route. No doubt to deal with the custody of CJ, as Sheldon had told her he intended to do.

Poor kid, she thought fleetingly. There wasn't much of a life for him to look forward to with nobody to act as a buffer between him and his father. Sofia was genuinely fond of CJ and had tried hard to give him some fun away from his father whenever she could. Lessons and learning were all Sheldon could think about. He didn't have a clue about the emotional welfare of the son he professed to love so much.

And, as far as she could tell, Pearl was even worse. Sofia could now see clearly where Sheldon had inherited his ideas of dictatorship parenting.

The second she had seen the note and the money,

Sofia had understood that she would have a fight on her hands and that she would have to play tough. Almost immediately she also realised angrily that his departure had been all too predictable. The signs had been flashing the night before as Sheldon had lain in silence and wide awake with his eyes focused firmly on the ceiling. Sofia had convinced herself he was thinking about the baby but now it was obvious to her he was only thinking about himself.

Annoyed with herself for letting it happen under her nose, she stormed out to the small, cool outhouse that was attached to the kitchen and, sliding her hand up over the partially exposed beam she pulled down her insurance envelope – a manila foolscap envelope that contained all the information and details she had been able to gather while they were there. Just in case she might need it.

And now, unfortunately, she *was* going to need it.

A sensible girl who was all too aware of how things could go wrong, especially after she had seen at first-hand how Sheldon had tried to excise Jess from his life, Sofia had made some provisions. In the envelope was nearly five thousand US dollars that she had systematically squirrelled away from the housekeeping allowance that Sheldon had given her, unaware that the cost of living in Mexico was far less than in either England or the States.

She smiled to herself as she thought how arrogant he had been with her. So arrogant that it simply hadn't occurred to him that Sofia was a far smarter cookie than Jess. Manipulating and dominating Jess had been so easy for Sheldon because she was in love with him and trusted him completely. Sofia's big advantage was that she hadn't trusted him and wasn't in love with him.

She had, without doubt, been infatuated with him at a distance in England, but living with him had given her a completely different perspective on his personality.

Her love was for the whole lifestyle that surrounded Sheldon Patterson; Sheldon himself was irrelevant. He could have been anyone.

Shaking herself back to the present, she thought about where she stood at that precise moment. She had nearly eight thousand dollars and the rent had been paid in advance for the next three months. That was plenty of time for her to plan her next move, which she knew would be to LA although she still had some groundwork to do before she headed off to confront him.

She also wanted to leave enough time to stop an abortion from being a viable option.

Despite his specific written instructions, Sofia had no intention of checking into the clinic. The baby she was carrying was her passport to the life that she wanted and the Pattersons, like it or not, would provide it for her and her child.

Also in the envelope was a handwritten list of all the names and details she had surreptitiously gathered from Sheldon's correspondence. Among them was Pearl, Sheldon's attorney, Kay his ex-wife and, of course, Jess and her lawyer. The list wasn't as comprehensive as she would have liked but she had never had the opportunity to get into his personal computer.

Taking the envelope through into the dining room, she spread everything out on the table along with a blank piece of paper.

Sofia intended to plan her assault carefully.

'Well, the sun is shining and there's not a cloud in the sky. Doesn't it look just so tempting?' Pearl looked back from the aircraft window and smiled at Sheldon and CJ.

'The sun was shining in Mexico and I'm damned sure it's shining in LA as well.'

Pearl sucked her cheeks in and then continued as if Sheldon hadn't spoken. 'I think this would be just perfect for you both. Far better than going back to LA, don't you think? Just imagine it, you could start up from scratch here. It would all be yours – a new office, a new house, a new life, in fact.'

Neither of them answered but, for the first time in weeks, CJ grasped his father's hand tightly, almost as if he knew Sheldon needed some support.

As the plane continued to circle over Miami airport prior to landing, Pearl Patterson felt comparatively happy. Everything was going to plan and she would make sure that it continued to do so. Although they didn't know it, everything was already in place for Sheldon and CJ to stay in Miami and, like it or not, that was where they were going to stay. Pearl had phoned ahead to make sure the company apartment was prepared and stocked. She had even arranged for clothes and toys to be ready and waiting.

When Sheldon and CJ walked into the apartment it would already be home for them.

Since her husband's death Pearl had settled into a comfortable routine of cruise and widowhood, but now her life was changing course to include a gentleman friend that Sheldon, as yet, knew nothing about.

At seventy-nine, Hank was old, even by Pearl's standards, but he was also a billionaire potential husband who would take Pearl straight onto the LA 'A' list. When his third wife had died a few weeks previously Pearl had been first off the starting block with her sympathies and now she knew she had to move quickly if she was going to hook him while he was still grieving and vulnerable.

Hank wasn't a great one for dependent family, she had discovered, so the last thing she needed at that moment was a son and grandson hanging around and causing problems. She wanted the custody dealt with and Jess paid off, maybe even Sofia as well if needs must, and Sheldon and CJ ensconced in another state where none of the mud would attach itself.

Eventually, when it was all over and forgotten, Sheldon and CJ would be allowed to return home and she would be able to loosen her hold on the reins of the family firm. But that was all in the future, part of Pearl's long-term plan that she had no intention of sharing with Sheldon at that moment.

When the chips were down, Pearl always put Pearl first.

'Right, boys, here we are. I just know you're both going to love it here!'

Again Pearl was up and away, leaving Sheldon and CJ with the hand luggage. She only had forty-eight hours to get them settled before she had to get back to Hank.

Chapter Twenty-Six

Cambridge, England

To Jess it was a case of déjà vu. Booking flights to Los Angeles once again, still hoping to find her son but with very little more to aid her search than on her previous trip.

Now suddenly Christmas was looming and nobody had seen hide nor hair of either Sheldon or CJ. Kay communicated regularly but she told Jess she was 99 per cent certain that they weren't in LA. She was convinced that if they were around then someone somewhere would have seen them and told her.

Pearl, meanwhile, was the talk of the town after being seen out and about with the recently bereaved Hank Rushforth, acting for all the world as if they were an established couple. Kay concluded, to Jess's amusement, that she had taken him off to keep him under wraps until she could drag him up the aisle and grab herself a few million to top up her own bank balance in the process.

Sheldon and his son had disappeared into thin air, Pearl was taking no calls, and as far as Jess could see, no one in officialdom seemed to care. Certainly they all made the right noises and promised action as soon as CJ was located, but nothing actually happened apart from a swathe of paperwork flying back and forth between all the interested parties.

Jess had heard no more from Sheldon and even her bluff of contacting Pearl to discuss the agreement hadn't worked. No matter when she called, or what message she left, the robotic response from Pearl's housekeeper was always the same: 'Mrs Patterson is away. I will pass on your message when she contacts me. I don't have a contact for Mr Patterson.'

The frustration was difficult for everyone but the most devastating effect was on Jess, who was finding it harder and harder to deal with. The initial adrenaline rush of activity had been replaced by an overwhelming inertia that made everything she tried to do feel like an assault on Mount Everest.

Because of her previous experience Jess had immediately been employed by the first nursing agency that she applied to but the job had only lasted a couple of weeks. Her concentration was poor and it was apparent very quickly that her heart wasn't in it. Both Jess and Sara had had to accept that working wouldn't be a viable option for Jess in her fragile mental state.

That left Sara working all the hours that she physically could. Both financially and emotionally Sara had to support them both, which also meant leaving Jess to her own devices for long periods of time. Too much time when Jess, who had stepped back from reality into the past, would go over and over every little detail from the first time she had set eyes on Sheldon Patterson.

Day in and day out she would try to analyse what

exactly had gone wrong, when it had gone wrong and why it had gone wrong.

The constant repetition was wearing to an already exhausted Sara and she sometimes wondered when it would all end.

Even for something as important as booking the tickets for the flights Jess hadn't wanted to go out, but in an attempt to get her daughter out of the house for a while, Sara had insisted.

'I can't do it, I won't do it. What's wrong with booking online? That way I can do it all from here.'

'No, Jess. I want you to go into town and get it done properly. With security as it is I want the tickets in my hand well in advance and I really haven't got time to do it myself.'

Jess had prevaricated with every excuse she could find but in the end Sara had won out. Under duress, Jess had agreed to drive into the city centre to the travel agents to book the flights. And again, after much tactful persuasion from her mother, she had also arranged to meet Barry for lunch.

Her initial reaction was to go as she was in jeans and trainers, but something made her get dressed up but in an understated way. Nearly all her clothes were too big so she had left them packed up in Carla's garage, making her choice limited. With very little deliberation she settled for a knee-length denim skirt teamed with long black boots and a black roll-neck sweater. She didn't bother to check herself out in the mirror; she was more concerned with actually getting there.

The trip had started off okay and Jess had booked the flights, but when she started to head for the restaurant the panic that had begun to sweep over her without any warning had soared, making Jess think seriously about going straight home. However, she really wanted to catch up with Barry to see if he had any news so, with her chest pounding and her legs wobbling, she steeled herself to enter the porticoed entrance to a deceptively large restaurant just one street away from Barry's office.

Looking at her watch as she approached the maitre d' at his desk, she realised with a sickly lurch that she was actually ten minutes early. Ten minutes when she would have to sit alone and make one glass of juice last, just in case he didn't turn up and she had to settle the bill. But as she took her seat and ordered, her mouth started working of its own accord and she ordered a double vodka to go with the juice. She hated herself for giving in, but by the time the glass, with ice and lemon, was glistening in front of her it was too late to turn back.

At two minutes past Barry rushed across to her, his face red with beads of sweat growing on his forehead. His unbuttoned coat flapped wildly and his tie was skewed over his shoulder.

'Jess, I'm so sorry, had a client I couldn't chase away. Have you been here long?' He brushed her cheek with his lips and handed his coat to the waiter.

'Yes and no. I've been here about ten minutes but I was early, which was stupid of me.' Aware of the vodka nestling in the juice her tone was edgier than she had intended. 'Anyway, I've got the tickets, Mum has agreed to come with me, so we're going to LA for Christmas. I just hope the holiday will tempt Sheldon out of his hole. The bastard. God, I hate that man so much.'

Fiddling nervously with an errant curl of hair that hung in front of her face, Jess blinked rapidly as she spoke erratically. 'I don't mean to start before you've barely got your bum on the seat, but I can't take much more, I really can't.'

Barry sat down. Reaching out, he took her hand away from the strand of hair and continued to hold it. 'We're closing in, Jess. I've told you that it's only a matter of time now.'

'How can you be closing in? You know nothing, I know nothing, we all know nothing. It's like they've been whisked away by aliens.' Clutching tightly at his fingers Jess stared down at the table as Barry tried to look her in the eye.

'I've got someone working on it. As each day passes we're getting nearer, I'm sure, but I know the waiting is a nightmare for you.'

'That's what Kay said, but I don't understand why we've found nothing, absolutely nothing.' Deep inside, Jess knew that none of it was Barry's fault but he was there in front of her, Sheldon wasn't. She took a mouthful of her drink before continuing. 'Surely it shouldn't be that hard? Isn't there a so-called paper trail you can follow? His business dealings? Credit cards? Surely there must be more you can all do?'

Barry's tone was casual and non-committal as he replied, 'You have to trust me, Jess. We're on it, I promise, but we're doing what we can within the confines of the law. You know the complexities, the main one being that Sheldon and CJ are both US citizens.'

He patted her hand and smiled. The last thing he wanted was to sound patronising so he tried to change the subject slightly. 'What are you and Sara going to be doing in LA over the holiday apart from the obvious?'

'Nothing, probably. It'll be strange really, just me and Mum in someone else's house with not a spare cent between us and not a clue about what to do next. Sounds like fun, huh?' Her smile was forced and feeble.

'I'm at a loose end over the holiday. Would you mind very much if I called in on you both?' Barry was hesitant as he spoke. 'I was thinking about following up some work contacts out there.'

Jess could instantly see Carla and Kay's faces in front of her. Both smiling knowingly, their heads bobbing back and forth like a pair of nodding dogs. But because Jess was so very down and confused, she couldn't see any humour in it. Instead, a feeling of paranoia swept over her.

'What work contacts? Barry, you're starting to make me feel like a scrounger. If you're pretending that you have work there to stop me from feeling guilty about your time, then don't. I don't want any favours.'

As the words tumbled out she realised just what she was saying and stopped, her face red with embarrassment. 'I'm sorry, I didn't mean it like it sounded. I'm just so aware that you're doing far, far more than I can possibly pay you for—'

'It's okay,' he interrupted her swiftly. 'I know you're strung out at the moment. It was just a suggestion. I'll be at a loose end, that's all. No problem, really.'

'What do you usually do at Christmas then?' Jess had to force herself not to be confrontational to the kindly man sitting opposite her. She knew it wasn't his fault her life was a complete shambles.

'Believe it or not, I've got in the habit of spending it with my ex-wife and her husband in their very opulent country mansion. Terribly modern and trendy, I know, but the kids have always enjoyed it. However, this year they're both off gallivanting so I don't think a threesome of me, the ex and her old man would be a recipe for a great Christmas.'

The first real smile swept over Jess's face. 'How old are your children?'

'Emma and Piers? Twenty-two and twenty. So far they're well-balanced individuals – that is, they're as well balanced as students can be. Actually they're good fun to be with. I miss them when they're not around, but hey! They're happy and I'm sure they'll pass through the house at some point with their washing and debts!'

Jess went quiet. Why couldn't Sheldon have been like that as a father, she wondered, instead of being so domineering and ambitious for poor little CJ? She imagined that Barry had been a very good father, and he even seemed to be an exemplary ex-husband!

'Come to LA with us then.' The words were out of her mouth before she could think about it. 'We could all travel together and stay at Kay's. There's bags of room and she won't mind, I'm sure. Then we could work together. Two heads are better than one, or rather three are better than two!'

A nervous giggle from the back of her throat took her by surprise.

'Now suddenly *I'm* not so sure.' Barry looked across at her with his head slightly to one side. 'I don't want you to feel sorry for me. I just fancied the idea of getting away and justifying it by combining it with work. I'm not usually so spontaneous. Mr Predictable, that's me.' Folding his arms in front of him he leaned on the table and grinned sheepishly.

'I am sure! You'd be doing me a favour instead of the other way round. My own personal lawyer travelling with me again. That will give Pearl Patterson something to think about, won't it?'

'I suppose it will.' Barry smiled contentedly. 'Would you like a dessert?'

'No, thanks. If there's one good thing to come out of all of this it's the two stone I've lost.'

'Maybe, but you don't want to overdo it. I thought you looked terrific when you first came to see me—' He stopped short and started to redden as he realised what he'd said. 'And you look great now, of course. I mean . . . oh God, I'm making this worse.'

'There's a wise old saying that goes *when you're in a hole stop digging*. But I take it as a compliment however cack-handed, so stop digging!' Jess laughed and wagged her forefinger at him.

'I never was smooth and sophisticated, more of the open mouth and put foot straight in brigade!' he chuckled. 'And now I'm making myself out to be a pratt, aren't I?' The flush continued rising up to his hairline but Jess found it strangely attractive.

'I'd sooner receive a clumsy compliment that someone means,' she said, 'than a load of dodgy old flannel, so thank you. Now let's change the subject.'

All too soon for Jess, Barry was rising from his seat.

'I have to get back, loads of work to sort out if I'm going to join you in LA. And I'll have to clear it with my partner but I don't see a problem. I'm looking forward to it already. Come on, I'll walk you to your car. By the way, has Sheldon's car been fixed yet?'

Barry put his hands in his pockets and Jess gripped hers together around her handbag as they walked.

'Yes, it's done and back on the drive but I can't use it because the tax has run out and the car is registered to him. He took the bloody documents with him so I can't even sell it. All we've got is Mum's old banger that's about to die a painful death.'

'If you promise not to be offended I can offer you the use of my spare car. I keep it for the kids but they're off travelling so it's just standing in the garage.' He stopped, shrugged his shoulders and grinned. 'Anyway, think about it when you get back from LA. Maybe your finances will be a bit healthier by then and you won't even need it.'

'Thanks for the offer. I appreciate it and I'll bear it in mind.' Jess was determined not to sound ungracious again.

In companionable silence they continued their walk to the car park.

'Remember the last time I headed for a car park? Pearl Patterson's pet monkey jumped me!' Barry rubbed his head theatrically.

'I know. I still feel so guilty about that as well.'

'Well, don't. It gave me some street cred when I got back to the office. They're still talking about it even now.'

They turned into the car park and walked over to the car.

'Right, here you are. Now you take care, Jess. I'll let you know if I can get on the same flight as you and Sara . . . if you're sure you want me tagging along?'

'I'm sure!'

Again he kissed her on the cheek and although Jess was tempted to turn her face to him, she resisted. It was still too soon, she thought, but the idea of something in the future had started to germinate in her mind.

Almost on a high, the first thing she did when she got home was fire up her laptop to email Kay with the confirmation of their travel dates and to ask her about Barry. The last thing she wanted to do was let Kay and Ryan think she was taking advantage of their hospitality.

But Kay had beaten her to it. Jess opened the mail and read it through several times.

In haste. Friend of a friend has heard a whisper that sheldon and cj are holed up in miami. Not confirmed so don't get too excited. I've asked someone to try and check it out but unsure where to start.

Any suggestions where they could be staying? Friends? Family? Let me know asap. Hope all's well and maybe cross over with you for a few days at christmas. Love kay.

p.s. brad is doing good and hopes to see you.

Miami. Why on earth would they be in Miami? To the best of her knowledge Sheldon didn't know anyone down there and, if she remembered correctly, he had always said he hated Florida. Jess reached for the phone to call Barry and then stopped, telling herself firmly that she couldn't just ring him with every little snippet that came her way. It wasn't fair on him.

Miami . . . Miami . . . There had to be a connection somewhere but for the life of her she couldn't think of it. While she was chewing it over the phone rang. It was Barry.

'Hi there, I was just thinking of calling you. I've had—'

But before she could finish the sentence he interrupted her sharply. Barry Halston was back in his lawyer mode.

'Jess, this is important. Just as I got back to the office I had a phone call from the Spanish nanny, Sofia. She said she had *quote* information of interest *unquote*. But she wants paying.'

Chapter Twenty-Seven

The phone call from Sofia Martinez had excited Barry more than he would ever admit to Jess. He knew he had to play it cool and not appear to be prepared to jump through hoops for the information, but his expectations of finding CJ had soared dramatically.

He was angry with himself for not being able to keep her on the line longer but the call was so unexpected she had caught him completely on the hop. Despite the brevity of the call, Barry had sensed an angry break in the girl's voice and his instincts told him that something had gone wrong. If everything was fine between her and Sheldon then Barry doubted she would endanger the relationship for the sake of ten thousand pounds; a sum that would be mere chickenfeed to the Pattersons.

Next time, he knew he would be prepared for her call, prepared to get as much information from her as he could without handing over any cash. An angry twenty-two year old would be easy to trip up.

Smothering his instant response, which had been to agree to pay the girl, had been difficult, and Barry had to consciously force himself back into the role of lawyer to Mrs Jessica Patterson. As such he knew he had to be calm and logical and not let his response be a knee-jerk reaction to his feelings for Jess. He didn't even want to ring and tell Jess but he knew he must; he was her lawyer after all.

When he cautiously gave her the news Jess could hardly speak as the potent mixture of excitement and anger blended together, causing her to hyperventilate down the phone line.

'Jess? Did you hear what I said? Sofia rang, she wouldn't leave a number, said she'll call again and then hung up.'

Breathing short and fast Jess regained her voice. 'Did you say she wanted money?'

'Ten thousand pounds.'

'Ten thousand pounds? What the fuck for?'

'Information, she said, presumably to do with Sheldon and CJ. I wonder if they're not together now. There's no reason for her to do it otherwise.'

'So you're saying we just have to sit and wait until she deigns to call back? What if she doesn't?' Her incredulity resounded down the line.

'I have to turn that question on its head and ask you, what if she does? You're in no position to pay out ten thousand and it's a bad idea anyway to pay for information. It could just be a try on.'

'Yes, but supposing it isn't? She may be having second thoughts about Sheldon. Perhaps she thinks CJ should be with me.'

The hint of optimism in Jess's voice warned Barry to play it down.

'Then in that case she should be volunteering the information out of the goodness of her heart, not trying to blackmail you, which is how I shall play it if and when she calls again.'

'What am I going to do, Barry?'

'Nothing, nothing at all. We'll wait and see if she calls back and work from there.'

'I'll find the money.' The break in her voice told Barry she was close to tears.

'No, Jess. That's not the way it works, is it? You know that. I'll try to hold her on ice, I think. If we let her believe we're not that interested, then maybe she'll try and negotiate, or even have second thoughts. Moral thoughts. We may not need her in the long run anyway.'

'Supposing she's frightened off and doesn't call again?'

'Oh, I think she will. If she went to the trouble of getting my number . . . I've just thought, Pearl must have given my details to Sheldon. Now that's good. It's all coming together.'

'I had an email from Kay today. The rumour is that Sheldon is in Miami!' Jess gave him the information as an afterthought.

'See what I mean?' Barry deliberately made himself sound upbeat. 'The net's closing and suddenly I'm optimistic about Christmas. Tell me everything you know about Miami or, better still, have dinner with me tonight, Jess. We can really talk then, plan a strategy.'

The words were out before Barry's brain could assimilate what he was saying, and suddenly the fifty-year-old lawyer felt like a hesitant schoolboy cautiously asking out a girl that he had a crush on. His heart was thumping and he was disproportionately fearful of rejection.

'That sounds like a good idea.'

'Pardon?'

'I said okay. Where shall we meet?'

'I'll pick you up, say seven thirty?'

'Okay. Have you booked your flight yet?'

Barry laughed nervously, trying hard not to show his growing pleasure at the thought of an evening with Jess Patterson. 'Give me a chance! It's next on my list.'

For the rest of the afternoon Barry might just have well not stayed in the office. His concentration was 100 per cent on his forthcoming night out.

Jess was almost in a trance as she sat down on the lumpy sofa, put her feet up sideways and tried hard to concentrate her mind on Miami and Sofia. She didn't want to think about Barry immediately. If Sheldon and CJ were in Miami, where was Sofia?

Jess wished she had taken more interest in the family firm, or rather she wished she had been allowed to. Now she could see that in many ways she had never been part of her husband's life. All the business trips away, all the travelling, Jess had innocently accepted it as part and parcel of marriage to the man she loved.

But that wasn't how it had been really. It had been secrecy and now she had no idea why Sheldon would be in Miami. If he was. And if he was, then where was Sofia? Her mind was whirring with the turn in events and it wasn't long before she gave up and thought about Barry.

Dinner with Barry. Not very many hours after lunch with Barry. Then Christmas in LA with Barry.

Sliding her hand down the back of the sofa she pulled out a still sealed half-bottle of vodka that she had put there the day before. Holding it up high she looked through the bottle as if it was a magnifying glass and studied the light fitting on the ceiling before moving on to the pictures on the wall. She pondered the way everything was distorted; nothing was as it seemed through the glass of the bottle.

Maybe that was the way the alcohol affected her brain. It changed her perception of reality so much that she wasn't sure any more what was real and true and what wasn't. CJ, her son, was real but he wasn't there; her marriage to Sheldon wasn't real and her perception of him had been distorted.

Her mind jumped to Brad. That was obviously why Brad drank. His reality was so bleak he didn't want to see it clearly so he lived his life in the permanent blackout of inebriation. Did she want that for herself? It would certainly dull the pain. But it would also dull any pleasure and for a split second, when Barry had asked her out to dinner, she had felt a wave of real pleasure for the first time in months.

Her fingers rolled around the seal, knowing that as soon as she twisted and cracked it then that would be it, all the contents would slide down her throat. The one solitary drink at lunch had whetted her appetite for the clear liquid that looked, and smelled, so harmless. She held it up again and in the bottle she could see Brad Walden, shuffling along the beach, head down with his filthy polythene dragging along the ground.

Then her thoughts drifted back to Barry. Still holding the bottle she tried to analyse her feelings for him and also the guilt she felt at those feelings. When she had first set eyes on Sheldon it had been an instant and spontaneous attraction, and within days she had been in love with him. An all-consuming love that had taken over her life from that moment on. The stirrings of feelings that she had for Barry were nothing like that at all. He was a nice man whom she was gradually getting to know, of whom she was fond and possibly even fancied a little, but the flashing fireworks and gut-wrenching aches weren't there.

Frowning deeply, she tried to guess which of the two was the better start to a relationship. She also tried to think about how she would feel if he wasn't her lawyer, if CJ wasn't missing, but her mind was too confused to make sense of any of it.

Slowly and carefully she turned the top until the seal split. Raising the bottle she sniffed at the contents for a few seconds before running out to the kitchen, with tears streaming down her face, and emptying it all down the sink.

'Hey, Brad, you scrub up okay, my man.' Ryan looked him up and down and smiled. 'You getting used to being sober?'

Holding out his hands in demonstration Brad shook his head. 'Nope, I feel like shit. Still shaking like a naked Eskimo in Alaska. I can't do this, it was a crazy idea.'

'Bull! You're doing just fine. How long is it now?'

'I dunno, too long. I just know I feel real bad, worse than when I was at my lowest.'

Two quick paces and Ryan was across the tiny room grabbing him by his emaciated shoulders.

'You *can* do it! Look at you – the worst of the detox is over, the alcohol is clean out of your system, now you have to eat and get some strength back. Come on, I'll give you a ride down to the centre. I can speak with your counsellor.'

Brad looked at Ryan but his eyes weren't really focusing. 'Why do you want to speak to him?'

''Cos we've got a deal. You get clean and dry and we help you, but we can only help if you carry on co-operating. I've got a free day, so let's go talk with the counsellor, see what we need to do to help you along.'

As a teenager Ryan Cacherton had spent huge swathes

of time running wild on the streets of LA, but after a spell of trouble with the law and the subsequent punishment he had headed off in the opposite direction. He had found religion and then became over-zealous in his desire to do good and convert the world to his thinking, but eventually age and experience taught him to take the middle road of just doing his best and keeping in mind the words, *There but for the grace of God go you or I.*

In the beginning he had briefly tried to resist Kay's idea of getting involved with Brad Walden because he thought it was all too close to home both literally and personally, but as always she had talked her husband round.

Almost immediately Ryan found himself spending more time than he cared to calculate hand-holding Brad back to a semblance of normality. He had listened and tended and even prayed that Brad would make it. For the first time Brad himself wanted to make it which was a bonus, but his history was against him.

The counsellor from the Veterans Association that Ryan had contacted was being a support. He had found Brad a room in a nearby shared house with some other vets who were prepared to help with his rehab and set it up for him to attend Alcoholics Anonymous.

As far as Ryan could see it was a case of so far so good. One day at a time.

The two men were now standing face to face in that room. Small and cramped, it was as basic as it could be but Ryan knew it was better than roaming the streets day in and day out. Brad didn't necessarily agree. On the streets he had no responsibilities, plenty of freedom and was answerable to nobody other than the local Police Department.

Now there was a counsellor, a landlord, Ryan and Kay. Not to mention Jess.

'When's Jess coming back?' he asked as he concentrated on tying the laces on his trainers. Ryan watched Brad's hands shaking but resisted the urge to help him.

'For the holiday, two weeks I think, but I'm not sure of the dates. She's staying at our house with her mother and also her lawyer.'

'I want to have something by then. I want to find that kid for her, have him back for Christmas.'

'One thing at a time, yeah? You need to get some strength back first.'

'I can do it. I know what it's like to lose your kids. Okay I know they aren't my kids but I didn't know that then and it hurts so bad. I know how she feels.' The pain in Brad's voice was palpable and Ryan could feel his emotions surfacing.

'I know you do.' Ryan touched his arm. 'Maybe the counsellor can work with you, help you come to terms with it, help you come to terms with everything and move forward. Then you can help Jess.' Ryan smiled at the intense figure who was almost folding in on himself. 'Come on, let's go visit the centre. We'll stop en route and grab a coffee and a doughnut.'

Ryan didn't hold any hope at all that Brad would be able to fulfil his ambition of taking off like Rambo and heroically bringing CJ back to his mother. He was too ill and frail, even without the alcohol problems, but if it gave Brad an aim, something to focus on, then it was worth nurturing the fantasy.

Hopefully Sheldon and CJ would be found in the meantime and Brad could keep what little self-esteem he had intact.

*   *   *

Sofia Martinez was angry. Not with Barry Halston, nor even with Sheldon Patterson. Sofia was angry with herself for being so mean. She really didn't know what had made her make that call except that in a flash of true frustration at her circumstances she had wanted to lash out. At anybody.

Sofia had saved the money, copied out everything she could and kept a record of everything she could get her hands on that she thought would be useful. Unfortunately she had failed to keep track of the most important things: her passport, her ID card and her birth certificate. Sheldon had taken them all with him.

The rosy future that had beckoned her a few short months before had turned into a dark nightmare and now Sheldon had disappeared on her the same way he had on Jess.

Her plans for retribution were, so far, going nowhere, and neither was she.

When she had first dialled the number her initial plan had been to tell all, to explain what had happened and why. To make sure that Jess took CJ away from Sheldon. Sofia couldn't bring herself to phone Jess directly so she had gone for the third party option. But when Barry had answered it was as if she had a brainstorm; all she could see was her secure future slipping away.

So she had asked for the money. And she didn't even know where Sheldon and CJ were anyway.

Jumping up, Sofia picked up a bright multi-coloured vase and threw it at the wall. She followed it with two decorative plates and a china lamp. The feeling of satisfaction as the china smashed around her was so great that she headed into the kitchen and systematically smashed every piece of crockery she could find. All the things that she had bought to make the bungalow more homely, she destroyed.

Despite the voice inside her telling her to stop she couldn't, and by the time she had finished wrecking everything that connected her to Sheldon she felt strangely euphoric.

She knew he had done it on purpose, leaving her stranded in Mexico, pregnant with no documents and, as far as he knew, with only three thousand dollars.

Revenge would be very sweet, she decided, just as soon as she found him.

Chapter Twenty-Eight

Jess's spirits were good as their plane soared high over the Atlantic en route to California once again. Despite the warnings of caution from Sara, Jess had convinced herself that the trip was going to be a success. Barry and Sara were both concerned that by being overly optimistic Jess was setting herself up for disappointment but she didn't agree.

She couldn't agree because that would mean admitting that the whole thing was yet another waste of time and money.

They were seated together in a row of three with Jess in the middle and Sara by the window because Barry had mildly insisted that his long legs needed to stretch out in the aisle from time to time.

'This is just the longest flight ever,' Jess sighed as she fidgeted around in her seat and drummed her fingers on the armrests. 'Last time I was dreading getting there, but this time, because I can't wait, it's neverending. I'm getting all twitchy.'

Barry smiled and put his hand on top of hers. 'You need to chill out. Be calm. Take a few deep breaths of your lavender oil and then pass it to me, I'd be interested to know if it works. You're starting to make me feel jumpy as well!'

As he curled his fingers loosely around hers, Jess noticed Sara start to smile, then turn her head and pretend an interest in the passing clouds outside.

Jess and Barry had become as close as she would, could allow. A few casual evenings out on the pretext of discussing the case as well as daily phone calls was as intimate as it had got, but a comfortable closeness was slowly developing. However, the wariness was still there for Jess. A predictable wariness of getting too close to someone again, coupled with an overwhelming guilt, made Jess put the shutters up but she silently appreciated the way he accepted the invisible boundaries without question.

'Tell me honestly, Barry, how do you rate my chances? I'm pinning my hopes on Sheldon going home for Christmas, but now I wonder if I should be heading for Miami instead.' Turning towards him, she frowned and chewed her bottom lip as Barry chose his words carefully before answering.

'Miami is a big place. If he is there he could be anywhere. We need to know for certain then it might be worth sending an investigator, but in the meantime you may be right – he may just head home for Christmas. I really hope so.'

'I can't believe that bitch Sofia never called back, that was just so cruel. I wonder if Sheldon put her up to it? Maybe it was just another twist of the knife.'

Gripping her hand just a little tighter Barry paused and looked at her affectionately. 'Possible. It was rather strange, I have to say. Well, let's hope you're right and Sheldon will surface, providing of course that he doesn't get wind of us being there. This time we need to lay low and let someone else do the donkey work.'

'Mmm, I guess you're right, but I don't know how I'm going to do that. I would love to go up to Pearl and smash her straight in the mouth.'

'Jessica!' Sara smiled reproachfully.

'Well,' Jess glared, 'she deserves it. I'm sure, even if she wasn't part of his initial plot to do a runner, that she is definitely the driving force behind him hiding out now.'

'Tell me about this chap Brad,' Barry jumped into the conversation, 'the one you're so eager to catch up with. What is it about him specifically? I just wondered what it is that caught your interest when there are so many others in the same situation?'

Barry looked genuinely interested but Jess didn't answer straight away. She herself wondered why it was so easy to conjure up an instant image of Brad and why she felt so protective of him. She imagined that a psychiatrist would have a field day trying to analyse it.

'It's so hard to explain, Barry. I think it was something in his eyes. If I was talking, which I did a lot, as you can imagine,' Jess smiled, 'he listened and his eyes were just so alive, but when I tried to turn the conversation around to him his eyes closed off, he literally just shut down in front of me.'

'What did you find out about him?'

'Not a lot really, although I know more now because Kay has been updating me. He's doing okay apparently, he's trying, but it must be hard after so many years. Maybe I feel he just needed something in his life, maybe just someone to show they cared.' Jess's expression was distant as she thought about the man on the beach.

'What made you think it had to be you? I mean, you were buried under the weight of your own problems, why did you want to take on someone else's emotional baggage?'

Jess glanced sideways at Barry before answering, unsure if there was a disguised barb in the question, just the slightest tinge of jealousy.

'Because he actually helped me more than I helped him, I think. I found I could talk to him because he wasn't involved, he had no part in my life. Also he didn't offer advice nor did he interrupt; he would just sit quietly and let me shoot off at the mouth.'

Barry frowned. 'Are you saying that's what I do?'

Jess laughed. 'Don't twist it round, Barry. It's your job to advise and point me in the right direction, to rein in my excesses and I appreciate you so much, more than you can imagine but I can't help you in return, can I?' Leaning across the armrest she kissed him on the cheek. 'You're my lawyer, you're also my friend. Brad is my conscience and he needed to be needed at the same time I did, I suppose. It was a mutual thing.'

For the first time Sara sat forward and joined in the conversation. 'That's a good sentiment, just so long as you don't blame yourself if he fails, which he might well do. One swallow doesn't make a summer, as they say.'

'I know he may fail,' Jess responded firmly. 'I don't think of myself as Mother Teresa. Anyway, Kay and Ryan are doing all the work, not me. I just think there's something there that can be turned around.' Her voice was rising. 'If you had one cake and there were fifty starving people, would you ignore them all because there wasn't enough to go round? No, you wouldn't, you'd do the best you could with what you had. That's how I feel. I can't help everyone but that doesn't mean I should turn my back on Brad.'

Heads turned as Jess tried to make her point emphatically, causing Barry to intervene quickly. 'You still haven't really told me anything about him. Mind you, I haven't asked you before, have I?'

'Thumbnail sketch, okay? Imagine this and think about how you would cope. Young man in the military, the Marines I think, wife, two daughters, went to the Gulf War, saw the horrors, came back, wife had gone off with friend she'd been having an affair with for years. The two daughters he thought he had weren't his at all and his health took a nose dive.' Jess's hands moved rapidly back and forth as she made her point. 'Think about it, within a few months he went from having everything to no job, no wife, no children, no home and he was sick as a dog. It's amazing he is even still alive, isn't it?'

Barry and Sara sat silently, both sharing the same sheepish expression.

'Okay, lecture over. You can both smile again,' Jess laughed. 'But you did ask, so I told you!'

'I'm looking forward to meeting him now,' Sara grinned. 'He won't know what's hit him when mother *and* daughter both get stuck in and take him in hand.'

Sheldon was stretched flat out on an oversized lounger on his roof terrace when a shadow appeared in front of him. Irritably he opened his eyes to see Isabella, the new nanny that Pearl had employed, standing over him.

'Mr Sheldon, I need to speak with you about CJ.' Crossing her arms across her vast bosom she deliberately stood directly between Sheldon and the sun's rays.

'Can't it wait? Now is not a good time, Isabella. I'm just trying to snatch some sun before I have to go into work, even if it's supposed to be a goddamned day off for me.'

The round, unattractive and middle-aged house-keeper that Pearl had employed to look after both her son and grandson glared down at him, her tightly pursed lips imparting her unspoken disapproval.

'This is very, very important, Mr Patterson. I really do have to speak with you.'

'Is CJ sick?'

'No, he's not sick, but—'

'Is he doing drugs?'

'Of course not! He's only five years old!' The lack of humour made Sheldon smile despite his irritation.

'Then it's not very important after all, is it? Now go away, you're in my light.'

Isabella firmly stood her ground. 'It *is* important – he misses you, you haven't spoken with him for so many days and he thinks you're mad at him.'

'Well, I'm not mad, just busy. Now go and tell him that and then look after him like you're paid to do. Give him some homework, that's part of your job.'

'But he needs to play! It's Sunday.'

'So? I have to work, so can he. Haven't you ever heard of character building?' Shielding his eyes he looked her up and down and sighed loudly for effect. 'No, probably not!'

The woman glared angrily before turning away and motioning with her hand to the boy, who was standing miserably inside the glass doorway, to go back inside.

Sheldon closed his eyes again and smiled, completely oblivious to his son in the background. He enjoyed bait-ing the woman. Much as he hated to admit it, his mother had again been right about Miami as a base. It was certainly a lot more fun than LA, far more laid back, and he had found himself relaxing enough to enjoy himself.

After Pearl had taken off back to LA Sheldon had quickly decamped from the company apartment and rented himself a duplex penthouse overlooking South Beach. It was expensive and luxurious but large enough for CJ, Isabella, and several typed pages of instructions, rules and regulations to be out of his way most of the time.

His initial fantasy of father and son had soon faded as reality turned into a chore and it was only his inability to be in the wrong, combined with his irrational fear of his mother, that stopped him from putting CJ on a plane back to Jess.

Sheldon's latest new life had started to emerge within a few days of his arrival although it had been more by accident than design. When it first dawned on him that his mother had presented him with a fait accompli Sheldon had been steaming mad, but Pearl had firmly put him back down in his place by threatening to cut him out of the business. She had even threatened to amputate his financial lifeline if he didn't comply. Everything had been set in motion before they even arrived for her son to start up the new office. The premises were leased and the key staff employed; all he had to do was oversee the running of it.

Sheldon had made sure his mother knew he was angry that she had arranged it all behind his back, but secretly he was pleased at the way things had turned out. In fact, Miami was turning out to be better than he could ever have anticipated.

Smiling, he thought back to the first couple of weeks when he had still been angry. Angry enough to head out to a bar after work with the sole intention of drinking himself into oblivion.

'Hey, man, you don't want to be drinking alone like that. Come and join us.'

Sheldon had already downed several straight bourbons one after the other when the young man had approached him at the bar, a friendly smile on his face.

'Don't man me, I'm okay. I want to drink alone.'

The man slid onto a vacant stool alongside Sheldon and held out his hand. 'Let me introduce myself. I'm Antonio. I've not seen you here before. You new in town?'

Sheldon ignored both the outstretched hand and its owner who carried on regardless.

'This is Miami Beach, everyone is a friend here and we don't let strangers drink alone. Come and join us. Look, my friends and I . . . we're over there.'

Sheldon couldn't resist looking over at the group of young men who were all laughing and drinking and enjoying themselves. All smart-looking businessmen in their thirties having a good time after work.

'Yeah, okay, why not? I'm Sheldon, Sheldon Patterson.' On the spur of the moment he had walked with Antonio over to the crowded booth. The young man introduced his friends who all smiled and shook hands and, after his initial discomfort, Sheldon started to enjoy himself for the first time in months.

Antonio Liastros, a handsome, snake-hipped young man of Cuban extraction, was the life and soul of the party all evening and went out of his way to put Sheldon at ease and include him in the conversation. After a couple of drinks Sheldon made his excuses and left but he had got into the habit of calling in at the bar after work and Antonio was there more often than not.

Sheldon had soon started to realise that his life could actually be far more enjoyable without Sofia hanging around, or Jess, or his mother, probably even CJ, if the truth be told. His mother had again been right. He was a fool when it came to women. Sofia had been a silly mistake, as had Jess and Kay. Marriage? Kids? he asked himself. Who needs them?

In the beginning he had gone along to the bar out of boredom and with no expectation of anything more than a couple of beers, but the two men had quickly connected and became friends.

'Would you like me to introduce you to the real Miami? I've lived here nearly all my life and I know all the best places – you know, the clubs,' Antonio had asked him casually after a couple of bar-room sessions.

'No way. I already know enough about Miami, thank you very much.' Sheldon had instantly dismissed his suggestion, taking offence that the young man would think he needed any help. 'It's not really my kind of place and as soon as my office is up and running successfully then I'm heading back to LA.'

Instead of being offended Antonio shrugged his shoulders and grinned. 'Sure, I understand that. LA is your home, but this is my home and I was brought up here so I know the real places to go, the best places, but hey, it's okay. I just thought we could have fun.'

Sheldon thought on his feet. Maybe it would be fun after so much time with just Sofia and CJ.

'On second thoughts, Antonio, perhaps I could use a social life. I've been tied down and locked up for too long.'

'Hey, man, that's great.' Antonio had swung a friendly arm around Sheldon's shoulder and grinned. 'I can show you how to have a great time!'

They had arranged to meet in a fashionable 'see and be seen' bar in the Art Deco area and when Sheldon arrived, Antonio and his friends were already seated in a booth by the window. He had suddenly felt decidedly staid and old in comparison to the smartly dressed group of younger men who all seemed to have opted for either black or white tight T-shirts that were tucked in black chinos held up by expensive leather belts. It was almost a uniform.

All of them jumped up as one as he approached the table and greeted him like a long-lost friend. After more introductions and a few beers the group, including a hesitant Sheldon, had headed off to a Latino club with an entrance jealously guarded by a troop of Arnie and Sylvester lookalike doormen who, as luck would have it, knew Antonio and allowed them all in.

The dark interior was lit spasmodically by dancing strobes and flashing lights, and males and females alike took to the sprung wooden floor that moved and swayed under the weight of the mass of moving bodies.

'Hey, Sheldon, you wanna hit the floor and dance?' Antonio had mouthed at him.

'Who with?' he mouthed back.

'With us. Everybody dances with everybody here, no protocol!'

So Sheldon had danced until he could dance no longer and started to make a move to leave.

'You leaving already?'

'Sure am.'

'But it's still so early! This place stays open all night for the right people and we are right, my man!'

'So does mine but it's quieter. Do you all want to come back for a nightcap?'

They had all piled into a couple of cabs and rolled back to his penthouse at 3 a.m. where they had stayed on the roof terrace until dawn watching the sunrise.

From then on Sheldon was out and about most nights of the week, leaving the general running of the office to the new manager, Daniel, who was ambitious enough to want to work all the hours that his boss didn't.

A whole new world had opened up to Sheldon Patterson, a world of gratuitous enjoyment that was far removed from his previous life of married responsibility.

Sheldon dragged himself up from the lounger. He didn't want to go into the office on a Sunday, but Daniel was working and he had called with a problem he wanted some help and feedback on. He certainly wasn't in the mood for any more of either Isabella or CJ so he dressed quickly and slipped out without saying a word.

'Thanks for coming in,' Daniel grinned as he arrived at the office. 'Didn't want to call you but I need to go over some details. This is a big one and I'm sweating.'

'No problem. Is the coffee machine on?'

'Sure, I'll get some while you look over the papers. Let me know what you think.'

The two of them then tossed a few ideas around and worked out a plan of approach that they were both happy with. Just as they were finishing off their discussion Antonio came through the door, casually dressed in shorts and deck shoes.

'Hey, man, just passing so I thought I'd drop in and say hi and ask if I can take your car again? Just for a couple of hours.' Antonio smiled, fluttering his eyes girlishly. 'Mine is still in the garage and your car is just so fast and cool. I love it and so does my girlfriend!'

Sheldon only hesitated for a second before tossing him the keys. 'No speeding, Antonio, I mean it, and I'll be ready to leave here by four so be back!'

Antonio laughed and, with a hugely exaggerated swing

of his hips, he left the office juggling the keys from hand to hand. Sheldon had never met anyone like him before. From nanny to mother to Kay to mother to Jess to Sofia, his life had been quite sheltered and he had always had a woman to care for him. Not once had he rebelled as a teenager; he hadn't touched drugs, got drunk or slept around, and he had never been a party animal.

Until now.

Antonio was all the things that Sheldon wished he himself was. Tall and exceptionally slim with hips the size of an average male thigh, his handsome darkly tanned face was etched with a permanent designer stubble over a well-defined jawline. Dark, sexy eyes looked out from under jet black hair that was neatly styled into a close cut that was maintained on a weekly basis.

From top to toe Antonio was seriously beautiful and attracted everyone around him. One sweep of a room with his magnetic eyes and he could take his pick. Sheldon could easily understand it; he himself found him attractive in a very non-sexual way.

Life in Miami wasn't so bad, after all, he thought to himself as he pulled a few folders across his desk and fired up his computer.

Chapter Twenty-Nine

Jess smiled as the hire car pulled up at the familiar beach house and Kay and Ryan both came out to greet them. It was almost like coming home and, convinced that he was, or soon would be, nearby, she felt nearer to CJ.

Kay and Ryan were leaving the next day on their trip so for one night they were all going to be there together. Jess was really looking forward to catching up with the couple who had become surprisingly good friends to her.

First out of the car, she ran forward and hugged them both alternately.

'It's so good to see you again,' she said, 'and we're going to find him this time, I just know it. I can feel it in my bones.'

'I hope so. It's time for things to come right for you and I'm sure they will.' Kay smiled then looked over to Sara and Barry who were still by the car pulling out the suitcases. 'Barry, good to see you also, and Sara, good trip?'

'Not bad but neverending!' Sara joked. 'Jess was like a cat on hot bricks throughout, all arms and legs and fidgeting. It was like sitting next to an octopus. A nightmare!'

With the ice instantly broken they all laughed and made their way indoors.

'So, how's Brad getting on?' Jess threw the question out after looking in the direction of the beach. 'Still holding up?'

Kay and Ryan exchanged looks that immediately told everyone something wasn't right.

'What's wrong?' Jess asked quickly. 'Has something happened to him?'

Ryan looked at his wife before responding hesitantly. 'I was hoping you wouldn't ask too soon. I'm afraid Brad has disappeared. He just took off some days ago and hasn't been seen since. Not at the centre, nor on the beach, nor at the apartment. He's dropped back out on us, I think, and he was doing so well.'

Shocked at the revelation Jess looked out at the spot where they had met on her last visit. She was more upset than she would ever admit. Superstitiously, she had associated Brad with CJ. With Brad gone, would she be able to find CJ? Despite knowing she was being irrational her optimism plummeted.

'Have you looked for him?' she asked. 'Did he give you any clue that he was about to take off? Even if he's fallen off the wagon I can't believe he'd leave the beach. It's been his home for so long.'

'We've looked all over.' Ryan held his hands up and sighed. 'So has his counsellor. He's left some stuff at the apartment so maybe it's just a blip on the radar and he'll come back. I hope so. I've paid his rent up for another two weeks in case.'

Kay jumped into the conversation. 'It's possible we pushed him too far too soon. Maybe he was feeling a little boxed in and has gone off for a break. He knew you were coming so I'm sure he'll be back. Don't worry about him. Brad is a survivor.'

Jess grimaced and stuck her chin forward. 'But he's not, is he? You know that, Brad is certainly not a survivor. If he was, he wouldn't have spent the last God knows how many years trudging the sand and living in the underbelly of society.' Jess's disappointment was obvious to them all. She was a whisper away from tears but it wasn't just Brad's disappearance, it was everything that was interconnected to it.

'Okay! There's nothing we can do right now.' Ryan held up both hands. 'So shall we put Brad to one side for a moment and concentrate on Sheldon. Any more news since we last spoke?'

Pulling a face, Jess put her hand up to her mouth, 'I can't believe that for a moment I was so caught up with Brad, I'd completely forgotten Sheldon and CJ. I don't know, I wonder whether I should be scouring the streets of Miami myself instead of listening to the authorities. They are all just so against any personal involvement, not that they seem to be doing much themselves.'

'They're doing all they can, I'm sure,' Kay responded gently.

'Hardly!' Jess proceeded to put on a silly voice. '"*We're dealing with it, Mrs Patterson. We know what we're doing, Mrs Patterson. Leave it to us, Mrs Patterson.*" It's always the same old crap! What about you, have you heard any more?'

Barry and Sara sat silently as the conversation went on around them, each aware that Jess had to let off steam occasionally.

'Nothing new, although I'm inclined to agree with your original assumption, Jess. Sheldon is a homing pigeon, he'll go home to Mom for Christmas, I'm sure.'

'If Mom is around, that is,' Kay said with distaste.

'That's true. Now tell us about this new boyfriend she's managed to hook for herself. Did she toddle off in the middle of the night and dig him up from the local graveyard?' Jess flicked the bottom of her nose with her finger and puffed out her cheeks.

'That's really not very nice, you know,' Sara joined in, a slight smile playing on her lips which was enough to break the tension and set everyone laughing.

The evening sun was fading as the group sat on the deck drinking coffee and snacking from the spread that Kay had prepared. They were all enjoying themselves so much they didn't see the same man in a different base-ball cap, tucked away behind a wide palm tree snapping rapidly away at them all with a long-range lens.

As soon as he had finished clicking he moved away and pulled out his mobile phone.

Pearl Patterson took her phone out of her bag and snapped it open impatiently. 'Yes?' she said crossly. 'This had better be good, Al, I'm in a meeting.'

'Trust me, you want to hear this. Your daughter-in-law is back, also the lawyer and another woman who I guess is her mother. Older but same shape and same red hair. Definitely mother and daughter.'

'Staying at the same place?'

'Yes, ma'am. They're all partying out on the deck right now. I'm just across the street.'

'Okay, Al. I'll be in touch.' Pearl snapped shut her phone and slid it back into her bag before leaning across the restaurant table towards her companion diners. 'I'm so sorry, but I have a major business problem I have to go and deal with.' She shrugged her shoulders and smiled. 'They just can't get through a day without calling me! Whatever will they do when I retire?'

She pushed back her chair and sailed regally away from the table with her smile in place until she was out of view; but by the time she climbed into the back of her car, her expression had changed dramatically to one of white fury. There was enough going on in her life at that moment in time without Jess coming back to stir everything up about Sheldon and CJ, and once again she was in cahoots with Kay and Ryan Cacherton.

She called Al back. 'I can talk now. Stay on their tails, I want to know everything. Find me a hook that I can use to hang them all out to dry on. What about the filthy down and out that Jessica poured her heart out to?'

'I've paid him off. A grand and he was away, out of town, gone.'

'Good. Keep me updated. I want this resolved once and for all. I haven't got time for all this. I want to know where they go and what they do. If there's the slightest hint of them booking flights down to Florida then I want to be informed.'

Pearl slammed into her house and threw her handbag across the room. Only two days previously she had received a visit from two of Hank's children demanding that she keep away from their father. They had even gone so far as to threaten legal action to prevent her taking advantage of Hank who, they inferred, was becoming a little senile and not able to make his own decisions.

Taking advantage of Hank? Senile? How dare they!

When her husband had died Pearl had been left very comfortable indeed with more than enough inheritance to allow her to live a life of luxury. But Hank had offered her so much more. Being married to him would heighten her social standing no end and open up all the other doors to which she craved access.

Now that she was busy focusing her mind on how to get round this delicate issue, she could really do without having to deal with any more problems that involved Sheldon and both his wife and ex-wife.

And Sofia! She had temporarily forgotten her. Again she picked up the phone.

'Al, I may need you to send someone to Mexico. Let me know when they can go and I'll give you the details.'

'Sure thing, Mrs Patterson. I'll get on it straight away.'

First thing the next morning Jess and Barry walked across to the beach. Each had their hands in their pockets as they scuffed through the golden sand to the water's edge. The sun was starting to brighten but there was still a chill in the air.

'This is winter in California,' Jess smiled as Barry closed his eyes and turned his face towards the sun. 'Look, even the true fitness fanatics are wrapped up.'

'I could live with this. I only wish winter in Cambridge were as good. Even just a little warm sun lightens the spirits, don't you think?' Barry crouched on his haunches and put his fingers in the water. 'That's freezing!' he laughed as he flicked it at her. 'No swimming today then!'

'Splash me like that again and you will be swimming, like it or not!' She flicked water back and they both laughed and ran off in opposite directions before meeting up away from the shoreline.

'It's good to see you laugh,' Barry suddenly said. 'So

much has happened to you, you deserve a little nonsense in your life.'

'Yes, but every time I laugh or start to enjoy myself, the guilt hits me. I feel I shouldn't be having fun while CJ is missing.'

'Yes, you should. You have to get in there and rebuild your life so that when CJ comes back, as I know he will, you can then concentrate on your relationship with him because everything else will be in order in your life.'

'How do you suggest I go about that then?' It was a loaded question and Jess knew exactly what she really meant; it was just a question of whether Barry did as well.

'I don't really know. I'm sure you know how I feel about you, Jess, but I also know it's too soon in lots of ways. But we can build on it, can't we? I think the foundations are there. Let's see how it goes.'

Jess turned away from him, not because she was angry but because she was smiling. 'What foundations are they then?' she asked.

'I'm very attracted to you. I was straight away, the first time you came in to see me.' Barry went up close and took her arm, pulling her gently round to face him. 'I think, in fact I know, we've become quite good friends and we get on well which is so important; we're on the same wavelength. I don't know how you feel about me. Am I just a friend or could I be something else?'

'If I'm totally honest I'd like to think so, but I'm not sure it's something I can deal with right now. I still have too many unresolved emotional issues around Sheldon and CJ. If we had separated, divorced or whatever before all this,' she paused and looked him directly in the eye, 'it would be different, but I had no idea anything was wrong and I still haven't been able to speak to him to find out why. I don't know why he did something so unbelievably cruel.'

'Jess, I know all that and I understand, truly I do. I just would like to know if you think we may go somewhere in the future?'

'It's possible, Barry, definitely possible, but first I have to find out just what it was I did that pushed Sheldon into doing what he did.'

'I doubt you pushed him into anything. As far as I can see, it's Sheldon who has the problem with commitment, not you.' He took her hand and gently raised it to his lips. 'It's enough for me that you're not totally against the idea of *us*, that's all I wanted to know.'

'Just one thing, Barry. Did you really have to come to LA the first time?'

'No. I came because I wanted to help you, to be with you when you most needed someone to lean on.' He looked at her sheepishly.

'And this time?'

'Apart from wanting to spend some time with you? Nope!'

Clasping his hand tightly she lowered it and turned slightly. 'Let's walk.'

As they strolled along closely, hand in hand in comfortable silence, the long-range lens was clicking away in the distance.

That afternoon they all gathered for a final drink together before Kay and Ryan left to pick up Ryan's children en route to the airport for their flight to New York.

Kay had packed the freezer to its limits and filled the pantry to overflowing.

'You just help yourselves. It's our Christmas gift to you.'

'But you've already given us the use of your home. I'm never going to be able to repay you both.' Jess rushed over and spontaneously kissed them one after the other.

Kay smiled widely then lowered her eyes coyly. 'Now you're embarrassing me! Just bring CJ to meet us, that's all we want for repayment, to see you and him back together. We really hope this is going to be *the* trip – and you make sure you call us if anything happens. We'll be thinking of you.'

'I'm just so disappointed about Brad.' Jess's eyes wandered over to the beach. 'I can't believe he would run off just before I got here. You don't think anything has happened to him, do you? None of this makes sense.'

'You always knew there was a high chance of failure, though. You did your best, we all did our best but for it to work Brad had to want to help himself.'

'I thought he did.'

'We all did, but there you go, people are unpredictable.' Ryan smiled.

Piling their luggage in the car, Kay and Ryan hugged everyone and then drove off leaving Jess, Sara and Barry with the house to themselves for two weeks.

'Right, that's it then. What shall we do?' Jess demanded. 'I can't just sit here and wait it out. How are we going to keep track of Pearl and possibly Sheldon?'

'Put a private investigator on Pearl?' Barry's tone was tentative as he made the suggestion.

'I can't afford it,' Jess sighed. 'I can't run up any more bills.'

'No, but I can afford it.'

Jess visibly bristled as she responded to his offer. 'I can't let you pay – I'm already in hock to you and your company.'

'Look on it as a loan then. You can pay me back if and when your divorce settlement is finalised, which it will be sooner or later.'

Sara's head turned from side to side as she tried to keep track of the conversation.

'What happens if I have to stay in the States?' Jess suddenly asked. 'Supposing that's one of the conditions?'

'We'll cross that bridge when we get to it.' He smiled confidently.

'Anything further from the police?' Jess asked, still avoiding having to accept or refuse his offer.

'Not a lot really. I did call again but let's face it, it's low priority to them. CJ is with his father who, as we've all admitted, isn't a threat to him. No, I think we have to stay low key and keep out of sight. We don't want the lovely Pearl to know we're here, do we? But someone somewhere will eventually trip up.'

The three of them sat in companionable silence for a few minutes until Sara jumped up.

'Okay, let's get down to business. Where are we going for dinner? My treat!'

'There's a freezer full of food out there, Mum. Isn't it a bit gratuitous to eat out?'

'Not a bit of it. I've got good vibes so don't be a party pooper!'

Chapter Thirty

When the man in the baseball cap had approached him in a dark, deserted side street, Brad Walden had recognised him immediately although he chose to look vague and uncomprehending.

'Hey, you're looking good, man. I've seen you hanging around the beach looking like shit.'

'Yeah?' Brad had deliberately avoided eye-contact. 'What's it to you?'

'Just making conversation. You look clean and sober. Last time I saw you, you were a fucking mess. You off the alcohol?' The smile on the man's face was insincere to say the least.

'I'm trying, one day at a time.' Brad started walking away but the man fell in step beside him, uncomfortably close beside him.

'I saw you at the beach some time back, always talking to a redhead.'

'Maybe. I don't know what I do when I'm out of it.'

The man grabbed his arm tightly and swung him round putting his face so close that Brad could feel his breath. The urge to break his neck was overwhelming but he wanted to know exactly what the man was after.

'Don't fucking give me maybe. I saw you there with her nearly every fucking day, gassing away like old friends . . . lovers even. Wanted to screw her, did you?'

Staring at the ground looking downtrodden, Brad tried to get a handle on where the meeting was going. Despite the way he had assaulted his brain cells over the years he could still smell real trouble when it confronted him. He knew it wasn't just a conversation and he could feel the excitement rising and adrenaline surging. It was a rush that he hadn't experienced since the war.

'So what? We were just talking. I talk to whoever will hand over a dollar.'

The grip tightened. 'Not just talking. You were talking real intimately. You see, I have hypersensitive hearing and I was listening to every word.'

'Come on, I just told you, I was out of it. I don't remember.' Brad added an element of pathetic pleading to his voice.

'That's good. Now you're getting the picture. You don't remember her, you don't remember what she said. She's a loser and she'll get you in trouble.'

'Whatever you say, man. I don't want no trouble.' A whine coupled with eyes firmly focused on the ground and Brad started to enjoy himself.

'Good. Now how would you like to get away from here? Disappear completely? Then you can drink yourself to death without any do-gooders on your tail. I've seen them all checking up on every move you make.'

'Sounds good to me but I can't afford to go nowhere. I've not got a dime.'

The man fumbled in his pocket and instantly Brad was on high alert, he thought he was going to pull a gun but instead he pulled out a wad of notes rolled up in an elastic band.

'Here's a grand – you get out of town now. If I see you here again I'll break your fucking scrawny little neck and dump you under the fucking boardwalk.'

Brad continued to look vague but his antennae twitched as he assimilated the information that he had. The man was obviously connected to the Pattersons and they didn't want him around because Jess had confided in him, told him all about Sheldon and Pearl Patterson. Even an old dosser as a friend was being seen as rocking the Patterson boat.

Brad wanted to smile but knew he couldn't. He needed to look really stupid if he was going to get anything. Hadn't Jess mentioned Miami in her email?

'Sure. I got a thing about Florida in the winter. Maybe Miami, I got family there.'

The grip on his arm came again. This time it was even tighter, threatening to cut off the blood supply.

'Not Miami. You got that? Not fucking Miami.'

'South Carolina?'

'South Carolina's good.'

'South Carolina it is then, man. Gee, thanks, I can't wait to get out of here.' Brad pocketed the money and carried on looking at the ground as the man disappeared as quickly as he had appeared a few minutes before.

As soon as he was out of sight Brad grinned. The stupid jerk had virtually confirmed where Sheldon was and had also given him the cash to get there! The Pattersons had obviously never understood that if you pay peanuts then you get monkeys! Really stupid apes, in fact, judging by Mr Baseball Cap.

His initial reaction was to contact Kay and Ryan but, after giving it some more thought, he decided against it. His old military gung ho kicked in. He wanted to be the one to do it for Jess, but he also wanted to do it for himself, for the restoration of his long-lost pride.

If Sheldon and CJ were in Miami then without a doubt he would find them one way or another.

He desperately wanted Jess to know that it was him, and only him, who had got her son back, whatever the consequences.

Back at the apartment he gathered together a few things and stuffed them into an old rucksack they had given him at the centre. Slipping silently out of the back door while the others were watching television he ran as fast as he could to the end of the street and hailed a cab to take him to the airport.

As Brad Walden was flying out of Los Angles en route to Miami, Sofia Martinez was midway on a flight from Cancun into Los Angeles. Both were travelling courtesy of the Patterson family's arrogance in thinking that money was all that was needed to buy people off. Both were travelling with the intention of stirring it up for the Pattersons.

She was still pregnant.

Sofia was incensed about the way she had been dumped, but she was also steaming mad that Sheldon had taken her passport and put her to the trouble of getting another one. It had caused no end of problems but she had reported it stolen and managed to get a replacement from the Spanish Embassy and was now on her way over to see Sheldon for a confrontation.

The problem was, she wasn't sure where to go first.

Throughout her flight she had smiled at the thought of turning up on the Patterson doorstep but her mind kept going over and over the curt note that Sheldon had left for her. She had kept it as proof that he was the father of her child, but the more she thought about it the more she realised that it actually proved nothing other than that he was giving her the money for an abortion. It made no mention of responsibility. In fact, reading between the lines, it actually inferred the opposite and there was the distinct possibility that Sheldon would buy himself time by denying paternity.

Digging into her flight bag she pulled out her list of information and names and went through them all again.

Jess Patterson, Sara Wells and Barry Halston were all in the UK.

Pearl Patterson, the family attorney and Kay Cacherton were all in and around LA. Sheldon and CJ could be anywhere.

After checking and rechecking the list, Sofia tried to decide who would be her most likely ally and possible source of a sympathetic hearing when she turned up looking abandoned, pathetic and pregnant. She even wondered about going back to England and throwing herself at Carla's mercy . . .

To give herself time to plot out her best course of action, she left the airport and booked herself into a cheap hotel for the night.

'I'd like to book a room.' His lack of confidence made Brad approach the Miami motel desk clerk tentatively but she didn't even bother to look up, she just pushed a registration slip towards him indifferently.

'How long for?' she asked as she flicked the page of a magazine.

'Erm, I'm not sure. I'll pay up front for three nights and take it from there, is that okay with you?'

He counted out the money and held it out. She took

it, counted it quickly and stuffed it in a drawer before letting her eyes drift back down.

'Whatever, it's your choice. Room Twelve, out and to the left.'

'Do you have a phone directory I could use? Can I take it to the room?'

'Sure.' Still she didn't raise her head from the magazine she was reading. 'Bring it back when you're done.'

Brad filled in the registration form and handed it back in exchange for a key and the phone book.

'I want to find out about Miami. Got any maps?'

Raising her bored eyes, Brad suddenly noticed a flicker of interest flash across her face. The woman was probably in her late thirties, with dull bleached hair backcombed up high and pulled into a haphazard pleat at the back. Her make-up was thick and badly applied and she looked rough in a work-weary way. He could sense hard times within her. Brad Walden had developed a keen awareness of need during his time on the beach.

'Do we look like we have maps?'

'How can I find out what's what?'

For the first time her expression changed and she laughed. Her flabby over-tanned face lit up and Brad could see the attractive woman she would have once been.

'Check out the book under your arm and start walking!'

Brad smiled back. For the first time in many years someone was looking at him and relating to him as a fellow human being instead of either expressing pity or rushing past and avoiding any interaction.

It made him feel good.

By the time Brad had arrived in Miami his hands

were shaking and his mouth was as dry as sandpaper. He wanted a drink, his body needed a drink and his faith in himself was shattered. He had started out on his journey on a high, unrealistically confident that he would find CJ and just take him home. Now, as reality kicked back in, he wasn't so sure.

Pushing his key in the lock he looked around furtively as the feeling that he shouldn't be there washed over him. So many years on the streets had eroded all his social confidence. The dingy motel was on the main street that ran up the coast but it was on the opposite side to the beach and set back behind a neglected strip of concrete. The room was sparse but clean and sounded as if it was occupied by a tractor as an old ceiling fan clunked away noisily. To Brad though, it was five star.

His immediate instinct had been to sleep rough and save the money, but he knew that he would inevitably get caught up in the street culture again and he didn't want that; he really wanted to stay away from bad influences if he could.

Thoughout that first night in Miami he was awake and restless as he stayed locked in his room, desperately trying to stay away from his demons. But he managed another dry night and in the morning he was ready to start searching out Sheldon Patterson and CJ which, he reasoned, would be easy for someone with his military training.

Brad got ready to go out.

He had run out of cigarettes and needed a hard hit of caffeine to bring him round so, letting himself out of the room quietly he went in search of somewhere that preferably didn't sell liquor.

Catching sight of himself in the mirror still shocked him. So many years had passed since he had really seen himself and the man in the mirror looked nothing like Brad Walden. The person in front of him wasn't a former Marine. It was someone else with an emaciated body topped by a newly shaven face that looked like a skull with skin pulled taut across it as it looked back at him. The jeans and polo shirt, previously Ryan's, hung loosely off his bones but were at least clean and fresh. Only the shoes on his feet were new, a present from the centre.

Despite the warm Florida sun he still felt cold so he pulled on a check fleece jacket and a baseball cap before going out.

As he rounded the corner of the building the desk clerk was just coming out of the office. In reverse to him, her jeans were a couple of sizes too small and a roll of fat had escaped over the top and was showing through the skin-tight scarlet T-shirt that was slashed so low her breasts were struggling to stay constrained.

She caught his eye and smiled. He smiled back.

'Hi there,' she shouted. 'Where are you heading?'

'Coffee shop. Where's the nearest?'

'There's one on the next block. Come on, I'll show you. I'm Enid, by the way.'

'I'm Brad.'

'I know,' she smiled, 'I checked you out. Brad Walden from California. What brings you to Miami, Brad Walden?'

'I'm looking for someone.'

'Is that good or bad? You looking for trouble?'

'Nope, I stay away from trouble now. Just looking for someone for a friend.'

'Maybe I can help?' She smiled expectantly and Brad felt a warm surge of normality.

'How long have you worked here?'

'Too long, but it's work.' She smiled wide, showing off surprisingly white teeth.

'You married?' he asked curiously.

'Divorced,' she laughed, 'twice. Still looking for the good one, so far only the bad and the ugly have come my way. And you?'

'Divorced. Once.'

'Hey, that's good for California! Here's the coffee shop. Come on, I'm buying. Looking at you I can see you need some good feeding up. I've seen more fat floating on my cheerios.'

'Oh no, *I'm* buying and then I'm going to pick your brains about Miami!'

'I'm getting truly pissed off with this. I feel as if we're wasting time just sitting around like we're on holiday. That's not why we're here.' Stretching her legs out, Jess hooked her feet into the rail of the deck. 'We should be battering down doors and threatening Pearl. It would be much easier, and certainly more enjoyable than waiting for the powers-that-be to shift their bits of paper around.'

Sara smiled. 'Be fair, Jess, I know how you feel, but Barry has been flitting around like a madman.'

'I know, and that's another worry. How can I ever pay his bill? I can't expect him to fork out for everything, it's putting me under an obligation.' She peered into the distance before continuing. 'This business with Brad has me spooked as well. I can't believe he would take off just like that. This is all just too much.'

'Come on, we've only been here a few days. Christmas is coming and sooner or later this will all come right.'

'I know Christmas is coming, don't I?' Jess looked at her mother sadly. 'But that makes it even worse. I focused on Christmas as the time I would get CJ back, but now I wonder how I'll cope if it doesn't happen. Suppose all this is wrong and he's still in Mexico? I might never get CJ back from there.'

Jess was getting more and more frustrated with each passing day. She knew it was only a matter of time before she ignored Barry and Sara's advice and hot-footed it off to a confrontation with her mother-in-law.

As far as they had been able to find out, there was, as yet, no sign of Sheldon or CJ. Pearl herself was in LA but apparently spent a lot of her time in her fiancé's high security mansion surrounded by walls, lights and a posse of highly trained Doberman guard dogs.

Jess really wanted to connect with someone who would update her on all the local gossip but she was frightened to approach anyone in case they told Pearl.

'You will get him back, Jess. You know what Barry said.'

'How come Barry is suddenly one step from being canonised in your eyes? He might be a bloody good lawyer but he's not a miracle worker.' Jess lit another cigarette from the butt of the last one.

'Oh, come on,' Sara answered, her tone very short. 'Considering everything he's done for you, is still doing in fact, you should be down on your knees giving thanks. If you alienate him then you're really being very silly. We are getting somewhere.'

'Where exactly? What's the difference between now and the beginning of September? That's three and half months and I'm no nearer to knowing where CJ is. The courts, the lawyers, the police, the bloody massed bands as well for all I know, are after them, and still Sheldon has CJ we know not where. So tell me – what's different?'

Sara didn't answer.

They both waited in silence for Barry to get back, each fearful of saying the wrong thing to the other. Jess felt mean but she knew she was right: they really were no further on as far as she could see.

'I'll make a drink and then I'm going for a walk up to the shopping mall. Do you want to come?' Sara murmured as she eventually stood up to go indoors. But she stopped in her tracks as a cab pulled up outside. 'Who's that?' she asked curiously, screwing up her eyes.

'I don't know. Probably someone for Kay or Ryan. We'll have to let them know they're away.'

Disinterestedly Jess watched as the back door of the cab opened and someone stepped out onto the pavement. It took a few moments for Jess to register who it was and then she literally sprang to her feet.

Chapter Thirty-One

'Oh my God, Mum, look! It looks like Sofia! It is, it's Sofia – what the hell is *she* doing here?' Jess nearly fell over her feet to get down the steps and to the gate. She could see the panic on the girl's face when she realised who was heading towards her but by then it was too late for her to do anything. The cab was pulling away.

Sara stumbled down after her daughter and reached out to grab her arm. 'Don't do anything, Jess – don't do anything you'll regret. This may just be the key to it all. Now take a deep breath . . . calmly, calmly, that's it.'

Jess didn't feel in the slightest bit calm, in fact she felt positively murderous but Sara's iron grip on her elbow held her back.

'Careful now, Jess, she's looking for an escape route. She obviously didn't expect you to be here. Don't frighten her off. In fact, you stay right here and let me deal with it.'

Sara pushed past her daughter and opened the gate. 'Well, well, what exactly brings you here, Sofia?'

'Who are you?' the girl asked, looking bewildered. 'I am looking for Kay Cacherton. What is going on?'

'Come on inside, Sofia,' Sara smiled grimly, 'and we'll tell you all about it. Come on.'

'But Jess is there, why is she there?' Sofia's eyes flickered around in panic as Sara started to lead her through the gate.

'It's okay, I'm Jess's mother and we're just staying here for Christmas. Now come inside. We all need to talk, don't you think?'

Sofia's eyes were fluttering from side to side obviously looking for a way out of her predicament but Sara was blocking her in very gently, leaving her no alternative but to walk on towards where Jess was standing.

White as a sheet and feeling quite sick Jess watched the scenario going on in front of her. She felt as if she was caught up in some bizarre nightmare. What on earth was Sofia doing *here*?

'I'm so sorry, I really am so sorry,' Sofia muttered as they came face to face.

'What are you doing here?' Jess asked, her eyes cold.

'I didn't know where to go. I have a list of names and Kay's name was there. I thought she might be able to help me.'

'Help you how?'

'I'm pregnant and I have nowhere to go.'

'What about Sheldon?'

'He left me, I don't know where he is. I'm sorry, I'm so sorry.'

Jess shook her head repeatedly. 'I don't believe this, I don't bloody believe it. What is going on here? Come on, Mum, do something.'

'What we're going to do is go indoors and talk this through between us. Calmly and quietly!' Sara looked hard at her daughter who got the message straight away.

'Okay, we'll go in, then Sofia can tell me what's been going on,' she replied grudgingly.

'Come on then, and I'll try to get hold of Barry.' Sara spoke gently and quietly.

On the way up the wooden steps Sofia started to hyperventilate and the second they got inside she sighed and slid almost gracefully to the floor.

'Oh really! This is getting ridiculous.' Jess turned her back on the girl who was groaning in front of her. 'Get her out of my sight, the gold-digging little slut. This is all her fault. All this mess is *her* fault.'

'Listen to me,' Sara snapped with naked panic in her voice. 'She's the one most likely to know where Sheldon and CJ are, yes? *Comprendez?* Now try and be reasonable, just for a short while. This is our secret weapon and she's hand-delivered herself straight to our door!'

Sara helped Sofia to her feet and led her over to the sofa before going through to the kitchen to fetch her a glass of water and quietly calling Barry. Jess just stared at the girl from across the room. She didn't trust herself to get any closer.

'Where are they?' she demanded, her face screwed up with fury. 'Where is CJ? Tell me, WHERE IS MY SON?' Her voice reverberated around the room, causing Sara to run back in as fast as she could.

'I do not know.' Looking terrified, Sofia pushed herself back into the sofa. 'That's why I'm here. I am looking for Sheldon also. I think they are with Mrs Patterson.'

'No, they're not, so don't give me that crap. You ran off with Sheldon, you must know where he is.'

'I do not know! Mrs Patterson, his mother, came to Mexico and took them away when I was out. I think they are here in Los Angeles, and that's why I came. His mother said he must go to court here, for CJ. They tell me to have an abortion.'

As Sofia started to cry Sara took over and threw a warning look at her daughter.

'Come on, Sofia, it's okay, we just want to know what's going on. Now sit quietly and get your breath back. I don't want you to feel intimidated.'

'I do, I want her to feel really intimidated, shit scared even,' muttered Jess with a face like thunder.

The three of them sat around in an emotion-fuelled group, each looking from one to the other as Sofia relaxed just a little and the colour came back into her face.

'Where is Kay?' she suddenly asked.

'She's not here. Anyway, why do you want Kay? Do you know her?'

'No, but I thought she might help me. I know no one here.'

'Hmm, she probably would have, she's a kind person. Timed it all wrong, didn't you?' Jess laughed but there was no humour on her face.

'Tell us exactly what happened from start to finish,' Sara said calmly. 'We need to know everything. We need to find CJ as soon as we can.'

The door flew open and Barry hurled himself in like a large, out of control tornado. 'Wait, let me deal with this. Let me talk to her properly.'

'Gently does it, Barry. The girl's pregnant,' Sara interrupted.

For the first time Jess took in the implications of the sentence. It hadn't registered fully with her before but in that instant she realised. 'You're pregnant? With Sheldon's baby?'

Sofia nodded miserably.

For Jess it was a pivotal moment in her life, the moment when she realised the depth of the betrayal.

'What does Sheldon think about it?' The question was quiet and cold.

'He told me to get rid of it.' Sofia looked up sadly, her face begging for sympathy but Jess just looked bewildered.

'That doesn't sound like Sheldon. He's always been obsessed with having children – dozens of little Pattersons. Women are walking wombs to him.'

'I think it was his mother, she told him—' Before she could finish Jess launched herself across the room and leaned forward, her face just inches away from Sofia's.

'Yes, well don't expect me to feel sorry for you. You wormed your way into my home and my marriage and then helped the bastard steal my son. If I had a gun I'd shoot you stone dead without a second thought, you selfish little bitch.'

Sofia's eyes welled up.

'Don't bother with the tears,' jeered Jess. 'Whatever has happened to you, you deserve every single bit of it.'

Barry took Jess by the arm and pulled her away. 'It's okay, Jess, I understand how you feel but now I want you and Sara to leave me alone with Sofia for a while. I want to talk to her privately.'

'Oh no, you're not going to get rid of me. Read my lips, Barry, not a chance. I want to know everything, I want to find CJ.' Jess was screaming at the top of her voice.

'And we will, but you're too close to it. Let me—'

'I don't want to talk to you.' Sofia started crying. 'I do not want to talk to anyone here. I am leaving now, you have no right to speak to me like that. This is all Sheldon's fault, not mine. Now I am going.'

'You fucking bitch. If you'd told us where you were instead of trying to blackmail me, I'd have my son back by now. So no, you're not going anywhere,' Jess snarled and Barry had to grab her again as she started back towards Sofia.

'You cannot stop me!' Sofia jumped up and started towards the door. 'I shall call the police. You cannot make me stay here!'

'Try me and I'll have you arrested for blackmail!' Jess laughed again without humour.

'Jess! Sara! Leave me with Sofia now. This is all getting out of hand.' The expression in Barry's eyes left them in no doubt that he was deadly serious. 'I mean it,' he continued. 'Do you want to find CJ or not?'

'Of course I do! What kind of stupid ass question is that?'

'Then go away! Now!'

Sheldon was once again in a club with Antonio and his friends. It was an exclusive lap dancing club that only allowed entry to selected clientèle. Antonio was, somehow, one of them. As a bevy of beautiful long-limbed girls gyrated in their G strings and golden tans Antonio was throwing money around like confetti.

It fleetingly passed through Sheldon's alcohol-befuddled brain that the money Antonio threw around didn't equate with his job as a 'financial adviser' but he was enjoying himself too much to give it any real thought.

One particular girl had obviously caught Antonio's eye and he handed over wadfuls of dollars for her to wave her surgically enhanced breasts around his face.

Then, to Sheldon's initial embarrassment, she danced seductively over in front of him and leaned forward. Taking a large slug of his drink, he smiled nervously before starting to enjoy it.

Her perfectly honed body swayed and spun in time to the throbbing beat that bounced around the walls of the darkened room as she edged nearer and nearer but, as the men were all well aware, touching was strictly forbidden. One small breach of the rules would find them out on the pavement.

She shimmied closer and closer until her body was a cigarette paper away from his; her eyes half-closed she looked into Sheldon's eyes and ran her tongue slowly over her glossed lips.

The next morning, before he even opened his eyes, the first thing Sheldon noticed was the thumping pain that started at the top of his skull and slowly spread down to his extremities. He had the mother and father of all hangovers.

The second thing he noticed, as he gingerly opened his eyes, was the blonde dancer from the club sitting in the armchair by the window, wrapped in a bathrobe and staring straight at him.

The third thing he noticed was that it wasn't his bedroom.

Panic swept over him as he realised he couldn't remember a thing. Lying rigid in the bed, too scared to move, he racked his brain to try and remember something, anything, but it was all a blank.

'What happened?' He looked at her, sensing something dramatically wrong.

'You raped me,' she stated calmly. 'You raped me – you're an animal.'

'I didn't! I don't even remember getting here. Where am I?'

'Don't try that one, asshole. You invited me here for a drink and raped me.' The girl jumped to her feet and started screaming at him, accusations, obscenities, threats.

Threats. Despite his throbbing head the implications of what was happening seeped through and he was scared sick. Literally. Falling out of the bed he stumbled to the bathroom and threw up. Rinsing his mouth afterwards he looked at the beautifully prepared basket of toiletries set out on a full-width marble vanity unit and realised he was actually in an expensive hotel room.

The girl banged on the door. 'Don't try hiding in there. If you don't get your ass out here I'm calling the cops.'

He wondered why she hadn't already called them if she had been raped. Why had she sat in a chair, patiently waiting for him to wake?

Blackmail. That must be the answer. Just thinking the word scared him. He knew he had to ring Antonio and find out what had happened.

'I certainly didn't rape you. This a set-up – I can smell it. You're trying to roll me, aren't you? Well, it won't work. Call the cops, go on, and then we'll see. They'll examine you and then we'll know.'

But as he was saying it he realised the futility of it as a threat. He couldn't remember a thing. He might have slept with her, might have had consensual sex and then the proof would be there anyway. Then it hit him. If he couldn't remember a thing, maybe he had forced himself on her. But as soon as he thought it, he dismissed it. No way, he told himself firmly.

Unlocking the bathroom door, he ignored her and

went straight to the phone and dialled Antonio. There was no answer on his home number so he dialled the mobile.

'Antonio? I'm in a hotel room with a woman who says I've raped her,' Sheldon bleated. 'You have to help me! Get yourself over here now.'

Antonio sounded shocked. 'Sure, man, where are you?'

'Not a clue. I'm in a fucking hotel room somewhere. Hang on, I'll check out where it is.' Sheldon picked up the folder of hotel information and flicked through before reading it out.

'Be there right away, man. Don't panic, we can deal with this.'

The girl pulled the robe tighter and looked at him with a very slight but almost victorious smile playing around the edge of her mouth. The night before, he had thought she was gorgeous, but in the cold light of day with her face bare of stage make-up she looked as ordinary as any other girl.

His mouth felt as if something had crawled in there and died. Something was definitely out of sync. Sheldon wasn't a drinker and had never been rolling drunk in his life. He had never lost control and certainly never lost his memory.

He dressed and turned on the coffee-machine but didn't speak to the girl. Surely the hotel would never have let him book in if he was paralytic? None of it made any sense.

The knock on the door nearly sent him through the roof but looking through the spy-hole he was relieved to see Antonio.

'Jesus Christ, you've got to do something. I've been set up, I just know it.'

'Hey, take it easy. We can deal with this. Let me speak to her.' Antonio put his arm around Sheldon's shoulder and hugged him before turning his attention to the girl. 'Now what happened here?'

'This . . . this animal invited me up for a drink. I thought he was all right,' the girl sniffed and dabbed at her eyes with a tissue. 'But then he just jumped me and . . . and . . . and then he raped me. Then he just went to sleep. I couldn't leave, I didn't want to go out past the desk. I didn't know what to do so I waited.'

'What's your name?' Antonio asked.

'Laura. Laura Howardson.'

'Well, Laura, what are we going to do about this? I'm sure my friend here would like to keep this quiet.' Antonio's voice was unusually gentle as he smiled at her.

'I don't know. I've been raped – why should I keep it quiet?'

'Because if this gets out you'll lose your job.'

She looked as if she was considering everything he had said. Dabbing at her eyes again she glanced over at Sheldon who was standing silently by the window.

'What do you think?' she asked Antonio, her eyes wide and innocent.

'Money, darling, money. I'm sure that will help ease your recovery.' Antonio smiled.

'No way!' Sheldon shouted. 'This is a set-up! I never raped anyone in my life and I certainly didn't rape you, that's for sure. I reckon my drink was spiked. I'm going to check the desk, see what happened when I – we – arrived. This is a five-star hotel – they don't let in drunks and hookers without reservations.'

'Not a good idea, Sheldon,' Antonio shook his head, 'you making it public. Let's see how much it'll cost you to keep it under wraps. Laura? What do you think?'

'Half a million dollars!'

Sheldon spat his coffee across the room and laughed. 'See? I told you it was a set-up. No way, not a dime. I'm calling the cops now – let them deal with it.'

Antonio went back to his side. 'Not so fast – just think about it. What about your son and your custody case? How will it look in court if they find out you've been accused of rape? I think you should try and cut a deal here.' He looked back at the girl. 'Half a million is pushing it, Laura, but I'm sure there's room for negotiation here. A quarter of a million and that's it. Take it or leave it.'

'Hang on there, this is my money you're talking about. Why should I pay this two-bit hooker for setting me up?' Sheldon knew he was fast losing control.

'It's your word against mine, mister. Who would you believe?' She smiled nastily. 'A child abductor? Or me?'

'How do you know all that?' The cogs in his brain went into overdrive. 'No one knows that except for Antonio, no one.'

'I've got big ears,' Laura boasted. 'I know all about you, Mr Sheldon Patterson. I've been watching you, listening to you and asking about you.' Suddenly she changed tack and went back to her girly voice. 'You raped me, you brought me to your hotel room, a pre-booked hotel room, and raped me and now you're going to pay. You promised me I would be safe with you and then you took advantage – you forced yourself on me.'

Sheldon knew he was caught between a rock and a hard place. He'd been well and truly set up and could think of no way out of it.

'I'm going home. Give your details to Antonio and I'll

think about it.' Grabbing his jacket up from the floor he stormed out and slammed the door.

Down at the checkout desk he paused, unsure if he owed for the room. 'I'm checking out of Room 914 in about half an hour. Anything due?'

'No, sir, we have your card details.'

'Did you swipe it last night? It's slipped my mind.'

'Yes, sir, but you gave us all your details when you booked.'

'When did I book the room? Sorry, my mind's been on other things lately.'

The clerk checked the computer. 'During the week, sir – Tuesday. You booked two adjoining rooms.'

'Are you sure?'

'Yes, sir. Here.' He handed over a printout. 'Here are all the details but we'll forward a receipt.'

'Thank you.'

Sheldon went to go back up to the room but as the lift doors opened on his floor he spotted Antonio and Laura laughing as they went into the lift opposite. Antonio had a large bag slung over his shoulder.

Chapter Thirty-Two

Very grudgingly Jess and Sara went out on to the deck, leaving Barry alone with a very defensive Sofia. He really wanted her to relax, to feel at ease with him so he turned to her and smiled. He watched carefully as Sofia turned her wide teary eyes to him and let her lips wobble, and in that split second he could see how she had got together with Sheldon Patterson.

He also realised that she thought he was only a lawyer, she didn't know anything about him and Jess, so he decided to play the game for a while.

'It's all right, Sofia,' he said. 'I know this is hard for you and I'm sorry Jess had a go at you, but she's distraught over her son. I'm sure you understand that. It's all been really hard on her.' Perching carefully alongside her, he smiled and patted her hand. 'But then this is hard for you as well, isn't it? I can understand completely how you're feeling right now.'

He watched her relax and lean back in her chair for the first time and decided to play it cool.

'It must seem as if everyone is against you. Why don't you tell me what happened? I'm a lawyer, maybe I could help you as well.' His voice was soothing.

'We were in Mexico,' Sofia sniffed, 'and his mother came to see him. She was not happy that I was there – he had told her I was the nanny employed to look after CJ. She offered me severance pay!' A half-smile edged around her mouth. 'I told her I was having Sheldon's baby. She was very angry.'

Barry tried not to smile, too. He could just imagine Pearl's distaste at finding her son shacked up with a girl young enough to be his daughter who, even worse, was pregnant.

'That must have been awful for you. What happened next?'

'The following day she came back when I was out and then when I got home they had all gone. Sheldon left the money for an abortion and paid some rent on the house. Here, I have the letter.'

Sofia handed it to Barry. He was stunned at the callousness of the wording.

'Where did they go? Do you know?'

Sofia smiled. 'My friend, a taxi driver, told me they flew from Cancun on a flight to Miami. I thought maybe that was to stop me following them. I thought they were going to carry on to Los Angeles. Are they really not here?' Her eyes became persuasively wider.

'Pearl is, but Sheldon and CJ are not. No one knows where they are, although it has been suggested that they are in Miami, which fits with what you've just told me. Do you think that's right?' Barry patted her hand reassuringly. Two could play at that game, he decided.

'I do not know. Sheldon didn't speak of Miami, only of going to the court in Los Angeles. I have to find him, I am carrying his baby. He will pay for what he has done to me, he will pay. He is a pig, his mother is a pig . . .'

'I'm sure that's true, Sofia. Now, just to put Jess's

mind at rest, tell me about your time with CJ. Anything you can tell us would be so great.' He patted her hand again and set his face into his kindly uncle expression. The expression he used in his office for recalcitrant youngsters.

'Do you mind if Jess comes in now?' he went on. 'I promise she'll be okay with you. She was just so upset – I'm sure you can understand that. It wasn't a good idea to phone like that, you know. She was quite rightly concerned, especially when you didn't call back.'

'I know it was wrong – that is why I didn't call again. I should not have phoned – it was stupid, but he had already left. It would not have helped for me to call again.'

Sofia shrugged and looked at him directly; her whole body language shouted hurt innocence. Even self-effacing Barry knew that she was hitting on him, hoping to get him on side against Jess.

Before his face reddened completely he opened the door on to the deck and went out to Jess.

'If you want to know everything then come in now and be nice,' he whispered. 'One wrong word and she'll be gone and you won't be able to stop her. So, be nice, invite her to stay and we have our bait. Okay?'

Jess opened her mouth but before she could speak, he raised his fingers to his lips. 'Sshhh, think before you speak. Pearl will go ape when she hears about this . . . can you just imagine it? Play the game and I'll have CJ back here by Christmas for you.'

Jess and Sara walked back into the house and smiled through gritted teeth.

'I'll make us all a drink,' Sara said pleasantly.

'And you can tell me all about CJ. I'm sorry I was so

angry. It's Sheldon I'm angry at really, not you.' As Jess sat down beside her, Sofia smiled in relief.

Brad Walden was actually starting to enjoy himself and for the first time in many years he felt alive. Way back when, he wouldn't have given the loud and brassy Enid a second glance, but now, with his self-confidence non-existent, Enid was pulling him together, albeit unwittingly.

He had been selective with the information he had shared with Enid, but she seemed to be enjoying the hunt for Sheldon Patterson. In fact, she was proving a very good detective because, unlike Brad, her brain hadn't been addled by years of substance and alcohol abuse.

'You want to get that cough checked out, Brad, it's real bad.' Enid looked at him as he hacked and hacked.

'I'm okay. I had a real bad bout of flu before I came down here. It'll clear.'

'You need some antibiotics, you seem sick to me.' Her face told him she understood more than she was saying.

'I'm fine. Let's get back to Mr Patterson.'

'Okay. We've tried the random search. Nothing. Now you say his family is big in real estate – maybe that's what he's doing here? Maybe Momma's bought him a new toy! How about we check out the realtors that sell top of the range? That'll be a start. Jeez, I'm really having fun here.'

'Yeah,' Brad smiled. 'Me too, Enid. Let's go check out some realtors. What time does your shift start?'

'Free day, free two days . . . free however many days you want.'

'You'll lose your job.'

'No way. There's no one else in town that can crunch roaches like me, and also my brother owns the motel and he's real scared of me!'

Laughing, they walked off down the road arm-in-arm to Enid's car. Brad was suddenly optimistic about finding Sheldon Patterson and, more importantly, Jess's son.

Sheldon was pacing the floor in panic. He knew that, this time, there was nowhere to turn. He couldn't face the thought of telling his mother, nor did he want to confront Antonio. Not yet.

Picking up the phone he called Antonio. Again no answer at home, again he answered his mobile.

'Antonio. How did it go? Did you get anywhere with her?'

'Jeez, this is a hard one, my friend, but I'm doing my best for you. The girl is insistent you raped her. I don't know, tell me what you remember.'

'No, you tell me first what happened in the club, after you paid the girl to dance for me.' It was difficult for Sheldon not to make any accusations to Antonio but he knew he had to play it tight to his chest if he wanted to dig his way out of the trap into which he had walked so willingly.

'You said you were going home with her, then . . . Mmm, I have to think.' As Antonio feigned thought Sheldon steamed. 'I thought you meant to go home because you got up and left. I didn't see anything more. I guessed you were meeting her outside the club, as the girls can't date clubbers, not officially. That is as much as I know.'

'So what you're saying is that you think I could have

attacked her? Was I still on my feet? Was I falling down drunk? You must have noticed.'

'No, man, you looked fine to me but then we weren't taking too much notice. We were having a ball and stayed till late.'

'So? Do you believe her?'

'Don't ask me that. How do I know what went on? Why not just pay her off and put it down to experience. Shit happens.'

Sheldon was clenching his fist. He wanted to scream and shout at the man who he had thought was a friend, and he desperately wanted to smash him to a pulp. But he knew he couldn't. There had to be another way to get back at the pair of them. He certainly had no intention of handing over a quarter of a million dollars to them.

'Not to me it doesn't, Antonio. I'm going to the cops. Let her try and prove it – let her prove that she was with me.'

Antonio sighed. 'I didn't want to tell you this, but she said she has proof.'

'What proof can she have? It was just her and me, and I know you'll stand by me, won't you, Antonio?'

'Of course, but I think it would be better to pay her off and put it behind you. Next time, I'll take better care of you. I should have gone with you when you left the club. I'm sorry.' Antonio sounded genuinely concerned and for a moment Sheldon wondered if he had misjudged him.

'I'll have to think about exactly how I'm going to play this. Have you got her details?'

'Just a phone number.'

'That will do for now. Thanks, Antonio, I appreciate your support.'

'No problem, my friend, no problem. I'll call in later and we can decide where we're going from here.'

Sheldon replaced the phone angrily and carried on pacing.

He wondered if he should just pack up, go back to LA and hope for the best. But if he did, he wasn't going to give his mother any advance warning. He and CJ would just turn up on the doorstep. If she thought a pregnant Sofia was a problem then he could only imagine what she would make of his current predicament.

A quarter of a million dollars! There was no way he could lay his hands on that amount of cash without asking his mother. No, he decided, paying them wasn't an option. He wouldn't give them the satisfaction of ripping him off like that.

There had to be another way.

Al! The name flashed into his brain. Al. His mother's pet gorilla. Suddenly there was a way out for him to focus on, but first he wanted to suss out Laura Howardson. Providing, of course, that that was her real name.

He called the first name on a list of private investigators that he had torn from the phone book.

'I'm being blackmailed,' he explained curtly. 'I want to know who, what, when, where and why. The lot. I'll give you everything I have on both of them, then you do the rest. Forget the cost, just get the information, preferably today or even yesterday!'

There was no way that Sheldon was up to going into work. His head was still thumping and he felt physically sick every time he tried to remember exactly what had happened but couldn't.

For the next couple of days Sheldon smiled and played friends with Antonio who smiled and played friends back while at the same time trying to persuade him to pay the money.

The more he refused, the harder Antonio pushed and it took all Sheldon's willpower not to admit what he knew. But he had to wait.

Two flights were booked to LA in four days' time. He was going to get out of Miami, he was going to take CJ home for Christmas, and if Antonio pushed him then Al would just have to deal with him. Permanently.

'Surely he wouldn't be that dumb?' Brad was bewildered.

'Is it dumb? Maybe he thinks everyone else is dumb.'

Brad and Enid had been checking out all the real-estate offices they could find, to no avail until Brad picked up a selection of local free papers.

'Surely he wouldn't set up a business in his own name if he was on the run?'

'But if it's a family business then maybe he had no choice. It's worth checking.'

'How? No offence, Enid, but we can't go in there, they'd throw us straight out. Look at the properties they're advertising. Millions of dollars – do we look like we could be interested?'

'Okay. We could follow him. What does he look like?'

'I've seen a photo, I reckon I'll know him if I see him.'

'Are you in love with this Jess woman, Brad?' The question came clean out of the blue and took Brad completely by surprise.

'No way!' Genuinely shocked by the question, he laughed. 'Oh jeez, no way. She is way out of my league, but it's not like that anyway. She was real good to me and I want to repay her. That's it. End of story. If you met her you'd know what I mean.'

'Yoh!' Enid stepped back and held both her hands up. 'Just a question, don't snap my head off. You coming back to mine for a good meal? You need feeding up, you're all skin and bone. I do a mean fried chicken.'

'What about Sheldon Patterson?'

'He can wait till the morning, honey. He won't be going nowhere tonight. If it *is* him, that is.' Leaning forward she laughed, a long, loud and humorous laugh that echoed around the motel room and then kissed him full on the lips.

Brad awoke next morning with a smile on his face and leaning over, looked silently at Enid who was snoring loudly beside him. Sex had been off his mind for so many years that when Enid had made the first move she had frightened him witless. Fear of the unknown, fear of failure and fear of her being turned off by his abused and skeletal body had combined to turn him into a quivering wreck gasping for a drink.

But it hadn't been like that. She had been gentle and understanding and made him feel almost good about himself. It certainly hadn't been a complete success, but Enid had chosen to ignore his initial failure with a laugh, a joke about crushed bones and a takeout pizza.

The next attempt was short and sweet but it worked and they both collapsed in a heap and slept through the night.

He reached out and stroked her cheek gently until she woke.

'Hi there, loverboy. Again?'

He smiled at her. 'Breakfast first. I'm cooking.' He kissed her gently then eased himself painfully out of the bed. Snatching up his boxers and T-shirt he walked into the small kitchen and carefully exercised his aching bones. He was in pain but happy.

Enid lived at the back of the motel in a staff unit that consisted of two small rooms, a tiny utilitarian kitchen and a bathroom which were all unexpectedly clean and tidy.

Brad looked at himself in the mirror on the shelf. After the night before he expected to see a change, but his face was still as gaunt and drawn, and his shoulders were still hunched and bony. However, he could see a change in his eyes. There was an element of life that had been missing and his mouth turned up instead of down. Even his hands weren't quite as shaky.

For the first time Brad wondered if he had actually turned the corner. One day at a time, he told himself over and over again. One day at a time.

'Can I use your phone?'

'Sure, honey, who are you going to call?'

'Sheldon Patterson, of course!'

He dialled the number from the advert and waited.

'Can I speak with Sheldon Patterson, please?' he asked in his best voice.

'Mr Patterson isn't in the office this morning. Can I take your name and get him to call you?'

'No, I'll call back later, maybe even drop in. When are you expecting him?'

'At around two p.m. this afternoon.'

Brad put the phone down and raised his fist in the air. 'Yeeees! We have lift-off.'

'You going to call Jess?' Enid asked curiously.

'Not yet. I'm going to get that motherfucker myself.'

'I know what you're thinking and you can't do it.'

'Do what?'

'Snatch the kid. He doesn't know you, you'll scare the shit out of him and then get yourself arrested.'

'What do you suggest then?'

'We'll follow him, find out where he lives and then you'll call the mother. It's only right, Brad. Whatever else you do, you can't scare the kid.'

Brad smiled at her, his lips pressed tightly together to hide his disintegrating teeth. 'You're a good one, Enid.'

Chapter Thirty-Three

That afternoon Enid drove Brad downtown and they parked in a side street near to the office that they hoped was Sheldon's and waited, taking it in turns to check out the entrance.

At 2.30 someone looking like Sheldon roared up in a new sports car and skidded into the car park at the back. Brad watched carefully. He was 99 per cent certain it was the man he was looking for, but he needed to be sure.

'Enid,' he smiled, 'how good's your acting? Can you play an eccentric millionaire widow with her skinny but able bodyguard in tow?'

'Sounds like fun!' she laughed. 'Let's go home and play dressing up.'

Within the hour they were back and marching confidently into the office. All eyes turned in their direction.

'Well, hello there,' Enid drawled to the receptionist. 'I'm looking for a property, on the beach, triplex I think, about two million dollars. What have you got?'

It wasn't long before Sheldon and Daniel were entertaining the unlikely couple in an inner office with Enid telling the long complicated story of her huge widow's inheritance. Brad stood upright by the door with every opportunity to study Sheldon because neither Sheldon nor Daniel were taking any notice of him whatsoever.

'Excuse me, madam,' he interrupted politely after a viable interval, 'but can I remind you that you have another appointment?'

'Gee, is that the time?' She smiled widely and stood up. 'I'll be in touch when I've given these some thought.' Enid picked up the wad of property details and fanned herself with them then, turning gracefully, she swept out of the building with Brad following at a respectful distance. Until they got round the corner and both laughed themselves silly.

'Now we have to follow them.'

'No, Brad, now you have to call Jess. You've found him, let her deal with it, yeah?'

'As soon as I've found out where he's living. We'll just do that first and then I'll call her, okay?'

'Okay!'

The coffee shop over the street on the opposite corner didn't give them a clear view of the car-park entrance but it was less conspicuous than hanging around outside. Again they took it in turns to go outside for a cigarette and check around, constantly ready to run for the car if he came out.

And, many cups of coffee later, he did.

Brad and Enid bolted for the car as fast as they could and pulled out into the traffic several cars behind.

'Nice car,' Brad wheezed. 'Easy to follow.' The run to the car had taken its toll and he struggled to get air into his lungs.

'You have to see a doctor, Brad. You're real sick, aren't you? Are you going to tell me about it?'

'It's a long story and now isn't the time. Just stay on his tail.'

★　　　★　　　★

Sheldon was worried sick. The girl Laura had called him at work and at home several times. Although he didn't ask, he knew that the only way she could have got hold of both numbers was from Antonio. And all the while Antonio was acting the concerned friend and trying to persuade him to pay up.

He wondered how many times the pair of them had pulled the scam before. It certainly would explain Antonio's expensive lifestyle. It was a good con, because no man ever wanted to be accused of rape; whatever the circumstances, the allegations would always be there, haunting the accused.

So far, the investigator had found nothing criminal connected to either of them. He had told Sheldon it was early days but time was running out. Sheldon couldn't make up his mind whether to run back to California and hope they would forget about it or take Antonio on. But how? He had arranged to meet Antonio at his apartment that evening but he still wasn't sure how to play it.

At that moment he really wished he had stayed put in England with Jess and CJ. No pregnant Sofia to haunt him, no mother on his case and no Laura Howardson threatening to have him locked up for years.

Pulling into the private car park he noticed Antonio outside his building with Laura; they were both sitting in the sun on a long semi-circular marble seat with their legs stretched out casually in front of them. Looking as if they didn't have a care in the world. Sheldon was so incensed at the sight of them that he didn't notice Enid's old wreck of a car cruise to a stop on the edge of the visitors' parking area, nor did he notice Brad get out and saunter over in his direction.

'What's she doing here?' Sheldon snarled at Antonio.

'You weren't supposed to bring her here. It was meant to be just you and me.'

'She insisted.' He smiled and put a comforting arm around Sheldon's shoulder, just like an old friend. 'I thought maybe we could strike a deal to get you out of this mess. I really want to help, man. Come on, let's go up and talk – try to negotiate a deal. Better than a stretch inside as a rapist, yeah?'

As they started to walk to the entrance Sheldon suddenly lost control. All he could see was Antonio's sparkly smile and Laura's smirk enlarged before his eyes, and before he could stop himself, his fist flew out and cracked Antonio on the jaw, sending him sprawling across the manicured lawn.

'Don't give me this crap, you asshole. You think I'm that fucking stupid? I know you're behind this. Well, tough shit, now take your girlfriend and get out of here.'

'You're going to regret this. I'm telling you, it's you in the wrong, not me.' Antonio struggled to his feet. 'I tried to help you. Come on, Laura, we're going to the cops, we'll get this rapist locked up now.'

'You're blackmailing me!' Sheldon screeched. 'I never touched her and you know it.' He threw himself headfirst into Antonio's stomach and took him down.

'You just try and prove it!' Laura laughed as the two men slugged it out on the grass. 'Go on, call the cops and I'll show them the photos of what you did. Done deal, mister, now hand over the cash.'

Brad wandered across the grass with his cap pulled down low. 'Got a problem here, fellas?' he asked.

'Too right, this asshole's blackmailing me.' As soon as the words were out, Sheldon stopped. 'What the fuck's it to you?'

'Just passing, man.'

As Sheldon's attention was momentarily diverted, Antonio dipped his hand into his jacket pocket and Brad's Marine instincts took over. Before Antonio even registered him moving, Brad had the man in a headlock and his wrist in an iron grip.

'Drop it,' he muttered into his ear as the wail of sirens came closer. Antonio slowly let his fist open and a sparkling flickknife fell onto the grass. Brad picked it up, and shouted to Sheldon, 'Let's go, man – *now*.'

As Antonio and Laura scampered off towards the beach shouting obscenities, Sheldon scrambled to his feet and, with Brad in tow, darted inside the building and hopped into the lift.

As it rose up through the floors Sheldon looked quizzically at Brad. 'Weren't you in the office today?'

'Yeah,' he wheezed, 'I came in with my boss. I was just checking out a condo in this block for her when it all kicked off.' Brad leaned forward and put his hands on his knees as he struggled for breath.

'Lucky for me, huh?' Sheldon sighed.

'You could say that.'

The doors opened and Brad waited expectantly while Sheldon looked decidedly confused about what to do next.

'Do you want a drink? So I can thank you?'

'Sure, best to lay low for an hour or so, but not alcohol, I'll get fired. Coffee would be good.'

Sheldon's apartment was the kind of place Brad had dreamed of when he was a young man but he'd never even visited inside one before. He wandered around with his hands in his pockets taking in everything without appearing to. His eyes settled on a framed photograph. It was CJ, he was sure.

'That your kid?' he called to Sheldon.

'Yep.'

'He live with you?'

'Yep. He's due in from school soon but he has his own rooms with his nanny. I don't see too much of him.' Sheldon smiled and passed Brad a glass mug. 'Here's your coffee. I need something stronger after all that shit downstairs.'

'What's the deal with the knifeman outside?'

'Long, long story. I was real stupid and got set up by him and the whore. She wants cash or she's going to report me for rape. They set me up and I was stupid enough to let it happen.'

Brad could hardly contain his excitement. He had Sheldon Patterson cornered 100 per cent.

He took his coffee out onto the balcony that overlooked the beach and ocean and immediately Sheldon followed him. Brad knew it was just a matter of time before he had the whole story. Just a matter of time before he could call Jess and put her out of her misery, but he also had to keep Sheldon safe and well and away from Antonio. The last thing he needed was for Sheldon to do another disappearing act.

He felt guilty about leaving Enid outside but knew she would understand. He just hoped she would wait. Suddenly she was important to him.

He looked at Sheldon Patterson out of the corner of his eye. This was the man that he had heard so much about, the man he desperately wanted to find and now he was on his balcony and they were chatting like old friends. Everything about him shouted money. The clothes, the careful grooming of his hair and nails, not to mention the slightly arrogant swagger that was still there, despite the recent encounter.

Brad wondered how any man could treat his wife the way Sheldon Patterson had treated Jess, let alone someone who could easily afford to be generous to his abandoned wife. Perhaps Jess was right. Sheldon Patterson was a puppet whose strings were manipulated by his mother.

'How did you get to be a bodyguard? You don't look like one.' As Sheldon's voice seeped into his brain Brad had to shake his head to get back to where he was standing.

He smiled. 'That's why I'm good – nobody notices me. I was in the military.'

'We could offer you a job, you know,' Sheldon said. 'We need someone that good.'

'We?' Brad asked. 'Who's we?'

'The company. It's a family company – my mother and I own it but I run it. We've got offices all over. Miami is new to us, but we have several in California.'

'Sounds interesting.' Brad was still looking thoughtful, as if he was genuinely considering the offer when the loud ringing on the door made them both jump.

'Careful,' Brad warned Sheldon. 'That asshole may be back.'

They both went to the door and Sheldon peered through the spy-hole before sighing with relief and opening the door.

'It's okay, it's the porter.'

'A package for you, sir. It was dropped off downstairs.'

As soon as he closed the door Sheldon ripped open the large envelope. 'Jesus Christ,' he groaned. His face paled and he grabbed at the doorframe.

'What is it?'

'Nothing for you to worry about. It's none of your business,' Sheldon snapped. 'I don't know you.'

'Sure, no problem.' Brad shrugged his shoulders as if he wasn't in the least bit interested. 'I'll just get my jacket.'

'No, wait.' The defeat on Sheldon's face made Brad feel almost sympathetic. 'I'm sorry. It's from those two who were downstairs. It's photographs, incriminating photographs. Jeez, this is real bad. I am in *so* much trouble!'

Brad kept his face straight. *Yep,* he thought, *and you don't know the half of it. You'll be in even bigger trouble now that you've been found.*

'Do you want to show me? Or is it too personal?' Brad spoke softly as he revelled in his new, powerful role.

Sheldon thought for a moment and then handed them over. 'Get me out of this and you've got yourself the best paid job in security. I promise.'

Again Brad kept his face straight as he pulled out half a dozen blown-up colour photographs of Sheldon with Laura, Sheldon with Antonio, and Sheldon with both of them. The photos were excellent quality, almost professional in detail and focus. They were pure pornography and Sheldon didn't remember a thing.

'How did they get these? If you were supposed to be alone and raping her, then why would there be these photographs?'

'Look at the note. They've changed tack. I'm supposed to have assaulted her after Antonio left. See this one of her looking battered and bruised? I'm supposed to have done that as well. None of this will stand up in court, will it?'

'Nope, but they certainly won't do your reputation any good if they're made public, will they? Now it's a case of straightforward blackmail. You're in big trouble.'

'Can you help?'

'Yes, sir, I'm sure I can help. Just you leave it with me.'

Brad hung around until he got the opportunity to slip just one of the photos inside his jacket. By the time he left, Brad had been with Sheldon Patterson for over three hours and knew everything there was to know.

His first thought was to phone Jess and bring her up to speed.

His second was for Enid. He shielded his eyes from the sun as he left the building and was pleased out of all proportion to see her car with Enid still behind the wheel reading a magazine.

Chapter Thirty-Four

'I am sorry,' Sofia sobbed. 'I don't know what to do. I did not want this, I did not want to upset you. I came to see Kay for help.'

Grimfaced, Jess and Sara looked at each other. Both were furious but they each realised that nothing was to be gained by ripping into Sofia, much as they wanted to.

'You'll have to go and see Pearl. She'll do something for you – maybe she'll pay you off,' Jess stated indifferently.

'Sheldon will say it's not his baby, I know he will. You saw the letter.'

'Then you'll just have to go home to Spain. You can't stay here.'

'I could go back to England, to Carla.' Her voice was childishly expectant.

'Don't be silly. Who's going to want a pregnant nanny? You had a bloody good job with Carla and Toby – whatever possessed you?' Suddenly Jess found herself taking on a mothering role to the girl in front of her, who looked like a child herself.

'I don't know,' she gulped and looked from Jess to Barry to Sara, hoping for a glimmer of support and sympathy. 'I was stupid but Sheldon has to pay also. I will stay in California until the baby is born and then I will have a test to prove it is his. He will have to help.'

'I doubt it, Sofia. Look what he did to me, and I'm married to him.' Jess laughed dryly.

'No! He will pay. I will make him pay.'

Sofia's dark eyes shone with anger and for a split second Jess admired her courage. She was only a young girl, after all, and Sheldon had lured her away with promises of a life she could never have anticipated before that. She wondered how she herself would have reacted to Sheldon if he had been married already? She had been more than willing to believe everything he told her about Kay; no doubt he had told similar tales to Sofia.

'I'll come with you to see Pearl, if it'll help.'

'No, Jess,' Barry interjected sharply. 'You can't – you mustn't let her know you're here. Sheldon will never come back then.'

'Yes, but if Sofia goes to see her alone, then Pearl will tell him anyway – catch twenty-two.'

'I think, for the moment, the best thing is for Sofia to stay here. Then if Sheldon does come home, you and she can go together – you can back each other up. A rather nice little Christmas gift for him and his mother.' Barry smiled and paused before continuing. 'And if he doesn't, then both of you have to see an attorney here – safety in numbers, so to speak. Jess, I know it wasn't what you wanted but surely now, after hearing all this, you have to think about filing for divorce here, in California.'

'I can't divorce him if I can't find him, can I? Anyway, I don't want to talk about this, not now.' Jess nodded her head in the direction of Sofia who was almost crouching in her chair looking completely dejected. Or acting completely dejected? Jess wasn't completely sure.

Barry smiled an acknowledgement and moved the subject away. 'Have you rung Kay and Ryan to see how they feel about yet another extra house guest?'

'No, I'll do it in a while. I'm going for a walk. I need to think this through, it's all too much. I really think I want to go to Miami.'

'For what? To walk the streets on the off-chance that you might just bump into Sheldon? Or even CJ? Come on, Jess.'

'I'm going out.' Jess headed for the door.

Barry held out his hand. 'I'm coming with you then.'

'What about her?' Jess glanced over at a silent Sofia.

'I'll keep an eye on her.' Sara smiled grimly. 'I'd like to have a chat with her alone.'

'Take it easy on her, she really looks shattered,' Barry whispered cautiously to Sara.

'I will. I'm just going to chat. Honestly. Come on, I could be her grandmother almost. Now *that's* scary.'

As they were talking the phone started ringing in the background.

'I bet that's Kay. What shall I tell her? She'll think I've gone mad.'

'Just tell her the truth.'

Jess snatched up the phone. 'Hello?'

'Is that Jess?' A familiar voice came down the line. 'It's Brad. Guess what, I'm in Miami and I've found CJ for you!'

Jess couldn't speak, she couldn't even breathe and as her hands started to shake Barry took the phone from her.

Five minutes later, after Barry had made a note of every bit of information he could elicit from Brad, all hell broke out in the Santa Monica beach house.

As Jess and Barry rushed to the airport to catch a flight

to Miami, Sara stayed behind with Sofia. The girl had wanted to go with them to confront Sheldon on her own behalf, but Jess was adamant that this was going to be her moment alone. It was far more important to get CJ than to end up in a free-for-all.

'But what about me?' she asked Sara. 'I am pregnant with his baby, I should be going also.' Her face was a picture of misery as she looked at Sara.

Sara's initial concern was for her daughter. It had to be after all that she had been through, but her heart went out to the young girl sitting in front of her with her life in ruins.

'Sofia, we know where he is now, and once Jess has CJ then Sheldon doesn't have to sneak around any more. You can catch up with him anytime.' Sara felt almost sympathetic to the girl who, in her eyes, was little more than a child herself. 'I know you don't want to hear this, but do you not think a termination might be a good idea under the circumstances? You're so young.'

'I know about children, I can look after them.' Indignantly she pulled herself up straighter and stared at Sara. 'This is to be my child, mine and Sheldon's. I cannot kill it.'

'Oh Sofia, Sofia.' Sara shook her head sadly. 'Surely you can see from all this exactly what Sheldon is like? Do you think he's going to stand by you? As soon as you leave America you'll be history.'

'Then I shall stay here. I shall stay here and *make* him look after us.'

'But you can't stay – you don't have a visa, do you? You'll have to go home and then that will be it for you.'

The tears that were filling up Sofia's eyes suddenly overflowed but she didn't wipe them; it was as if by ignoring them slowly sliding down her face that they didn't exist.

'He said we would always be together. He told me he wanted many children and that Jess wouldn't give them to him.'

'And you believed him?' Sara looked at her incredulously and then sighed. 'I suppose you did. I can understand that. Everyone seems to believe Sheldon Patterson and his mother.'

Sofia didn't answer so Sara continued. 'What about your family? Will they help you?'

'No!' She spoke loud and clear. 'My family cannot know this has happened. They will never speak to me again. I have disgraced them, Sheldon has disgraced me.'

Sara smiled. 'I have to agree with you there! Oh well, we'll leave it for the moment. Let's just see what happens when Jess and Barry get to Miami. Maybe you'll get the opportunity to talk to Sheldon soon and sort something out.'

On the spur of the moment Sara went over and sat beside the girl then hugged her tight. 'Come on, let's go and sit outside. I'll make some tea.'

As she took the tea out and sat with Sofia in silence, Sara heard a whirr. She stood up and looked around, then heard another one. Glancing in the direction of the sound she caught sight of someone across the street with what looked like a professional camera pointed right at them. As she looked directly at the man holding the camera she saw him turn very slowly and start shooting the view across the beach.

Something wasn't right, but she wasn't sure what. Why would someone be taking photographs of them?

'Pearl!' Sara sighed.

'Pardon?' Puzzled, Sofia looked at her.

'It's okay, Sofia. I've just realised how Pearl knew everything that was going on. I bet someone is following Jess and Barry as we speak. Bugger!'

First Sara tried phoning Jess's rental mobile but it was switched off so she flicked through the notepad beside the phone where Barry had been making notes and found a contact number for Brad at his motel.

But he wasn't available. Sara left a message for him to call her urgently. She knew that if Pearl spoke to Sheldon he would be off again with CJ. She also knew that Jess would be devastated beyond belief if she got there to find the pair of them gone.

'Sofia, you haven't a clue what you have got yourself into,' she murmured, almost to herself. 'Same as Jess didn't, and the same as Kay didn't. You have to think very carefully about this. The whole Patterson family are either mad or bad or both.'

Sofia managed a watery smile. 'Yes, I know that. But he said he loved me, he said he would provide for me.'

'And I'm sure he meant it at the moment he said it. Now you have to look on it as a lucky escape. If you have the baby then you have to make sure you go through all the right procedures. We'll help you.'

'Jess will not help me. She hates me.'

'Of course she does at the moment, but in the long run your baby will be a brother or sister to CJ and I know Jess would want them to know each other.' Sara smiled at her. 'We'll sort something out!'

It was a while later, long enough for Sara to get really nervous, when the phone rang. It was Brad again.

'Jess and Barry are on their way but I think they may have been followed to the airport. Can you keep an eye on Sheldon and CJ? Make sure they don't do a runner.' She paused. 'And by the way, we can never thank you enough for what you've done. You're a good man.'

Brad listened as Sara spoke and had to blink back the tears before Enid saw them.

'You okay, Brad?' Enid asked from across the room.

'Sure, but I got to go out. That asshole Sheldon may be about to do a runner before Jess gets there.'

'I'll drive you. Now you take it easy, you're sick and he's not. Don't you go getting yourself beat up. You were lucky last time.'

'I'm just gonna watch the building, make sure he doesn't take CJ anywhere. You okay about driving me again?'

Laughing, she jumped over the coffee table and kissed him full on the lips. 'No problem, honey, no problem. This sure beats sitting at that desk reading magazines all day.'

'I don't know how I'm going to hold on to him for all that time. Even if they got on the flight now it'll still be hours before they get here. It takes about half a day from California. Jeez, how can I keep hold of him for that long?'

Brad could feel the panic washing over him. Instant and spur-of-the-moment events he could deal with, things he had to think about first made him jumpy. His hands started to shake and beads of sweat bubbled up on his forehead just at the thought of it. For the first time in days he desperately wanted a drink, just to help him get through it.

Enid looked at him, concern written all over her face. 'This isn't your war, Brad. You don't have to do it if it's going to make you sicker. You've done your bit, you found them.'

'I want to do it. I have to do it, for Jess, and for myself.'

'Then we'll do it together, honey. Somehow we'll do it.'

Like a madwoman Enid drove her car in and out of the busy traffic to get to the condo block that was a world away from where she lived. But she got them there and again parked on the outer edge of the car park, out of sight of the porter of the block but within sight of the main entrance.

Sheldon's car wasn't anywhere to be seen.

'I hope they haven't gone already. We've got no way of checking him out.'

'We'll wait and see, that's all we can do right now.'

Pearl Patterson could feel everything closing in on her. As if it wasn't bad enough that Jess was in cahoots with Kay, now it seemed as if that Spanish girl was there as well. None of it made any sense.

When Al had phoned in with the information about another girl at the beach house, Pearl had ordered him to get the photos to her instantly. She was on the verandah waiting for him as she tried to decide what to do for the best. For herself, of course.

After a few hiccups with his interfering family, her desperately desired relationship with Hank the billionaire was back on track and she was on the verge of persuading him up the aisle. The last thing she needed was a huge family scandal to derail it, and she knew that the deadly combination of Kay, Jess and Sofia could do just that. Each of them individually she could handle – but all three? And that was without the mother, the lawyer and Kay's husband. She knew Kay and Ryan were away in New York for the holiday but she also knew that they would hotfoot it back to gleefully watch the floorshow if everything kicked off.

When Al turned up with the digital photos Pearl's worst fear was realised. It was the Spanish girl chatting away to Jess's mother.

'And you say your guys followed Jess and her lawyer to the airport?'

'Yes, ma'am. They took a flight to Miami.'

'Oh, for God's sake. This is getting worse by the minute.'

'Do you want me to get someone down there to meet them in Miami? Follow them?'

Pearl thought about it then shook her head. 'Not sure. Set it up and I'll let you know what I want you to do. You can go now, but I want prints of all the shots right away.'

'Yes, ma'am. I'll bring them back in about an hour.'

After he had gone Pearl changed into her swimsuit and slid into the heated pool to relax and think. She realised Jess must have got wind of where Sheldon and CJ were living. She rationalised that they probably didn't have an exact address but even if they did, they still had to get there first.

The whole episode was driving her crazy, her son was driving her crazy. It had all got way out of hand.

Elegantly she swam breast-stroke up and down the pool with her head out of the water as she pondered the easiest route to take. Up and down she swam, thinking and waiting impatiently for Al to get back with the prints. Pulling herself delicately out of the pool she wrapped herself in an enormous fluffy white towel just as Al arrived back.

'I've been thinking about our situation, Al, and I don't think you need send anyone to Miami. I'm going to call

Sheldon and tell him to move back to the company apartment. They can lie low there for a while and then come back to LA and deal with the custody after the Larkins have gone back to England.'

'The Larkins?' Al put his head on one side as he tried to figure out what she was talking about.

'Yes, Al, the Larkins, a none too clever English family immortalised in English literature as . . .' She stared at the none too clever man in front of her looking bewildered. 'Never mind, Al, it doesn't matter. Just leave all this to me for the time being.'

Pearl picked up the phone and dialled Sheldon's number in Miami.

Chapter Thirty-Five

Brad and Enid kept up their watch on Sheldon's building. They saw CJ go out with an older woman and Brad quickly took off in pursuit but they only went for a walk to the adjoining play area and back.

Then Sheldon pulled up with a wheelspin and went inside, looking slyly from side to side checking all around, but despite Brad and Enid being ready to roll, none of them came out again.

The day ticked on and it was getting closer and closer to the time that Jess should arrive, but there was no more movement for another couple of hours until Antonio turned up and swaggered through the main doors.

Brad knew he had no choice but to follow him in, not for Sheldon's sake but for CJ and Jess. Antonio equalled trouble and he knew for certain that the little boy was in the apartment.

Fast and silent, Brad made his way around the edge of the car park towards a round stone pillar that was part of the edifice and tucked himself behind it, before peering round to see Antonio disappearing out of sight towards the lifts.

After allowing enough time for him to get on board

and start going up, Brad got himself together enough to swagger confidently into the vast lobby and around the security desk looking for all the world as if he belonged in a building like that.

Antonio was already out of sight so Brad pushed the button and waited for the next lift. The doors opened on the top floor just in time for Brad to see Antonio disappearing inside. He tried to listen but the solid wood double doors were soundproof so he made a snap decision and rang the bell several times.

'Just called by to talk about the job you offered me. Is it a good time or would you prefer me to come back later?'

Sheldon looked completely bewildered and Brad could see him trying to figure out exactly what was going on. First Antonio and then Brad.

'Why now? Are you in this with him?' Sheldon said suspiciously and then flipped his head round to where Antonio was standing just inside the door. 'That's twice now you've both turned up here at the same time.'

'Yeah, right, man, like I associate with that kind of lowlife.' Brad turned as if to leave. 'Forget it. See you around.'

'No. Come in, you can show me what you're made of.' Brad could see he was thinking safety in numbers but before he could move a step Antonio was there blocking the doorway.

'Fuck off right now, asshole. Me and Mr Patterson have got business, private business, nothing to do with you.' Antonio moved forward to edge Brad out but he stood his ground.

'Not that private, *asshole*. I know all about it already. Now move.'

'So he told you he was a rapist? Did he tell you he

raped a dancer? Just because she's a lap dancer he thought he could fuck her and get away with it.'

Brad smiled and moved forward. 'Whatever. Now I either go past you or through you – your choice, my friend.'

He was bluffing, of course. Brad had accepted that on a one-to-one where he didn't have the advantage of surprise, he would be no match for the fit young man in front of him but there was a chance Antonio believed the bodyguard bullshit he had previously spun.

With his eyes still firmly on Brad, Antonio moved aside.

'I swear that if this plane went any slower it would drop clean out of the sky. How much longer can it take?'

Once again Jess was in the air on a flight that seemed to take for ever. For a change, luck had been on their side and they had caught a flight almost immediately despite the vigorous security checks at the airport. And once again Barry had come up trumps and paid for the tickets, leaving Jess to mentally add another big chunk to her debt to him. But thoughts of what she owed to whom were far from her mind once they were in the air.

'Do you think this really is it? Do you think I'm going to find CJ this time?'

'I'm sure of it, and it just goes to show that life really is full of surprises. Who'd have thought that your Brad would come up trumps like this? I'm amazed.'

'Me, too – how on earth did he do it? I mean, there was so little to go on and while we hummed and haahed he just went off and did it. I owe him so much.'

'And he owes you, don't forget. He told me he was just returning the favour.' Barry reached his arm up and wrapped it around her shoulders. 'Who's Enid?' he asked.

'Haven't a clue, why do you ask?'

'He said several times "me and Enid" – seems like she's helping him. She's got a car.'

'Oh well, let's hope they can stay on Sheldon's tail until we get there. God, I hope this works out. I hope he doesn't get wind of us and disappear again. I want to see CJ so much it hurts, but I also want to see Sheldon and ask him why he did this to me. And then I'm going to castrate him with a rusty knife and fork.' Jess tried to smile but wasn't entirely successful.

'Well, hopefully you'll get your chance very soon, but I really don't want to watch.'

Jess looked at Barry tearfully. Was it all about to end? She wanted to believe it but was scared to; there was suddenly so much at stake.

Barry pulled her closer to him. 'Not long now.'

'I know, and I'm scared, more scared than at any time in the last few months. It's nearly Christmas and then it will be the New Year. I can't imagine how it's going to be for me and CJ. I'm nearly thirty-seven years old and I thought my life was pretty much mapped out, and now I have no idea about the future.'

'Just so long as I'm in it somewhere.' As he looked at her Jess could see the insecurity he was feeling written all over his face.

'Oh, I think you will be, I hope you will be.' Jess leaned in towards him. 'Anyway, I must owe you a small fortune so I can't disappear off into the night or you'll have the debt collectors after me, won't you?'

As the plane came in to land Jess's level of nervous excitement reached an all-time peak that had her bordering on mania. She tried to breathe slowly to calm herself down but she didn't know what she'd do if things didn't go as she and Barry anticipated. So much was hinging on it.

The stand-off between Sheldon, Antonio and Brad was an equilateral triangle as each took his seats in a position where he could watch the others.

'I don't know what you're doing here again, Antonio. I told you there's no deal. Oh, and just in passing, you're dead as well.'

A slow smile spread over Antonio's face as he leaned back and crossed his legs. 'But Sheldon,' he drawled sarcastically, 'I was only trying to help you. You got yourself in this mess, *my friend*.'

'Do I look that stupid? Have I got asshole written on my forehead? No, Antonio *my friend*, it's you who's stupid. You haven't learned that no one fucks around with the Pattersons. You screwed yourself by sending those photographs. Anyone with half a brain can see they're a set-up.'

Antonio threw his head back and laughed. 'Sheldon *my friend*, I know nothing about photographs. Did someone sneak up on us and take them? Maybe this gentleman here, perhaps? I don't know. You'll have to go to the police and let them authenticate them, won't you?'

'And the blackmail? You know as well as I do that I never raped that girl. I was drugged and set up by both of you, that's when you took the photos, so how could I have raped her with you in the room snapping away?'

As Antonio smiled Brad realised exactly what a reptile he really was.

'No, no, no, you've got it all wrong. That was a different night, don't you remember? We both took Laura back to the hotel on another night – you arranged for the camera, right? That was the night you booked the room again and planned to take her back, alone, to viciously and violently rape her.'

Sheldon tried to laugh it off but his temper was bubbling away just under the surface, as he looked at the man who he had thought was his friend.

'So you're saying she willingly went to a hotel with me to be raped? You'll have to do better than that.'

'How was she to know you would get violent? How was she to anticipate that you are a sadistic little pervert who gets his rocks off beating up on women? No, let's face it, you're screwed, so you may as well pay up now and we'll forget about it all.' Again the smug smile as Antonio flexed his shoulders.

'Not a dime,' Sheldon ripped back. 'What have I got to lose? I'm a businessman not a fucking rock star. Who cares about me and a cheap hooker?'

Fascinated, Brad watched the exchange. At least while they were batting words back and forth like kids arguing over whose turn it was to hold the ball, it was buying him time, giving him a legitimate reason for being there.

'But Laura is not a hooker, she is my girlfriend. You took advantage of my girlfriend!' Antonio almost sounded plausible as he paused to let the information sink in before continuing, 'And what about your wife? What if she finds out? You'll never get to keep your kid then.'

'Like that would break my heart.'

Brad went on alert as Antonio stood up. 'There's still your mother. Does Mommy's Boy want her to see what her precious son gets up while she's not around?'

Sheldon's face changed. It was only a slight flicker but enough to cause Antonio to smile and Brad to move forward to the edge of his seat expectantly.

'You are really pissing me off now,' Sheldon hissed. 'No deal! Whatever you try and pull.'

'Okay, man, if that's the way you want to play it. I'll tell Laura to make the complaint. It'll cost you millions . . . trust me.'

'In your dreams, you slimy little spic.'

In a flash Antonio was across the room to Sheldon.

'Jesus Christ, not again,' Brad sighed. 'You two trying to finish me off?'

Antonio almost reached Sheldon and then, in one quick movement, he pulled out a switchblade and flicked it open. Sheldon and Brad froze.

'Now let's really talk. Let's talk hard cash.'

'You're right, let's talk,' Brad said, trying to calm the situation. 'Come on, cool it both of you before someone gets hurt. Let's find a way out of this before it's too late.'

Brad was suddenly scared. Not of Antonio and his stupid knife and certainly not of Sheldon who obviously had no idea how to handle the situation. No, Brad was scared for himself in the situation he was in. If it all kicked off then the chances were he would end up getting the blame. Sheldon and Antonio were both lying, cheating con artists, neither better nor worse than the other, so who better to lay it on than the alcoholic down and out with a grudge against society?

Neither of them moved. Both had their eyes firmly set on each other until the ringing of the phone momentarily distracted them both. As Sheldon went to answer it Antonio took a casual step forward and, with the blade that was open in his hand, cut the wire to the socket.

'That was just fucking ridiculous.' Sheldon looked incredulous.

'No, man, it was a necessity. We need some peace here to discuss my financial settlement, *my friend.*'

'Okay, unless you back off each other I'm leaving,' Brad said firmly. 'You two can kill each other if that's what you want, but I'm out of here now.'

He looked over at the wall clock and tried to calculate the time that Jess and Barry would arrive. Another couple of hours at most. He didn't want Antonio to be there with a knife in his hand to greet them and he certainly didn't want Sheldon lying in a pool of blood.

'Come on, man, put it away.' He directed his gaze at Antonio. 'You're getting in too deep for a few lousy dollars. Ripping him off is one thing, but cutting him? That'll get you locked away for the rest of your life. Give me the blade.'

Antonio thought about it for several long seconds before clicking it shut and returning it to his pocket. 'Nobody calls me a spic. I'm telling you, say it again and I'll slit you from ear to ear. Understand?'

'Yeah, okay, I'm sorry I called you a spic but you're still a miserable hooker-fucking blackmailer,' Sheldon said contemptuously.

Brad expected it to start again but Antonio merely smiled. He didn't seem to mind being called that.

'Maybe. What's the deal?'

'Ten grand for the photos and negatives and a signed agreement that there are no copies.' Sheldon threw the words across the room.

'No way,' Antonio snarled. 'Two hundred and fifty grand it is. Two fifty or Laura goes public.'

'Okay, go public. Like I care any more – I'm going back to LA.'

Once the knife was away Brad started to enjoy himself. At least he was there. As far as he knew, Sheldon had no idea that Jess was on her way and it was entertaining to watch two grown men fighting like kids.

He stood up. 'I'm going to leave you to it, while I go down to make a call to my boss and have a smoke. No knives, okay? Or I'll call the cops.'

Neither of them took any notice so he slipped out. Dropping a disposable lighter in the edge of the frame so the door couldn't quite close he ensured he would be able to get back in again. Providing neither of them spotted it.

He banged on the car window, making Enid jump. 'I need a break. They're both off their heads in there.'

'And the kid?'

'Haven't seen him – seems like there's a separate area for him and the nanny. What sort of life is that? Everything that money can buy but no mother and no father. The guy's crazy, I'm telling you.'

'You going back up?'

Brad smiled at the concern in Enid's voice. 'Not if I can help it. The cavalry should be here soon. You got the photo?'

'Yessir! Ready and waiting, but all I really want to do is shred it. It's disgusting.'

'Well, it was the pick of the bunch!' Brad laughed and brushed the beads of perspiration off his brow, trying at the same time to ignore the other signs of alcohol withdrawal. He watched Enid as she pretended not to notice.

'You don't think he's likely to run before they get here, then?'

'Seems not, but who knows? I couldn't stay in there for ever, it'd look too suspicious. Anyway, right now he's got other things on his mind. Like his bank account.'

'Good. The little shit deserves a few sleepless nights.'

Chapter Thirty-Six

After much foot-hopping and finger-tapping from an impatient Jess, they cleared the arrivals hall and jumped straight into a cab.

Throughout the drive Jess was silent as her nerves jangled so violently she was sure Barry would hear. So near yet so far was all she could think. She didn't dare contemplate the best scenario; she could only consider the worst.

Trying to picture her son, she wondered how much he might have changed in nearly four months. Had he missed her? Had he been happy with his father? And worst of all, supposing he wanted to stay with him? What if CJ didn't want to go with her?

Her superstitions made it impossible for her to put her thoughts into words so she scrunched herself up in the corner of the car far away from Barry, wishing she was alone. She knew it was a selfish thought but she couldn't help it.

The traffic was stacked all the way to South Beach and the journey seemed to take for ever but eventually they pulled up outside the building Brad had directed them to.

As she threw herself out of the door ready to run inside she stopped in her tracks when someone came up to her. 'Jess!' Uncomprehending, she looked at the man beside her, the man who knew who she was. It took a few moments to register. '*Brad?*'

'Sure is.' He smiled shyly.

'Good God, I'd never have recognised you. You look great.' Jess reached forward and kissed him on both cheeks.

Brad kept his arms by his side and looked at his feet. 'They're in there, both of them.'

'Are you sure it's them? You can't have made a mistake?'

He shook his head. 'No mistake, ma'am, I'm sure of it. They're in there unless they skydived out. I've been here since your mom phoned. We've been watching both exits.'

'Mum phoned you? Why?'

'Too complicated to explain. Are you going in there now?'

Barry came alongside and held out his hand. 'I'm Barry Halston, Jess's lawyer.'

Brad shook his hand. 'I left his apartment door ajar so that you can just get in, but beware the sleazeball, he's real mean.'

'How did you get to fix the door open?'

'Still too complicated, I'll explain later.' He smiled. 'Okay? Then let's go. I'll keep a check on the sleaze that's in there with him.'

Relieved to see the lighter still wedged in the door, Brad carefully pushed it open.

'What are you back for, asshole?' Antonio sneered. 'Don't you know when you're not fucking wanted?'

Brad held his hand out. 'Sheldon's got some more

visitors who really want to see him, though I doubt he wants to see them!' As he pushed the door wide and stood back to let Jess and Barry through, Brad was certain he would never again enjoy a moment so much.

Sheldon sat open-mouthed as Jess flew across the room and started beating him about the head with both fists until Barry firmly pulled her off.

'You bastard, I hate you! Where's CJ? Where is he? I want my son!'

'That's tough, Jess. He's not here.' Sheldon was cowering in his chair with his arms protecting his head.

'Oh yes he is,' Brad laughed. 'Through that door, down the stairs into the nanny's den. CJ lives there, tucked away out of sight and out of mind!'

As Jess ran through, Sheldon jumped up but Brad and Barry both blocked his way.

'Stay right there,' Barry commanded.

'Who the fuck are you?'

'Your wife's lawyer. We're here to collect CJ.'

'You're not taking my son anywhere.'

'Oh yes, we are. If you've got a problem then take it to the court,' Barry stated emphatically.

Antonio was silently open-mouthed as he watched the surreal events going on around him. Brad went over to him and put his mouth to his ear. 'Beat it, man, *now*. This is your one and only chance.'

'No way. I want my cash and I'm staying right here until I get it. I don't give a fuck about their domestics.'

'I said beat it. I'm FBI and this is a kidnapping investigation. Get your butt out of here now and I'll forget I ever saw you.'

Barely had Brad finished speaking when Antonio was across the room and out of the door.

おはよ

Jess ran two at a time down the stairs to the lower level and started pushing open doors and screaming, 'CJ! CJ! Where are you, CJ? Mummy's here. *CJ?*'

Within seconds a small whirlwind of a child spun out of a door and wrapped himself around her legs.

'Mummy, Mummy.' The little boy burst into tears; big gulping sobs escaped his throat and she tried to peel him off to pick him up. But he clung fast.

'It's okay, Mummy's come to take you home.' Jess opened her eyes and for the first time noticed the woman standing inside the room. 'Who are you?'

'I'm Isabella, CJ's nanny.'

'You're not going to stop me taking him.' Jess started to back away but found it hard with CJ wrapped around her knees.

'I don't want to,' the woman smiled happily. 'This is what I have been wishing for CJ, he has been so unhappy and his father is a pig. I would have contacted you myself if I'd known where to find you! You want a witness in court then use me, I'm your woman.'

Jess carefully unwrapped the child from her legs and, kneeling down, looked at him closely. 'You have grown so much – and just look at all those gorgeous freckles! Just like Mummy's and Nana's.'

Stroking his hair, she couldn't believe that her child was back in her arms. Mother and son were still clinging together and sobbing when Barry came down to find them.

'Hello, CJ,' he smiled but the little boy wouldn't look at him, wouldn't remove his face from his mother's neck.

'Is it okay to go back through? I don't want CJ upset any more than he already is,' Jess asked him tearfully.

'Yes, it's all clear. Sheldon has calmed down and the

other creep has bolted. Brad whispered something in his ear and he was off like a bat out of hell.'

'And where is Brad?'

'He's still there but getting jumpy. I think all this is taking its toll on him – he's shaking a bit.'

'Okay, I'll go and see him. If it wasn't for him . . .' The tears started again and that got CJ sobbing even louder. 'Come on, CJ, come and meet Brad.' As she said it she saw the veiled disappointment on Barry's face. 'And this is Barry, Mummy's best friend in the whole wide world. He's been helping me look for you.'

'Why didn't you visit me?' the boy sobbed.

'I didn't know where you were, but it's all over now. I just have to talk to Daddy for a bit first.'

'I don't want to stay with him. I hate him, I hate him!'

Sheldon appeared as if from nowhere. 'Ungrateful kid, after all I've done for you. Well, let me tell you, boy, you're going nowhere. You're staying here where you belong.'

The sobs were getting excruciating. 'I'm not, I'm not.'

'It's okay, CJ, you're right. You're not staying here.'

As Jess went back up to the main area with CJ round her neck Sheldon followed.

'You are *not* taking him! I'll get an emergency order – *you're not taking him.*' Sheldon moved forward with his arms outstretched to try and take CJ from Jess.

'Oh, I think she is.'

Sheldon spun round to see Brad with a wide smile on his face and a large photograph in his hand. He was holding it up facing towards him; all that the others could see was the plain white backing. 'Wow! This really is something. Jeez, the judge will just *luurvve* this.'

Sheldon walked over and tried to snatch it but Brad held it tight while at the same time letting Sheldon see what was on the other side. It was the best of the bunch that Brad had stolen. Sheldon, Laura and Antonio were all naked on a vast bed indulging athletically in an explicit, sadistic sex scene that left nothing to the imagination.

'Give me that! You know it was a set-up. I don't even fucking remember it.'

'Prove it to the judge!' Brad laughed. 'Now we're all going to leave and you're going to be civil about it. Say goodbye to your son nicely, just like any good father would and we'll be out of your hair.'

Sheldon dropped his hands to his side and looked at the floor in defeat. 'You're going to regret this.'

'Oh no, *my friend*. You are the one that will regret it if I stick this up all over LA.'

Jess noticed Isabella standing smiling in the background. 'Give me a contact number and we'll let you know how it's going. Sorry about your job.'

'No problem. I would have left long ago but for CJ. Now I'll look for a job with a human being as a boss!'

'CJ, say goodbye to Isabella.' Jess tried to make CJ turn his face to the woman.

'It's okay.' Isabella planted a kiss on the back of his neck. 'He's too bewildered by it all but he'll be okay now he's back with his mom.'

Sheldon glared at them all one by one. 'I'm going to call my mother, she won't let you get away with this.'

'Good for you, Sheldon. You go ahead and call her. I'm sure Pearl will be delighted to hear from you – that's if she's got time to talk to you now she's hooked herself a new old man.'

'What do you mean by that?'

'What? Hasn't Mommy Dearest told you? Oh well, I'm sure she will, after she's married. Now I'm going to get CJ settled somewhere and then I'll be back. We have unfinished business, much unfinished business in fact, that we can't discuss in front of our son.'

'I might not be here later.' He tried to look disinterested.

'That's fine. By the way, as your mother will no doubt also tell you, Sofia is staying with me at Kay's. How's that for an interesting mix of conversation?'

'I didn't know you could be such a bitch.' Sheldon actually looked shocked.

'Then congratulate yourself, Sheldon. You made me like it.'

Once outside, the euphoria of the moment quickly passed and a more rational mood took over. Jess looked pensive.

'What are we going to do now?' she asked. 'We can't fly straight back. I have to talk to Sheldon – I can't do what he did and just drag CJ off into the sunset, but I have to get away from here.'

'I think we need to book into a hotel for a couple of nights to tie up all the loose ends and then go back to LA for Christmas.' Barry led her away from the entrance as he was speaking. 'I'll have to get some new papers filed for custody and then there's the divorce. You have to get something from Sheldon immediately.'

'I'm not a money grabber!' Jess snapped angrily.

'Jess, will you get rid of that mindset? This is about what is owed to you, not to mention support for your son, but we'll talk about that later. First thing is a hotel, agreed?'

'Agreed.' Jess looked across to Brad who was quietly

watching from a distance. 'Where are you staying, Brad? You're not sleeping rough, are you?'

'Nope. I'm in a motel.'

'You'll have to come with us, stay with us.'

'Thanks all the same but no, I'm okay where I am.' He held up his hand and waved to Enid in her car, then he beckoned her over. 'Without Enid I couldn't have done any of this. She drove me about, pretended to be a crazy widow heiress and generally took good care of me. I'll stay with her.'

Jess watched as the woman tottered over towards them, large and brassy with skin-tight clothes and wobbly high heels, but all that was overshadowed by the smile on her face and the look of admiration on Brad's.

'Jess, this is Enid. Enid . . . Jess.'

Jess smiled and held out a hand, which was difficult with CJ still hanging grimly and silently round her neck like a limpet with arms and legs.

'Good to meet you, Enid. I understand I have you to thank as well for helping Brad find CJ.' Jess could feel her face stretching into a wide grin. 'I am just so grateful. This has been a nightmare for me and now it's over, thanks to you. Thank you both.'

'And I've got you to thank for helping me find Brad!'

Everyone stood around in embarrassed silence for a few minutes until Barry came to the rescue.

'Right, Enid, you live here, where's the best place? Not as posh as this, that's for sure.'

'And certainly not as trashy as where I live, that's for sure also.' Enid smiled openly; there wasn't a hint of malice in her response but Barry gasped in horror.

'No offence. I didn't mean anything by that – I don't know where you live.'

'I know that!' Her raucous laugh made Jess and Barry

jump. 'I was just kidding. Now how about the almost classy joint that isn't too far from my not so classy joint, then we can all get to know each other!'

'Sounds good to me,' Jess smiled. 'We can all go out and eat. I'm starving now!' She whispered in CJ's ear, 'What about you, my little man? Are you hungry?'

'I want my blanket.'

'I'll go up and get it. Where is it?'

'In Mexico.'

'Oh dear.' Jess smiled and kissed his head. 'That might take a little bit longer. How about a burger with lots of ketchup?'

'I'm not allowed.'

'You are now, CJ. Let's go!'

'You've got to call Sara right away, Jess.' Barry touched her elbow. 'She'll be hopping by now and I think Sofia needs to know where Sheldon is, don't you?'

Jess nodded then looked back to Brad. 'What was that photo you were waving around? The one that stopped Sheldon in his tracks?'

'Oh, nothing important. Shall we go? I could eat a burger.'

As Jess immersed herself in making soothing noises to her son, Brad took the opportunity to slip the photo to Barry. 'Maybe this will help if the asshole plays hard to get, but I don't want Jess to see it. This is real, real sleazy.'

Barry sneaked a look. 'Ah! I see what you mean. I'll file it under *in the event of*. Thank you. You know,' he paused and looked at Brad curiously, 'I really admire you.'

Brad looked back at him. 'What do you mean?'

'Just that. From what Jess has told me, you've been to hell and back, literally. How did you claw your way back from that? I mean, look what you've done here, for Jess.' Barry looked over his shoulder to check that Jess wasn't in earshot. 'When she came back from LA the first time she told me you were the one who stopped her from doing the unthinkable. She was on the edge and you pulled her back.'

'No, no, no, man, you've got it all wrong, I told you,' Brad interrupted him mid-sentence, 'Jess helped *me*. She gave me a reason to get up from the ground.'

'Come on, guys!' Jess shouted. 'Let's get away from here before Big Momma Patterson calls the cops and has us all arrested.'

Barry reached out to shake Brad's hand. 'Anything I can do for you, anything at all to help, you let me know!'

Jess had intended to go back to see Sheldon that evening but CJ wouldn't let her out of his sight. He even followed her to the toilet and squatted on the floor outside. She knew it would take a long time for the scars Sheldon had inflicted on him to heal. Her own confrontation with her husband would just have to wait.

Looking around her, Jess realised how much she owed to Brad and to Barry. And also to the people who weren't around the table – her mother, Carla, Kay and Ryan. Between them they totally negated the poison of the Pattersons.

In a strange way Jess felt sorry for Sheldon. He wasn't bad, he wasn't even really nasty, he was just weak and indulged. Her image of him was now perfectly clear and she knew without doubt that with a mother like Pearl he had never really stood a chance.

It was just unfortunate that none of the women he got involved with realised until it was too late.

She nudged Enid. 'I'm going to the rest room.'

Enid smiled. 'Me too.'

Again CJ was stuck like glue. 'Darling, Mummy's coming back, I promise. I just have to go to the ladies again. You talk to Barry, tell him all about Nana Wells. You'll be seeing her again soon.'

Jess slipped away and Enid followed.

'Tell me about you and Brad. I'm dying to know.' Jess perched herself on the edge of the wash basin. 'I'm really fond of him and I can see you are too.'

'Sure am,' Enid smiled, 'but I'm not stupid. I know he's got problems of the *one day at a time* variety, but then I've had my share of shit also. We'll see what happens.'

'I hope it works.' Jess reached out and gave the woman a hug. 'Is Brad going back to LA?'

'Not if I can help it. Brad needs to keep away from his old buddies and anyway, I think he's real sick. He needs to see a doctor and the warmth is good here. Get some sun on his back and some colour in his scrawny cheeks.' Enid's loud belly laugh made Jess smile; she could see instantly that Brad stood more chance of making it with a woman like that alongside him.

'You know I'll pay – well, Barry will pay for the time being, till I get my cash flowing again!' Jess laughed. 'Whatever it takes. But meanwhile I know you'll take good care of him, and you take care of yourself and you both keep in touch.'

'Thanks, we sure will.'

'Mummy, Mummy, where are you?' The plaintive voice slid under the door.

'Coming right now, darling.' Jess smiled at Enid. 'You've no idea how good that sounds. I thought I'd never hear it again. I'd better go back.'

'I'm right with you, honey. Let's get back to the party!'

That night Jess snuggled down in her bed with her son and savoured every minute of the sleepless night. Aware of Barry in the next room she thought about him. There was a lot of work to do with CJ but she knew there was something there. In fact, she really wanted to be with him, to have him in the bed with her, not necessarily in a sexual way at that moment but definitely as a comfort. She could imagine his arms around her, holding her close. She wondered if he was asleep.

Sliding quietly from the bed where CJ lay exhausted and all cried out, Jess crept over to the phone and, after carefully stretching the cable into the bathroom, she sat on the edge of the bath and dialled the room next door.

'Barry?' she whispered. 'Can you hear me?'

'Of course. I've been lying here thinking about you, wishing I was with you.'

'Me, too. Barry, we have to talk. Not now, there's too much still to go through, but I know we've got something between us. Can you wait?'

'Of course I can wait, as long as it takes. I love you, Jess, But you already know that, don't you?'

She smiled. 'Yes, I do know!'

In time, she thought as she gently replaced the receiver and slipped back in beside her sleeping son.

In time it would happen.

Epilogue

Santa Monica, Christmas

'Christmas in Los Angeles – it's not quite the same as Christmas at home but I have to admit this is my best ever. It's exactly what I hoped for, to have CJ back with me, but deep down I didn't dare believe it would happen!'

Jess looked around the overflowing and highly decorated table that had been lovingly prepared by everyone for the extraordinary Christmas celebration. She was aware of her still raw emotions bubbling away just under the surface and desperately wanted to keep control, for CJ's sake.

Barry was seated on one side of her and CJ was on the other; opposite were Sofia and Sara.

Jess stood up and smiled brightly. 'I'm going to do this whether you like it or not, and I am *not* going to cry. No more crying!'

Raising her glass high she looked slowly from one to the other. 'This is a toast to everyone both present and absent, who has supported and helped me, especially to Barry and Brad, my heroes who each came charging to the rescue in different ways. But not forgetting my mother who I've been mean to more often than not, and Kay and Ryan who put themselves on the line for me. Oh, and not forgetting Enid, the crazy heiress, or as Brad put it, the driver from hell!'

Jess paused and made a series of exaggerated tutting noises. 'Oh silly me, I nearly forgot, and of course CJ, my own little man. Back with his mum at last.'

As they made their toasts a little voice piped up.

'To everyone,' CJ announced solemnly as he raised his glass of lemonade amid much tipsy laughter.

Jess sat down quickly and Barry clasped her hand under the table and smiled before standing up himself.

'To a brilliant New Year in England and a Happy Summer back here next year with all our new friends.'

As the toasts carried on and excited phone calls went back and forth across the Atlantic Ocean, Jess slipped unnoticed out onto the deck and leaned her elbows on the rail, looking out across the beach towards the gentle waves that ebbed and flowed on the moving sand. Back and forth they lapped, just like her emotions.

Mesmerised by the movement she thought back over the previous few months and it was as though those events had happened to someone else. For the first time Jess could look at the events rationally.

After she had arrived back from Miami with CJ and Barry, it had taken several days for the enormity of their experience to sink in, and Jess had initially found it hard to adjust. CJ still clung to her and wouldn't let her move more than a few feet away, but Jess didn't mind, she felt the same. She couldn't bear to let him out of her sight as long as they were still in the vicinity of Pearl Patterson.

After much difficult discussion amongst them all

and some persuasive argument from Sara, Jess had grudgingly agreed that Sofia, pregnant, penniless and homeless, could go back to England with them. Then, as soon as the baby arrived and was proved to be Sheldon's, she could start proceedings against him for support.

Sara's argument in favour of the girl was that the baby she was expecting would be a sibling to CJ, and there was no disputing that Sofia had been good to CJ and that he was fond of her. In fact, when he could be peeled away from Jess it was to Sofia that the boy turned.

Jess wasn't sure if she could ever truly forgive Sofia her betrayal but for CJ's sake, and for the new baby, she was going to do the best she could.

Perversely, despite everything, Jess found it far harder to forgive Sheldon for denying that Sofia's baby was his. It was at the precise moment of denial when he had demanded that a DNA test be performed immediately after the birth, that Jess saw the true colours of the man she had thought she knew.

He might have been her husband and the father of her only child, but with an overwhelming sadness she realised she didn't know him at all.

Sheldon had left Miami shortly after Jess and was already back in LA licking his wounds after his experience at the hands of Antonio and sheepishly staying at his mother's home.

Jess had adamantly refused to go to the house either with or without CJ, but there had been a meeting at the Patterson lawyers' offices where a tentative agreement had been drawn up that Barry, and Jess, had approved.

Sheldon would pay off the mortgage on the Cambridge house straight away and then sign it over to Jess. As soon as Jess was back in her own home Sheldon would be allowed supervised access to his son. She and CJ would also, if all went well, spend some time in LA during the summer holidays.

Predictably no formal divorce settlement could be agreed because Pearl Patterson, ever the manipulator, was still standing right behind her son and pulling his strings, although Barry was hopeful that they would be able to find a compromise sooner rather than later. Sheldon did, however, agree to an immediate cash transfer to tide Jess over and to allow her to pay Sara back.

Jess could see that Pearl Patterson viewed situations in straightforward black and white. Deals were either won or lost, and as far as she was concerned, the Pattersons had lost the battle for CJ – and it wasn't easy to accept.

The grey area of compromise was alien territory to Pearl.

Brad and Enid were together in Miami and hoping that Brad's health would improve in time. Enid had told Jess she was going to make sure that he attended the local AA meetings and made contact with other Gulf War veterans who suffered similar illnesses. She was also determined to get him to a specialist doctor as soon as she could persuade him.

Jess guessed that Enid's powers of persuasion were quite considerable.

Looking out across Brad's old territory Jess smiled as she thought about the couple, how fate had helped them find each other and the way they had clicked together in a flash. She desperately hoped it would work out for Brad, not just with Enid but with life.

Her man from the beach deserved a lucky break.

Thinking of Brad and Enid as a couple made her mind jump to Barry, but her emotions were still too raw for her to think about where they would go together; however, she had no doubts it would be somewhere.

Jess jumped in shock as a hand touched her shoulder and then stroked her hair.

'Hello, you. How's it going? I saw you sneak out but thought you needed some thinking time alone.'

'You were right. It's just so sad, isn't it? I've tried to get to the bottom of why Sheldon behaved as he did, but I still can't work it out. Deep down I know that whatever plans we put in place, as soon as Sheldon finds someone else he'll forget about CJ and then they'll both miss out on so much.'

Barry hooked his hand into the lapel of her denim jacket and pulled her close. 'It might not be ideal, but CJ will be okay, and you never know, Sheldon may dig deep into himself and find a sense of responsibility. Anyway, you did all right growing up without a dad, didn't you?'

'Maybe, but it's not the best way. CJ needs to know his dad, even Pearl who is his grandmother after all, but I fear it will all fade away in time.'

Barry turned Jess around to face him. 'He'll always have you and Sara, and maybe even me! I'm a good dad to my two even if I do say it myself. I could be a half-decent substitute.'

'I'm sure you could. I don't think CJ will miss out too much, but Sheldon will. And Pearl!'

'That will be their choice. We all have to take responsibility for our own actions, even the Pattersons.'

'Yes, I know.' Jess hesitated and looked out to the ocean again. 'Barry, I've had a germ of an idea growing in my brain for the last few months and it just won't go away. I want to try and find my own father. It never bothered me before but now it's important to me and to CJ. Somewhere he has a grandfather he knows nothing about and I have a father whom I've never met, or not that I can remember. I'm going to try to find him.'

'How do you think Sara will feel about that? She's been mother and father to you all your life.'

Jess smiled. 'I know, and it's time she had a break now, isn't it? No, seriously, I have to do this. Same as I have to do everything in my power to help CJ know all of his family. Mum will understand, I'm sure.'

Carefully Barry leaned down and kissed Jess on the end of her nose. 'You're probably right, but can we have some stress-free time to ourselves first? Get to know each other properly? We could go out on dates, go to the cinema, take trips to the seaside, even go on a dirty weekend to Brighton. We could do normal!'

'Sounds good to me. After all this upheaval it would be nice to do normal. I don't think we'll ever be the Waltons but we could give it a try.'

They both turned at the same time and looked back into the house that was bedecked with fairy lights; the tree that stood tall and wide in the corner of the room flickered its lights eerily from red to green and back again.

Just at that moment, Sara looked up from the book that she and CJ were reading together and locked eyes with her daughter through the glass.

Jess and Barry both smiled, raised their hands in tandem and waved.

'Happy Christmas,' Jess mouthed to her mother.

'And to you, to both of you,' Sara mouthed back as she lifted an imaginary glass to them and smiled before wrapping an arm around CJ and kissing the top of his head.